PENGUIN CLASSICS

HONORÉ DE BALZAC

Old Man Goriot

A new translation by OLIVIA MCCANNON

PENGUIN CLASSICS

OLD MAN GORIOT

HONORÉ DE BALZAC was born at Tours in 1799, the son of a civil servant. He spent nearly six years as a boarder in a Vendôme school, then went to live in Paris, working as a lawyer's clerk, then as a hack writer. Between 1820 and 1824 he wrote a number of novels under various pseudonyms, many of them in collaboration, after which he unsuccessfully tried his luck at publishing, printing and type-founding. At the age of thirty, heavily in debt, he returned to literature with a dedicated fury and wrote the first novel to appear under his own name, *The Chouans*. During the next twenty years he wrote about ninety novels and shorter stories, among them many masterpieces, to which he gave the comprehensive title *The Human Comedy*. As Balzac himself put it: 'What he [Napoleon] was unable to finish with the sword, I shall accomplish with the pen.' He died in 1850, a few months after his marriage to Eveline Hanska, the Polish countess with whom he had maintained amorous relations for eighteen years.

OLIVIA MCCANNON is a literary translator and writer based in London and Paris. She studied at the Queen's College, Oxford (French/German), then at the Sorbonne Nouvelle (Paris III), on an Entente Cordiale scholarship. Her translation work includes nineteenth- and twentieth-century French poetry and contemporary Francophone plays (Royal Court theatre). She has received various awards, including a Hawthornden Fellowship (2005). Her writing has been broadcast on BBC Radios 3 and 4 and her poetry collection *Exactly my own Length* is published by Carcanet/ Oxford Poets (2011).

GRAHAM ROBB studied French and German at Oxford and took his doctorate at Vanderbilt University. His books include *Balzac* (1994), *Unlocking Mallarmé* (1996), *Victor Hugo* (1997), *Rimbaud* (2000) and *Strangers: Homosexual Love in the Nineteenth Century* (2003). *The Discovery of France* (2007), based in part on 14,000 miles' cycling in France, won both the Duff Cooper Prize and the 2008 Royal Society of Literature Ondaatje Prize. *Parisians: An Adventure History of Paris* came out in 2010.

HONORÉ DE BALZAC
Old Man Goriot

Translation and Notes by OLIVIA MCCANNON
Introduction by GRAHAM ROBB

PENGUIN BOOKS

PENGUIN CLASSICS

Published by the Penguin Group
Penguin Books Ltd, 80 Strand, London WC2R ORL, England
Penguin Group (USA) Inc., 375 Hudson Street, New York, New York 10014, USA
Penguin Group (Canada), 90 Eglinton Avenue East, Suite 700, Toronto, Ontario,
Canada M4P 2Y3 (a division of Pearson Penguin Canada Inc.)
Penguin Ireland, 25 St Stephen's Green, Dublin 2, Ireland (a division of Penguin Books Ltd)
Penguin Group (Australia), 250 Camberwell Road, Camberwell, Victoria 3124, Australia
(a division of Pearson Australia Group Pty Ltd)
Penguin Books India Pvt Ltd, 11 Community Centre, Panchsheel Park, New Delhi – 110 017, India
Penguin Group (NZ), 67 Apollo Drive, Rosedale, North Shore 0632, New Zealand
(a division of Pearson New Zealand Ltd)
Penguin Books (South Africa) (Pty) Ltd, 24 Sturdee Avenue, Rosebank, Johannesburg 2196, South Africa

Penguin Books Ltd, Registered Offices: 80 Strand, London WC2R ORL, England

www.penguin.com

First published in French as *Le Père Goriot* 1835
This translation first published in Penguin Classics 2011

1

Translation and notes copyright © Olivia McCannon, 2011
Introduction copyright © Graham Robb, 2011
All rights reserved

The moral right of the translator and author of the introduction has been asserted

Set in 10.25/12.25 pt PostScript Adobe Sabon
Typeset by Jouve (UK), Milton Keynes
Printed in England by Clays Ltd, St Ives plc

ISBN: 978-0-140-44972-3

www.greenpenguin.co.uk

Contents

Acknowledgements

My most grateful acknowledgements are due to the impressive scholarship of the many reference works I consulted at the British Library and the Bibliothèque Nationale de France, and above all to that of the Pléiade edition and the *Oxford English Dictionary (OED)*.

I'm extremely grateful to Mrs Drue Heinz for the opportunity to work on the translation without interruption at Hawthornden Castle, and to the Centre National du Livre, for enabling me to do the same in Paris.

I owe a particular debt to Graham Robb, for his inspiration, generous guidance and expert scrutiny; and to Sasha Dugdale, and David and Helen Constantine, for their skilful advice on both my translation and the art and craft of translation itself.

I've been very lucky to be supported by such a talented team at Penguin and am especially grateful to Laura Barber, for commissioning the translation; Monica Schmoller, for her sensitive copyediting; and Anna Hervé and Jessica Harrison, for putting the book to bed.

My warmest personal thanks are due to Mike Bradshaw, Juan Yermo and Rhianwen Bailey, for sharing their expertise; and to my parents, Dominic and Judith McCannon, for all their encouragement.

Finally, I'd like to thank my husband, Jamie Glazebrook, for his endless open-hearted support at every level.

This translation is dedicated to my father, Dominic, to my husband, Jamie, and to my son, Arthur.

Chronology

1799 *20 May*: Born at Tours, and put out to nurse until the age of four. His father is a civil servant, of peasant stock; his mother from a family of wealthy Parisian drapers.

Napoleon Bonaparte overthrows the Directory and becomes First Consul of France.

Hölderlin, *Hyperion*.

1804 First Empire: Napoleon becomes Emperor of France and starts conquering Europe.

Schiller, *William Tell*.

1805 Nelson defeats the French and Spanish fleet in the naval battle of Trafalgar. Napoleon defeats Austro-Russian troops at Austerlitz and then the Prussians at Jena.

Chateaubriand, *René*.

1807 Sent to the Oratorian college in Vendôme, where he boards for the next six years. Birth of his half-brother Henry. (Already has two younger sisters: Laure, Laurence.)

1812 Napoleon is defeated in his catastrophic Moscow campaign against Tsar Alexander I.

Byron, *Childe Harold's Pilgrimage*.

1814 Family move to Paris, where Balzac continues his education.

Allied troops enter Paris. Napoleon abdicates, and becomes King of Elba. First restoration: Accession of Louis XVIII to the French throne.

Austen, *Mansfield Park*. Goya, *The Second* and *Third of May 1808*.

1815 Napoleon returns in triumph to Paris and rules for 100 days before defeat at Waterloo. Second restoration: Louis XVIII is reinstated on the French throne.

1816–19 Begins his legal training, attending lectures at the Sorbonne; articled to a solicitor, Maître Guillonnet-Merville, then a notary, Maître Passez.

1819 Determined to make a career from writing, moves into a garret in Rue Lesdiguières.

    Scott, *Ivanhoe*. Géricault, *The Raft of the Medusa*.

1820 Finishes a verse drama, *Cromwell*, which is judged to be a failure by family and friends.

    Shelley, *Prometheus Unbound*. Keats, *Ode on a Grecian Urn*.

1821 Publishes novels of Gothic inspiration, many produced collaboratively, under the pseudonyms Lord R'hoone and Horace de St Aubin. Writes poems and plays.

    Constable, *Landscape: Noon (The Hay Wain)*.

1822 Becomes the lover of Laure de Berny, mother of nine and twenty-two years his senior.

1824 'Horace de St Aubin' is slated in the *Feuilleton littéraire*. Balzac contemplates suicide.

    Louis XVIII dies and is succeeded by Charles X.

    Beethoven, *Ninth Symphony*.

1825 Launches a publishing and printing venture, producing editions of Molière and La Fontaine. Meets Victor Hugo.

    Grillparzer, *King Ottokar's Rise and Fall*.

1828 Printing business collapses, leaving him in debt. His literary purpose strengthens.

    Schubert, *Schwanengesang (Swansong)*.

1829 Frequents the *salons*, introduced by the Duchesse d'Abrantès. His father dies. *The Chouans*, the first novel he signs with his own name.

1830 Publishes numerous short stories, including 'Gobseck', 'The Vendetta' and 'Sarrasine'.

    July Revolution. Charles X abdicates. July Monarchy. Louis-Philippe becomes king.

    Delacroix, *Liberty Leading the People*. Berlioz, *Symphonie fantastique*.

1831 Adopts a lifestyle beyond his means. *The Wild Ass's Skin* establishes his reputation. Begins systematically and publicly to use the particle '*de*' before his surname.

Victor Hugo, *Notre-Dame de Paris*. Pushkin, *Boris Godunov*.

1832 Travels widely. Begins corresponding with Eveline Hanska, a Polish countess. Joins the neo-legitimist (ultra-conservative) party and publishes political essays. Rumoured to be going mad. *Louis Lambert, Colonel Chabert*.

Goethe, final revision of *Faust* before his death.

1833 Meets Mme Hanska for the first time, in Switzerland. Signs a contract for the publication of *Studies of Nineteenth-Century Life*, a collective work which will stretch to twelve volumes over the next four years. *The Country Doctor, Eugénie Grandet*.

1834 Birth of Marie du Fresnay, his supposed daughter by Maria du Fresnay. Becomes Mme Hanska's lover. Meets Countess Guidoboni-Visconti. Has grand idea of recurring characters between novels and begins adapting previous works to establish continuity. *History of the Thirteen, The Quest of the Absolute*.

1835 Spends three weeks with Mme Hanska in Vienna, the last time for eight years. *Old Man Goriot, Seraphita* and collected *Philosophical Studies*.

Gautier, *Mademoiselle de Maupin*.

1836 Birth of Lionel-Richard Guidoboni-Visconti, his supposed son. Death of Laure de Berny. Liquidates *La Chronique de Paris*, the journal purchased the previous year.

Serial publication of Dickens's *Pickwick Papers* begins in England. Some months later, Balzac's *The Old Maid* is serialized in *La Presse*, the first *roman-feuilleton*.

1837 Countess Guidoboni-Visconti settles his debts to save him from imprisonment. His tilbury is seized by the bailiffs. Travels to Italy, staying at the best hotels. Exhibition of his portrait in a monk's habit by Louis Boulanger. *César Birotteau*.

1838 Visits George Sand (who begins a nine-year relationship with Chopin this year). Travels across Sardinia, Corsica and the Italian peninsula. Incurs further debt after speculating in Sardinian silver mines. *The Firm of Nucingen*.

1840 His play *Vautrin* opens and is banned. Launches the *Revue parisienne*, which folds; his review of Stendhal's *The Charterhouse of Parma* appears in the third and final issue. Moves to Passy with his mother and housekeeper/mistress Louise de Brugnol.

1841 Signs a publishing contract for *The Human Comedy*, his collective title since the previous year. *Ursule Mirouet*, *A Murky Business*.

1842 Compares human types to animal species in the preface to *The Human Comedy*. Has his portrait taken by a *Daguerréotypeur*. Mme Hanska's husband dies. *The Black Sheep*. His play *The Resources of Quinola* is a flop.

Gogol, *Dead Souls*. Verdi, *Nabucco (Nebuchadnezzar)*.

1843 Visits Mme Hanska in St Petersburg. Sits for David d'Angers. His health is poor. Writes a letter of introduction to Mme Hanska for Liszt, who tries to seduce her. Completion of *Lost Illusions*, in three parts. *Honorine*.

1844 Due to ill health, travels and socializes little. Collects furniture and paintings. *Modest Mignon* and publication of the beginning of *The Peasantry*.

Dumas, *The Three Musketeers*. Turner, *Rain, Steam and Speed*. Heine, *New Poems*.

1845 Travels in Europe with Mme Hanska, her daughter and her future son-in-law.

Poe, *The Raven and Other Poems*. Wagner, *Tannhäuser*.

1846 Mme Hanska delivers a stillborn baby, which would have been named Victor-Honoré. *Cousin Bette*.

1847 Mme Hanska visits for four months in Paris and he makes her his legal heir. They winter in the Ukraine. *Cousin Pons*. Completion of *A Harlot High and Low*.

Charlotte Brontë, *Jane Eyre*. Emily Brontë, *Wuthering Heights*.

1848 Returns to Paris. Witnesses the sacking of the Tuileries. His play *The Stepmother* is a success with critics. Ill health prevents him working regularly. Returns to the Ukraine.

February Revolution. Second Republic. Louis Bonaparte is elected President. Revolutionary uprisings across Europe. Final abolition of slavery in French domains.

Marx and Engels, *The Communist Manifesto*. Gaskell, *Mary Barton*. Thackeray, *Vanity Fair*.

1849 Health deteriorates seriously. Starts work on projects he will never finish.

1850 Marries Mme Hanska in March, at Berdichev. (They are married for only five months.) On return to Paris in May, Balzac can no longer read or write. *18 August*: Dies. A cast is taken of his writing hand. Hugo pronounces a funeral oration at Père Lachaise.

Courbet, *A Burial at Ornans*.

Introduction

Like most of Balzac's novels, *Old Man Goriot* began with a bare subject and the ghost of a character: paternal love, 'a sentiment so great that nothing can exhaust it'; 'a man who is a father in the same way that a saint or a martyr is a Christian'.[1] Almost as soon as the idea was in his head, a story began to weave itself around the ghost. He jotted down these phrases in his notebook: 'A decent man – middle-class boarding house – 600 francs annual income – Having sacrificed every penny to his daughters, who each have an income of 50,000, dying like a dog.'[2]

This was the protoplasmic novel that was taking shape in Balzac's mind when he set off for his country retreat, the little Château de Saché in the valley of the Indre, Touraine, at the end of September 1834. Five years before, Balzac had burst onto the Parisian literary stage with a historical novel, *The Chouans*, and an anthropological study of modern marriage presented as a self-help guide for husbands with unfaithful wives: *The Physiology of Marriage*. All his earlier novels had been published under pseudonyms. They were bloody melodramas and tearful romances written for undiscriminating readers. Since then, Balzac had written forty short stories, twenty tales in his own form of medieval French and five novels. He had also signed contracts for dozens of works that would never be written. His doctor had ordered a complete rest. He was not to read, write or think.

The prospect of comfortable idleness always had an energizing effect on Balzac's brain. 'Sometimes', he told a correspondent as he worked on several stories at the same time, 'I have the impression that my brain has caught fire.'³ At Saché he finished two other novels and saw the new work growing in his mind. Before a word of it was written, he knew that *Old Man Goriot* would be a masterpiece.

He sat at his desk on the top floor of the chateau, with a view of ancient oaks and peaceful fields, and thought of the city he had left behind, that 'valley full of genuine suffering and frequently counterfeit joy' (p. 3). He told his mother about the new novel as though it already existed on paper: 'It's a work even more beautiful than *Eugénie Grandet*.'⁴ (*Eugénie Grandet*, the tale of a miser and his daughter, had been published in 1833 to universal acclaim.) Later, when the new novel had been written and – to use Balzac's image – he could turn the tapestry over and see what he had made, he would describe it in different terms: '*Old Man Goriot* is a beautiful work, but monstrously sad. In order to be complete, it was necessary to depict a moral sewer in Paris, and it looks like a repulsive wound.'⁵

In mid-October, Balzac was back in Paris, settling into his story like a housekeeper into a new home. He had signed a contract with the *Revue de Paris*, which was to publish the novel in instalments. For Balzac, this newfangled mode of publication was a blessing and a curse. The advance from the journal helped him to pay the everlasting debts that seemed to other people to be his principal motive for writing. Though he wore a monk's robe and (as he put it himself) worked like a galley-slave, Balzac presented himself to the journalists and gossips of literary Paris as a bumptious *parvenu*, a conspicuous consumer who revelled in the new, socially mobile France, where money was a magic talisman and noble obscurity had no market value. As Vautrin tells Rastignac in *Old Man Goriot*, in order to succeed 'you either have to be rich to start with or appear to be so' (p. 99). When Balzac described the seedy boarding house where much of the novel takes place, he had just redecorated his home near the Paris Observatory with expensive wallpaper. He bought gold buttons for his blue suit, a powerful spyglass made for him by the Observatory optician and a jewel-encrusted walking-stick. A young observer of literary life called Antoine Fontaney saw him at a party: 'He is the commercial writer par excellence. "The *Revue de Paris*", [Balzac] said airily, "is the best journal in Europe: it pays the biggest fees." How disgraceful!'[6]

Unfortunately for his finances, while other novelists followed a simple recipe and could serve up a regular slice of plot for publication, Balzac worked from the inside out, inflating his sentences, evolving digressions and making room for characters who refused to remain two-dimensional. His novel grew like a complicated organism. The original short story on the agonies of paternal love turned into an astonishingly concise, encyclopaedic novel on modern society. This tale of a father abused by his children became a drama with a large cast of memorable minor characters and three main plots: the obsessively devoted father, Goriot, 'who resembles the murderer's dog that licks its master's blood-stained hand';[7] the beautiful, blue-eyed, dark-haired student from the provinces, Eugène de Rastignac, who sets sail 'across the ocean of Paris . . . fishing for his fortune' (p. 79); and the mysterious Vautrin, who seduces Rastignac with his sinister wisdom: 'You must either plough through this mass of men like a cannonball or creep among them like the plague' (p. 98). Several other plots were entwined around the main branches, as though Balzac were trying to cram a *Thousand and One Nights* of modern Paris into the space of a small novel: a young girl disowned by her father, a viscountess abandoned by her lover, a debt-ridden baroness married to a stingy millionaire.

Fuelled by endless cups of hallucinatingly strong coffee, Balzac produced the first draft of *Old Man Goriot* in just over three weeks. He then began the painful process of rewriting. In all, by his own account, he spent forty days on the novel. During that time, he slept, on average, only two hours in every twenty-four. The first of four instalments, made up of two parts, 'A Respectable Boarding House' and 'Two Calls are Paid', appeared in the *Revue de Paris* on 14 December 1834, six weeks before the novel was completed. As usual, Balzac tormented the typesetters with his expanding paragraphs and modifications. When proofs were delivered, he would ask his two little nieces to cut them out and paste them onto large sheets of

paper, which he quickly turned into a barely legible mass of corrections and additions. The corrected pages were deciphered,
reset and reprinted, and the whole process began again. Balzac
was, in effect, using a word processor consisting of a hydraulic
press and a team of exasperated typesetters.

The second and third instalments appeared on 28 December
1834 and 25 January 1835 under the titles 'An Introduction to
Society' and 'Cat-o'-Nine-Lives'. The final instalment appeared on
11 February 1835, also divided into two parts: 'The Two Daughters' and 'Death of the Father'. *Old Man Goriot* was published
by Edmond Werdet as a two-volume book on 2 March 1835.
Just as he had seen the finished novel in his mind several months
before it was written, he celebrated in advance its 'incompar-
able success'. The 'fools' who made up Parisian society were
buying hundreds of copies, he told his future wife.[8] Two new
editions were already being printed. His former mistress, Laure
de Berny, according to Balzac, had enjoyed the second part so
much 'that she had a heart attack'.[9]

Two years later, the *Figaro* newspaper offered unsold copies
of *Old Man Goriot* to new subscribers as a free gift, which was
a compliment to Balzac but hardly a sign of commercial success. A novel in which crime went unpunished and which
devoted as much space to food stains and peeling wallpaper as
to ball gowns and boudoirs was never likely to be a bestseller.
Novels were expected to provide light relief, not to analyse the
workings of society and the mind. Nonetheless, it was a not-
able victory. The publication in the *Revue de Paris* and the first
two editions (March and May 1835) earned Balzac a total of
10,000 francs, which is eighteen times more than old man Goriot
pays for a year's board and lodging. Even the criminal members of the 'Ten Thousand Club' (p. 151), who consider 10,000
francs the smallest amount worth stealing, might have been
forced to admit that virtuous hard work could be a lucrative
investment.

Just over a year before starting his novel, Balzac had conceived
a 'grand and extraordinary enterprise'.[10] He had decided that
all his novels, past and future, would form a vast tableau of

modern society. This was the monumental oeuvre that he later called *La Comédie Humaine* (*The Human Comedy*). Unfinished at Balzac's death in 1850, *The Human Comedy* in its published form contains over a hundred novels, short stories and studies of human behaviour. He defined its scope while working on *Old Man Goriot*: 'all social effects, including every situation of human life, every physiognomy, male or female personality, way of life, profession, social zone, region of France, and anything to do with childhood, old age, middle age, politics, justice and war'.[11]

As he explained in the preface to *The Human Comedy* (1842), he wanted to produce the epic, eye-witness social history that was missing for earlier civilizations. He would do for nineteenth-century France what no historian had done for Ancient Rome, Greece or Egypt. *Old Man Goriot* was the first big test of this scheme. Like a preview of the whole *Human Comedy*, it opens doors into almost every layer of Parisian society: the salons of aristocrats – both those whose noble ancestors predate the Revolution and those who owe their ennoblement to money; the halfway house of the middle class – tradesmen, civil servants, students and retired people; and some shadowy figures from the criminal underworld. There are glimpses of theatres, casinos, government offices, the fashionable fortress-mansions of the extremely rich, defended by etiquette and liveried servants, and the semi-rural plots that lay behind the squalid house fronts of the Latin Quarter.

Balzac would have been delighted, but not surprised, to learn that historians still plunder his novel for documentary evidence. A reader of *Old Man Goriot* acquires, almost by accident, a vast amount of information about daily life in Restoration Paris. Thanks to Balzac, we know the muddled human contents of a typical Latin Quarter boarding house; we know what the boarders kept in their wardrobes and drawers, and how they talked to one another. We know that city-dwellers missed appointments when fog prevented them from correctly guessing the time of day, that tailors gave credit while hatters did not and that some of the dazzling young dandies who sat in theatre boxes sporting spectacular waistcoats were too deeply in debt to afford a pair of socks. We even know how much a grave-digger might have expected as a tip.

Balzac's aim, however, was not just to document but also to diagnose the ills of the modern world. *Old Man Goriot* takes place between November 1819 and February 1820. It depicts Parisian society a generation after the French Revolution and Louis XVI's 'little accident' (as Madame Vauquer calls the King's decapitation, p. 195) and five years after the fall of Napoleon. The economy was still recovering from the Napoleonic Wars. The restoration of the monarchy in 1815 gave a misleading impression of stability. It suggested that France would now return to those 'eternal truths' which Balzac saw as the basis of civilized society and the twin pillars of his *Human Comedy*: Catholicism and Royalty.

Balzac's political conservatism may reflect a desire to flatter his aristocratic friends, but it also reflects his view of human nature. The human race, in Balzac's view, is directly analogous to the animal kingdom (*Old Man Goriot* is dedicated to a zoologist, Geoffroy Saint-Hilaire). Like all species, the various types of human animal have a common origin, but they evolve and diversify according to their environment. The leafy calm of the provinces is the natural habitat of the virtuous Rastignac family. The city of Paris 'is like a forest in the New World', infested with 'savage tribes' (p. 101), where rapacious individuals, unchecked by religion and monarchy, thrive at the expense of the weak. Humans, of course, are more sophisticated than beasts: 'In the animal kingdom, there are few dramas and little confusion: animals simply attack one another. Humans attack one another too, but the intelligence that they possess to varying degrees makes the struggle more complex.'[12] Humans have arts and sciences; they surround themselves with furniture, and their behaviour changes from one period to the next.

In the urban jungle, a few remarkable individuals rise above the mass by exercising the mysterious power of will. For Balzac, as for Vautrin, thought or will-power (*volonté*) was a material substance which, at a sufficient degree of intensity, could have a visible effect on physical reality. Wielded by a monomaniac, *volonté* could be more destructive than an army. The 'thin lips' and 'greedy teeth' around the table at the Maison Vauquer (p. 11) are examples of the individual human animal focusing its will-power on a particular, petty object to the detriment of the community. A monarchical system of government, in Balzac's view, prevents the mass of ravenous individuals from imposing the tyranny of its animal desires, while Christianity – whether or not a god exists – has a civilizing effect on behaviour. 'Christianity, and especially Catholicism,' he wrote in the preface to *The Human Comedy*, 'is a complete system of repression of the depraved tendencies of man.'

In *Old Man Goriot*, the fixed, feudal society, which the French Revolution had weakened but not destroyed, is being further undermined by poorly regulated capitalism. Baron Nucingen, the husband of Goriot's younger daughter, is able to make a killing, quite legally, by bankrupting the entrepreneurs who build houses on his land. Money contaminates almost every relationship in the novel. The word *argent* (money) appears as often as the word *amour* (love), sometimes in the same sentence. Madame Vauquer judges people by the size of their purse and treats them according to their income. Vautrin gives Rastignac a detailed estimate of the cost of happiness (one million francs). Gondureau, the Chief of the Sûreté, serves the State by having criminals secretly assassinated, thereby saving the cost of trials, prison meals and legal executions. Goriot himself believes that 'Money is life' (p. 205). Cash has replaced the complicated moral arithmetic of vice and virtue with a single currency of success and failure. It encourages crime and cleanses consciences like an indulgent confessor.

This socio-economic view of human relations was something quite new in the French novel. To most critics of the time, mentioning sums of money in a serious work of fiction was intolerably vulgar. Balzac was accused of writing like an auctioneer drawing up a sales catalogue or like a commercial traveller displaying his wares. He was compared to his own comic character 'the Illustrious Gaudissart', who can sell anything from hair-restorer to insurance. Years would pass before this apparent obsession with material details was widely recognized as a mark of Balzac's historical accuracy. It was new in the French novel because it corresponded to something new in French society.

In the early nineteenth century, France was still a rural economy. Less than a quarter of the French population lived in towns and cities. There was practically no heavy industry: the entire country had fewer than forty functioning steam engines. Cash and credit played no role in the lives of most French people. In Rastignac's home region (the Charente), according to Vautrin there are 'more chestnuts [poor people's food] than hundred-sou coins' (p. 98). The fortunes of the richest characters are either inherited (Madame de Beauséant) or based on commerce, property and speculation (Goriot and Baron Nucingen). Paris, which was the biggest city in continental Europe, with a population larger than that of the next six biggest French cities combined, was still a collection of villages. The sound of traffic barely reaches the boarding house in *Old Man Goriot*, and the quartier has yet to be sanitized by modern sewers and building regulations. Pigs, chickens and rabbits live in the little courtyard at the rear of the house. The household waste is swept out into the street. The seamy districts described by Balzac in that 'illustrious valley' of crumbling plaster and 'mud-clogged gutters' (p. 3) are easier to imagine today in half-abandoned hamlets of the southern Massif Central than in Paris itself.

The inmates of the boarding house are like a microcosmic provincial population, a complete society with its own dialect, customs and folklore. Yet even that small society is falling apart. Social mobility brought the characters together and social mobility will scatter them to other parts of the city. The brief appearance, in the opening pages, of a bogus countess who runs off without paying her bill is a warning that the old hierarchy is collapsing. Goriot himself began as a worker, then grew rich during the Revolution by exploiting fears of famine and selling his pasta flour at extortionate prices. Now, an embarrassment to his wealthy daughters, he is a stranger to the world that his money created, alienated from every level of society. By the time the novel opens, in the Maison Vauquer, he has already moved from his three-room, first-floor apartment

to a cheaper one on the second floor and finally to a room on
the third floor, beneath the servants' attic. He may look like an
anachronism to his fellow boarders, but old man Goriot is a
man of his time.

Many of Balzac's admirers, including Victor Hugo and Friedrich
Engels, noticed that his characters often seemed to contra-
dict the author, and that, although Balzac often presented his
novels as political morality tales, his reactionary views were
not necessarily a reliable guide to the true significance of his
work. Balzac himself talked about his characters as real people,
as though he had as little control over them as Goriot has over
his daughters.

As well as exemplifying life in nineteenth-century France,
each character plays a symbolic role, which Balzac frequently
underlines like an artist adding captions to his drawings, just
as he heightens the contrasts of his tableau: age and youth,
poverty and wealth, the glittering Faubourg Saint-Germain and
the festering Latin Quarter. Goriot is a 'Christ of Paternity'
(p. 192), an incarnation of Fatherhood. He expresses Balzac's
own opinion: 'If fathers are to be trampled underfoot, the country will go to the dogs' (p. 240). Goriot's devotion to his daughters
appears to be a dazzling exception in a world where families are
cliques and marriages are business deals, where a virtuous girl
like Victorine Taillefer is abandoned by her father and an ambitious young man like Rastignac uses his family as a bank.

But Goriot is not a simple advertisement of Balzac's convic-
tions. His love is not a model but an aberration. He pictures
himself sitting in his daughters' laps like a puppy. He dreams of
rubbing up against their dresses and kisses Delphine's feet while
she talks to her lover. He funds her adulterous liaison with
Rastignac and fantasizes about living above the lovers' nest,
listening to their movements when they return in the evening.

The 'Christ of Paternity' has reduced his life to a grim obsession. Like a strange bacterium, he feeds on lies and self-deception.
As the frighteningly perspicacious Vautrin points out, Goriot is
quite normal. The city is full of people who are 'thirsty [only] for
a certain kind of water drawn from a certain well', which is 'often

stagnant' (p. 42). To satisfy their secret passion, they would sell their families into slavery and their soul to the devil. They may be gamblers, stock-market speculators or collectors. They may have a passion for music or an all-consuming desire for sweets. 'Old Goriot', says Vautrin, 'is one of those fellows.' In Vautrin's view, Goriot is not a tragic hero but 'a dull stick' (p. 43).

Balzac's novels are remembered for their grand passions and extremes of vice and virtue, but even in his saintliest characters he also shows the frailty of true love and the extraordinary resilience of misguided devotion. He describes heroic self-sacrifice but also the insidious anaesthetic of habit, the tenacity of trivial addictions and the inexorable force of stupidity. For every luminous genius in *The Human Comedy*, there is an indestructible idiot like the mechanical Poiret. In a preface to the first edition of *Old Man Goriot*, Balzac answered complaints that his depiction of society was too bleak by publishing a sarcastic list of all his female characters. It looks like a financial statement, with virtue in the credit column and vice in the debit column. The result was thirty-eight 'virtuous' women and twenty 'criminal' women, 'omitting on purpose more than ten virtuous women, so as not to bore the reader'. The implication was that his characters are not caricatures but human beings who muddle through, adapting their morality to circumstances. They are neither entirely virtuous nor entirely corrupt. The impressively small-minded and ultimately excusable Madame Vauquer appears in the 'virtuous' list, though she is marked as 'doubtful'.

The boarding house itself, ironically, is the closest thing in the novel to a functioning urban family. For all their foibles and obsessions, the boarders form a society which is capable of acting for the general good. Perhaps, as Madame Vauquer believes, the decline of her boarding house is a greater tragedy than the demise of Old Goriot. Here, too, Balzac was conveying a historical truth. He was analysing a relatively recent state of affairs which has since become a social norm. The enormous nineteenth-century Larousse encyclopaedia found his description of a typical boarding house 'too gloomy' ('usually, these modest establishments are clean, pleasant and discreet'), but it agreed with him that the boarding house played a vital role in the city of strangers and misfits: a secular cloister 'for those who like to eat invariably the same thing, from the same plate, in front of the same faces . . . It replaces the missing family with a kind of adopted family.'[13]

The greatest irony of all is that Balzac's novel about paternal love contains one of the first sympathetic depictions of a form of love that was associated with the disintegration and 'demoralization' of society. Vautrin is the first three-dimensional homosexual character of modern fiction whose love is not automatically condemned and whose personality is not defined exclusively by his 'vice'. Unlike most of the other characters, Vautrin is capable of true devotion. Compared to Goriot's violent obsession, his love is silent, discreet and devastatingly effective, as Rastignac discovers.

This surprising aspect of the novel passed unnoticed for over a century after its publication, just as it escapes Rastignac's attention until Mademoiselle Michonneau shines 'a terrifying light into his soul' by hinting at the nature of his attachment to Vautrin (p. 184). If anyone had noticed, the novel would certainly have been banned. In Balzac's hands, the practical impossibility of writing openly about a 'sodomite' became a literary advantage. Vautrin's love is one of the secrets that Rastignac must discover for his 'education' to be complete. Like the reader, he must follow clues and decipher innuendos: the words 'My angel', Vautrin's predilection for tales of passionate male friendship or the expression 'men who have their passions' ('*des hommes à passions*') (pp. 42, 146), which was prostitutes' slang for 'homosexuals'.

Old Man Goriot revealed the extent of Balzac's ambition as a chronicler of modern life. It also introduced a device that would help to hold this teeming universe together. Other novelists had toyed with the idea of making characters recur from one novel to the next, but no one had applied it in such a full and systematic fashion. Rastignac had already appeared as a young dandy in *The Wild Ass's Skin* (1831). In *Old Man Goriot*, he appears at an earlier stage of his career. The tale of Madame de Beauséant's abandonment had already been told in 'The Abandoned Woman'

(1833). The medical student Bianchon, who eats at the Maison Vauquer, would appear in thirty other stories. Vautrin himself, as Balzac wrote in *Splendeurs et misères des courtisanes* ('A Harlot High and Low'), became 'a kind of spinal column who, by his horrible influence, joins, so to speak, *Old Man Goriot* to *Lost Illusions* and *Lost Illusions* to *Splendeurs et misères des courtisanes*'. The end of the novel looks forward to the continuing adventures of Eugène de Rastignac.

So many of Balzac's characters are related to one another that the genealogical tree of *The Human Comedy* covers three walls of the Balzac museum in his house at Passy. A few heroic scholars and monomaniacal readers have managed to commit this gigantic human web to memory. However, all of Balzac's stories can be read quite separately, without any knowledge of the others. The point was not to create a soap opera with a cast of two thousand but to reproduce the three-dimensional effects of real life. Characters become known to us, like real acquaintances, little by little, at different stages of their lives. They show the effects of passing time.

The vital importance of this device lies in the impression of interconnectedness. Every character has hypertextual connotations, just as every inanimate object vibrates with significance. The opening description of the boarding house, which is probably one of the most famous settings of a scene in the history of fiction, serves as an introduction to this alluringly consistent world of material and spiritual unity. Madame Vauquer is not a figure in front of a painted backdrop but a zoological specimen in its natural environment. The creature and its habitat are described simultaneously. Each is explained by the other. Madame Vauquer not only ties the various characters together, she also proves that there is nothing random in the world.

Balzac's total descriptions struck many of his contemporaries as a quirky conceit. One newspaper, the *Gazette des femmes*, parodied his method by telling the story of a house that died of a chest complaint because its walls were thin and damp.[14] Almost two centuries later, his intimation of unity in the infinitesimal bric-a-brac of daily life looks like an aspect of the novel's modernity. His method gave the slightest detail an air of mysterious importance. It redeemed the tawdriness and the clutter. The description of the Vauquer boarding house, that Aladdin's cave of worthless objects, has a curiously inspiring effect. It suggests that the new world of mass-produced objects had an organic life of its own, that there was mystery in streets where every house had a number and every ornament a manufacturer's name. Even before Vautrin's true identity is revealed, the boarding house is a crime scene in which everything is a clue to everything else. It is no coincidence that the inventor of the detective story, Edgar Allan Poe, was an avid reader of *The Human Comedy*. Balzac's characters snuffle about, sifting trivial evidence, prying into private lives. Rastignac peers through Goriot's keyhole, Madame Vauquer investigates his savings, Mademoiselle Michonneau seems to see through walls. Like a highly specialized Sherlock Holmes, Goriot can sniff a crust of bread and identify the quality and provenance of the flour. The narrator himself thinks like a detective, even when no crime has been committed and when the object of forensic investigation is something of no apparent interest, such as a piece of wallpaper or a wooden box of numbered pigeon holes containing napkins.

In a world that seems to be governed by the minor deities of money and sex, this minute omniscience suggests a higher intelligence beyond the moral chaos of the novel. The question of God's existence hovers over the whole drama. Both Goriot and Rastignac are troubled by God's apparent refusal to order the world as morality and their own desires would demand. Goriot claims to have understood God when he became a father, though he barely understands his own daughters. Vautrin is closer to the sceptical spirit of the novel when he gleefully imagines the disappointment of the virtuous if God fails to turn up on the Day of Judgement. Vautrin plays the role traditionally assigned to fairy godmothers and dispensers of divine justice. He penetrates and moulds the minds of the characters like a novelist. He knows how to make their dreams come true. To Rastignac, he reveals the inner workings of society. To the reader, he gives a glimpse of the ferocious intelligence that created him.

*

For most of his professional career, Balzac was admired as a writer of short stories. After his death, he was celebrated as France's pre-eminent novelist. *Old Man Goriot* was seen as one of the great nineteenth-century novels, long before that century had ended. George Eliot thought it 'hateful',[15] but she read it aloud from beginning to end. *Old Man Goriot* showed that the novel was a more capacious genre than anyone had supposed and that an analysis of modern society could be an enthralling tale. One day, Balzac's innovations would appear to be the normal substance of the novel: the effects of environment and physiology on human behaviour; the depiction of social types and the accurate reproduction of their language; the attempt to catalogue the trivia of modern life, and especially the seamy side of urban life.

The idea that Balzac was a realist was already so well established in 1859, nine years after his death, that the poet and critic Charles Baudelaire thought it necessary to emphasize the supernaturalism of his characters:

> I have often been amazed that Balzac's great glory was his reputation as an observer, for it always seemed to me that his principal merit lay in his being a visionary, and an impassioned visionary. All his characters are gifted with that ardour of life that animated himself. All his fictions are as deeply coloured as dreams . . . In Balzac, even the door-keepers have genius. All his minds are weapons loaded to the muzzle with will – just like Balzac himself.[16]

Now that *Old Man Goriot* is well established as a monument of Western literature, the arguments that once surrounded it seem quaint and unimportant. Many critics believed that it was a profoundly immoral work. They thought – as Poiret says of convicts who live with their mistresses – that it 'set an extremely bad example to the rest of society' (p. 151). According to some writers of the time, young men were treating Rastignac as a role model and criminals were using Vautrin's advice as an instruction manual. Balzac himself took accusations of immorality quite seriously. He insisted that 'vice' should be accurately portrayed in alluring colours, and that the morality of a tale lay in its truth not in its social acceptability. 'The author is not deliberately moral or immoral,' he wrote in the preface to the second edition of *Old Man Goriot*. 'The general plan that joins his works one to the other . . . compels him to depict everything.' Of course, he knew that his novels would be read for enjoyment, not for moral improvement, and that *The Human Comedy* could inspire in its readers the kind of obsessional fervour that destroys his fictional families. As Oscar Wilde observed, when he compared Balzac's full-blooded realism to the ghostly reality of life: 'A steady course of Balzac reduces our living friends to shadows, and our acquaintances to the shadows of shades.'[17]

The real story of *Old Man Goriot*'s critical reception lies in the unrecorded pleasure of its countless readers and in the afterlife of its characters. Rastignac and Vautrin are a shadowy presence in a hundred other 'education' novels: Hugo's *Les Misérables*, Dickens's *Great Expectations*, Flaubert's *Sentimental Education*, Dostoevsky's *Crime and Punishment*. Academic critics recognized *Old Man Goriot* as one of the best introductions to Balzac's colossal work and ensured that it was read, or slowly deciphered, by generations of schoolchildren. Histories of literature presented Balzac as the progenitor of Realism and Naturalism. Madame Vauquer's boarding house found itself at the centre of modern literary history.

Graham Robb

NOTES

1. Balzac, *Lettres à Madame Hanska*, ed. Roger Pierrot (Paris: Laffont, 1990), I, p. 195 (18 October 1834).
2. Quoted by Rose Fortassier in *La Comédie Humaine*, ed. Pierre-Georges Castex (Paris: Gallimard, 1976–81), III, p. 5.
3. *Lettres à Madame Hanska*, I, p. 268 (23 August 1835).
4. Balzac, *Correspondance*, ed. Roger Pierrot (Paris: Garnier, 1960–69), II, p. 553 (28 September 1834).
5. *Lettres à Madame Hanska*, I, p. 208 (26 November 1834).
6. Antoine Fontaney, *Journal intime* (Paris: Les Presses françaises, 1925), p. 30 (7 September 1831).

7. Preface to the second edition of *Le Père Goriot* (1835): *La Comédie Humaine*, III, p. 46.

8. *Lettres à Madame Hanska*, I, p. 234 (11 March 1835).

9. *Lettres à Madame Hanska*, I, p. 221 (4 January 1835).

10. *Lettres à Madame Hanska*, I, p. 52 (end of August 1833).

11. *Lettres à Madame Hanska*, I, p. 204 (26 October 1834).

12. Preface to *La Comédie Humaine*, I, p. 9.

13. 'Pension', in Pierre Larousse, *Grand Dictionnaire universel du XIXe siècle*, XII (1874), p. 565.

14. 'La Famille maigre', *Gazette des femmes*, 2 December 1843.

15. Quoted by Donald Adamson in '*Le Père Goriot* devant la critique anglaise', *L'Année balzacienne* (1986), p. 274.

16. Charles Baudelaire, *Oeuvres complètes*, ed. Claude Pichois (Paris: Gallimard, 1975–6), II, p. 120.

17. Oscar Wilde, 'The Decay of Lying', *Intentions* (1891; London: Methuen, 1913), pp. 15–16.

Further Reading

BIOGRAPHY

Hunt, Herbert J., *Honoré de Balzac: A Biography* (1957; New York: Greenwood Press, 1969). A short summary of Balzac's life by one of his most scrupulous translators.

Maurois, André, *Prometheus: The Life of Balzac* (London: The Bodley Head Ltd, 1965). An engaging life by the biographer of Shelley, Proust, Hugo and Sand.

Robb, Graham, *Balzac: A Biography* (1994; London: Picador, 2000). The most recent to appear in English; Robb skilfully interweaves Balzac's life with his work.

Zweig, Stefan, *Balzac* (1946; London: Cassell, 1970). Insightful and pays tribute to Balzac's immense creative energy and vision.

INTERPRETATION

Butler, Ronnie, *Balzac and the French Revolution* (London and Canberra: Croom Helm; Totowa, NJ: Barnes and Noble, 1983). A study of Balzac's preoccupation with the society that emerged from the Revolution.

Kanes, Martin (ed.), *Critical Essays on Honoré de Balzac* (Boston: G. K. Hall & Co., 1990). A collection of modern criticism and essays, with literary vignettes and letters by various authors.

Prendergast, Christopher, *Balzac: Fiction and Melodrama* (London: Edward Arnold; New York: Holmes and Meier,

1978). An exploration and appreciation of the 'melodra-
matic' aspects of Balzac's writing.

Tilby, Michael (ed.), *Balzac* (Modern Literatures in Perspective
series) (London and New York: Longman, 1995). Critical
essays presenting reactions to Balzac's work from the time of
its publication to the present day.

HISTORY

Hemmings, F. W. J., *Culture and Society in France, 1789–1848*
(Leicester University Press; New York: Peter Lang, 1987). A
study of cultural change and social development in the period
between the two revolutions.

Perrot, Michelle (ed.), *A History of Private Life: 4. From the
Fires of Revolution to the Great War*, ed. Philippe Ariès and
Georges Duby (London and Cambridge, Mass.: Belknap
Press of Harvard University Press, 1990). A Balzacian
approach reflected in the title: a history of the private, every-
day lives of individuals.

Note on the Text and Translation

The translation follows the text of the Pléiade edition of *Le Père Goriot*, edited by Rose Fortassier (Gallimard, 1976). This is based on Balzac's personal copy of the 1843 Furne edition, which contains his final corrections in the margins.

The six sections take the titles of the four instalments of the novel as it appeared in the *Revue de Paris* (1835). The first and last instalments were made up of two chapters each. See Introduction pp. xvii–xviii.

The main source of nineteenth-century English equivalents for thieves' cant and slang in the translation is Eric Partridge's *Dictionary of the Underworld* (1949). Not all slang is explained in the Notes, especially where its main purpose has been to add colour or tone.

Note on Money

Financial references abound in *Old Man Goriot* (see Introduction pp. xviii–xxiii on Balzac's innovative 'socio-economic view of human relations'). Many of them are fairly complex and specific explanations, or interpretations, have been attempted in the notes. A number of general points are dealt with below.

Throughout the novel, characters refer to different currency systems, which it might be useful to clarify here.

The official currency in France at the time was the decimal (Germinal) franc, introduced by the Republican government in 1795 but not minted (due to a shortage of bullion) until 1803. The franc was divided into decimes and centimes and issued in 1-franc, 5-franc (écu) and 20-franc (napoléon) pieces.

This system replaced the Ancien Régime *livre tournois* (3 deniers to the liard, 12 deniers to the sou, 20 sous to the livre, 6 livres to the écu, 24 livres to the louis d'or). However, the *livre tournois*, exchangeable at a rate of 81 livres to 80 francs, remained in circulation until 1834.

During the Bourbon Restoration, the 20-franc piece, or napoléon, was renamed the louis.

Banknotes were issued by the Bank of France from 1800, in denominations of 500 and 1,000 francs. These replaced the unpopular revolutionary *assignats*, whose swift devaluation led to a long-term distrust of paper money and preference for stable coinage in France.

To give an idea of the relative worth of money in the novel: Vautrin tips the postman 20 sous (1 franc); Rastignac pays Madame Vauquer 45 francs a month for food and lodging (540 francs per year) and receives an allowance of twelve hundred a year from his cash-strapped family; Goriot's daughters have (or are supposed to have) annual incomes of 36,000 or 50,000 francs (Goriot cites both figures); Madame Vauquer has 40,000 francs in savings; Monsieur d'Ajuda-Pinto has a carriage and pair worth 'at least thirty thousand francs'. See also Vautrin's rundown, for Rastignac's benefit, of the cost of living as a man of fashion in Paris (pp. 137–8).

OLD MAN GORIOT

To the great and illustrious Geoffroy Saint-Hilaire,[1] as an admiring tribute to his work and his genius.

de Balzac

I

A RESPECTABLE
BOARDING HOUSE

For the last forty years, an old woman by the name of Madame Vauquer, *née* de Conflans, has run a boarding house in Paris, in the Rue Neuve-Sainte-Geneviève,[2] between the Latin Quarter and the Faubourg Saint-Marceau.[3] Although this respectable establishment, known as the Maison Vauquer, accepts both men and women, young and old, its habits have never once excited malicious gossip. But then, no young lady has been seen there for thirty years and a young man who lodges there must have a very small allowance from his family. However, in 1819, the year in which this drama begins, one poor young woman was to be found there. Now, the word drama has fallen into some disrepute, having been bandied about in such an excessive and perverse way, in this age of tear-strewn literature,[4] but it does ask to be used here. Not that this story is dramatic in the true sense of the term, but by the end of it, perhaps a few tears will have been shed *intra muros et extra*.[5] Will it be understood outside Paris? There is room for doubt. The peculiarities of this scene packed with commentary and local colour may only be appreciated between the hills of Montmartre and the heights of Montrouge, in that illustrious valley of endlessly crumbling stucco and black, mud-clogged gutters; a valley full of genuine suffering and frequently counterfeit joy, where life is so frantically hectic that only the most freakish anomaly will produce any lasting sensation. Nonetheless, here and there, in this dense web of vice and virtue, you come across sufferings that seem grand and solemn: the selfish, the self-interested stop and feel pity; although for them such things are no sooner seen than swallowed, as swiftly as succulent fruit. A stouter heart than most may put a temporary spoke in the wheel of the chariot of civilization, which resembles that of the idol of Jaggernaut,[6] but will soon be crushed as it continues its glorious progress. You will react in much the same way, you who are holding this book in your white hand, you who are sinking into a soft-cushioned chair saying to yourself: 'Perhaps this will entertain me.' After reading about old man Goriot's secret woes, you will dine heartily, blaming your insensitivity firmly on the author, accusing him of exaggeration, pointing the finger at his feverish imagination. Well! Let me tell you that this drama is neither fiction nor romance. *All is true*,[7] so true that we may each recognize elements of it close to home, perhaps even in our hearts.

The premises used for the business of the boarding house are owned by Madame Vauquer. The building stands at the foot of the Rue Neuve-Sainte-Geneviève, just where the ground shelves into the Rue de l'Arbalète so sharply and inconveniently that horses rarely go up or down it. This circumstance contributes to the silence which prevails in these streets wedged between the domes of the Val-de-Grâce and the Panthéon,[8] two monuments which modify the atmospheric conditions, giving the light a jaundiced tinge, while the harsh shadows cast by their cupolas make everything gloomy. The pavements are dry, the gutters are empty of either water or mud, grass grows out of the walls. Every passer-by – even the most carefree man in the world – feels dejected here, where the sound of a carriage is a momentous event, the houses are drab and the walls make you feel boxed in. A Parisian who strayed this way would see nothing but boarding houses and institutions, tedium and wretchedness, old age dying, blithe youth forced to toil. No district of Paris is less attractive, nor, it must be said, so little known. The Rue Neuve-Sainte-Geneviève itself is like a bronze frame, the only one that fits this tale, for it prepares the mind only too well with its murky colours and sobering thoughts; just as, step by step, the daylight fades and the guide's patter rings hollow, when the traveller descends into the Catacombs. A fitting comparison! Who is to say which sight is the more horrible: shrivelled hearts, or empty skulls?

The front of the building overlooks a small patch of garden, while the boarding house as a whole stands at a right angle to the Rue Neuve-Sainte-Geneviève, where you see its depth in cross-section. Between the house and the garden, a sunken gravel strip a fathom wide runs the length of the façade, fronted by a sandy path bordered with geraniums, oleanders and pomegranate trees planted in large blue and white porcelain vases. The entrance to this path is through a secondary door, above which is a sign declaring: MAISON VAUQUER, and underneath: *Lodgings for persons of both sexes et cetera*. During the day, at the end of the path, through an openwork gate with a strident bell, you might glimpse a green marble arcade painted by a local artist on the wall facing the street. A statue of Eros stands in the recess suggested by the painting. Those fond of symbols might see in its blistering coat of varnish a kind of love more Parisian than mythical, one which is cured a stone's throw away.[9] Beneath the pedestal, this half-eroded inscription, with its fashionable enthusiasm for Voltaire on his return to Paris in 1777,[10] reveals the ornament's age:

> *Whoever you are, your master you see:*
> *For that's what he is, was, or shall be.*

At nightfall, the openwork gate is covered with a solid one. The patch of garden, as wide as the façade is long, is boxed in by the street wall and the adjoining wall of the house next door, whose thick curtain of ivy is so unusually picturesque for Paris that passers-by find their eye drawn to it. The garden walls are covered in espaliers and vines, whose spindly and powdery attempts at fruit each year provide Madame Vauquer with a source of concern and conversation with her lodgers. Along each wall a narrow path leads to an area overshadowed by lime trees, which Madame Vauquer, albeit *née* de Conflans, obstinately calls *ly-ums*, despite her boarders' remarks on her pronunciation. Two paths run either side of a bed of artichokes bordered with sorrel, lettuce and parsley, and flanked by tapering fruit trees.[11] A round table, painted green and surrounded by seats, stands beneath the spreading lime branches. On

sweltering summer days, those boarders who can afford to take
coffee come and sip it here, in heat strong enough to hatch
eggs. The front of the building, three storeys high and topped
with garrets, is built of rough stone daubed in that shade of
yellow which gives a dingy air to almost every house in Paris.
Each floor has five small-paned windows, whose slatted blinds
all hang aslant so that no two line up as they should. The building has two windows to its depth; those on the ground floor are
furnished only by iron bars, covered with mesh. At the back is
a yard about twenty feet across, where pigs, chickens and rabbits live together companionably, with a shed stacked with
wood at one end. Hanging between the shed and the kitchen
window is the pantry; the slops from the sink flow out beneath
it. The yard has a narrow door leading to the Rue Neuve-
Sainte-Geneviève, through which the cook sweeps away the
household's waste, sluicing the cesspool that forms there with
water to keep the stench at bay.

The ground floor is naturally appointed to the activity of
a boarding house. A French window opens into the front
room, whose two street-facing windows let in some light. The
drawing room communicates with the dining room, which is
separated from the kitchen by a flight of wooden stairs laid
with scrubbed and re-stained tiles. There is no more dispiriting
sight than that drawing room furnished with easy and hard-
backed chairs upholstered in haircloth[12] with matt and shiny
stripes. In the middle is a round table with a grey-and-white
marble top bearing the obligatory white porcelain coffee
service with worn gilt trim found everywhere these days. This
room, whose floor is rather crooked, is wainscoted to elbow
height. The remaining wall space is covered with glazed wallpaper showing scenes from *Telemachus*,[13] whose classical
characters appear in colour. In the panel between the barred
windows, the boarders may contemplate the scene of the ban-
quet given by Calypso for Ulysses' son. For forty years this
picture has provided material for endless quips by the younger
boarders, who make believe they're superior to their circumstances by mocking the dinner to which poverty condemns
them. The stone fireplace, whose permanently spotless hearth

attests to the fact that no fire is ever kindled there except on special occasions, is adorned with two vases crammed with decrepit artificial flowers, set on either side of a bluish marble clock in the worst taste. Our language has no name for the odour given off by this first room, which ought to be called 'essence of boarding house'. It smells of all that is stale, mildewy, rancid; it chills you, makes your nose run, clings to your clothes; it repeats like last night's dinner; it reeks of the scullery, the pantry, the poorhouse. If a method were invented for measuring the foul and fundamental particles contributed by the catarrhal conditions specific to each boarder, young and old, perhaps it really could be described. And yet, despite these dreary horrors, if you compare it with the dining room next door, you will find the drawing room as elegant and fragrant as any self-respecting boudoir. This room, panelled throughout, was once painted a colour which can no longer be discerned, providing a backdrop for the grime which has printed over it in layers, forming intriguing patterns. It is crammed with an assortment of sticky sideboards upon which you see nicked, stained carafes, round *moiré*[14] stands and stacks of thick china plates with blue edging, made in Tournai. In one corner is a rack of numbered pigeon holes housing each boarder's food- or wine-stained serviette. In this room you find those indestructible pieces of furniture that nobody else will have, stranded here like the debris of civilization in a Hospital of Incurables. You might see a weather house with a Capuchin monk that comes out when it rains, tasteless prints that spoil your appetite, all framed in varnished black wood with gilt-piping; a tortoiseshell wall-clock with copper detail; a green stove, Argand lamps[15] coated in a blend of dust and oil, a long table covered with oilcloth greasy enough for a facetious diner to write his name on using his finger as a pen, warped chairs, shabby rush placemats, forever uncoiling but just about holding together; and finally, pitiful plate-warmers with broken grates, slack hinges and charred wood. A full explanation of how old, cracked, rotten, shaky, worm-eaten, armless, seedy, creaking and generally on its last legs the furniture is would require a description so lengthy it would delay the main interest of this story, something that those of you in a hurry would find unforgivable. The floor, laid with red tiles, is pitted with craters caused by repeated scrubbing and staining. In all, an unpoetic wretchedness reigns throughout; a mean, reduced, threadbare wretchedness. Although there is not yet filth, there are stains; although there are neither holes nor rags, everything is sliding into decay.

The room may be seen in all its splendour at around seven in the morning, at which time Madame Vauquer's cat, running ahead of its mistress, jumps up onto the sideboards, sniffs at the milk kept in various jugs covered with plates and makes its morning *prrruing* sound. Now the widow herself appears, shuffling along in her puckered slippers, a crooked hair-piece poking out beneath the tulle bonnet perched on her head. Her flabby, sagging face, her protruding parrot's beak of a nose, her stubby, pudgy hands, her plump tick of a body, her overstuffed, wobbling bodice, are all entirely in keeping with this room, where the walls sweat misfortune, where enterprise kicks its heels and whose fetid fug Madame Vauquer breathes in without gagging. Her face is as cold as the first autumn frost, the expression in her crow-footed eyes shifts between the fixed smile of a dancer and the baleful glower of a discounter;[16] in all, everything about her points to the boarding house, just as the boarding house leads to her. There can be no prison without a warder, the one is unimaginable without the other. The pallor and portliness of this small woman are the products of the life she leads, just as typhus emanates from the vapours of a hospital. Her knitted woollen petticoat, drooping below an overskirt made from an old dress and poking out through the slits where the cloth has worn away, epitomizes the drawing room, the dining room, the garden, anticipates the cooking and prefigures the boarders. Once she's here, the scene is set, the show can begin. Madame Vauquer, who must be about fifty years of age, resembles all *women who have seen better days*. She has the unflinching stare, the self-righteous manner of a Madam who will lay down the law to raise her fee, but is otherwise prepared to stop at nothing to improve her lot, to inform on Georges or Pichegru[17] (if Georges and Pichegru hadn't already been shopped). Nonetheless, the boarders would say that she was a *good woman at heart*, believing her to be as down on her luck as they were, hearing her groan and cough as they did. What kind of a man was Monsieur Vauquer? She tended to be uncommunicative on the subject of the deceased. How did he lose his fortune? In the troubles, she would reply. He had treated her shabbily, leaving her with only her eyes to weep with, this house as her livelihood and the right not to sympathize with anyone else in a tight spot, because, as she would say, she had suffered all that a body can suffer. Recognizing her mistress's shuffling step, big Sylvie, the cook, would hurry out to serve *déjeuner* to the lodgers.

The boarders, who lived out, usually only came for dinner, which cost thirty francs a month payable in advance. At the time when this story begins, there were seven lodgers. The best apartments in the house were on the first floor. Madame Vauquer lived in the smaller of the two and the other was occupied by Madame Couture, the widow of a Commissary-General[18] of the French Republic. She had in her charge a young lady of a tender age, called Victorine Taillefer, whom she cared for as a mother. These two ladies paid eighteen hundred francs for their board and lodging. The first of the two apartments on the second floor was occupied by an elderly man called Poiret; the other by a man of around forty years of age, known as Monsieur Vautrin, who wore a black wig, dyed his side-whiskers, and was by his own account a former merchant. The third floor was divided into four rooms, two of which were rented, one by an elderly spinster called Mademoiselle Michonneau; the other by a retired dealer in vermicelli, Italian pasta and starch, who had come to be known as old man Goriot. The other two rooms were intended for birds of passage, for students down on their luck who, like Goriot and Mademoiselle Michonneau, could only afford forty-five francs a month for food and lodging, but Madame Vauquer had little desire for their custom and only took them in for want of anyone better: they ate too much bread. At the time, one of these two rooms was occupied by a young man who had come to Paris from the Angoulême area to study law and whose large family were tightening their belts and making endless sacrifices in order to send him twelve hundred francs a year. Eugène de Rastignac, as he was called, was one of those young men whose lack of fortune requires them to develop an aptitude for work, who, from an early age, fully understand what their parents expect of them and prepare for greatness by calculating how far their learning will take them and adapting it in advance of shifts in society, thus ensuring they will be the first to benefit. Without his inquisitiveness and the skill with which he engineered his entry into the most exclusive Parisian society, the present account would not have been painted in such true colours, and for this we must undoubtedly thank his shrewdness and his desire to fathom the mysteries of an appalling situation, as carefully concealed by those who had created it as by the man who endured it.

Up from the third floor was an attic where the laundry was hung out, and two garrets, where Christophe the errand boy and big Sylvie the cook slept. Besides the seven lodgers, year in, year out, Madame Vauquer took eight students of law or medicine and two or three regulars who lived nearby, all of whom paid for board alone. In the evening, eighteen people sat down to eat in the dining room, which could hold up to twenty, but in the morning, only the seven residents were to be found there, so that *déjeuner* almost felt like a family meal. They would come downstairs in slippers and venture to make confidential remarks about the dress or appearance of the non-residents, discussing the events of the previous evening, their privacy encouraging them to speak freely. These seven lodgers were Madame Vauquer's spoilt children and she measured out the level of care and respect due to each, depending on how much they paid, with the precision of an astronomer. The residents may have ended up under the same roof by chance, but they were all motivated by the same consideration. The two second-floor lodgers paid only seventy-two francs per month. Rates as cheap as these are only to be found in the Faubourg Saint-Marcel between the hospitals of La Bourbe and La Salpêtrière.[19] Indeed, with the exception of Madame Couture, who paid more, all of the lodgers were more or less obviously down at heel. And so the dingy-looking interior of this establishment was matched by the equally shabby clothing of those who occupied it. The men wore frock-coats whose colour you'd be hard pressed to define, shoes of the kind found discarded in the road in fashionable districts, linen hanging by a thread, clothes stripped of all but their soul. The women wore faded, re-dyed, washed-out dresses, old darned lace, gloves shiny with wear, collarettes that always looked soiled and frayed *fichus*.[20] Yet despite these clothes, almost without exception, they had solid physiques, constitutions which had survived life's storms, and cold, hard faces, as worn as écu coins withdrawn from circulation. Their thin lips concealed greedy teeth. Each lodger's appearance hinted at a tragedy, either fully played-out, or in progress; not a tragedy performed in the glare of the footlights against a backdrop of painted scenery, but a silent, real-life tragedy, so chilling it stirs and warms the heart, a tragedy with no final curtain.

The elderly, weary-eyed Mademoiselle Michonneau was never seen without a grubby green taffeta eye-shade edged with wire, which would have scared off the Angel of Mercy. Her shawl, with its balding, drooping fringe, appeared to be draped over a skeleton, so angular were the shapes it clung to. What acid had eaten away this woman's feminine curves? She must have been pretty once, and shapely too: was it vice, grief, cupidity? Had she loved too much? Perhaps she had been a dealer in second-hand finery,[21] or simply a whore? Was she atoning for a shameless youth spent in pursuit of profit and pleasure, with an old age which made passers-by turn away? Her blank expression chilled, her scraggy face threatened. Her voice was as shrill as a solitary cicada scraping in the undergrowth at the approach of winter. She said that she had cared for an old gentleman suffering from an inflammation of the bladder and abandoned by his children who believed him to be destitute. This old man had bequeathed to her a life annuity of one thousand francs, which was periodically disputed by his heirs, who called her every kind of name. Although her face had been ravaged by the passions that had distorted it, the texture of her skin was still delicate and white in places, perhaps indicating that her body also retained some vestigial beauty.

Monsieur Poiret was a kind of blundering automaton. To see him – looming like a grey shadow along a path in the Jardin des Plantes, a drooping old cap on his head, barely able to grip the yellowing ivory handle of his stick, the crumpled skirts of his frock-coat flapping, miserably failing to hide his empty, sagging breeches and blue-stockinged legs that gave way like a drunkard's, and revealing his dirty white waistcoat and the concertinaed coarse muslin shirt frill which had worked loose from the tie twisted round his scrawny turkey's neck – you wouldn't be alone in asking yourself whether this pantomime figure could possibly belong to the audacious tribe of the sons of Japet[22] who flit about on the Boulevard des Italiens. What kind of employment had knocked the stuffing out of him? What passion had left such a stamp of bewilderment on his bulbous face, which would have seemed overdone drawn as a carica-ture. What kind of a man had he been? Perhaps he'd been employed by the Ministry of Justice, in the office to which exe-cutioners addressed their memoranda of expenses, accounts of supplies of black veils for parricides, of sawdust for baskets, of rope for the guillotine. He might have once been a receiver at the entrance to an abattoir or an assistant health inspector. In all, he appeared to have been one of the mill-horses that keep the great wheel of society turning, one of those Parisian cats that never know for which monkeys they are pulling chestnuts out of the fire,[23] one of many pivots on which some public tragedy or controversy has revolved, one of those men that we look at and say: *After all, someone has to do it.* The fine folk of Paris are oblivious to faces such as his, drained by mental or physical suffering. But then Paris is an ocean. Heave in the lead as often as you like, you'll never sound its depths. Explore it, describe it: however exhaustive your exploration or descrip-tion, however numerous and inquisitive the explorers of that sea, there will always be virgin territory, an unknown cave, flowers, pearls, monsters, something unheard of, forgotten by literary divers. The Maison Vauquer is one of these curious monstrosities.

Two faces stood out in striking contrast to the majority of the boarders and lodgers. Although Mademoiselle Victorine

Taillefer had the sickly complexion of a young lady suffering from chlorosis,[24] and her habitual melancholy, troubled countenance and air of weakness and fragility blended seamlessly into the background of general suffering, at least she wasn't old and her tongue and her movements were agile. This young unfortunate resembled a shrub with yellowing leaves, recently planted in the wrong kind of soil. Her sallow features, her slick of tawny hair, her painfully thin waist, gave her the kind of grace which modern poets have found in medieval statues. Her grey eyes flecked with black expressed a Christian gentleness and resignation, while her simple, inexpensive clothes showed off her youthful curves. Compared with the other boarders, she was pretty. If she had been happy, she would have been ravishing: happiness is a woman's poetry, as powders and pomades are her persona. If the exhilaration of a ball could have imparted a rosy bloom to her pale face; if the sweet delights of an elegant life could have filled out her cheeks – already somewhat hollow – and made them glow; if love could have rekindled some spark in her downcast eyes, Victorine would have been the equal of the most beautiful of young women. She lacked what creates a woman anew: fine clothes and love letters. Her story would have made a good novel. Believing he had good reason not to recognize her as his daughter, her father refused to have her under his roof, gave her only six hundred francs per year and had wound up his estate so that his son would be the sole inheritor. Victorine's mother had died of despair in the house of a distant relative, Madame Couture, who had cared for the orphan ever since as if she were her own child. Unfortunately the widow of the Commissary-General to the Armies of the Republic had nothing to her name but her dower and her pension; one day she might have to leave this poor girl, entirely without experience and resources, to the mercy of the world. The worthy woman took Victorine to Mass every Sunday and to Confession once a fortnight, to make her pious, if nothing else. With good reason. Her religious fervour gave the disowned child some hope for the future. She loved her father and tried, every year, to deliver in person her mother's letter of forgiveness to him; but every year without fail she found the door of her father's house closed to her. Her brother, her only possible intermediary, hadn't once come to visit her in four years and sent her no assistance. She implored God to open her father's eyes, to soften her brother's heart, and prayed for both without condemning either. As far as Madame Couture and Madame Vauquer were concerned, there weren't enough words in the dictionary of insults to describe such barbaric conduct. Whenever they spoke ill of the infamous millionaire, Victorine murmured words as gentle as the call of a wounded dove whose cry of pain still expresses love.

Eugène de Rastignac's looks were typically southern: pale complexion, black hair, blue eyes. His bearing, his manners, his unfailing poise, all indicated that he had been born into a noble family, where every effort had been made to educate him in traditions of good taste. Although he was careful with his coats, although on a normal day you would find him still wearing out last year's clothes, nonetheless, from time to time he was able to go out dressed like any fashionable young gentleman. Most days he wore an old frock-coat, a shabby waistcoat, the limp, sorry-looking, badly knotted black tie favoured by students, trousers in keeping with the rest and resoled boots.

Vautrin, the forty-year-old man with dyed side-whiskers, slotted in somewhere between these two characters and the other boarders. He was one of those men people call 'the life and soul!'. He had broad shoulders, a powerful chest, bulging muscles and thick, square hands marked with distinctive growths of tufty, flame-red hair between the finger joints. His face, lined with premature wrinkles, showed signs of an intransigence which belied his accommodating and sociable ways. His bass-baritone voice, as booming as his hearty laugh, was far from displeasing. He was obliging and cheerful. If a lock was playing up, he would dismantle it, get it working, oil it, file it and put it back together again in an instant, saying, 'I know a thing or two about that.' Indeed, he knew a thing or two about everything: ships, the sea, France, foreign parts, business, men, current affairs, laws, grand houses and prisons. If someone had a fit of the grumbles, he offered them his services on the spot. He had on several occasions lent money to Madame

Vauquer and some of her boarders; but despite his good-natured manner, those in his debt would have died rather than fail to return what they owed him, due to a certain piercing and steely look[25] he had, which struck fear into the heart. His skill at aiming a stream of saliva hinted at unshakeable sang-froid, suggesting that he would stop at nothing, not even a crime, to get himself out of a tight situation. His eyes seemed to penetrate right to the heart of all matters, all consciences, all feelings, with the severity of a judge. He usually went out after *déjeuner*, coming back for dinner, then would disappear for the entire evening and return towards midnight, letting himself in with a master key which Madame Vauquer had let him have. He was the only one to enjoy this privilege. But then, he was on the best of terms with the widow, whom he would seize around the waist, calling her 'Ma', a baffling piece of flattery. The old bird still believed this feat to be within the reach of any man, but only Vautrin had long enough arms to squeeze her bulky circumference. One typically extravagant gesture of his was to pay fifteen francs a month for the *gloria*[26] he took at dessert. Had any of the boarders been less superficial – the young caught up in the whirlwind of Parisian life, the old indifferent to anything which did not affect them directly – they might have looked beyond the ambiguous impression that Vautrin made on them. He knew or guessed the business of all those around him, while not one of them was able to read either his thoughts or his actions. Although he might cast his apparent conviviality and jollity, his constant willingness to oblige, as a barrier between himself and the others, he frequently revealed glimpses of the fearsome depths of his personality. Often, a flash of wit worthy of Juvenal[27] – showing that he revelled in scoffing at the law, lashing out at high society, exposing its fecklessness – suggested that he had some score to settle with society and that there was some carefully buried mystery in his life.

Attracted, perhaps without realizing it, by the strength of the one and the beauty of the other, Mademoiselle Taillefer divided her furtive glances, her secret thoughts, between the forty-year-old man and the young student; but neither appeared to show any interest in her, even though, from one day to the next, chance might improve her lot and make her a wealthy match. None of these people, as it happened, ever bothered to question whether the alleged misfortunes of this or that person were genuine or false. They all felt a kind of mutual indifference mingled with distrust that arose from their respective situations. They knew they were powerless to do anything about their sufferings, and by dint of recounting them to each other had all drained the cup of sympathy dry. Like old couples, they had nothing left to say to each other. And so all that was left between them were the interrelated parts of the machinery of life, the cogs and wheels without the oil. They would all of them walk straight past a blind man in the road, listen unmoved to tales of woe and view a man's death as a solution to the problem of the poverty which left them insensible to the most agonizing death throes. The happiest of these forlorn souls was Madame Vauquer, who reigned over this poorhouse with paying guests. She alone believed the little garden – silent and cold, parched and dank, and thus as monotonous as any steppe – to be a pleasant grove. For her alone this drab yellow building, smelling as strongly of verdigris[28] as a counting-house, was a source of delight. These cells belonged to her. She fed these convicts – lifers sentenced to endless punishment – and they respected the authority she exerted over them. Where else in Paris would these poor creatures have found, at the price she was asking, adequate, wholesome food, and lodgings which they were at liberty to make, if not elegant or comfortable, at least clean and salubrious? Had she ever allowed herself some blatant act of injustice, the victim would have suffered it in silence.

Such a gathering should and did present in microcosm the elements that make up society as a whole. Among the eighteen boarders was to be found, as in every school, or throughout the world, one poor rejected creature, a figure of fun and the butt of all humour. At the start of his second year, this man began to stand out for Eugène de Rastignac from the rest of those among whom he was condemned to live for a further two years. Their whipping boy was the retired vermicelli dealer, old man Goriot: a painter would have shone all the light in the scene upon his face, as this historian will. What twist of fate had caused such a confusion of scorn and hatred, persecution and pity, such a lack of concern for his suffering, to rain down on the head of the oldest boarder? Had he brought it upon himself through one of those acts of ridicule or eccentricity that we find less pardonable than actual vice? Such issues lie behind many a social injustice. Perhaps it's in human nature to reserve all suffering for the person who quietly endures everything, whether out of genuine humility, weakness or indifference. Don't we all love to prove our strength at the expense of someone or something else? Even that most pathetic of creatures, the street urchin, rings all the doorbells when it's freezing cold outside or shins up a gleaming monument to write his name on it.

In 1813, at around sixty-nine years of age, old man Goriot had withdrawn from business and retired to Madame Vauquer's establishment. He had initially rented the rooms now occupied by Madame Couture and had paid twelve hundred francs for board and lodging with the air of a man for whom five louis more or less was a trifle. Madame Vauquer had spruced up the three rooms of this apartment on receipt of an advance payment, which covered, he was told, the cost of the tawdry furnishings: yellow calico curtains, varnished wooden armchairs upholstered in Utrecht velvet, a couple of cheap distemper-paintings and wallpaper at which suburban taverns would turn up their noses. Perhaps it was the casual generosity with which old man Goriot – at that time respectfully referred to as Monsieur Goriot – allowed himself to be duped that made her decide he was a fool without an ounce of business sense. Goriot arrived fitted out with an opulent wardrobe, the magnificent *trousseau* of a merchant with the means to treat himself on retiring from trade. Madame Vauquer had admired eighteen cambric shirts, whose exquisite quality she found all the more remarkable for the two pins joined by a fine chain, each set with a huge diamond, that the vermicelli dealer wore on his shirt frill. It was his custom to wear a cornflower-blue morning coat, and every day he chose a fresh white *piqué* waistcoat, beneath which his pear-shaped, protuberant belly would wobble around, causing a heavy gold chain hung with watch-charms to bounce up and down. His snuffbox, also made of gold, contained a locket full of hair, appearing to suggest he had stolen a few hearts. When his hostess accused him of being a bit of a *ladies' man*, his lips widened into the glad smile of the bourgeois whose soft spot has just been touched. His armoires (which he pronounced '*ormoires*'[29] as those of humble station do) were crammed with an abundance of his household silverware. The widow's eyes lit up as she obligingly helped him to unpack and tidy away the ladles, serving spoons, cutlery, cruets, sauce boats, miscellaneous dishes, silver-gilt breakfast services, all more or less splendid pieces, worth a considerable weight in marks,[30] and from which he couldn't bear to be separated. These presents reminded him of special occasions in his family life. 'This', he said to Madame Vauquer, clutching a platter and small dish with two kissing turtle-doves on its cover, 'is the first present my wife ever gave me, on our anniversary. Poor darling! It cost her every penny of her maiden's savings. Let me tell you, Madame, I would rather scrape a living from the earth with my bare nails than part with this. Thank the Lord! I'll be able to drink my coffee from this bowl every morning for the rest of my life. I have nothing to complain about, my bread will be buttered on both sides for a good while yet.' Indeed, Madame Vauquer, with her magpie's eye, had taken a good look at certain entries in the Grand-Livre,[31] which, roughly totted up, indicated that the excellent Goriot had an income of around eight to ten thousand francs a year. From that day on, Madame Vauquer, *née* de Conflans, who only admitted to thirty-nine of her forty-eight years, began to get ideas. Although the lower lids of Goriot's eyes were turned out, swollen and drooping, so that he was forever wiping them, she found his manner agreeable and proper. Moreover, his fleshy, bulging calves, not to mention his long square nose, betokened certain fine qualities the widow seemed to find attractive, and which were borne out by the old man's moon-like and naively foolish face. He appeared to be a solidly built beast, more likely to be led by his heart than his head. His hair dressed in pigeon-wings, which the barber from the Ecole Polytechnique came to powder for him each morning, formed five points on his low forehead and framed his face well.

Although a little countrified, he was so well turned out and took such generous pinches of snuff, inhaling it with the air of a man whose snuffbox is always bound to be full of Macouba,[32] that on Monsieur Goriot's first night under her roof, Madame Vauquer rolled in her blankets like a partridge wrapped in bacon and roasted in the flames of an overwhelming desire to throw off the shroud of Vauquer and rise out of the ashes as Goriot. To be married, sell her boarding house, give her arm to this prime specimen of the bourgeoisie, become one of the local worthies, collecting money for the poor, driving out to Choisy, Soissy, Gentilly[33] on Sundays; going to the theatre whenever she felt like it and sitting in a box, without having to wait for some boarder to pass on a free ticket in July:[34] the Eldorado she dreamed of was that of any modest Parisian householder. She had told no one about the forty thousand francs she owned, scraped together penny by penny. In terms of wealth, she confidently believed herself to be a decent match. 'As for the rest, I'm certainly good enough for that old chap!' she said to herself in bed, turning onto her side as if to provide herself with evidence of the alluring contours which big Sylvie found moulded into the hollows of the mattress each morning. From that day on, for around three months, the widow Vauquer took advantage of Monsieur Goriot's barber and spent a fair amount of money on her appearance, which she justified by the need to ensure that the standing of her establishment was in keeping with the dignitaries who patronized it. She plotted and schemed to bring in a different class of boarder, and made no secret of the fact that, from now on, she would only accept persons of the highest distinction in every respect. If a stranger showed up, she boasted to him of the preference that Monsieur Goriot, one of the most important and respected merchants in Paris, had shown for her establishment. She distributed brochures with the heading MAISON VAUQUER. 'It was', she wrote, 'one of the most longstanding and highly esteemed boarding houses in the vicinity of the Latin Quarter. It had a charming view over the Gobelins valley (you could just about see it from the third floor) and a *delightful* garden, at one end of which was a LONG ARBOUR of lime trees.' She also mentioned the clean air and seclusion. This brochure brought her Madame la Comtesse d'Ambermesnil, a thirty-six-year-old woman, who was awaiting completion of the settlement and payment of a pension due to her as the widow of a general who had died in the *fields* of battle. Madame Vauquer introduced certain refinements to her table, lit a fire in her drawing room for almost six months and kept the promises made in her brochure so well that she really *invested herself*. The comtesse even told Madame Vauquer, whom she called her *dear friend*, that she would bring her the Baronne de Vaumerland and the widow of Colonel Comte Picqoiseau, two friends of hers, who would, at the end of the quarter, be leaving a boarding house in the Marais that cost more than the Maison Vauquer. Of course, these ladies would be extremely well off once the War Office had sorted out their affairs. 'But', she said, 'the paperwork is always interminable.' The two widows would retire to Madame Vauquer's rooms after dinner, where they had little chats, drinking cassis and nibbling delicacies reserved for the delectation of the mistress of the house. Madame de l'Ambermesnil greatly approved of her hostess's views on Goriot, excellent views, which she had of course guessed from the start; she thought he was just perfect.

'Oh! My dear lady! A man as sound as a bell,' the widow said to her, 'a man in mint condition, with plenty left for a woman to enjoy.'

The comtesse generously gave Madame Vauquer the benefit of her opinion: her wardrobe needed to be brought in line with her aspirations. 'We must set you on a war-footing,' she said to her. After much calculation, the two widows set off together to the Galeries de Bois[35] at the Palais-Royal, where they bought a plumed hat and a bonnet. The comtesse then took her friend to La Petite Jeannette,[36] and at this shop they chose a dress and a shawl. When the ammunition had been loaded and the widow presented arms, she bore a striking resemblance to the signboard of the Boeuf à la mode.[37] Despite this, she found her appearance so much improved that she felt she owed the comtesse, and although *not one for giving presents*, begged her to accept a hat costing twenty francs. As it happened, she wanted to ask her a favour: to sound out Goriot and sing her praises to him. Madame de l'Ambermesnil went along with this little game most obligingly. She cornered the old vermicelli dealer and managed to confer with him; but finding that her efforts, inspired by her particular wish to seduce him on her own behalf, were met with prudishness, if not consternation, she came out disgusted by his rudeness.

'My angel,' she said to her dear friend, 'you won't get anything out of that man! He's absurdly suspicious; he's a skinflint, a brute, a fool, who will bring you nothing but trouble.'

Such things had passed between Monsieur Goriot and Madame de l'Ambermesnil that the comtesse could no longer bear to remain under the same roof as him. She left the next day, forgetting to pay six months' rent and leaving personal effects worth all of five francs. Despite the grim determination with which Madame Vauquer carried out her enquiry, she was unable to track down the Comtesse de l'Ambermesnil's whereabouts in Paris. She often talked about this deplorable affair, bewailing her trusting nature, although she was warier than a she-cat. However, she wouldn't be the first person to mistrust her nearest and dearest yet confide in the first stranger who comes along: a strange but true quirk of behaviour, whose root is easily traced to the human heart. Some people perhaps have nothing left to gain from those they live with; having revealed the emptiness of their souls, they secretly feel themselves to be judged with deserved severity; however, as they have a powerful craving for the flattery they need but lack, or a burning desire to appear to possess qualities they do not have, they hope to take by surprise the heart and esteem of those who are strangers to them, at the risk of one day falling from grace. Meanwhile, there are some individuals who are born mercenary, who never do a kind deed for friends or family, because they owe it to them; but who will bend over backwards for people they don't know in a bid to salvage some scrap of self-esteem: the narrower the circle of their intimates, the less they love them; the wider it is, the keener they are to offer their services. Madame Vauquer's nature had something of both these types, at bottom loathsome, deceitful and mean.

'If I'd been here,' Vautrin would say to her, 'that's one mishap you'd have been spared! I'd have soon seen through that trickstress of yours. I'd recognize one of their *boat-races* anywhere.'

Like all narrow-minded people, Madame Vauquer tended not to look beyond her own version of events or to examine root causes. She preferred to blame others for her own failings. At the time when she incurred her loss, she decided that the honest vermicelli dealer was the source of her misfortune, and from then on, she said, began to come to her senses about him. Once she realized that her pointed coquetry and showy dress were getting her nowhere, it didn't take her long to work out what the reason was. She noticed that her lodger already had his carryings-on, as she called them. This proved that the hope she had cherished so fondly was based on sheer fantasy and that she'd never get anything out of that man, as the comtesse had so forcefully put it, and after all, she had appeared to be something of an expert. Inevitably, she took her aversion further than she had her attraction. The intensity of her loathing was proportionate to her thwarted expectations, rather than to her love. Although the human heart may stop and rest as it climbs the peaks of an attachment, it rarely pauses on the slippery downward slope of hatred. But Monsieur Goriot was her boarder, and so the widow had to repress the outbursts of her wounded self-esteem, smother her sighs of disappointment and swallow her desire for vengeance, like a monk nettled by his prior. The small-minded satisfy their urges, good or bad, with endless pettiness. The widow channelled all her female cunning into inventing covert ways of persecuting her victim. She began by putting a stop to the extravagances which had found their way onto her table. 'No more *cornichons*, no more anchovies: it's all a perfect swindle!' she said to Sylvie, on the morning when she resumed her original modus operandi. Monsieur Goriot had frugal tastes: the prerequisite parsimony of the self-made man had become a habit with him. Soup, boiled meat, a dish of vegetables were, and always would be, his favourite dinner. As Madame Vauquer was unable to deprive him of what he liked best, she found it hard to make her lodger's life a misery. In desperation at her failure to make a dent in Goriot's armour, she began to belittle him, infecting her boarders with her loathing, and as they made him their sport, they dished up her revenge. By the end of the first year, the widow had come to view him with such suspicion that she would wonder why this wealthy merchant, with a private income of seven to eight thousand livres, who owned such splendid silverware and jewels fine enough for any dancing girl, was staying at her boarding house and paying her such a paltry sum of money in proportion to his wealth. For most of this first year, Goriot had tended to dine out once or twice a week; until, little by little, it came to the point where he would dine in town only twice a month. *Mister* Goriot's intimate little dinners out suited Madame Vauquer's interests far too well for her not to be irritated by the increasing frequency with which her lodger took his meals in the boarding house. She attributed this change as much to a desire to annoy his hostess as to the gradual attrition of his wealth: one of the most unattractive habits of Lilliputian minds is to imagine that others share their pettiness. Unfortunately, at the end of the second year, Monsieur Goriot lent some substance to the gossip about him by asking Madame Vauquer if he could move up to the second floor, reducing his rent to nine hundred francs. His need to save money was so great that he went without a fire in his room all winter. Widow Vauquer wished to be paid in advance; Monsieur Goriot consented, and from then on she called him old man Goriot. The reasons behind his decline were anyone's guess. No easy investigation! As the counterfeit comtesse had put it, old man Goriot was secretive, a dark horse. According to the logic of the empty-headed, who keep nothing secret because they hold nothing sacred, those who keep themselves to themselves must have something to hide. So it was that the highly respected merchant became a charlatan, the ladies' man became an old rogue. Sometimes, according to Vautrin, who came to live at the Maison Vauquer around that time, old man Goriot was a *lamb* who, having been shorn of his fortune in the stock-market, would try and recoup his losses as a *stag*,[38] in the forceful phraseology of financial language. At other times, he was one of those

lightweight gamblers who have a flutter with ten francs every
night and never win more than the same amount back. Sometimes, they decided he must be a spy with high-level police
connections; but Vautrin said he wasn't cunning enough to be
one of them. Old man Goriot was also a miserly, small-time
lender or a man who would always bet on the same number in
the Lottery. Every kind of shady behaviour that vice, shame and
impotence could produce was laid at his door. Only, however foul
his behaviour or his vices might be, the general loathing he
inspired did not extend to kicking him out: he paid his rent.
Besides, he was useful – each boarder's good or bad mood found
an outlet in the little digs and jokes they aimed at him. The most
widely credited and accepted opinion was that held by Madame
Vauquer. To her mind, that man, in mint condition, as sound as
a bell and who still had plenty left for a woman to enjoy, was a
rake with unnatural appetites. These were the facts on which
Madame Vauquer based her smear-mongering. When she was
still in bed one morning – a few months after the departure of the
catastrophic comtesse who had managed to live at her expense
for six months – she heard the rustle of a silk dress on her staircase and the light tread of a dainty young woman, who then
slipped through Goriot's door, which had been conveniently left
ajar. Big Sylvie immediately came to inform her mistress that a
young lady who was too pretty to be proper, *dressed like a goddess*, wearing laced prunella[39] boots without a spot of mud on
them, had slipped like an eel from the street into her kitchen
and asked for Monsieur Goriot's room. Madame Vauquer and
her cook duly pressed their ears against the door and detected a
number of tenderly spoken words during the visit, which lasted
some time. When Monsieur Goriot escorted out *his lady friend*,
big Sylvie grabbed her basket and pretended she was off to
market, so that she could shadow the loving couple.

'Madame,' she said to her mistress on her return, 'Monsieur
Goriot must be rolling in it, all the same, to be keeping them in
that style. Just fancy! There was a splendid carriage waiting at
the corner of the Rue de l'Estrapade,[40] which *she* got in to.'

At dinner, Madame Vauquer went to draw a curtain, to
block out a ray of sun that was shining in Goriot's eyes.

'Beauty loves you, Monsieur Goriot, even the sun comes looking for you,' she said, alluding to the visit he had received. 'My! What good taste you have; she was a pretty one.'

'That was my daughter,' he said proudly. The boarders interpreted this as the foolishness of an old man keeping up appearances.

A month after this visit, Monsieur Goriot received another. His daughter, who had come in morning dress the first time, appeared after dinner decked out for an evening in society. The boarders, busy gossiping in the drawing room, caught a glimpse of her, a slim-waisted pretty blonde, graceful and far too distinguished to be the daughter of someone like old man Goriot.

'That makes two of 'em!' said big Sylvie, failing to recognize her.

A few days later, another daughter, a tall, shapely brunette with dark hair and sparkling eyes, asked for Monsieur Goriot.

'That makes three of 'em!' said Sylvie.

This second daughter, who also visited her father in the morning the first time round, arrived in a carriage a few evenings later, wearing a ball gown.

'That makes four of 'em!' said Madame Vauquer and big Sylvie, unable to see in this grand lady the slightest trace of the girl who had been dressed so simply on the morning of her first visit.

Goriot was still paying twelve hundred francs for his board and lodging. Madame Vauquer thought it quite natural for a rich man to have four or five mistresses and even thought it very clever of him to pass them off as his daughters. She saw nothing wrong in him receiving them at the Maison Vauquer. However, because these visits provided her with an explanation of her lodger's indifference to her, from the second year onwards she allowed herself to call him an *old goat*. Finally, following her lodger's descent to nine hundred francs, when she saw one of these ladies coming downstairs one day, she curtly asked him exactly what kind of establishment he thought this was. Old man Goriot replied that the lady was his eldest daughter.

'Got thirty-six daughters, have you?' said Madame Vauquer, sourly.

'Just two,' replied her lodger, with the meekness of a man who has come down in the world, his spirit broken by destitution.

Towards the end of the third year, Goriot reduced his costs still further, moving up to the third floor and dropping to forty-five francs a month. He went without snuff, dismissed his wigmaker and stopped powdering his hair. The first time old man Goriot appeared without powder, his landlady gasped with surprise when she saw the colour of his hair, a dirty, greenish grey. His face, upon which suppressed grief had, imperceptibly, day by day, left its stamp of sadness, now seemed the most woebegone of all those round the table. There could no longer be the slightest doubt. Goriot was an old rake and, without the skill of a doctor, the adverse effects of the treatments his diseases required would have cost him his eyesight. His vile hair colour was the consequence of his excesses and the drugs he had taken to allow him to prolong them. The old man's physical and mental condition gave substance to these old wives' tales. When he had worn out his *trousseau*, he bought calico at fourteen sous an ell[41] to replace his fine linen. One by one, his diamonds, his gold snuff-box, his chain, his jewels all disappeared. Instead of his cornflower-blue coat, his opulent-looking outfits, he now wore, winter and summer, a frock-coat of coarse brown drab,[42] a goat-hair waistcoat and grey woollen trousers. He became increasingly thin; his calves sagged; his face, once plump and satisfied with the pleasures of bourgeois life, became inordinately wrinkled; his forehead furrowed, his jaw sharpened. Four years after moving in to the Rue Neuve-Sainte-Geneviève, he was no longer the same man. The worthy sixty-two-year-old vermicelli dealer who looked not a year over forty, the pot-bellied, prosperous bourgeois, with his frank and foolish face, whose jaunty bearing gladdened those he passed, whose smile still bore the trace of his youth, now had the appearance of a vacant, meandering, pasty-faced seventy year old. His blue eyes, once so full of life, took on a dull iron-grey tinge; they had faded, no longer watered, and their red rim seemed to weep blood. He inspired revulsion in some, pity in others. Some of the young medical students, having noted the droop of his lower lip and measured the extension of his facial angle,[43] diagnosed him as suffering from cretinism, after their prolonged efforts to provoke him came to nothing. One evening, after dinner, when Madame Vauquer mockingly enquired, 'Don't they come and see you any more, those daughters of yours?' in a way that cast doubt on his paternity, old man Goriot twitched as if his hostess had run him through.

'They come from time to time,' he replied, his voice choked with emotion.

'A-ha! So you still see them from time to time!' the students shouted to each other. 'Bravo, old Goriot!'

But the old man didn't hear the mockery his reply had earned him; he had sunk back into a pensive mood, which those observing him superficially assumed to be a kind of senile torpor due to his lack of intelligence. Had they known him well, perhaps they would have taken a keen interest in the problem underlying his physical and mental state; but nothing could have been harder for them. Although it would have been easy enough to find out whether Goriot really had been a vermicelli dealer and how much money he had made, the older boarders whose curiosity he aroused never left the neighbourhood and clung to the boarding house like oysters to a rock. As for the others, as soon as they left the Rue Neuve-Sainte-Geneviève, the relentless pace of Parisian life made them forget the poor old man they mocked. For the old and narrow-minded, as for the young and thoughtless, old man Goriot's desiccated wretchedness and air of bemusement were incompatible with wealth or ability of any kind. As for the women he called his daughters, everyone agreed with Madame Vauquer, who said, with the unswerving logic of an old woman well practised in the art of conjecture, after so many evenings spent gossiping: 'If old man Goriot's daughters were as rich as all his lady visitors seem to be, he wouldn't have taken lodgings on the third floor of my establishment, at forty-five francs a month, and he wouldn't go round dressed like a pauper.' There was nothing to give the lie to the facts as she presented them. And so, at the end of November 1819, when this drama began to unfold, everyone in the boarding house had already made up their mind about the poor old man. He had never had either a daughter or a wife; his overindulgence in the pleasures of life had made him a slug, an anthropomorphic mollusc to be classified among the *Capiferae*,[44] said the museum clerk, one of the regular diners, a real card. Poiret was an eagle, a gentleman next to Goriot. Poiret could speak, reason, reply; true, he said nothing when he spoke, reasoned or replied, because he usually repeated in other words what someone else had just said; but he contributed to the conversation, he was alive, he seemed capable of feeling; while old man Goriot, the museum clerk continued, was constantly at zero-point on the Réaumur scale.[45]

Eugène de Rastignac had returned to Paris in a frame of mind well known to all young men of superior ability or those spurred on by difficult circumstances to achieve greatness. As law students are required to do very little work to pass their preliminary papers at the Faculty, during his first year, Eugène had been free to sample the obvious material delights of Paris. A student has no time to waste if he wishes to familiarize himself with the repertoire of each theatre, memorize each twist and turn of the Parisian labyrinth, know what is and isn't done, learn the language and appreciate pleasures unique to the capital; exploring smart and seedy districts, attending the most entertaining lectures, ticking off lists of treasures in museums. This is a time when a student is excited by insignificant things which to him seem very grand. He has his great man, a professor of the Collège de France who is paid to stoop to the level of his listeners. He straightens his cravat and poses to attract the attention of a woman in the dress circle of the Opéra-Comique. As his initiation proceeds, he becomes more thick-skinned, broadens the scope of his expectations and finally works out how the human strata of society overlay each other. Although at first he merely admires the carriages that parade along the Champs-Elysées on fine days, he soon begins to covet them. Without knowing it, Eugène had already completed this apprenticeship when he left for the vacation, after receiving his bachelor of arts and of law. His childhood illusions, his provincial mentality, had disappeared. On his return to the paternal manor-house and the bosom of his family, his sharpened intelligence and heightened ambition made him see both in a clearer light. Living on the small estate of Rastignac were his father, his mother, his two brothers, his two sisters and an aunt whose wealth consisted solely of annuities. These lands, with a yearly income of around three thousand francs, were subject to the insecurity which governs the laborious industry of wine-growing, and yet each year twelve hundred francs had to be pressed out of this sum for him. The sight of the constant hardship so generously hidden from him, the comparison he was forced to make between his sisters, who had seemed so beautiful to him as a child, and the *Parisiennes* who now fulfilled his dream of ideal beauty, the uncertain future of this large family, one that rested on his shoulders, the parsimonious care with which he watched them eke out the meagrest yield, keeping for themselves only the dregs of the wine-press, in all, a whole range of circumstances, which there is no need to list here, fuelled his desire to succeed and tripled his yearning for distinction. Like other noble souls, he wanted to succeed on merit alone. But he had the temperament of a Southerner; when the time came to act, his resolve would be weakened by the hesitation that paralyses a young man who finds himself on the open sea knowing neither how to put his energy to best use, nor how to trim the sails so they swell with wind. Although, at first, he resolved to throw himself wholeheartedly into his studies, he was soon side-tracked by the need to make the right connections, and having remarked how much influence women have on life in society, immediately decided to venture into the world and win himself a few female protectors: surely there'd be no shortage of takers for a passionate, witty young man, whose wit and passion were further enhanced by elegant bearing and a kind of highly strung beauty which women readily fall for. These thoughts filled his head as he walked through the fields with his sisters, who found him much changed from the cheerful companion he had once been. His aunt, Madame de Marcillac, who had been presented at court in days gone by, had known the most prominent aristocrats of the time. Suddenly, the ambitious young man saw, in the memories with which his aunt had so often lulled him to sleep, the raw material for several social victories at least as significant as those he was working towards at the law school; he questioned her about family connections which might still be revived. After shaking the branches of the family tree, the old lady deemed that, of all the people who might be of service to her nephew among their self-serving tribe of rich relatives, Madame la Vicomtesse de Beauséant would be the least recalcitrant. She wrote a letter in the old style to this young lady and handed it to Eugène, saying that if he succeeded in his dealings with the vicomtesse she would put him in touch with his other relatives. A few days after he arrived, Rastignac sent his aunt's letter to Madame de Beauséant. The vicomtesse replied the following day with an invitation to a ball.

This was how things stood in the boarding house at the end of November 1819. A few days later, Eugène attended Madame de Beauséant's ball, returning at around two in the morning. As he danced, the indefatigable student had promised himself that he would study until morning, to make up for lost time. He was about to stay awake all night for the first time in this silent neighbourhood: entranced by his glimpse of the splendours of society, he was full of a deceptive energy. He hadn't dined at Madame Vauquer's and so the lodgers were unlikely to expect him back from the ball until the next morning at first light, as he had sometimes been known to return from those at the Prado or the Odéon,[46] his silk stockings splashed with mud and his pumps trodden out of shape. Before shooting the bolts across the door, Christophe had opened it to look out into the road. Rastignac turned up at the same time and was able to slip up to his rooms without making a sound, followed by Christophe, who made plenty. Eugène undressed, put on slippers and a worn old coat, lit his tan-turf[47] fire and made ready to start work so swiftly that Christophe, still clattering around in his clumpy books, drowned out the young man's quiet preparations. Eugène remained pensive for a few moments before immersing himself in his law books. He had just discovered that Madame la Vicomtesse de Beauséant was one of the most fashionable women in Paris and that her house was deemed to be the finest in the Faubourg Saint-Germain.[48] Furthermore, her name and fortune made her one of the leading lights of the aristocratic set. Thanks to his aunt, Madame de Marcillac, the penniless student had been warmly received in her house, without realizing the extent of the favour. Being admitted to those glittering salons was tantamount to a certificate of the highest nobility. By appearing in such company, the most exclusive of all, he had gained the right to go anywhere. Dazzled by the brilliance of the assembled company, after exchanging only a few words with the vicomtesse, Eugène had contented himself with singling out from the crush of Parisian deities thronged together at this rout,[49] one of those women whom a young man will inevitably worship at first sight. Comtesse Anastasie de Restaud, tall and well formed, was thought to have one of the prettiest waists in Paris. Picture to yourself deep dark eyes, flawless hands, shapely ankles, movements full of fire, indeed, a woman the Marquis de Ronquerolles had termed a thoroughbred. Her energy and spirit in no way detracted from her charm; although she had full, rounded contours, no one would have accused her of excessive embonpoint. *Pure-blooded horse, thoroughbred woman*: expressions such as these were beginning to replace the heavenly angels, the Ossianic figures, the old mythology of love brushed aside by the dandies. But for Rastignac, Madame Anastasie de Restaud was everything he imagined a desirable woman to be. He had contrived to put his name down for two dances on the list of partners written on her fan and managed a few words with her during the first quadrille.[50] 'Where might a man see you again, Madame?' he asked bluntly, with that passionate candour women find so attractive. 'Why,' she replied, 'in the Bois, at the Bouffons,[51] at home, everywhere.' And the intrepid Southerner did everything he could to become intimate with the charming comtesse, in so much as a young man can become intimate with a woman in the space of a quadrille and a waltz. When he mentioned that he was related to Madame de Beauséant, this woman, whom he took for a great lady, invited him to call, and he thereby gained his introduction to her house. The last smile she tossed his way gave Rastignac reason to believe that his call was indispensable. He had been fortunate enough to make the acquaintance of a man who didn't laugh at his ignorance, an unforgivable failing in the eyes of the haughty, well-born rakes of the time, men of the ilk of Maulincour, Ronquerolles, Maxime de Trailles, de Marsay, Ajuda-Pinto, Vandenesse, who were there in all their conceited glory, mingling with the most fashionable women, Lady Brandon, the Duchesse de Langeais, the Comtesse de Kergarouët, Madame de Sérisy, the Duchesse de Carigliano, Comtesse Ferraud, Madame de Lanty, the Marquise d'Aiglemont, Madame Firmiani, the Marquise de Listomère and the Marquise d'Espard, the Duchesse de Maufrigneuse and the Grandlieus. Luckily for him then, the naive student happened upon the Marquis de Montriveau, the lover of the Duchesse de Langeais,[52] a man as uncomplicated as a child, from whom he learned that the Comtesse de Restaud lived in the Rue du Helder. What it is to be young, to have a thirst for the world, to be hungry for a woman and to see two grand houses open up to you! To have a foot in the door of the Vicomtesse de Beauséant's house in the Faubourg Saint-Germain and a knee in that of the Comtesse de Restaud in the Chaussée d'Antin![53] To see one Paris salon lead to another like so many interconnecting rooms and think yourself handsome enough to find in a woman's heart the help and protection you need there! To feel ambitious enough to kick out imperiously on the tight-rope along which you must walk with the confidence of a sure-footed acrobat who never falls, and to have found an attractive woman to be the best possible balancing pole! With these thoughts in his head and the vision of a magnificent woman rising out of the tan-turf fire before him, suspended between the Code[54] and poverty, who wouldn't have mused on what the future held, as Eugène did, who wouldn't have filled it with success? His roving imagination began cashing in future joys thick and fast, so that he was already picturing himself at Madame de Restaud's side, when a sighing groan worthy of a Saint Joseph[55] disturbed the stillness of the night and resonated with such feeling in the young man's heart that he took it for the last gasp of a dying man. He quietly opened his door and as he stepped out into the corridor saw a trickle of light spilling out beneath old man Goriot's door.

Fearing that his neighbour might be unwell, Eugène put his eye to the keyhole, looked into the room and saw the old man engaged in an activity which seemed so obviously criminal that he felt obliged to do society a service by taking a careful look at what the so-called vermicelli dealer was getting up to by night. Old Goriot, who appeared to have tied a silver-gilt platter and what looked like a tureen to the cross-bar of the upturned table, was winding a kind of rope around the intricately embossed pieces, winching it in so tightly and powerfully as to shape them, most likely, into ingots. 'Gracious! What a man!' Rastignac said to himself, watching the old man's sinewy arms, as, with the help of the rope, they noiselessly kneaded the silver-gilt like dough. 'Does this mean he's a thief, or a fence, who pretends to be foolish and helpless and lives like a pauper, as a cover for his operations?' Eugène asked himself, straightening up for a moment, before returning to his post at the keyhole. Old man Goriot unfastened the rope, spread his blanket on the table, put the lump of silver on it and rolled it into the shape of a bar, completing the task with incredible ease. 'He must be as strong as King Augustus of Poland,'[56] Eugène said to himself, as the round bar took shape. Old Goriot contemplated his handiwork sadly, tears trickled from his eyes, then he blew out the wax taper by the light of which he had shaped the silver, and Eugène heard him lie down on his bed and heave a deep sigh.

'He's mad,' thought the student.

'Poor child!' said old Goriot, aloud. On hearing these words, Rastignac decided he would be wise to keep quiet about this incident and not condemn his neighbour too hastily. He was about to return to his room when he suddenly heard an indescribable sound, like the muffled tread of men in list slippers[57] coming up the stairs. Eugène listened carefully and managed to pick out the rasp of two men breathing in turn. Although he had heard neither the creak of the door nor the men's footsteps, he suddenly saw a faint light on the second floor, coming from Monsieur Vautrin's room. 'So many mysteries in one boarding house!' he said to himself. He went down a few stairs, listened, and the clink of gold reached his ears. Before long the light went out and he heard the breathing again, without the door having creaked. The sound faded away gradually as the two men went downstairs.

'Who's there?' shouted Madame Vauquer, opening her bedroom window.

'Just me coming in, Ma Vauquer,' replied Vautrin, in his booming voice.

'That's odd! Christophe had bolted the door,' said Eugène to himself as he went back to his room. 'In Paris you have to stay up all night if you want to know what's really going on around you.' His ambitiously amorous train of thought having been diverted by these little events, he now set to work. Distracted by his misgivings about old man Goriot, distracted still more by visions of Madame de Restaud, who kept appearing before him like an augury of future greatness, he ended up lying down on his bed and falling fast asleep. A young man will sleep soundly through seven out of ten of the nights he means to spend working. A man must be over twenty to stay awake all night.

The next morning, Paris was smothered by one of those thick fogs which envelop and befuddle it so completely that even the most punctual people get the time wrong. Business appointments are missed. Everyone thinks it's eight o'clock when the clock strikes twelve. At half past nine, Madame Vauquer still hadn't stirred from her bed. Christophe and big Sylvie, who had also risen late, were calmly drinking their coffee, made with the cream off the top of the milk meant for the lodgers, which Sylvie then boiled for a long time, to ensure that this illegally levied tithe did not come to Madame Vauquer's notice.

'Sylvie,' said Christophe, dipping his first piece of toast in his coffee; 'Monsieur Vautrin, who's a decent sort, all things considered, had two more chaps round again last night. Best say nothing to Madame, if she starts her inquisition.'

'Did he give you anything?'

'He gave me a hundred sous just for this month, his way of saying: "keep your mouth shut".'

'There's only him and Madame Couture who put their hands

in their pockets; the others take away with the left hand what they give us with the right at New Year.'

'It's not like they give us much, either!' said Christophe. 'One measly coin, I ask you! A hundred sous, if you're lucky. Old man Goriot's been cleaning his own boots for two years now. That cheapskate Poiret does without polish; he'd drink it before he put any on his filthy old shoes. As for that runt of a student, he gives me forty sous. Forty sous don't even pay for my brushes, and to cap it all, he sells his old clothes. What a dump!'

'Well!' said Sylvie, sipping at her coffee, 'I still say we've got the best positions of any round here: we're doing all right for ourselves. But Christophe, speaking of old uncle Vautrin, has anyone been asking you about him?'

'Yes, they have. I met a gent in the street a few days ago who said: "Haven't you got a large chap who dyes his side-whiskers staying at your place?" So I said, "No, sir, he don't dye 'em. A gay dog like him don't have the time." So I told Monsieur Vautrin, and he said: "You did the right thing, my boy! Always give them a smart answer. There's nothing worse than having other people know your weaknesses. That sort of thing can ruin your marriage prospects."'

'One of 'em tried to catch me out too, at market, asking whether I'd ever seen him putting his shirt on. The cheek of it! Listen!' she said, breaking off, 'there's the Val-de-Grâce striking a quarter to ten and not a soul stirring.'

'Why, they've all gone out! Madame Couture and the young lady went off at eight to partake of the Almighty at Saint-Etienne.[58] Old man Goriot went out with a parcel. The student won't be back until after his lecture, at ten. I saw them leave when I was doing my stairs; old man Goriot bashed me with his bundle, hard as iron, it was. What's his game I wonder, the old gaffer? The others are always on his back, but if you ask me, he's a harmless old soul and worth more than the rest of them put together. He don't give me much himself; but the ladies he sends me to sometimes stretch to a handsome tip; nicely turned out they are too.'

'The ones he calls his daughters, eh? There's a dozen of them.'

'I've only ever seen two ladies, the same two as have been here.'

'I can hear Madame stirring; she'll be kicking up a rumpus soon: better go up. Keep an eye on the milk, Christophe, on account of the cat.'

Sylvie went upstairs to her mistress's room.

'Gracious, Sylvie, it's a quarter to ten; you've let me sleep in like a sluggard! I've never known such a thing.'

'It's the fog; you can cut it with a knife.'

'What about *déjeuner*?'

'If you ask me, the devil's got into your lodgers; they all cleared out at cock-croak.'

'Speak proper please, Sylvie,' said Madame Vauquer reprovingly; 'one should say at the cock o' dawn.'

'Ah! Madame, anything you say. Either way, you can have your *déjeuner* at ten. No sign of Michonnette and Poireau[59] yet. There's only the two of 'em left in the house and they're sleeping like logs.'

'But Sylvie, you're pairing them together, as if . . .'

'As if what?' repeated Sylvie, with a foolish snort of laughter. 'They are a right pair, after all.'

'It's very strange, Sylvie: how did Monsieur Vautrin get in last night after Christophe had bolted the door?'

'Not at all, Madame. Christophe heard Monsieur Vautrin and went down to open the door for him. And there you were thinking . . .'

'Pass me my shift, hurry, and see to *déjeuner*. Fix up that leftover mutton with some potatoes and give them some stewed pears, the ones that cost two liards[60] each.'

Madame Vauquer came downstairs a few moments later, just as her cat, with a paw, had flipped off the plate covering the bowl of milk and was lapping it up as fast as it could.

'Mistigris!' she shouted. The cat sprang away, then came back and rubbed up against her legs. 'Don't try and butter me up, you old coward!' she scolded. 'Sylvie! Sylvie!'

'Yes, Madame. What is it?'

'Look what the cat's been drinking.'

'It's that dimwit Christophe's fault. Where's he got to? I told him to lay the table. Don't worry, Madame, it'll do for old man Goriot's coffee. I'll put some water in it, he won't notice a thing. He's oblivious to everything, even what he eats.'

'So where's he gone, the old nincompoop?' said Madame Vauquer, laying out the plates.

'Who knows? He's up to all sorts.'

'I've had too much sleep.'

'Why, Madame is as fresh as a daisy . . .'

At that point the doorbell was heard, and Vautrin came into the drawing room singing in his booming voice:

I've been a-roving all over the world
And I've been seen in every land . . .

'Ho-ho! Good day, Ma Vauquer,' he said, catching sight of the landlady and gallantly taking her in his arms.

'Now, now, that'll do.'

'Call me a *saucebox*!' he replied. 'Go on, say it. Pretty please? Very well, I'll help you lay the table. Now! Isn't that kind of me?

Courting the brunette and the blonde,
Loving, sighing . . .

I've just seen a peculiar thing.

. . . for either one.'

'What's that?' said the widow.

'At half past eight old man Goriot was at the goldsmith's, the one in the Rue Dauphine that buys old plate and gold braid. He got a tidy sum of money for a silver-gilt piece he sold them, nicely twisted it was, for an amateur.'

'Well I never!'

'Yes, I was on my way back after escorting a friend of mine, who's leaving the country, to the packet-boat;[61] I waited for old man Goriot to see where he'd go next, for a lark. He headed back this way, to the Rue des Grès,[62] where he went into the house of a notorious usurer, name of Gobseck, an out-and-out villain, who'd make dominoes out of his own father's bones; a Jew, an Arab, a Greek, a Bohemian,[63] a man you'd be hard put to burgle; he keeps his stash in the Bank.'

'What's he done then, this Goriot of ours?'

'It's not so much what he's done, as undone,' said Vautrin. 'He's a rattle-brain soft enough to bankrupt himself for the kind of girls who . . .'

'Here he comes now!' said Sylvie.

'Christophe,' cried old man Goriot, 'come upstairs with me!'

Christophe followed old Goriot and came back down shortly afterwards.

'Where are you off to?' said Madame Vauquer to her servant.

'To run an errand for Monsieur Goriot.'

'What do we have here?' said Vautrin, snatching a letter out of Christophe's hands and reading aloud:

'*To Madame la Comtesse Anastasie de Restaud.*'

Handing the letter back to Christophe, he continued, 'And you're going to . . . ?'

'Rue du Helder. I'm under orders to give this to no one but Madame la Comtesse.'

'What's inside?' said Vautrin, holding the letter up to the light. 'A banknote? No.' He opened the envelope slightly. 'A quietus,'[64] he exclaimed. 'Well, I'll be hanged! How very gallant of the old beau. Go on, be off, you rascal,' he said, knocking Christophe's hair flat with his huge hand and spinning him round; 'you'll get a good tip.'

The table was laid. Sylvie had put the milk on to boil. Madame Vauquer was lighting the stove, helped by Vautrin, who was still humming:

'*I've been a-roving all over the world*
And I've been seen in every land . . .'

Everything was ready by the time Madame Couture and Mademoiselle Taillefer came back.

'Where have you been so early, fair lady?' said Madame Vauquer to Madame Couture.

'We've been at our devotions at Saint-Etienne-du-Mont, as we shall be calling on Monsieur Taillefer today. Poor little mite, she's shaking like a leaf,' continued Madame Couture, sitting herself down by the stove and warming her steaming shoes at its opening.

'Come and warm yourself, Victorine,' said Madame Vauquer.

'It's all very well, Mademoiselle, to pray to the Almighty to melt your father's heart,' said Vautrin, pulling up a chair for the orphan. 'But that's not enough. You need a friend who'll make it his business to give that villain a piece of his mind; he's worth three million, so it's said, and the brute won't give you a dowry. A beautiful young woman needs a dowry these days.'

'Poor child,' said Madame Vauquer. 'You'll see, poppet, your monster of a father will get his come-uppance before too long.'

Victorine's eyes welled up with tears at these words and the widow was brought up short at a sign from Madame Couture.

'If only we could see him, if I could just talk to him and give him his wife's last letter,' the widow of the Commissary General went on. 'I've never dared try sending it by post; he'd recognize my handwriting . . .'

'*O innocent, unfortunate and persecuted women*,'[65] declaimed Vautrin, interrupting. 'You have come to a pretty pass! I'll apply myself to your affairs in the next day or so and put things to rights.'

'Oh, Monsieur!' said Victorine, casting a fervent, moist-eyed glance at Vautrin, whom it left unmoved; 'should you manage to gain an audience with my father, be sure to tell him that his affection and my mother's honour are more precious to me than all the wealth in the world. If you convinced him to relax his rigour even a little, I would remember you in my prayers. Let me assure you of my gratitude . . .'

'*I've been a-roving all over the world*,' sang Vautrin, ironically.

At that point, Goriot, Poiret and Mademoiselle Michonneau came downstairs, perhaps drawn by the smell of the *roux*[66] that Sylvie was making to thicken the mutton leftovers. Just as the seven guests sat down to their *déjeuner*,[67] greeting each other, the clock struck ten and the student's footsteps were heard in the road.

'Ah, Monsieur Eugène,' said Sylvie; 'so you'll be joining the others for *déjeuner* today.'

The student greeted the lodgers and sat down next to old man Goriot.

'I've just had the strangest adventure,' he said, helping himself to a generous serving of mutton and cutting himself a piece of bread, whose size Madame Vauquer, as usual, measured with a beady eye.

'An adventure!' said Poiret.

'Well, I don't see why you should be so surprised, old boy,' said Vautrin to Poiret. 'The young gentleman is certainly cut out for one.'

Mademoiselle Taillefer glanced shyly at the young student.

'Tell us your adventure,' demanded Madame Vauquer.

'Yesterday, I went to a ball held by Madame la Vicomtesse de Beauséant, a cousin of mine, who has a magnificent house, apartments hung with silk draperies; to cut a long story short, she gave a wonderful party, where I was as happy as a king . . .'

'. . . fisher,' said Vautrin, cutting him off.

'Monsieur,' replied Eugène sharply, 'what are you trying to say?'

'I said *fisher*, because kingfishers are much happier than kings.'

'That's very true: I'd much rather be a little bird without a care than a king, because . . .' said Poiret, the human echo.

'So anyway,' continued the student, cutting him off mid-flow, 'I danced with one of the most beautiful women at the ball, a ravishing comtesse, the loveliest creature I've ever seen. She wore peach blossom in her hair, with the finest spray of flowers on the side, real flowers that filled the air with their delicate scent; but it's no use, you would need to have seen her, it's impossible to describe how dancing lights up a woman's face. Well, this morning at around nine, I came across the divine comtesse on foot, in the Rue des Grès. Oh! My heart was racing, I imagined . . .'

'That she was on her way here,' said Vautrin, giving the student a piercing stare. 'She was probably on her way to see uncle Gobseck,[68] the usurer. Search the heart of a Parisian woman and you'll find the usurer before the lover. Your comtesse is called Anastasie de Restaud and she lives in the Rue du Helder.'

When he heard this name, the student returned Vautrin's stare. Old man Goriot suddenly raised his head and gave the two speakers a lucid, concerned look that surprised the other lodgers.

'Christophe will arrive too late, she'll have already left,' Goriot groaned to himself, stricken.

'Just as I thought,' murmured Vautrin in Madame Vauquer's ear.

Goriot ate without thinking, oblivious to what he was eating. He had never seemed more confused or vacant than he did now.

'Who the devil told you her name, Monsieur Vautrin?' Eugène asked.

'Hah! There I have you,' replied Vautrin. 'Old man Goriot knew it, didn't he? So why wouldn't I?'

'Monsieur Goriot!' exclaimed the student.

'Hmm?' said the poor old man. 'Was she very beautiful last night?'

'Who?'

'Madame de Restaud.'

'Just look at the old skinflint,' said Madame Vauquer to Vautrin; 'see how his eyes light up.'

'So he'd be keeping her then?' said Mademoiselle Michonneau to the student, in a low voice.

'Oh yes! She was dazzlingly beautiful,' Eugène continued, watched eagerly by old Goriot. 'If Madame de Beauséant hadn't been there, my divine comtesse would have been the queen of the ball; the young men had eyes only for her. I was the twelfth on her list; she danced every quadrille. The other women were furious. If anyone was happy yesterday, she was. Now I understand why they say that there's nothing more beautiful than a frigate in full sail, a horse at full gallop and a woman full of the dance.'

'Yesterday, at the top of the wheel, received by a duchesse,' said Vautrin; 'this morning, at the bottom of the ladder, calling on a pawnbroker: that's Parisian women for you. If their husbands can't fund their unbridled pursuit of luxury, they sell themselves. Those who can't sell themselves would disembowel their mothers if they thought they'd find anything in there that glittered. In a word, they're up to a billion tricks. Everyone knows that . . .'

Old Goriot's countenance, which had beamed like the sun on a fine day as he listened to the student, now clouded over at Vautrin's harsh remarks.

'Is that it?' said Madame Vauquer. 'Where's the adventure in that? Did you speak to her? Did you ask her if she was coming to study law?'

'She didn't see me,' said Eugène. 'But don't you think it's strange to meet one of the prettiest women in Paris at nine in the morning in the Rue des Grès, a woman who must have left the ball at two in the morning? That's the kind of adventure you can only have in Paris.'

'Hah! That's just the tip of the iceberg!' retorted Vautrin.

Mademoiselle Taillefer had barely listened to a word, pre-occupied by the attempt she was about to make. Madame Couture gestured to her to leave the table to go and dress. When the two women went out, old Goriot followed suit.

'Well, did you see that?' Madame Vauquer said to Vautrin and the other lodgers. 'It's obvious that he's bled himself white for those women.'

'You will never convince me', cried the student, 'that the beautiful Comtesse de Restaud belongs to old man Goriot.'

'Why,' said Vautrin, interrupting him, 'we're not trying to convince you. You're still too young to really know Paris; later, you'll discover that it is full of what, for now, we shall call *men who have their passions* . . .' (At these words, Mademoiselle Michonneau gave Vautrin a knowing look, like that of a sol-dier's horse when it hears the bugle call.) 'A-ha!' said Vautrin, breaking off to give her a hard stare; 'so we've had our little passions too, have we?' (The old spinster lowered her eyes hastily like a nun catching sight of a statue.) 'So,' he continued, 'our man finds one idea that fits and wears it out. He is only thirsty for a certain kind of water drawn from a certain well, often stagnant; he's prepared to sell his wife, his children, to sell his soul to the devil, so that he can drink from it. For one man the well is gambling, the stock-markets, a collection of paintings or insects, music; for another, it's a woman who knows how to titillate his fancy. If you were to offer such a man every woman on earth, he wouldn't care, he only wants the one who can satisfy his passion. Often, the woman in question cares little for our man, treats him harshly, makes him pay a high price for the tiny scraps of satisfaction she sells him; well! he can't get enough and would pledge his last blanket at the Mont-de-Piété[69] if it meant he could give that woman his last écu. Old Goriot is one of those fellows. The comtesse exploits him because he keeps his head down, and that's the smart set all over! The poor old fool thinks only of her. His passion aside, he's a dull stick, as you've seen for yourself. Get him started on his pet subject and his face sparkles like a diamond. It's not hard to guess the nature of his secret. This morning he sold some silver-gilt for melting down and I saw him go and call on uncle Gobseck in the Rue des Grès. Now, listen to this. As soon as he got back, he sent Christophe to the Comtesse de Restaud's house; that blockhead showed us the address on the envelope, which contained a quietus. If the comtesse also intended to pay the old bill-discounter a visit, it's obvious that the situation was urgent. Old Goriot has gallantly settled up for her. You don't need to put this and that together to see what's going on there. Which proves, my young friend, that while your comtesse was laughing, dancing, frolicking, flaunting her peach blossom and swinging her skirts, she was on tenterhooks, as they say, at the thought of the bills of exchange[70] that she or her lover had failed to honour.'

'You've given me a burning desire to find out the truth. I'll go and call on Madame de Restaud tomorrow,' cried Eugène.

'Yes,' said Poiret, 'you should call on Madame de Restaud tomorrow.'

'Perhaps you'll find our dear friend Goriot there, come to cash in on his gallantry.'

'Why,' said Eugène, with an air of disgust, 'this Paris of yours is a dunghill.'

'And a funny old dunghill it is too,' Vautrin continued. 'A man in a carriage who gets his hands dirty is honest, a man

who walks and gets his feet dirty is a rogue. If you're unfortunate enough to lift some trifle or other, you're paraded on the
square[71] in front of the law courts like a freak. If you steal a
million, you're pointed out in the salons as one of the Virtues.
You pay thirty million to the Police and to the Law to maintain
those moral standards there. A fine mess!'

'Well I never!' exclaimed Madame Vauquer; 'so old man
Goriot has melted down his silver-gilt breakfast service?'

'The one with two turtle-doves on the cover?' said Eugène.

'That's the one.'

'It must have been very dear to him; he wept when he'd
finished twisting the dish and platter. I happened to see him do
it,' said Eugène.

'It was as dear to him as his life,' replied the widow.

'So you see how the old man's passion rules him,' cried
Vautrin. 'That woman knows how to titillate his soul.'

The student went up to his room. Vautrin went out. Shortly
afterwards, Madame Couture and Victorine set off in a fiacre[72]
that Sylvie had found for them. Poiret offered Mademoiselle
Michonneau his arm and they left to make the most of the best
two hours of the day with a stroll in the Jardin des Plantes.

'Well I never! They'll be getting married next,' said big
Sylvie. 'Today's the first time they've gone out together. They're
both so dry that if they bump into each other, they'll go up like
touchwood.'

'Mademoiselle Michonneau should watch out for her shawl,'
said Madame Vauquer, laughing; 'it'll catch like tinder.'

When Goriot came back that afternoon at four, the first
thing he saw, by the light of two smoky lamps, was Victorine,
red-eyed. Madame Vauquer was listening to the account of that
morning's unfruitful visit to Monsieur Taillefer. Irritated by the
presence of his daughter and the old woman, Taillefer had had
them brought before him so that he could make matters plain.

'My dear lady,' said Madame Couture to Madame Vauquer,
'can you believe that he didn't even offer Victorine a seat; she
remained standing the whole time. Without raising his voice,
quite coldly, he said that we should spare ourselves the trouble
of calling on him; that to his mind, the young lady, without

calling her his daughter, wasn't doing herself any favours by importuning him (once a year, the monster); that, as Victorine's mother married without a fortune, she had nothing to hope for; indeed, he said the hardest things, which made the poor girl burst into tears. So she threw herself at her father's feet and bravely told him that she only kept trying for her mother's sake, that she would obey him without a murmur; but she begged him to read the poor dead woman's last testament. She took out the letter and gave it to him, saying the most heartfelt and beautiful things in the world; I don't know where she got them from, God must have been dictating to her; the poor child was so inspired that I wept like a baby to hear her. And do you know what that abominable man did? He trimmed his nails, then took the letter that poor Madame Taillefer had drenched in her tears and threw it on the fire, saying, "Enough!" He tried to pull his daughter to her feet and when she took hold of his hands to kiss them, he snatched them away. What a scoundrel! His great lump of a son came in without even greeting his sister.'

'Why, the monsters!' said old Goriot.

'And then', said Madame Couture, ignoring the old man's exclamation, 'father and son left, bidding me farewell and begging me to excuse them, as they had urgent business to attend to. That was our visit. At least he saw his daughter. I really don't know how he can deny her; they're as like as peas in a pod.'

The boarders arrived in dribs and drabs, residents and non-residents wishing each other good day and exchanging the kind of banter which, among a particular class of Parisian, passes for wit, involving a strong element of chaff and heavily dependent on pronunciation and delivery for its success. This kind of *argot* is in constant mutation. The shibboleth on which it turns never lasts longer than a month. A political event, a trial at the assizes, a street ballad, an actor's spiel, everything feeds into this game of wit, which mainly consists of throwing words and ideas into the air like shuttlecocks and batting them to and fro around the room. The recent invention of the *Diorama*, taking optical illusion to even giddier heights than the *Panoramas*,[73]

had, in some studios, inspired the conceit of ending words in
rama, a contagious skit that the Maison Vauquer had caught
from a young painter, one of the regulars.

'So, *meesteurr* Poiret,' said the museum clerk; 'still *aliverama*?'
Then, before he could reply: 'Ladies, you look down at heart,'
he said to Madame Couture and Victorine.

'How about some *deeneurr*?' cried Horace Bianchon, Rastignac's medical student friend. 'My poor tum has sunk *usque
ad talones*.'[74]

'The weather's mighty *coltorama*!' said Vautrin. 'Move
along there, old man Goriot. Damn it! Your great foot is filling
the whole grate.'

'Revered Monsieur Vautrin,' said Bianchon, 'surely you
can't mean *coltorama*? There must be some mistake, it should
be *coldorama*.'

'No,' said the museum clerk, 'it's *coltorama*, my feet are *colt*,
as in *coltsfoot*.'

'Har har!'

'Here comes H.E. the Marquis de Rastignac, Bachelor of
Lawlessness,' cried Bianchon, grabbing Eugène round the neck
and pretending to strangle him. 'Hey, everyone, look out!'

Mademoiselle Michonneau came in quietly, nodded to the
boarders without saying a word and went and sat down with
the other three women.

'She always gives me the creeps, that old bat,' said Bianchon
to Vautrin in a low voice, nodding towards Mademoiselle
Michonneau. 'As a student of Doctor Gall's system, I can see
that her head has the bumps of Judas.'[75]

'Monsieur has met him?' said Vautrin.

'Who hasn't bumped into him!' replied Bianchon. 'I swear to
you, that pasty-faced old maid reminds me of a long worm
steadily eating its way through a beam.'

'That's how it is, young man,' said the forty year old, strok-
ing his side-whiskers.

A rose, she lived as roses do,
Through a single dawn.'[76]

'A-ha! Here comes a glorious *soupeaurama*,' said Poiret, as
Christophe appeared, reverentially bearing a tureen.

'Pardon me, Monsieur,' said Madame Vauquer; 'it's not a *soupe au rama*, but a *soupe au cabbage*.'

All the young men burst out laughing.

'You're thrashed, Poiret!'

'*Poirrrrreette* is thrashed.'

'Two points to Ma Vauquer,' said Vautrin.

'Did anyone notice the fog this morning?' said the museum clerk.

'It was', said Bianchon, 'a freakish, feverish fog, a cheerless, melancholic, glaucous, broken-winded fog, a Goriot fog.'

'A *Goriorama*', said the painter, 'because you couldn't see what was staring you in the face.'

'Ay seh, Milord Gorriotte, one is tawking abowt yew.'

Sitting at the lower end of the table, near the service door, old man Goriot lifted his head, sniffing a piece of bread he had tucked under his napkin, an old business tic of his which resurfaced now and then.

'What's the matter?' Madame Vauquer bawled at him sourly, her voice cutting through the din of clattering spoons, plates and voices; 'is the bread not good enough for you?'

'On the contrary, Madame,' he replied, 'it's made with the finest quality Etampes flour.'

'How can you tell?' asked Eugène.

'By its whiteness, its taste.'

'Your nose can taste, then, seeing as all you ever do is sniff the bread?' said Madame Vauquer. 'You're getting to be so thrifty that one of these days you'll end up inventing a way to feed yourself simply by breathing in cooking smells.'

'Take out a patent,' cried the museum clerk; 'you'll make a fortune.'

'Ignore him, he's just trying to convince us he used to be a vermicelli dealer,' said the painter.

'So that would make your nose a *cornute*?'[77] asked the clerk, continuing regardless.

'Cor what?' said Bianchon.

'Cor-net.'

'Cor-nemuse.'

'Cor-nelian.'

'Cor-nice.'

'Cor-nichon.'

'Cor-bie.'

'Cor-bel.'

'*Cor-norama*.'

These eight retorts shot from each side of the room with the rapidity of a firing squad and caused such uproarious laughter that poor old Goriot looked at his companions with a bemused expression, like a man trying to understand a foreign language.

'Cor . . . ?' he asked Vautrin, who was next to him.

'Corns, old chap!' said Vautrin, banging on the crown of Goriot's hat and ramming it down over his eyes.

The poor old man, stunned by this swift attack, was paralysed for a moment. Meanwhile, Christophe came and cleared away the old fellow's dish, thinking he'd finished, so that when Goriot pushed his hat back up and went to pick up his spoon, he knocked his hand against the table. All the boarders roared with laughter.

'Monsieur,' said the old man, 'you are a cad, and should you attempt any further rammings of the kind . . .'

'What then, Pa?' said Vautrin, interrupting him.

'Well! You'll pay dearly for it one day . . .'

'In hell, is it?' said the painter; 'in the nasty dark corner where they put the naughty children?'

'Why, Mademoiselle,' said Vautrin to Victorine, 'you're not eating. Papa turned out to be intractable?'

'Abominable,' said Madame Couture.

'He needs to be brought to his senses,' said Vautrin.

'Although,' said Rastignac, who was sitting next to Bianchon, 'seeing as she's not eating, Mademoiselle could always start alimentary proceedings against the food. Hey! Look at how old man Goriot is staring at Mademoiselle Victorine.'

The old man left off eating, intent on studying the poor girl, whose face bore the stamp of genuine pain, the pain of a wronged daughter who loves her father.

'Dear chap,' said Eugène in a low voice, 'we've been mistaken about old man Goriot. He's neither a fool nor a zombie.

Apply your Gall system to him and tell me what you think. Last night I saw him twist a silver-gilt dish as if it were wax, and as he did, the expression on his face betrayed extraordinary emotion. His life seems too mysterious not to reward further study. Yes, Bianchon, laugh as much as you like; I'm not joking.'

'The man is a medical phenomenon,' said Bianchon. 'Very well; if he wants, I'll dissect him.'

'No, examine his skull.'

'Ah well! His stupidity appears to be contagious.'

TWO CALLS ARE PAID

The next day, Eugène dressed in his most elegant clothes and set off at around three in the afternoon to call on Madame de Restaud. On the way, he indulged himself in the recklessly madcap expectations which bring so much zest and emotion to the lives of young men: they anticipate neither obstacles nor dangers; all they can see is success, poeticizing their existence entirely in their imagination and feeling glum or discouraged at the failure of plans which had only ever existed in their wildest fancies; if they didn't also happen to be shy and ignorant, the social world would be insufferable. As he walked, Eugène took a thousand precautions to avoid being spattered with mud, but at the same time he planned what he would say to Madame de Restaud, he stored up witty remarks, he invented clever answers in an imaginary conversation, he prepared his subtle ripostes, his Talleyrand-esque sayings,[78] weaving in small opportunities conducive to the declaration on which he was staking his future. He ended up splashed with mud and had to have his boots polished and trousers brushed at the Palais-Royal. 'If I were rich,' he said to himself, pocketing the change from a thirty-sous piece which he had brought with him *in case of an emergency*, 'I would have gone by carriage and could have pursued my thoughts at leisure.' He finally arrived at the Rue du Helder and asked for the Comtesse de Restaud. With the icy fury of a man confident that one day he will triumph, he found himself on the receiving end of the servants' disdainful stares: they had seen him cross the courtyard on foot, without having heard the sound of a carriage at the gate. He felt these stares all the more keenly, as his inferiority had been brought home to him as soon as he entered the courtyard, where a magnificent horse stood champing at the bit, finely harnessed to one of those dashing cabriolets that announce a lavish and dissipated lifestyle and imply a familiarity with all the costly delights Paris has to offer. He proceeded, all on his own, to put himself into a bad mood. The open drawers of his brain, which he had banked on finding full of wit, slid shut, his aplomb deserted him. While he waited for a reply from the comtesse, as a valet went to announce the visitor's name, Eugène stood on one leg in front of a window in the antechamber, resting his elbow on the catch and looked blankly out at the courtyard. He found that the time passed slowly and would have left if he hadn't been blessed with that Southern tenacity which works wonders when it keeps a straight course.

'Monsieur,' said the valet, 'Madame is in her boudoir and otherwise engaged; she didn't give me an answer, but if Monsieur would care to come into the drawing room, another gentleman is already waiting there.'

As he marvelled at the awesome power of those who, with a single word, indict or try their masters, Rastignac resolutely opened the door the valet had come out of, intending to show these insolent servants that he already knew his way around, but instead stumbled clumsily into a room filled with lamps, sideboards and a contraption for heating bath towels, whose only issue was a dark corridor and a back staircase. The stifled laughter he heard in the antechamber brought his embarrassment to a peak.

'The drawing room is this way, Monsieur,' the valet said to him, with that false respect which comes across as yet another kind of mockery.

Eugène retraced his steps with such haste that he collided with a bathtub and only just managed to stop his hat falling into the bath. Just then, a door opened at the end of the long corridor lit by a small lamp, and all at once Rastignac heard the voice of Madame de Restaud, that of old man Goriot, and then the sound of a kiss. He went back into the dining room and crossed it, following the valet, and came to a reception room, where he paused in front of the window, noticing that it looked out over the courtyard. He wanted to find out whether this Goriot was, in reality, his old man Goriot. His heart beat strangely as he remembered Vautrin's damning remarks. The valet was waiting for Eugène at the door of the drawing room, when an elegant young dandy suddenly came out and said impatiently: 'I'm going, Maurice. Tell Madame la Comtesse that I waited for over half an hour.' This impertinent, who doubtless had reason not to stand on ceremony, hummed some Italian roulade or other as he strode towards the window where Eugène had positioned himself, as much to see the student's face as to look into the courtyard.

'Monsieur le Comte may prefer to wait a moment longer, as Madame has finished,' said Maurice, going back into the ante-chamber.

At this point, old man Goriot emerged from the exit at the foot of the back staircase, near the carriage entrance. The old fellow held out his umbrella and began to unfurl it, without realizing that the main gate had just opened to let in a young man wearing military decoration, driving a tilbury. Old Goriot barely had time to jump backwards to avoid being crushed. The taffeta of the umbrella frightened the horse, so it shied slightly as it sped towards the front steps. The young man turned his head angrily, saw Goriot and, without stepping down, gave him a nod conveying the affected courtesy you might show a usurer whose services you require, or, if it cannot be avoided, a man of blemished reputation, knowing you will blush for it later. Old man Goriot responded with a friendly little nod, full of affability. These events took place as quick as a flash. Too engrossed to realize that he was not alone, Eugène suddenly heard the comtesse's voice.

'Ah! Maxime, you were just leaving,' she said in a reproach-ful tone, mingled with a touch of pique.

The comtesse hadn't seen the tilbury arrive. Rastignac spun round and saw her, alluringly dressed in a white cashmere dressing-gown with pink ribbons, her hair loosely swept up in the style favoured by Parisian women in the morning; her scent filled the air, she must have taken a bath, and this had, as it were, soft-ened her beauty, making her seem even more voluptuous; her eyes were moist. A young man's eye drinks everything in: just as a plant absorbs vital substances from the air, so his spirit fuses with a woman's radiance. Eugène therefore sensed the fresh bloom of the comtesse's hands without needing to touch them. Through the cashmere, he saw the rose-coloured shades of her bosom which her dressing-gown, falling open here and there, left partially exposed, and on which his eyes lingered. The comtesse had no need for whalebone stays: a simple belt showed off her supple waist, her neck invited caresses, her feet looked pretty in their slippers. Maxime took her hand and kissed it, at which point Eugène noticed Maxime, and the comtesse noticed Eugène.

'Why! It's you, Monsieur de Rastignac, how delightful to see you,' she said, in a tone of voice to which a man with his wits about him knows the correct response.

Maxime looked from Eugène to the comtesse in a pointed manner intended to send the intruder packing. 'Really, dear girl, I hope you'll show this young whipper-snapper the door!' These words hung in the air, a clear and intelligible translation of the expression on the face of this haughtily proud young man, whom Comtesse Anastasie had called Maxime, looking searchingly at him with that melting concern which betrays a woman's secrets without her realizing. Rastignac felt a violent hatred for the young man. Firstly, Maxime's beautifully curled blond hair showed him how awful his own looked. And then, Maxime had spotless kid boots, while his, despite the care he had taken as he walked, were stained with a light coat of mud. Finally, Maxime was wearing an elegant frock-coat, fitted tightly at the waist, so he looked as pretty as a woman, while at half past two Eugène was wearing a black evening coat. The quick-witted child of the Charente[79] sensed the advantage that tailoring gave this tall, lean dandy, with his clear eyes and pale skin, a man capable of ruining any number of orphans. Without waiting for Eugène to reply, Madame de Restaud fluttered away into the other drawing room, the loose skirts of her dressing-gown furling and unfurling, so she looked like a butterfly; and Maxime followed her. Furious, Eugène followed Maxime and the comtesse. The three of them came face to face in the middle of the main drawing room, level with the fire-place. The student was well aware that he was going to annoy the odious Maxime; but he was determined to cramp the dandy's style, even if it meant incurring Madame de Restaud's displeasure. Suddenly, remembering that he had seen the young man at Madame de Beauséant's ball, he guessed the nature of Maxime's relationship with Madame de Restaud; and with the youthful audacity that leads a man to commit huge blunders or succeed with flying colours, he said to himself: 'He is my rival, I must triumph over him.' The fool! Little did he know that Comte Maxime de Trailles would solicit a challenge, then shoot first and kill his man. Eugène was a decent shot but hadn't yet managed to hit twenty out of twenty-two dummies at a shooting gallery. The young comte threw himself into a bergère[80] next to the fire, took up the tongs and poked the coals in such a violent, sullen way that Anastasie's beautiful face suddenly clouded over. The young woman turned towards Eugène and gave him one of those coldly enquiring looks which so clearly say: 'Why don't you leave?' that those of good breeding immediately take their cue and make what we might call their exit speech.

Eugène assumed a pleasant manner and said: 'Madame, I was keen to see you to . . .' He stopped short. A door opened. The man who had driven the tilbury suddenly appeared, without a hat. He didn't greet the comtesse, but looked askance at Eugène and held out his hand to Maxime, amicably wishing him 'Good day', which Eugène found most surprising. Young men from the provinces have no idea how sweet life can be as a threesome.

'Monsieur de Restaud,' said the comtesse to the student, gesturing towards her husband.

Eugène made a low bow.

'This gentleman', she went on, introducing Eugène to the Comte de Restaud, 'is Monsieur de Rastignac, related to Madame la Vicomtesse de Beauséant through the Marcillacs, and whom I had the pleasure to meet at her last ball.'

Related to Madame la Vicomtesse de Beauséant through the Marcillacs! These words, which the comtesse pronounced with a slight emphasis, attributable to the pride a hostess feels in proving that she only receives men of distinction, had a magic effect: the comte put off his coldly formal manner and bowed.

'Delighted, Monsieur,' he said, 'to make your acquaintance.'

As for Comte Maxime de Trailles, he looked at Eugène uneasily and his haughty manner immediately left him. This wave of the magic wand, for which he had to thank the power-ful intercession of a name, opened thirty drawers[81] in the Southerner's brain, and restored the wit he had planned to have at the ready. A sudden ray of light burst through the murky atmosphere of Parisian high society and he began to see his way more clearly. At this point, the Maison Vauquer and old man Goriot were far from his thoughts.

'I thought the Marcillacs had died out?' the Comte de Restaud said to Eugène.

'Indeed, Monsieur,' he replied. 'My great-uncle, the Cheva-lier de Rastignac, married the heiress of the Marcillac family. He had an only daughter, who married the Maréchal de Clar-imbault, Madame de Beauséant's maternal grandfather. We are the younger branch and became even poorer when my great-uncle, a vice-admiral, lost everything he had in the service of the King. The revolutionary government refused to acknow-ledge us as creditors when it liquidated the Compagnie des Indes.'[82]

'Didn't your esteemed great-uncle command the *Vengeur* until 1789?'

'That is correct.'

'Well then, he'll have known my grandfather, who had command of the *Warwick*.'[83]

Maxime shrugged his shoulders slightly and looked at Madame de Restaud, as if to say, 'If he gets started on navy talk with that man, we may as well call it a day.' Anastasie under-stood Monsieur de Trailles' look. With that admirable presence of mind with which women are blessed, she smiled, saying: 'Come with me, Maxime; I have something to ask you. Gentle-men, we will leave you to sail in convoy on the *Warwick* and the *Vengeur*.' She stood up and gestured to Maxime in a mock-ingly complicit way, and they headed off in the direction of the boudoir. This *morganatic*[84] couple, a neat German expression with no French equivalent, had barely reached the door, when the comte broke off his conversation with Eugène.

'Anastasie! I wish you would stay, my dear,' he exclaimed irritably; 'you know very well that . . .'

'I'll be back, I'll be back,' she said, interrupting him; 'it will only take me a second to tell Maxime what I want him to do for me.'

She returned quickly. Like any woman whose freedom to behave as she pleases is contingent on how well she can gauge her husband's moods, who knows how far she can go without losing his precious trust and who will therefore never thwart him over a triviality, the comtesse had understood from the comte's tone of voice that it would not be safe to remain in the boudoir. This *contretemps* was Eugène's fault, as the comtesse, her glances and gestures full of vexation, made clear to Maxime, who, in a pointedly brusque way, said to the comte, his wife and Eugène: 'Listen, you're busy, I'd rather not disturb you; goodbye.' He left.

'Stay, Maxime!' cried the comte.

'Come to dinner,' said the comtesse, leaving Eugène and the comte alone again and following Maxime into the reception room, where they stayed together long enough to give Monsieur de Restaud time to get rid of Eugène.

Rastignac heard them burst out laughing, talk and fall silent in turn; but the wily student was doing his utmost to keep Monsieur de Restaud entertained, flattering him or starting long-winded discussions, so that he would see the comtesse again and discover the nature of her relationship with old man Goriot. This woman, clearly in love with Maxime, this woman, who ruled over her husband, secretly connected to the old vermicelli dealer, was a complete mystery to him. He wanted to get to the bottom of the mystery, hoping in this way to reign supreme over such an eminently Parisian woman.

'Anastasie,' said the comte, calling his wife once more.

'Well, my poor Maxime,' she said to the young man, 'we must resign ourselves. Until this evening . . .'

'I hope, *Nasie*,' he murmured in her ear, 'that you'll dispatch this foolish young man, whose eyes glowed like hot coals each time your gown slipped open. He would make love to you, compromise you, and I'd be obliged to kill him.'

'Are you mad, Maxime?' she said. 'On the contrary, don't you think these little students make excellent lightning conductors? I'll make sure that Restaud takes a sudden dislike to him.'

Maxime burst out laughing and left the room, followed by the comtesse, who stood at the window to watch him climb up into his carriage, flourishing his whip and making his horse paw the ground. She waited until the main gate had closed behind him before returning.

'Just imagine, my dear,' the comte exclaimed when she returned; 'Monsieur's family estate is near Verteuil, on the Charente. His great-uncle and my grandfather were acquainted.'

'Delighted to be among familiar faces,' said the comtesse distractedly.

'More so than you think,' said Eugène in a low voice.

'Pardon?' she replied sharply.

'Why,' continued the student, 'I've just seen a man leaving your house who lodges next door to me, old man Goriot.'

On hearing this name spiced with 'old man', the comte, who was poking the fire, dropped the tongs as if they had burned his fingers and stood bolt upright.

'Sir, you might have called him *Monsieur* Goriot!' he exclaimed.

The comtesse turned white at first, seeing her husband's irritation, then she flushed and was clearly embarrassed. Making an effort to sound natural, and assuming an air of studied indifference, she replied: 'You couldn't know anyone we love more . . .' She broke off, looked at her piano as if overcome by a sudden urge and asked: 'Do you care for music, Monsieur?'

'Very much so,' replied Eugène, red in the face and paralysed by the mortifying realization that he must have committed some terrible blunder.

'Do you sing?' she cried, going to the piano and rapidly running her fingers the length of the keyboard from bottom C to top F. Rrrrah!

'No, Madame.'

The Comte de Restaud was pacing up and down.

'Such a shame: a man who can sing is always sure to be in demand. *Ca-a-ro, ca-a-ro, ca-a-a-a-ro, non dubitare*,'[85] sang the comtesse.

By mentioning old man Goriot, Eugène had once again waved a magic wand, but this time the effect was the exact opposite of that achieved by the words *related to Madame de Beauséant*. He found himself in the position of a man being shown around the house of a collector of curiosities, as a special favour, who, inadvertently colliding with a case full of sculptures, manages to knock off a couple of loose heads. He wished the earth would open and swallow him up. Madame de Restaud's face was cold, aloof, her gaze now impassive, and she avoided all eye contact with the unfortunate student.

'Madame,' he said, 'you have matters to discuss with Monsieur de Restaud; please accept my humble respects and allow me to . . .'

'Whenever you call,' the comtesse said hastily, interrupting Eugène with a gesture, 'you may be sure that both Monsieur de Restaud and myself will be delighted to see you.'

Eugène gave the couple a low bow and left, followed by Monsieur de Restaud, who, despite all his entreaties, accompanied him as far as the antechamber.

'Whenever that gentleman calls,' the comte said to Maurice, 'neither myself nor Madame will be at home.'

As Eugène set foot on the flight of steps leading down from the front door, he realized it was raining. 'Well,' he said to himself, 'all I've achieved by coming here is to put my foot in it, without understanding why or what the consequences will be, and to top it all, I'm about to ruin my suit and hat. I ought to stay in my corner slaving away at the law and concentrate on becoming a lowly magistrate. How can I make my way in society, when, to move in the right circles, you need scores of cabriolets, polished boots, all kinds of essential equipment, gold chains, white suede gloves at six francs a pair for the morning and another pair of yellow gloves in the evening? Goriot be hanged! The old rascal.'

As he stood in the doorway leading to the street, the driver of a hired coach, who had clearly just set down some newly weds and was hoping to sneak in a few illicit fares unbeknown to his master, gestured to Eugène, seeing him with no umbrella, dressed in black, wearing a white waistcoat, yellow gloves and polished boots. Eugène was smouldering with that suppressed rage which drives a young man to plunge still deeper into the hole he has dug for himself, as if he hoped to find some way out at the bottom. He took up the coachman's offer with a nod. With only twenty-two sous left in his pocket, he climbed up into the carriage, where a few strands of lametta and some orange blossom attested to its recent occupation by bride and groom.

'Where to, Monsieur?' asked the driver, who had already divested himself of his white gloves.

'Damn it!' Eugène said to himself; 'seeing as this is already costing me a small fortune, I may as well put it to good use! Take me to the Hôtel de Beauséant,' he added aloud.

'Which one?' asked the coachman.

Two sublime words which stumped Eugène. Our debutant dandy was unaware that there were *two* Hôtels de Beauséant, nor that he had so many relatives who were oblivious to his existence.

'The Vicomte de Beauséant, Rue . . .'

'. . . de Grenelle,' said the driver, nodding his head and interrupting him. 'You see, otherwise there's the Comte and the Marquis de Beauséant, in the Rue Saint-Dominique,' he added, drawing up the step.

'I know,' replied Eugène curtly.

'The whole world is mocking me today!' he said to himself, throwing his hat onto the cushions opposite. 'Now here's an escapade that's going to cost me a king's ransom. But at least I'll be able to call on this cousin of mine in a suitably aristocratic manner. Old man Goriot has already cost me at least ten francs, the old rogue! Well, I'll tell Madame de Beauséant about my adventure; perhaps it will make her laugh. She'll know the mystery of the criminal connection between this beautiful woman and that old rat without a tail. Better that I should win favour with my cousin than be spurned by that Jezebel, who in any case seemed to have rather expensive tastes. If the beautiful vicomtesse has such power in name, how much more must she have in person? Go to the top. When you've set your sights on something in heaven, you need God on your side!'

These words briefly summarize the thousand and one thoughts that were rushing through his mind. As he watched the falling rain, he regained some of his composure and self-assurance. He told himself that if he was going to squander two of the precious hundred-sous coins he still had left, they would at least be well spent in protecting his coat, his boots and his hat. He felt a surge of elation when he heard his coachman shout: *Gate please!* A red and gold porter[86] set the gate to the mansion groaning on its hinges and with sweet satisfaction Rastignac saw his carriage pass through the entrance, turn in the courtyard and come to a halt beneath the marquise roof over the front steps. The coachman, wearing a loose-fitting blue greatcoat with red trimmings, came and let down the step. As he stepped out of his carriage, Eugène heard stifled laughter coming from beneath the peristyle: a couple of valets had already made the vulgar wedding equipage the butt of their humour. The student soon understood why they were laughing, when he saw his carriage standing next to one of the most elegant coupés[87] in Paris, drawn by a pair of spirited horses with roses at their ears, champing at their bits, kept tightly reined in by a powdered coachman in a smart cravat, as if they might take flight at any moment. At the Chaussée d'Antin, Madame de Restaud had had the exquisite cabriolet of a twenty-six-year-old dandy in her courtyard. At the Faubourg Saint-Germain, here, awaiting the pleasure of a high-ranking nobleman, was a carriage and pair that must have cost at least thirty thousand francs.

'Who can that be?' Eugène wondered, belatedly realizing that there couldn't be many women in Paris who weren't already otherwise engaged and that it would take more than breeding to conquer one of these queens. 'Dammit! My cousin must also have a Maxime.'

He climbed the flight of steps leading to the front door with death in his heart. At his approach the glass door opened: he found the valets as long-faced as donkeys taking a thrashing. The ball he had attended had been held in the formal reception rooms on the ground floor of the Hôtel de Beauséant. Not having had time to call on his cousin between receiving the invitation and going to the ball, he had not yet visited Madame de Beauséant's private apartments. He was about to see, for the very first time, the wonders of that intimate elegance which reveals what a woman of distinction has in her soul and on her conscience. His curiosity was even keener now that he had a point of comparison in Madame de Restaud's drawing room. At half past four, the vicomtesse was at home. Five minutes earlier, she would not have received her cousin. Eugène, still oblivious to the subtleties of Parisian etiquette, was led up a grand flower-filled staircase, white in hue, with a gold handrail and a red carpet, to Madame de Beauséant – without having heard her word-of-mouth biography, whose latest instalment was passed from ear to ear each night in the drawing rooms of Paris.

For three years, the vicomtesse had been connected with one of the most famous and wealthy Portuguese noblemen, the Marquis d'Ajuda-Pinto. It was one of those harmless liaisons which have so much appeal for the two individuals involved that they cannot abide the presence of third parties. Whether he liked it or not, the Vicomte de Beauséant himself had set the public an example by respecting this morganatic union. In the early days of the relationship, anyone who came to call on the vicomtesse at two would find the Marquis d'Ajuda-Pinto there. Madame de Beauséant, unable to close her door, as this would have been most improper, received her callers so coldly and contemplated her mouldings with such a studious air that they soon realized how inopportune their visit was. When it became known in Paris that you would incovenience Madame de Beauséant if you called between two and four, she was left in the most complete solitude. She went to the Bouffons or to the Opéra accompanied by both Monsieur de Beauséant and Monsieur d'Ajuda-Pinto; but once they were seated, Monsieur de Beauséant, as a true man of the world, always left his wife and the Portuguese nobleman on their own. Monsieur d'Ajuda was about to be married. He was to wed a young noblewoman, one of the de Rochefides. Everyone who was anyone knew about the wedding, except for one person, and that person was Madame de Beauséant. A few of her friends had made some vague mention of it to her; she had laughed it off, believing that they were jealous of her happiness and sought to cloud it. But the banns were about to be published. Although he had come to tell the vicomtesse about his marriage, the handsome Portuguese lord had not yet dared to breathe a word about it. Why? Nothing is harder than presenting a woman with an *ultimatum* of this kind. Some men are happier in the field facing a man who has the tip of his sword against their heart, than facing a woman who reels off elegies for a few hours then faints dead away, calling for her smelling salts. So, at that precise moment, Monsieur d'Ajuda-Pinto was in a tight spot and keen to take his leave, telling himself that Madame de Beauséant would hear the news anyway; he would write to her, it would be easier to pull off this amatory assassination by letter than in person. When the vicomtesse's valet announced Monsieur Eugène de Rastignac, the Marquis d'Ajuda-Pinto quivered with joy. Make no mistake, a woman in love is even more adept at putting her finger on some suspicious circumstance than she is at finding new sources of pleasure. When she's about to be abandoned, she guesses the meaning of a gesture more swiftly than Virgil's stallion detects the scent of equine love on the breeze.[88] So you may count on the fact that Madame de Beauséant sensed his almost imperceptible, but utterly damning, involuntary quiver. Eugène was unaware that you should never call on anyone in Paris without having first asked a friend of the family to tell you the life-story of the husband, wife or children, to avoid committing the kind of blunder picturesquely referred to in Poland as *Harnessing five oxen to your cart*, no doubt because that's what it takes to pull you out of the bog your wrong turning has led you into. If conversational mishaps such as these do not yet have a name in France, it must be because no one believes they really exist, due to the sheer amount of gossip doing the rounds. Having first stepped into the mire by calling on Madame de Restaud, who barely gave him time to harness all five oxen to his cart, only Eugène was capable of ploughing on regardless, by calling on Madame de Beauséant. However, although he had been a hindrance to Madame de Restaud and Monsieur de Trailles, he was a great help to Monsieur d'Ajuda.

'Farewell,' said the Portuguese nobleman, hurrying towards the door, just as Eugène entered a small, stylish, pink and grey drawing room, in which luxury and elegance were all of a piece.

'But only until tonight,' said Madame de Beauséant, turning her head to look at the marquis. 'Aren't we going to the Bouffons?'

'I won't be able to come,' he said, taking hold of the door handle.

Madame de Beauséant stood up and summoned him back, without paying the slightest attention to Eugène, who, standing there, struck dumb by the dazzling splendour of such fabulous wealth, thought he must be in the Arabian Nights. He hardly knew where to put himself in the presence of this woman, who seemed not to have noticed him. The vicomtesse lifted the first finger of her right hand and, with a pretty flourish, pointed at the space in front of her. There was such a violent tyranny of passion in this gesture that the marquis let go of the door handle and went to her. Eugène watched him, not without envy.

'That's him,' he said to himself, 'the man with the coupé! But does that mean you need prancing horses, liveried coachmen and an endless supply of gold before a Parisian lady will look twice at you?' The demon of luxury gripped his soul, the fever of greed consumed him, the thirst for gold parched his throat. He had a hundred and thirty francs to last the quarter. His father, his mother, his brothers, his sisters and his aunt spent no more than two hundred francs a month between them. This swift comparison between his current situation and his future goal left him feeling even more dazed.

'Why', said the vicomtesse, laughing, 'won't you *be able* to come to the Italiens?'

'Business! I am dining with the English ambassador.'

'Make your excuses.'

When a man deceives, he is inevitably forced to pile one lie on top of another. Monsieur d'Ajuda replied, laughing, 'Is that an order?'

'Yes, of course.'

'That's just what I wanted to hear,' he replied, with a meaningful look which would have reassured another woman. He kissed the vicomtesse's hand and left.

Eugène ran his hands through his hair and turned awkwardly, as if to bow, thinking that Madame de Beauséant was about to direct her attention to him, when she suddenly rushed into the gallery, ran to the window and watched Monsieur d'Ajuda climb into his coupé; she listened for the order and heard the page repeat to the coachman: 'To Monsieur de Rochefide's.' These words, and the way Ajuda hurled himself into his carriage, were as thunder and lightning to this woman, who turned back in the grip of mortal fear. The most terrible catastrophes may amount to no more than this in high society. The vicomtesse returned to her bedchamber, sat down at her desk and took a sheet of elegant notepaper. She wrote:

'*Since you are dining with the Rochefides, and not at the English embassy, you owe me an explanation. I am waiting.*'

After straightening a few letters made crooked by the convulsive trembling of her hand, she wrote a C, for Claire de Bourgogne, and rang the bell.

'Jacques,' she said to her valet, who appeared immediately; 'at half past seven you are to go to Monsieur de Rochefide's house, where you will ask for the Marquis d'Ajuda. If the marquis is there, you will make sure this letter reaches him without waiting for a reply; if he's not there, you will come back and return the letter to me.'

'Madame la Vicomtesse has someone in her drawing room.'

'Ah! yes, so I have,' she said, closing the door.

Eugène began to feel extremely ill at ease. The vicomtesse eventually emerged and said, her voice so full of emotion it stirred the strings of his heart: 'Forgive me, Monsieur, I had to write a note; I am now entirely at your disposal.' She barely

knew what she was saying, because she was thinking: 'So! He
wants to marry Mademoiselle de Rochefide. But is he free to do
so? This evening the marriage will be called off, or I . . . But it
will no longer be an issue tomorrow.'

'Cousin . . .' replied Eugène.

'What?' said the vicomtesse, with such a haughty look the
student's blood ran cold.

Eugène understood her reaction. In the past three hours he'd
learned so much that he was now more circumspect.

'Madame,' he corrected himself, flushing. He hesitated, then
continued, saying, 'Forgive me; I'm so much in need of protection, that the smallest scrap of kinship would be a blessing.'

Madame de Beauséant smiled, but sadly: she could already
sense the first mutterings of tragedy in the air around her.

'If you knew the state my family is in,' he continued, 'you
might like to play the role of one of those fairy godmothers
who delight in spiriting away the obstacles that stand in their
godson's way.'

'So, cousin,' she said, laughing, 'how may I be of service to
you?'

'I hardly know. To be connected to you by an obscure family
tie is already a great fortune. You've flustered me and I've forgotten what I came to say. You're the only person I know in
Paris. Oh! I wanted to ask you to guide me and accept me like
a poor child who wants to cling to your skirts and who would
die for you.'

'Would you kill a man for me?'

'I'd kill two,' said Eugène.

'Child! Yes, you are a child,' she said, suppressing a few
tears; 'your love would be sincere!'

'Oh!' he said, nodding his head.

The student's bold reply sharpened the vicomtesse's interest
in him. The Southerner had made his first calculated move.
Between Madame de Restaud's blue boudoir and Madame de
Beauséant's pink drawing room, he had studied three years of
that unspoken *Parisian law*; a lofty social jurisprudence which,
properly learned and practised, opens every door.

'Ah! I remember now,' said Eugène. 'Madame de Restaud

came to my attention at your ball; I went to call on her this morning.'

'She must have found your visit rather irksome,' said Madame de Beauséant, smiling.

'Yes! indeed, I'm such an ignorant soul that I'll turn everyone against me if you refuse to come to my aid. I can't help thinking that in Paris it's very hard to meet a woman who is young, beautiful, rich *and* unattached. I need someone to teach me what women are so good at explaining: life. I'll come up against a Monsieur de Trailles wherever I go. So I came here to ask you to solve a mystery and to explain the nature of the blunder I made there. I mentioned a certain old man . . .'

'Madame la Duchesse de Langeais,' said Jacques, interrupting the student, who made the gesture of a man sorely vexed.

'If you wish to succeed,' said the vicomtesse in a low voice, 'you must learn to hide your feelings.'

'Ah! Good afternoon, my dear,' she continued, standing up and going to greet the duchesse, whose hands she squeezed with as much warmth as if she were her sister, and to which the duchesse responded with the most charming display of affection.

'Here are two good friends,' Rastignac said to himself. 'I'll have two protectors now; the two women must have similar loyalties and this lady will surely take an interest in me.'

'To what generous motive do I owe the pleasure of your call, my dear Antoinette?' said Madame de Beauséant.

'I happened to see Monsieur d'Ajuda-Pinto go into Monsieur de Rochefide's house and I thought you must be alone.'

Madame de Beauséant did not purse her lips or flush, her brow remained unruffled and her expression unchanged as the duchesse pronounced these lethal words.

'If I'd known you had company . . .' added the duchesse, turning to Eugène.

'This is Monsieur Eugène de Rastignac, a cousin of mine,' said the vicomtesse. 'Have you any news of General Montriveau?' she continued. 'Sérisy was saying yesterday that we hardly ever see him these days – perhaps he called on you today?'

The duchesse, who was believed to have been abandoned by

Montriveau, with whom she was desperately in love, felt the sharp point of this question pierce her heart. She flushed, replying: 'He was at the Elysée[89] yesterday.'

'On duty,' said Madame de Beauséant.

'Clara,' continued the duchesse, her eyes glinting with mischief; 'I expect you've heard about Monsieur d'Ajuda-Pinto and Mademoiselle de Rochefide? The banns are to be published tomorrow.'

The blow was too harsh, the vicomtesse turned white and replied, laughing: 'One of those rumours that keeps fools amused. Why would Monsieur d'Ajuda connect one of the noblest names in Portugal with that of the Rochefides, whose title dates from yesterday?'

'They say that Berthe brings with her an annual income of two hundred thousand livres.'

'Monsieur d'Ajuda is far too rich to care about such things.'

'But my dear, Mademoiselle de Rochefide is charming.'

'Really!'

'In any case, he's dining there tonight; all the arrangements have been agreed. I'm most surprised to find you know so little about it.'

'So what was this blunder of yours, Monsieur?' said Madame de Beauséant. 'This poor boy is so recently come into society, my dear Antoinette, that he has no idea what we are talking about. For his sake, let us speak no more of this until tomorrow. Tomorrow, you know, it will all no doubt be official, and your friendly communication will have the authority of a decree.'

The duchesse gave Eugène one of those disdainful stares which swallow a man whole, chew him up and spit him out.

'Madame, I have unwittingly dealt a blow to Madame de Restaud's heart. Unwittingly: there lies my mistake,' said the student, whose presence of mind had served him well, and who had detected the biting commentary hidden behind the affectionate exchange between the two women.

'You continue to receive – and you perhaps fear – people who secretly know how much pain they are causing you, whereas he who wounds without realizing how deeply he has wounded is seen as an oaf, a fool incapable of turning anything to account, and scorned by all.'

Madame de Beauséant gave the student one of those melting looks which great souls are able to imbue with both gratitude and dignity. Her look was a balm that soothed the blow the duchesse had struck to his morale by sizing him up with the eye of a bailiff's assessor.

'You won't believe', continued Eugène, 'that I had just managed to win favour with the Comte de Restaud; for', he said, turning to the duchesse and adopting an air that was both humble and mischievous, 'I must tell you, Madame, that I am still a poor devil of a student, very much alone, very poor . . .'

'Keep that to yourself, Monsieur de Rastignac. We women never want what no one else will have.'

'No matter!' said Eugène, 'I'm only twenty-two, a man must learn to bear the hardships that come with his age. Besides, I'm at Confession; and I could hardly be kneeling in a prettier confessional: this is where a man commits the sins he admits to in the other kind.'

The duchesse affected a cold expression on hearing such irreligious talk, whose poor taste she condemned by saying to the vicomtesse: 'Monsieur has just arrived . . .'

Madame de Beauséant began to laugh outright at both her cousin and the duchesse.

'He has just arrived, my dear, and is looking for a governess to give him lessons in good taste.'

'Madame la Duchesse,' Eugène continued, 'surely it's natural for a man to wish to learn the secret of that which enchants him?' ('Dear me,' he said to himself, 'I'm sure I must sound just like a hairdresser.')

'But Madame de Restaud is, I believe, the pupil of Monsieur de Trailles,' said the duchesse.

'A circumstance I was entirely unaware of, Madame,' continued the student. 'And so I rashly threw myself between them. As I was saying, I was getting along fairly well with the husband, I had been tolerated for a while by the wife, when I took it upon myself to tell them that I knew a man I'd just seen leaving by a hidden staircase and who had kissed the comtesse at the end of a corridor.'

'Who was that?' asked the two women.

'An old man who, like myself, poor student that I am, lives on two louis a month, holed up in the Faubourg Saint-Marceau; a truly wretched old man mocked by all, whom we call old man Goriot.'

'Child that you are,' cried the vicomtesse; 'Madame de Restaud was once Mademoiselle Goriot.'

'The daughter of a vermicelli dealer,' continued the duchesse, 'a woman of low birth who was presented at court on the same day as a pastry cook's daughter. Don't you remember, Clara? The King started to laugh and made a Latin *bon mot*, something to do with flour. People who are, how did it go? People who are . . .'

'*Ejusdem farinae*,'[90] said Eugène.

'That was it,' said the duchesse.

'What! He's her father?' the student responded, with a gesture of horror.

'Why, of course; the old fellow had two daughters, he dotes on them both, although they've near enough disowned him.'

'Isn't the other one', said the vicomtesse, looking at Madame de Langeais, 'married to a banker with a German name, a Baron de Nucingen or somesuch? Delphine, is that it? You know, that blonde woman with a side-box at the Opéra, who comes to the Bouffons as well and laughs too loudly in order to draw attention to herself?'

The duchesse smiled, saying, 'My dear, I do admire you. Why do you take so much interest in these people? You'd have to be madly in love, as Restaud was, to have covered yourself in flour for the sake of Mademoiselle Anastasie. Well! He'll end up with precious little to show for it! Monsieur de Trailles has got his hands on her now and will be her ruin.'

'They've disowned their father,' repeated Eugène.

'Indeed, yes, their father, the old man, a father,' continued the vicomtesse, 'a good father, who gave them, so I've heard, five or six hundred thousand francs[91] apiece so they'd make a good match and be happy, keeping an annual income of just eight to ten thousand livres for himself, believing that his daughters would always be his daughters, that he'd be able to divide himself between two lives, two homes in which he'd be pampered and adored. In the space of two years, the sons-in-law had banished him from their sight, as if he was the lowliest of wretches . . .'

Recently refreshed by the pure and sacrosanct feelings of his family, still in love with his youthful beliefs, Eugène's eyes welled up with tears: this was his first day on the battlefield of Parisian civilization. Genuine emotion transmits itself so clearly that the three of them looked at each other for a while in silence.

'Dear God!' said Madame de Langeais, 'how terrible that seems, and yet we see it every day. Is there not some underlying cause? Tell me, my dear, have you ever reflected on the nature of a son-in-law? A son-in-law is a man for whom we – you and I – will raise a dear little creature attached to us by a thousand bonds, who for seventeen years will be the family's joy, its swan-white soul, as Lamartine[92] might say, and who then becomes its scourge. When this man has taken her from us, the first thing he will do is wield love like an axe[93] and sever every feeling in our angel's heart that binds her to her family. Yesterday, our daughter was everything to us, we were everything to her; the next day she's our enemy. Do we not see this tragedy played out every day? Here, a daughter-in-law is breathtakingly rude to her father-in-law, who sacrificed everything for his son. Elsewhere, a son-in-law turfs out his mother-in-law. I hear people asking where all the drama is in society these days; well, there's the terrible tragedy of the son-in-law, not to mention the ridiculous farce of marriage. I know exactly what happened to the old vermicelli dealer. I think I recall that this Foriot[94] of ours . . .'

'Goriot, Madame.'

'Yes, this Moriot, was president of his section[95] during the Revolution; he had inside knowledge of the famous food shortage and made his fortune during that time by selling flour at ten times more than he bought it for. He was given any price he asked for. My grandmother's intendant[96] sold him vast quan-

tities of it. Goriot, like the rest of his kind,[97] probably shared
the proceeds with the Committee of Public Safety.[98] I remember
the intendant telling my grandmother she could stay at Grand-
villiers in all safety, wheat being a guarantee of good citizenship.
Well, this Loriot, who sold wheat to those butchers, has only
ever had one passion. They say he's besotted with his daughters. He found the elder daughter a perch in the house of
Restaud and grafted the other onto the Baron de Nucingen,
a wealthy banker with royalist leanings.[99] As you may well
imagine, under the Empire, the two sons-in-law didn't trouble
their heads too much about having the old veteran of '93[100] at
home; under Bonaparte, that still passed muster. But when the
Bourbons were reinstated,[101] the old fellow was a thorn in
Monsieur de Restaud's side, and even more so in the banker's.
The daughters, who still loved their father, perhaps, tried to
accommodate chalk and cheese, father and husband; they
received Goriot when no one else was there; they invented tender excuses. "Papa, come, we'll be more at ease because we'll
be alone!" and so on. As for me, my dear, I believe that true
feelings have eyes and an intelligence: and so the heart of this
poor veteran of '93 must have bled. He saw that his daughters
were ashamed of him; that they loved their husbands, but that
he was an embarrassment to his sons-in-law. He therefore had
to sacrifice himself. He sacrificed himself because he was a
father: he took himself into exile. Seeing his daughters happy,
he understood that he had done the right thing. The father and
his children were complicit in this petty crime. We see it everywhere. Wouldn't old Doriot have been like a greasy stain in his
daughters' drawing rooms? He would have felt embarrassed to
be there, it would have grieved him. What happened to this father
can happen to even the prettiest girl at the hands of the man she
loves most of all: if she importunes him with her love, he leaves,
he behaves like a coward to escape her. That's how it is with
feelings. A heart is a treasure chest: empty it in one go and you
are ruined. We are as unforgiving of a feeling for having revealed
its depth as we are of a man for being penniless. He was a
father who gave everything. For twenty years, he gave his soul,
his love; as for his wealth, he gave that away in a day. Once the

lemon had been squeezed dry, his daughters threw the peel into the road.'

'The world is foul,' said the vicomtesse, fiddling with the fringe of her shawl and without raising her eyes, for she was cut to the quick by the words meant for her that Madame de Langeais had slipped into this story.

'Foul! No,' countered the duchesse; 'it follows its course, that's all. If I'm talking about the world like this, it's to show you that I'm not fooled by it. I think as you do,' she said, pressing the vicomtesse's hand. 'The world is a quagmire, let us try to stay on high ground.' She stood up and kissed Madame de Beauséant on the forehead, saying: 'You're very beautiful at the moment, my dear. You have the prettiest colour I've ever seen.' Then she left, with a cursory nod in Rastignac's direction.

'Old man Goriot is sublime!' said Eugène, remembering how he had seen him twist his silver-gilt on the night of the ball.

Madame de Beauséant did not hear him; she was lost in thought. A few moments went by in silence and the poor student, paralysed with embarassment, dared neither to leave, nor to stay, nor speak.

'Society is foul and evil,' said the vicomtesse, at last. 'As soon as misfortune comes our way, there is always a friend ready to come and tell us about it, piercing our heart with a dagger even as they invite us to admire the handle. Sarcasm and mockery – so soon! Well! I will defend myself.' She raised her head like the noble lady she was, her proud eyes blazing. 'Oh!' she said, catching sight of Eugène. 'You're here.'

'Still,' he said sheepishly.

'Well, Monsieur de Rastignac, treat this world as it deserves to be treated. You want to succeed, and I will help you. You will plumb the depths of female depravity, you will gauge the breadth of the contemptible vanity of men. Although I've read widely in the book of society, there were a few pages even I knew nothing about. Now, I know them all. The more coldly calculating you are, the further you will go. Strike ruthlessly and you'll be respected. Accept that men and women are posthorses that you ride into the ground then leave at each stage, and you'll reach the pinnacle of your desires. Remember, you'll be nothing here without a woman to further your interests. You need one who is young, wealthy and elegant. But if you have a single genuine feeling, bury it like treasure; don't ever let others suspect its existence or you'll be lost. Instead of being the torturer, you'll become the victim. If you ever fall in love, guard your secret well! Don't reveal a thing until you have made sure of the person to whom you are opening your heart. From now on, to protect this love which does not yet exist, learn to be wary of this world of ours. Listen to me, Miguel . . .' (she innocently called him by the wrong name without realizing), 'there is something even more terrible than the neglect of the father by his two daughters, who wish him dead. And that is the rivalry between the two sisters. Restaud has birth, his wife has been recognized, she has been presented at court; but her sister, her rich sister, the beautiful Madame Delphine de Nucingen, the wife of a money-man, is dying of pique; she's consumed by jealousy, she's a thousand leagues behind her sister; her sister is no longer her sister; the two women disown each other just as each disowns her father. And that's why Madame de Nucingen would lap up all the mud that lies between the Rue Saint-Lazare and the Rue de Grenelle to enter my drawing room. She thought that de Marsay would help her reach her goal, so she has made herself de Marsay's slave and is boring de Marsay to tears. De Marsay cares little for her. If you introduce her to me, you'll become her favourite, she'll worship you. Love her afterwards, if you can, otherwise, make use of her. I'll acknowledge her once or twice at large parties, among the crowd; but I will never receive her in the morning. I'll bow to her, that will suffice. By uttering the name of old man Goriot you have ensured that the comtesse's door will always be closed to you. Yes, my dear, go and call on Madame de Restaud twenty times, and twenty times you will find she is not at home. You are in her black books. Now, let old man Goriot introduce you to Madame Delphine de Nucingen. The beautiful Madame de Nucingen will be your ensign. Be the man she singles out and women will fall at your feet. Her rivals, her friends, her closest friends, will all try and take you away from her. Some women prefer a man who has already been chosen

by another woman, just as a poor *bourgeoise* hopes that by
wearing the same hats as we do, she will acquire our poise. Be
successful. In Paris, success is everything, it's the key to power.
If the women find you witty and talented, that's what the men
will believe, if you don't undeceive them. Then you can set your
sights on anything you wish, you'll have a foot in everyone's
door. And then you will know what society really is, a bunch of
frauds and knaves. Do not join either one faction or another. I
will lend you my name; it will guide you through this labyrinth
like Ariadne's thread.[102] Do not compromise it,' she said, arch-
ing her neck and casting a regal glance at the student; 'I want it
returned to me in perfect condition. Go now, and leave me. We
women have our own battles to fight.'

'Should you ever need a man willing to spring a mine,' said
Eugène, interrupting her.

'If I should?' she asked.

He struck his heart, smiled to see his cousin smile and left. It
was five o'clock. Eugène was hungry; he feared he might not
arrive in time for dinner. This fear made him appreciate the
delight of crossing Paris swiftly in a carriage. The pleasure this
brought was purely automatic, leaving him at liberty to pursue
the thoughts jostling for position in his mind. When a young
man of his age is scorned, he loses his temper, he frets, he shakes
his fist at the whole of society, he wants to avenge himself, 'and
yet he is prone to self-doubt. Rastignac's head was still ringing
with the words: *You have ensured that the comtesse's door will
always be closed to you.* 'I will go there!' he said to himself, 'and
if Madame de Beauséant is right, if I am barred . . . I . . . Madame
de Restaud will find me in every drawing room she enters. I will
learn to fence, to fire a pistol, I'll kill her Maxime!' – 'And what
about money!' his conscience cried out to him; 'where will you
get that?' Suddenly the ostentatious wealth on display at the
Comtesse de Restaud's house glittered before his eyes. There,
he had seen the kind of luxury which a Mademoiselle Goriot
was bound to find attractive, gildings, showpieces that drew
attention to their cost, the undiscerning luxury of the *parvenu*,
the extravagance of the kept woman. This glittering mirage was
suddenly outshone by the majestic Hôtel de Beauséant. His

imagination, soaring among the highest peaks of Parisian society, sowed a thousand base thoughts in his heart, as it stretched his head and mind. He recognized the world for what it is – a place where laws and morality have no power over the rich – and he saw in wealth the *ultima ratio mundi*.[103]

'Vautrin is right: wealth equals virtue!' he said to himself.

As soon as he arrived at the Rue Neuve-Sainte-Geneviève, he ran up to his room, came down with ten francs for the coachman, then went into the unsavoury dining room where he found the eighteen diners feeding like animals at the trough. He balked at the room's appearance, at the sight of such wretchedness. The transition was too abrupt, the contrast too stark not to cause a sudden surge in his ambition. On the one hand, the fresh, delightful images of the most elegant creatures in society, young, animated faces, surrounded by the marvels of art and luxury, minds alive with passion and poetry; on the other, a series of murky portraits with begrimed edges, faces with nothing left showing but the ropes and pulleys of their passions. The teachings that the rage of a spurned woman had wrenched from Madame de Beauséant, her beguiling proposals, rose to the surface of his memory, and poverty provided a commentary on them all. Rastignac resolved to pursue two parallel lines of attack to make his fortune, to rely on both love and the law, to be a man of learning *and* a man of fashion. What a child he still was! These two lines are asymptotes[104] and can never meet.

'You seem rather solemn, Monsieur le Marquis,' said Vautrin, giving him one of those penetrating stares with which he seemed to make himself privy to the most deeply buried secrets of the heart.

'I'm not in the mood to put up with the jokes of those who call me Monsieur le Marquis,' he replied. 'In this city, to be a real marquis you need a hundred thousand livres a year, and when you lodge at the Maison Vauquer you're hardly the favourite of Fortune.'

Vautrin gave Rastignac a look that was both paternal and contemptuous, as if to say: 'Brat! I'd make light work of you!' Then he replied: 'Perhaps you're in a bad mood because you failed to impress the beautiful Comtesse de Restaud.'

'Her door will be closed to me from now on because I mentioned that her father ate at our table,' cried Rastignac.

The diners looked at each other. Old man Goriot lowered his eyes and turned away to wipe them.

'You flicked some snuff in my eye,' he said to his neighbour.

'From now on, anyone who upsets old man Goriot will answer to me,' replied Eugène, glaring at the man sitting next to the old vermicelli dealer; 'he's worth more than all of us put together. Apart from the ladies,' he said, turning to Mademoiselle Taillefer.

These words fell like a thunderbolt, Eugène's tone having silenced the diners. Only Vautrin replied, mockingly: 'If you're going to pick up old man Goriot's tab and make yourself his keeper, you'll need to know how to hold a sword and fire a pistol properly.'

'And so I will,' said Eugène.

'So the campaign starts today?'

'Perhaps,' replied Rastignac. 'But that's my business and I'll keep it to myself, seeing as I don't go sticking my nose into other people's goings-on at night.'

Vautrin shot Rastignac a sidelong look.

'Dear boy, if you don't want to be fooled by puppets, you have to get right inside the theatre and not be content with peering through holes in the scenery. That's enough talk,' he added, seeing that Eugène was ready to press the point. 'We can have a little chat about this whenever you want.'

Dinner became a cold and glum affair. Old Goriot, still grieving over the student's words, was unaware that the general attitude towards him had changed and that a young man capable of silencing his persecutors had come to his defence.

'So the latest on Monsieur Goriot', said Madame Vauquer in a low voice, 'is that he's the father of a comtesse?'

'And of a baron's wife,' Rastignac replied.

'What else could he be?' said Bianchon to Rastignac; 'I've felt his head and there's only one bump, that of paternity: he'll be an *Eternal* Father.'

Eugène was too preoccupied to laugh at Bianchon's joke. He

wanted to turn Madame de Beauséant's advice to good account and was wondering how and where he could get hold of some money. His brow furrowed as he pictured the savannahs of society stretching out before him, full and yet empty. After dinner, the others drifted out one by one, leaving him alone in the dining room.

'So you saw my daughter?' said Goriot, his voice choked with emotion.

Awoken from his daydream, Eugène took the old fellow by the hand and, looking at him with warmth and pity, said: 'You are a good and worthy man. We'll talk about your daughters later.' He stood up without waiting to hear old Goriot's reply and withdrew to his room, where he wrote his mother the following letter:

'Dearest Mother, see if you can't perform a miracle and make milk flow from a third breast for your son. I'm in a position to swiftly make a fortune. I need twelve hundred francs, and I need them whatever it takes. Don't mention my request to Father, as he may oppose it, and if I don't have the money I'll be racked with such despair that it may lead me to blow my brains out. I'll explain my motives when I next come home, for I'd need to write volumes to make my situation clear to you. I haven't been gambling, dear Mother, I have no debts; but if you care about preserving the life you gave me, you must find me this amount. You see, I'll be calling on the Vicomtesse de Beauséant, who has taken me under her wing. I'll be moving in the highest circles and I haven't a sou to buy myself clean gloves. I can get by on bread and water and go without food if I have to; but I can't do without the tools they use to tend the vines round here. For me, this is the difference between making my way or languishing in the mud. I know that you have placed all your hopes in me and I want to fulfil them just as soon as I can. Dearest Mother, sell some of your old jewellery, I will replace it shortly. I'm familiar enough with our family's position to appreciate the enormity of such a sacrifice, and you must believe that I am not asking you to make it in vain or I'd be a monster. Do not interpret my plea as anything other than a cry of urgent need. Our entire future hangs on

this grant with which I must open my campaign; for life in Paris
is an eternal battle. If, to make up the amount, there is nothing
for it but to sell my aunt's lace, tell her that I will send her other,
far more beautiful pieces.' Etc.

He wrote to each of his sisters, asking for their savings; and
to ensure that the rest of the family did not hear of the sacrifice
they would be only too happy to make on his behalf, he
appealed to their discretion by touching the chords of honour
which have such resonance and are so finely tuned in young
hearts. Nonetheless, once he had written these letters, he felt an
involuntary pang: his heart was racing, he was trembling. Despite his ambition, the young man recognized the nobility and
purity of these souls hidden away in their solitude; he was well
aware of the hardship he would cause his two sisters, and also
of the joy, the pleasure, they would take from discussing their
beloved brother in secret, deep in the vineyards. His heightened
awareness showed them to him, counting out their modest pile
of treasure in secret: he saw them using all the wily ingenuity
young girls have at their disposal, to send him the money *incog-*
nito, exalting themselves as they tried their hand at deceit for
the first time. 'A sister's heart is as pure as a diamond, its kindness knows no bounds!' he said to himself. He was ashamed of
what he had written. How heartfelt their wishes would be, how
pure the flight of their souls towards heaven! How exquisite
the delight of their self-sacrifice! What grief his mother would
feel, if she failed to send the full amount! These noble feelings,
these terrible sacrifices, would be the stepping stones that would
bring him to Delphine de Nucingen. A few tears, the last grains
of incense laid on the sacred altar of the family, splashed from
his eyes. He paced up and down in a torment of despair. Old
Goriot, seeing him in this state through the half-open door,
came in and asked, 'What's wrong, Monsieur?'

'Ah! Dear neighbour, I am still a son and a brother, just
as you are a father. You are right to tremble for Comtesse
Anastasie; she has fallen into the hands of Monsieur Maxime
de Trailles, who will ruin her.'

Old man Goriot withdrew stammering something Eugène

did not catch. The next day, Rastignac went out to post his letters. He hesitated right up to the last moment, but then threw them into the box, saying: 'I will succeed!' Such is the fatal motto of a gambler, or a great captain, one which destroys more men than it redeems.

A few days later, Eugène went to call on Madame de Restaud and was not received. He went back three times and a further three times found her door closed to him, even though he called when the Comte Maxime de Trailles wasn't there. The vicomtesse had been right. The student stopped studying. He turned up at lectures to answer the roll-call and took himself off as soon as he had been registered. He followed the same reasoning as most students. He would put off studying until it was time to sit his exams; he would let his second- and third-year courses pile up, then at the last minute apply himself seriously to learning law, in one short spurt. That left him at liberty to sail across the ocean of Paris for fifteen months, to throw himself into bartering for women or fishing for his fortune. During this week, he visited Madame de Beauséant twice, arriving just as the Marquis d'Ajuda's carriage was leaving. That illustrious woman, the most poetic figure of the Faubourg Saint-Germain set, held sway for a few more days, and the marriage between Mademoiselle de Rochefide and the Marquis d'Ajuda-Pinto hung in the balance. But these last few days, which the fear of losing her happiness made the most passionate of all, would only serve to precipitate the catastrophe. The Marquis d'Ajuda, together with the Rochefides, viewed this falling-out and reconciliation as fortuitous, hoping that Madame de Beauséant would become accustomed to the idea of the marriage and end up renouncing her afternoons in favour of the future a man expects in life. Despite the most heartfelt promises, made afresh each day, Monsieur d'Ajuda was acting a part and the vicomtesse was enjoying playing along. 'Instead of nobly throwing herself out of the window, she was letting herself be tricked into falling down the stairs,' concluded the Duchesse de Langeais, her best friend. Nonetheless, these dying rays shone long enough to keep the vicomtesse in Paris, where she could be of use to her young relative, for whom she felt a sort of superstitious affection. Eugène had shown himself to be full of devotion and sensitivity towards her, in a situation where a woman sees neither pity nor true consolation in anyone's eyes. If a man should speak sweet words to her at such a time, he does so from self-interest.

As he wished to chart the lie of the land before attempting to storm the house of Nucingen, Rastignac undertook to acquaint himself with the facts of old man Goriot's earlier life and collected a fair amount of reliable information, which may be summarized as follows.

In the days before the Revolution, Jean-Joachim Goriot was an ordinary workman in the vermicelli trade, skilful, thrifty and canny enough to purchase his master's business when chance made him a victim of the first uprising in 1789. He set up shop in the Rue de la Jussienne, near the Corn Exchange, and when invited to become president of his section, had the enormous good sense to accept, so that his business was protected by the most influential people at that dangerous time. This wise step was the making of him, when the food shortage, true or feigned, led to an exponential rise in the price of grain in Paris. Some people killed each other at bakery doors, while certain other people, without any uproar, went and bought Italian pasta at the grocers. During that year, citizen Goriot accumulated the capital which later allowed him to do business with the superior advantage that a vast quantity of cash confers on its owner. What happened to him is what happens to all men of only average ability. His mediocrity saved him. Moreover, as his wealth only became common knowledge at the time when it was no longer dangerous to be rich, he excited no one's jealousy. The grain trade appeared to occupy his entire mind. Whether he was dealing in wheat, flour, middlings – recognizing their quality or origin, taking care of their storage, predicting prices, forecasting a good or poor harvest, procuring cheap cereals, buying in supplies from Sicily or the Ukraine – no man was a match for Goriot. To see him running his business, analysing the laws governing grain imports and exports, working out their spirit, seizing upon their loopholes, any man would have thought him capable of being a Minister of State. Patient, active, energetic, steadfast, quick to dispatch, he had an eagle eye, he was always a step ahead, he saw everything coming, knew everything, concealed everything: a diplomat in his design, a soldier in his stamina. Away from his speciality, from his simple, obscure place of work – on whose steps he lingered during his leisure time, leaning against the door-post – he reverted to his former self: the dull-witted, brutish workman, incapable of following an argument, oblivious to all the pleasures of the mind, the man who fell asleep at the theatre, one of those Parisian Dolibans[105] who excel only in stupidity. Natures such as these are almost all the same. You will find that nearly all have some sublime feeling in their hearts. Two feelings alone had engrossed the vermicelli dealer's heart, had absorbed its humidity, just as the grain trade had soaked up all his intellect. His wife, the only daughter of a rich farmer in the Brie region, was the sacred object of his devotion and boundless love. Goriot admired her nature, both fragile and robust, sensitive and appealing, so very different from his own. If a man has any innate feeling in his heart, surely it is pride at offering protection to a weaker being at any time? If you combine that with love, the intense gratitude felt by all sincere souls towards the source of their happiness, you will understand a whole host of behavioural peculiarities. After seven years of unclouded happiness, Goriot had the great misfortune to lose his wife, just as her influence over him was beginning to extend beyond the realm of feeling. Perhaps she would have sparked off his inert nature, perhaps she would have sown in it some seeds of understanding of the world and of life. In these new circumstances, Goriot's paternal devotion deepened to an insane degree. He transferred his love, thwarted by death, to his two daughters, who at first fully satisfied his emotional needs. However brilliant the offers made by tradesmen or farmers eager to foist their daughters onto him, he preferred to remain a widower. His father-in-law, the only man he had any fondness for, claimed that he knew for a fact that Goriot had sworn never to be unfaithful to his wife. The men at the Corn Exchange, incapable of understanding this sublime piece of madness, cracked jokes about Goriot and gave him a grotesque nickname. The first man who thought fit to call him by it to his face, while raising his glass to clinch a deal, received such a blow on the shoulder from the vermicelli dealer that it sent him head first into a milestone in the Rue Oblin.[106] Goriot's unquestioning devotion, his easily triggered, delicately adjusted love for his daughters, was so well known that one day a competitor of his, to make him leave the Exchange so he would gain the upper hand in a deal, told him that Delphine had just been run over by a cabriolet. The vermicelli dealer, his face drained of colour, immediately left the Corn Exchange. The distressing feelings that this false alarm aroused in him laid him low for several days. Although he spared this man a lethal blow to the shoulder, Goriot did drive him out of the Corn Exchange by forcing him to go bankrupt in a critical situation.

Naturally, he gave his two daughters an extravagant education. With an income of over sixty thousand livres per year and personal expenses of less than twelve hundred francs, Goriot's only pleasure lay in granting his daughters' every wish: the very best masters were instructed to equip them with the accomplishments that are the markers of a fine education; they had a companion – happily for them, she was a woman of intelligence and good taste; they rode, they had their own carriage, they lived as the mistresses of a rich old lord would live; they only had to express some expensive desire to see their father fall over himself to fulfil it; all he asked for was some sign of affection in return for his offerings. Goriot elevated his daughters to the rank of angels, and so he ranked them above himself, poor man! He even loved the pain they caused him. When his daughters reached a marriageable age, they were able to choose their husbands to suit their tastes: they had half their father's fortune each as a dowry. Courted for her beauty by the Comte de Restaud, Anastasie's aristocratic aspirations led her to leave her father's house for the higher echelons of society. Delphine loved money: she married Nucingen, a banker of German extraction, who became a baron of the Holy Roman Empire.[107] Goriot remained a vermicelli dealer. Before long, his

daughters and sons-in-law couldn't bear to see him continue
his trade, even though it was his entire life. After resisting their
entreaties for five years, he consented to retire on the capital
raised by the sale of his business and the profits of the last few
years; resources which Madame Vauquer, in whose establishment he was to become a fixture, estimated would bring in an
annual income of eight to ten thousand livres. It was his despair at seeing his two daughters forced by their husbands to
refuse not only to have him to live with them, but even to
receive him in public, that drove him to remove himself to the
boarding house.

This was all the information that a certain Monsieur Muret,
who had purchased his business, was able to give him about
old man Goriot. It confirmed the conjecture that Rastignac had
heard from the lips of the Duchesse de Langeais. Here ends the
exposition of this obscure but terrible Parisian tragedy.

AN INTRODUCTION
TO SOCIETY

Towards the end of the first week in December, Rastignac received two letters, one from his mother, the other from his older sister. The familiar handwriting made him both quiver with relief and quake with terror. These two flimsy documents contained a verdict of life or death for his hopes. Although he felt some apprehension as he recalled his parents' penury, he had too much experience of their indulgence not to fear that he had finally bled them dry. His mother's letter ran as follows:

'My dear child, I am sending you what you asked for. Use this money well, for if I have to save your life a second time, I will not be able to find such a substantial amount without telling your father and that would cause a rift between us. We would be forced to mortgage the estate to raise the money. It is impossible for me to assess the merit of plans I know nothing about; but what kind of plans can they be if you are afraid to share them with me? Your explanation needn't have taken volumes; all a mother needs is a word, a single word to save her from the agony of uncertainty. I cannot conceal from you how much grief your letter caused me. My dear Son, what motive led you to strike such fear into my heart? You must have been suffering terribly as you wrote to me, for I suffered terribly as I read what you had written. What escapade are you embarking on? Your life, your happiness, seem to hang on passing yourself off as someone you are not, frequenting the kind of society you cannot be seen in without living above your means and without losing precious time meant for study. My dear Eugène, trust your mother's *instinct: tortuous paths do not lead to greatness. Patience and resignation must be the virtues of young men in your position. I am not scolding you, I do not wish to taint our offering with bitterness. I speak as a mother who trusts you as much as she fears for you. If you know what your duty is, then I, your mother, know how pure your heart is and how good your intentions. And so I may say to you without fear: "Go, beloved Son, walk on your own two feet." I tremble because I am a mother; but every step you take will be accompanied by our loving good wishes and blessings. Be prudent, dearest child. You must display the wisdom of a man; the destinies of five people who are dear to you rest on your shoulders. Yes, all of our fortunes are bound up in you, just as your happiness is ours. We all pray to God to help you in your endeavours. Your Aunt Marcillac has shown extraordinary kindness in this matter: she went so far as to find what you said about your gloves quite understandable. But then she has always had a soft spot for the eldest, she said cheerfully. Darling Eugène, show your aunt how much you love her. I won't tell you what she did for you until you have succeeded, otherwise her money would burn your fingers. You children don't know what it means to sacrifice memories! Yet, what wouldn't we sacrifice for you? She has asked me to send you a kiss on the forehead from her and to tell you that she hopes this kiss will give you the power to be happy time and again. The dear, kind woman would have written to you herself if she didn't have the gout in her fingers. Your father is well. The 1819 harvest is better than expected. Farewell dear child. I won't say a word about your sisters: Laure is writing to you herself. I will leave her the pleasure of chattering on about the family's little bits and pieces of news. May heaven send you success! Indeed, yes, you must succeed, dear Eugène, you have caused me such terrible pain I could not bear it a second time. I have known what it is to be poor and to wish I had riches to give to my child. Farewell, that's all for now. Don't leave us without news and accept this kiss your mother sends you.'*

By the time Eugène had finished this letter, he was in tears: he thought of old man Goriot twisting his silver-gilt and selling it to pay off his daughter's bill of exchange. 'Your mother has had her jewellery melted down!' he said to himself. 'Your aunt must have wept as she sold off her treasures! What right do you have to judge Anastasie? Out of selfish ambition you have just done exactly what she did for her lover! Who is the better person, you or she?' The student felt an unbearable burning sensation inside him. He wanted to turn his back on society, he wanted to refuse the money. He felt all the nobility and beauty of that secret remorse whose merit is rarely appreciated by men when they judge their fellow creatures, with the result that a criminal condemned by earthly judges is often absolved by heavenly angels. Rastignac opened the letter sent by his sister, whose innocent, flowing words refreshed his soul.

'Your letter came at just the right time, dearest Brother. Agathe and I wanted to spend our money in so many different ways that we couldn't make up our minds what to do with it. Like the King of Spain's servant, when he turned his master's clocks upside down, you made us see eye to eye. Really, we kept on squabbling over which of our wishes should be given preference and we had not yet managed, dear Eugène, to find a way of satisfying all our desires. Agathe jumped for joy. We were like two madwomen for the rest of the day, to such an extra-ordinary degree (as our aunt might put it) that Mother sternly asked us: "What is the matter with you, young ladies?" If we had been scolded a little, I think that would have made us happier still. A woman must enjoy suffering for the one she loves! For my part I was pensive and sad in the midst of my joy. I am bound to make a bad wife, I'm too much of a spendthrift. I had bought myself two sashes and a pretty bodkin for piercing eyelet-holes in corsets, silly trifles, which meant that I had less money than old Agathe, who scrimps and saves and hoards her écus like a magpie. She had two hundred francs! As for me, poor friend, I only have fifty écus. I have been suitably punished; I want to throw my sash down the well, I will never enjoy wearing it. I have cheated you. Agathe was a darling. She said: "Let's send him three hundred and fifty francs from us both!" But I can't wait to tell you what we did. This is

*how we carried out your orders: we took our fabulous wealth,
went for a walk together, and once we reached the main road,
ran to Ruffec, where we simply handed it all over to Monsieur
Grimbert at the post office! On our way back, we felt as free as
birds. "Is it happiness that makes us feel so light-hearted?"
Agathe asked me. We talked of a thousand things that I won't
repeat here,* Monsieur le Parisien, *for it was all about you. Oh!
darling Brother, we love you dearly, that is the long and short of
it. As for our secret, according to my aunt, dark horses like us are
capable of anything, even holding their tongues. Mother made a
mysterious journey to Angoulême with Aunt, and they both
refrained from commenting on the high politics of their trip,
which took place following long meetings from which we were
excluded, along with Monsieur le Baron. The great minds of the
State of Rastignac are busy pondering this. Work on the muslin
dress trimmed with openwork flowers that the Infantas are
embroidering for Her Majesty the Queen is proceeding in the
greatest secrecy. There are only two widths left to do. A decision
has been taken to put a hedge on the Verteuil side, rather than a
wall. The humble folk will lose fruit and espaliers, but strangers
will gain a fine view. Should the heir apparent require any handkerchiefs, he is to know that the Dowager de Marcillac, while
digging deep among her treasures and chests, known as Pompeii
and Herculaneum, found a length of fine holland cloth that she
didn't know she had; Princesses Agathe and Laure place needle
and thread at his disposal, along with their hands, which are
always a touch too red. The two young princes Don Henri and
Don Gabriel are still in the disastrous habit of gorging themselves
on grape jelly, driving their sisters to distraction, thwarting all
efforts by anyone to teach them anything, amusing themselves with
bird-nesting, making a racket, and despite the laws of the State,
cutting willows to make rods. The Pope's nuncio, otherwise known
as Monsieur le Curé, has threatened to excommunicate them if
they continue to neglect the sacred canons of grammar for belli-
cose cannons of elder.*[108] *Farewell, dear Brother, no letter has ever
borne so many wishes for your happiness, nor so much contented
love. You will have so much to tell us when you come home! You*

*must tell me everything as I am the eldest. My aunt has led us to
suspect that you have had some success in society.*

There is talk of a lady and silence as to the rest.[109]

*In our presence, at least! By the way Eugène, if you like, we could
do without handkerchiefs and make you some shirts. Send me
your answer as soon as possible. If you had a pressing need for
some fine, well-tailored shirts, we would need to start work
straight away; and if there are fashions in Paris that we are
unfamiliar with, you could send us a pattern, especially for the
cuffs. Farewell, farewell! I am planting a kiss on the left side of
your forehead, on the temple which belongs exclusively to me. I
will leave the other sheet of paper for Agathe, who has promised
not to read what I have written. But, just to make sure, I will
stand next to her while she is writing to you.
Your loving Sister,
    LAURE de RASTIGNAC.'*

'Oh! Yes,' Eugène said to himself, 'yes, I must make my fortune at all cost! No treasures could repay such devotion. I want
to bring them every kind of happiness at once. Fifteen hundred
and fifty francs!' he said after a pause. 'Every single coin of it
must strike home! Laure is right. Woman be praised! My shirts
are all made of coarse cloth. A girl becomes as wily as a thief to
bring about another's happiness. Innocent unto herself and
provident unto me, she is like some heavenly angel who par-
dons earthly sins without understanding them.'
    The world belonged to him! His tailor had already been sum-
moned, sounded out, won over. On seeing Monsieur de Trailles,
Rastignac had understood the influence that tailors exercise over
the lives of young men. Alas! There is no middle ground: depending on his skill, a tailor is either your worst enemy, or a friend in
need. Eugène found his to be a man who understood the paternal side of his trade, seeing himself as the link between a young
man's present and his future. The grateful Rastignac later made
this man's fortune with one of the witty remarks at which he
came to excel. 'I know', he said, 'two pairs of his trousers that
made matches worth twenty thousand livres per year.'[110]

Fifteen hundred francs and as many clothes as he could wear! With this thought, the last of the poor Southerner's doubts was dispelled and he went down to *déjeuner* with the undefinable air of a young man who finds himself in possession of a certain sum of money. As soon as a few notes slide into a student's pocket, an imaginary pillar of support rises up inside him. He walks taller than before, senses a fulcrum giving him leverage, he looks you in the eye, boldly, his movements are agile and alert; yesterday, timid and humble, he would have cowered under a shower of blows; today, he has it in him to punch a Prime Minister. All kinds of phenomenal changes take place inside him: he wants everything and is capable of anything, he burns with wild, indiscriminate desires, he is joyful, generous, extrovert. At last, the flightless bird remembers how to spread its wings. A penniless student snatches a scrap of pleasure as a dog snaps up a bone; threatened from all sides, he crunches it, sucks out the marrow and keeps on running. A young man who jingles a few fleeting gold coins in his fob, however, savours and itemizes his enjoyment, revels in it; he soars across the sky, he no longer knows the meaning of the word *poverty*. The whole of Paris belongs to him. A time when everything gleams, when everything blazes and sparkles! A time of elation and strength which no one else can turn to their advantage, neither man nor woman! A time of debts and terrible fears which increase pleasure tenfold! A man who has never known the Left Bank of the Seine, between the Rue Saint-Jacques and the Rue des Saints-Pères,[111] knows nothing of life! 'Hah! If they only knew!' Rastignac said to himself, as he wolfed down Madame Vauquer's one-liard-apiece stewed pears; 'the women of Paris would be flocking here in search of love.' At this point, the bell on the openwork gate rang and a postman from the Messageries Royales appeared in the dining room. He asked for Monsieur Eugène de Rastignac, then handed him two bags and a register to sign. Vautrin gave Rastignac a meaningful look that cut into him like the lash of a whip.

'You've enough there to pay for fencing lessons and shooting practice,' the older man said.

'Your ship has come in,' added Madame Vauquer, eyeing up the bags.

Mademoiselle Michonneau kept her eyes lowered, not daring to look at the money, for fear of revealing how she coveted it.

'Your mother is good to you,' said Madame Couture.

'Monsieur has a good mother,' Poiret echoed.

'Yes, your mother has bled herself dry,' said Vautrin. 'You can have all the fun you like now: go fishing for dowries in high society and dance with comtesses with peach blossom in their hair. But take my advice, young man, and put in some shooting practice.' Vautrin took aim at an imaginary enemy.

Rastignac put his hand in his pocket to tip the postman, and found it empty. Vautrin reached into his, and threw the man twenty sous.

'You've got good credit,' he said, looking the student in the eye.

Rastignac was forced to thank him, although he had found his presence unbearable since their harsh exchange of words on the day of his first visit to Madame de Beauséant. Over the past week, Eugène and Vautrin had kept silent in each other's company, watching one another warily. The student had pondered this mystery without getting to the bottom of it.

It seems likely that the force with which thoughts are projected is directly proportionate to that with which they are conceived, and they strike where the brain sends them, like the mathematical law that governs the trajectory of a shell shot from a mortar-piece. The effect they have varies widely. While some may become lodged and wreak havoc, as in the case of tender natures, others come up against strongly armed natures, skulls with bronze ramparts, upon which the wills of others are smashed and drop like bullets bouncing off a wall; or, again, there are those flabby, woolly natures which swallow up other people's thoughts, just as the soft earth of a redoubt absorbs cannonballs.

Rastignac had one of those heads packed with powder which explode on the slightest impact. His liveliness and youth made him only too susceptible to these projected thoughts, to the contagion of feelings whose many strange phenomena catch us unawares.[112] His mind had the sharpness and depth of his hawk-like eyes. Each of his double-edged senses had that mysterious reach, that fluid thrust and parry, which we find so awe-inspiring in people of superior note, those duellists skilled at finding the weak spot in every breast-plate.

Over the past month, Eugène had developed as many fine qualities as flaws. His flaws had been forced in the hot-house of society and by the need to pursue his burgeoning desires. Among his fine qualities was the hardiness of the South; a man from south of the Loire tackles obstacles head on and is incapable of remaining in a state of uncertainty. Northerners call this quality a flaw, maintaining that while this was the key to Murat's success, it was also the cause of his death.[113] From this we may conclude that if a man of the Midi[114] can combine the cunning of the North with the daring of the South, he is consummate and will become the King of Sweden.[115] Thus Rastignac was unable to remain under fire from Vautrin's batteries for long without ascertaining whether the older man was his friend or foe. It seemed to him that this extraordinary character was capable, from one moment to the next, of fathoming his passions and reading what he had in his heart, while himself remaining so tightly sealed that he appeared to have the inscrutable depth of a sphinx that knows and sees everything, and says nothing. Emboldened by the weight of his purse, Eugène rebelled.

'Do me the pleasure of waiting a moment,' he said to Vautrin, who was preparing to leave after savouring the last drops of his coffee.

'What for?' replied the forty year old, putting on his wide-brimmed hat and picking up a metal cane which he flourished like a man unafraid of assault by four footpads.

'I intend to pay you back,' continued Rastignac, swiftly untying one of the bags and counting out a hundred and forty francs to give to Madame Vauquer. 'An account paid is a friend made,' he said to the widow. 'We're square until New Year's Eve. Now, change a hundred sous for me.'

'A friend made is an account paid,' echoed Poiret, looking at Vautrin.

'Your twenty sous,' said Rastignac, holding out a coin to the bewigged sphinx.

'Anyone would think you were afraid to be in my debt,' exclaimed Vautrin, his all-seeing eyes burning into the young man's soul, giving him one of those mocking and cynical smiles which had come close to triggering Eugène's temper any number of times.

'Indeed . . . I am,' replied the student standing up, holding the two bags in his hand, ready to go upstairs to his room.

Vautrin made to leave through the door to the drawing room and the student turned to go out through the one that led to the square passageway and the stairs.

'Do you realize, Monsieur le Marquis de Rastigna*corama*, that what you said was not exactly polite?' said Vautrin, lashing out at the drawing-room door with his cane and walking over to the student, who surveyed him coldly.

Rastignac closed the dining-room door, bringing Vautrin with him to the foot of the stairs in the square passageway between the dining room and the kitchen, where a solid door topped with a barred fanlight led into the garden. There, in front of Sylvie, who had just come out of the kitchen, the student said: '*Monsieur* Vautrin, I am not a marquis, and my name is not Rastigna*corama*.'

'They're going to fight a duel,' said Mademoiselle Michonneau, with an air of indifference.

'Fight a duel!' repeated Poiret.

'Surely not,' replied Madame Vauquer, playing with her pile of écus.

'There they are, walking under the lime trees,' cried Mademoiselle Victorine, standing up to look into the garden. 'But the poor young man is surely in the right.'

'Let us go upstairs, dear girl,' said Madame Couture; 'these matters do not concern us.'

When Madame Couture and Victorine stood up, they found their way blocked by big Sylvie who had appeared at the door.

'What's to do?' she cried. 'Monsieur Vautrin said to Monsieur Eugène: "Let's settle this once and for all!" then he led him outside by the arm, and now they're trampling all over the artichokes.'

At this point Vautrin appeared. 'Ma Vauquer,' he said with

a smile, 'don't be alarmed; I'm just going to give my pistols an airing under the lime trees.'

'Oh! Monsieur,' said Victorine, clasping her hands together; 'why do you want to kill Monsieur Eugène?'

Vautrin took two steps back and stared at Victorine. 'Now here's an interesting development!' he exclaimed in a mocking voice, which made the poor girl blush. 'A charming young man, is he not?' he continued. 'You've given me an idea. I'll make you both happy, my pretty child.'

Madame Couture took her ward by the arm and steered her out, saying in her ear: 'Why Victorine, I really cannot make you out this morning.'

'I won't have any pistols fired in my house,' said Madame Vauquer. 'Don't you go frightening the neighbours and bringing the police round at this time of day!'

'Now, now, easy does it, Ma Vauquer,' replied Vautrin; 'nothing to worry about, it's just a little shooting party.'

He rejoined Rastignac and took him by the arm familiarly: 'Even after I've shown you that I can put a bullet in an ace of spades five times in a row at thirty-five paces,' he told him, 'you'll still be raring to go. If I'm not mistaken, you've lost your cool, and at this rate you're going to get yourself killed like an idiot.'

'So you're backing down,' said Eugène.

'Don't be so tiresome,' replied Vautrin. 'It's mild out this morning, come and sit down with me,' he said, gesturing towards the green-painted garden chairs. 'No one will hear us there. I've got a few things to say to you. You're a decent young man and I mean you no harm. I like you, or my name isn't Cat-o'- ... (blast it!) ... Vautrin. I'll tell you why I like you. Why, I know you as well as if I'd made you, and I'm going to prove it. Put your swag here,' he went on, pointing at the round table.

Rastignac put his money on the table and sat down, his curiosity powerfully aroused by Vautrin's abrupt change in manner: after threatening to kill him, he was now posing as his protector.

'You want to know who I am, what I've done and what I

do,' continued Vautrin. 'You want to know too much, my
young friend. Now, now, hold your horses. There's more! I've
had my share of misfortune. Listen to me first and then you can
have your say. Here's my life in a nutshell. Who am I? Vautrin.
What do I do? Whatever I like. Say no more. You want to
know what kind of a man I am? I'm good to those who are
good to me or whose heart speaks to mine. I'll let them get
away with anything, they can kick me in the shins without so
much as a *Watch it!* crossing my lips. But blow me if I'm not as
mean as the devil towards those who give me trouble or who
let me down. And it's as well for you to know that I'll kill a
man as easily as that!' he said, spitting on the ground. 'But I
make sure I kill him cleanly and only when he leaves me no
choice. I'm what you might call an artist. I've read the *Memoirs
of Benvenuto Cellini*,[116] in Italian at that, although you might
not think it to look at me! It was from him, the finest of fellows, that I learned to imitate Providence, which picks us off
without rhyme or reason, and to love beauty wherever it is
found. After all, what finer game is there than to take on the
rest of mankind and have luck on your side? I've thought long
and hard about the constitution of your present social disorder.
My dear boy, a duel is child's play, sheer folly. When one of two
living men must be eliminated, only an idiot allows chance to
decide which it will be. A duel? Heads or tails! That's all there
is to it. I can shoot five bullets in a row through the same hole
in an ace of spades, and I can do that at thirty-five paces! With
that little talent under your belt, you might feel pretty certain
of killing your man. Well, I fired at twenty paces and missed
mine. The knave had never touched a pistol in his life. Look!'
said this extraordinary man, unfastening his waistcoat and
baring his chest – as furry as a bear's back, but with a strange
tawny streak that inspired both repulsion and awe – 'that
greenhorn turned my hair red,' he added, pressing Rastignac's
finger against a hole in his chest. 'But in those days I was a
child, I was your age: twenty-one. I still had something to
believe in then, in the love of a woman, a heap of nonsense
you'll soon be up to the neck in. We were ready to fight each
other just now, weren't we? You might have killed me. Say I

was six foot under, where would you be? You'd have to clear out, go to Switzerland, squander Daddy's money, the little he has. Let me shed some light on your position, from the vantage point of a man who, having studied the world, has seen that only two courses of action are possible: slavish obedience or revolt. I obey nothing, is that clear? Do you know what you need, my young friend, at the rate you're going? A million, and fast. Without it, however handsome you are, you may as well hang around in the nets at Saint-Cloud[117] waiting to see if the Supreme Being shows up. I'll give you that million.' He paused to look at Eugène. 'A-ha! That's made you see your dear uncle Vautrin in a new light. I say the magic word and you look like a girl with "until tonight" ringing in her ears, preening herself and licking her lips like the cat that's got the cream. That's the spirit! Now, let's get down to the nitty-gritty. Here's what's in it for you, young man. At home, you have Papa, Mama, Great-aunt, two sisters (eighteen and sixteen), two little brothers (fifteen and ten). That's the crew inspected. Aunty gives your sisters some instruction. The parish priest comes to teach your brothers Latin. The family eats more mashed chestnuts than white bread, Papa darns his trousers, Mama is lucky if she has a different dress for summer and winter, your sisters scrape by the best they can. I know exactly what it's like, I've spent some time in the Midi.[118] That's how things stand at home, if they're sending you twelve hundred francs a year, and if your little estate only brings in three thousand francs. You have a cook and a manservant; Papa is a baron so one must keep up appearances. As for yourself, you are ambitious, you have an ally in the de Beauséants and you walk everywhere on foot; you want to be wealthy and you haven't a sou; you eat Ma Vauquer's messes and you have a taste for the fine dining of the Faubourg Saint-Germain, you sleep on a pallet and you want a mansion! I don't condemn you for your yearnings. Not everyone is lucky enough to have ambition, my sweet. Ask any woman what kind of man she wants – an ambitious one. An ambitious man's blood is richer in iron, his constitution stronger, his heart warmer than that of other men. And because a woman knows she's happiest and most beautiful when her influence is at its strongest, she will always favour a man whose power is great, even if she risks being crushed by him. I've drawn up this inventory of your desires in order to ask you a question. Here it comes. You're as hungry as a wolf, your fangs are newly cut and sharp; how do you catch a little something for the pot? First, you have to chew your way through the Code:[119] it's far from entertaining and you learn nothing from it, but it has to be done. So be it. You turn yourself into a lawyer with a view to becoming a magistrate, sending down poor devils worth far more than you, with T for thief[120] branded on their shoulders, merely to prove to the rich that they can sleep peacefully in their beds. It's not much of a lark, and what's more, it takes for ever. First, two years spent kicking your heels in Paris, eyeing up – but never touching – the *yum-yums* you're partial to. It wears you out, to be always craving without ever satisfying your desires. If you were pasty and of a sluggish disposition you'd have nothing to fear; but you have the raging blood of a lion and an appetite big enough to get you into twenty scrapes a day. Let's assume that you put yourself through this torture, the most horrible of all those to be seen in the good Lord's hell. Let's suppose that you're sensible, that you drink milk and write elegies; however noble you are, after enough tedium and privation to make you foam at the mouth, you'll have no option but to start right at the bottom, as assistant district attorney to some crook, in some dump of a town, where the government will throw you a salary of a thousand francs, as one might throw soup to a butcher's dog. Bark at thieves, defend the rich, send the stout-hearted to the guillotine. You'll have no alternative! Unless you have friends in high places you'll be left to rot in your provincial tribunal. At thirty or so, you'll be a judge on twelve hundred francs a year, if you haven't thrown in the wig by then. When you hit forty, you'll marry a miller's daughter with an annual income of six thousand livres. No thank you. With help from the right friends, you'll be appointed a Crown Prosecutor, with a salary of a thousand écus, and you'll marry the mayor's daughter. If you stoop to one of those despicable little political scams, like reading Villèle on a ballot paper instead of Manuel[121] (it rhymes, and that's good enough for your conscience), at forty you'll be a senior Crown Prosecutor and you might even have your own constituency. Note, my dear child, that you will have besmirched your precious conscience, that you will have had twenty years of tedium, of miserable obsurity, and that your sisters will be on the shelf.[122] What's more, allow me to point out that there are only twenty Crown Prosecutors in the whole of France and that there are some twenty thousand of you aspiring to that rank, including any number of ruthless scoundrels who would sell their families to crawl up a rung. Should that profession not be to your taste, let's take a look at another. Would the Baron de Rastignac care to become a lawyer? Oh! Delightful. You're required to live in poverty for ten years, with costs of a thousand francs a month, own a library and chambers, mingle in high society, kiss a solicitor's robes to get briefs, sweep the courts clean with your tongue. If this profession took you anywhere, I wouldn't say no; but can you find me five lawyers in Paris who, at the age of fifty, earn over fifty thousand francs a year? Hah! I'd rather be a corsair than belittle my soul that way. So – where will you get your écus? It's not easy. You resort to a woman's dowry. You want to marry? You'll hang a millstone around your neck; and then, if you marry for money, what will become of your honourable feelings, your nobility! You may as well start your revolt against human conventions today. It would mean grovelling like a worm before a woman, kissing her mother's feet, committing acts of servility at which even a sow would turn up its snout: ugh! If only that brought you happiness. But you'll feel as low as the stones that line the gutters with a woman you've married for those reasons. It's a far better thing to wage war against men than bicker with your wife. You are at life's crossroads, young man; now you must make your choice. You have already chosen: you went to call on your cousin Madame de Beauséant and had a taste of luxury there. You called on Madame de Restaud, old man Goriot's daughter, and breathed in the scent of a Parisian woman. On that day you came back here with one word written on your forehead, and I read it, clear as day: *Succeed!* Succeed whatever the cost. "Bravo!" I said to myself, "now here's a man after my own heart." You had to have

money. Where could you get it from? You bled your sisters dry.
All brothers *sharp* their sisters to a greater or lesser degree. The
fifteen hundred francs you have extracted – God knows how! –
from a region that yields more chestnuts than hundred-sou
coins, will vanish like soldiers gone a-pillaging. What will you
do then? Will you work? Work, as you define it at the moment,
will earn you, for your old age, an apartment at Ma Vauquer's
next door to men of the ilk of Poiret. So how can you get rich
quickly? That's the problem that fifty thousand young men, all
in the same position as you, are currently trying to solve. You
are one unit of that total. Now work out just how much effort
you'll have to make, how fierce the struggle will be. Given that
fifty thousand good positions don't exist, you'll be forced to eat
each other like spiders in a jam-jar. Do you know how a man
makes it to the top of the social pile? Through the brilliance of
his genius or the skill of his corruption. You must either plough
through this mass of men like a cannonball or creep among
them like the plague. Honesty will get you nowhere. They'll
yield to genius – they'll detest it, they'll try to malign it because
it keeps taking without giving back – but they'll yield if it prevails; in a word, they'll worship it on their knees when they've
failed to bury it in mud. Corruption is thick on the ground,
talent rare. Which means that corruption is the weapon of
mediocrity and you'll feel the tip of its blade wherever you go.
You'll see women whose husbands are paid six thousand francs
all told and who spend more than ten thousand francs on their
dress. You'll see employees on twelve hundred francs buying up
land. You'll see women prostitute themselves to climb into the
carriage of the son of some French peer who can drive in the
middle lane at Longchamp.[123] You've seen that silly goose of an
old man Goriot forced to pay a bill of exchange endorsed by
his daughter, whose husband is worth fifty thousand livres a
year. I defy you to take two steps in Paris without coming across
all kinds of machinations. I will wager you on my life that
you'll be fed a dish of wasp-infested lies at the home of the first
woman who takes your fancy, however rich, young and beautiful she is. They are all bridled by laws and at loggerheads with
their husbands over everything. We'd be here all day if I made

it my business to explain the shenanigans that go on over lovers, fripperies, children, the domestics or vanity – rarely virtue, you can be sure of that. Which makes the honest man the common enemy. So, what kind of a man is honest? In Paris, the honest man keeps his own counsel and refuses to share. I'm not talking about those poor slaves who do all the work everywhere without ever being rewarded for their effort; I call them the Brotherhood of the Good Lord's Holy Shoes. In them you see virtue in the full bloom of its stupidity, but also its poverty. I can already see the terrible look on the faces of all those poor people if God is shabby enough to renege on the Last Judgement. So if you want to get rich quickly, you either have to be rich to start with or appear to be so. To make your fortune in this city, you need to play for high stakes; otherwise you're going after chickenfeed, and may as well sign off *Your humble servant* etc. Among the hundred professions you might pursue, if there are ten men who succeed overnight, the public calls them thieves. Draw your own conclusions. That's life as it really is. It's no prettier than the kitchen, it smells just as foul, and if you want to cook something up, you have to get your hands dirty; just master the art of scrubbing them clean afterwards: that's what morality boils down to, today. If I'm talking about the world in this way, it's because it has given me cause to do so, I know it well. You think I blame it? Not in the slightest. Things have always been like this. Moralizing won't change them. Man is flawed. He is, at times, more or less of a hypocrite, making fools claim he's moral or immoral. I don't point the finger at the Rich in favour of the People: man is the same at the top, the bottom and in-between. For every million sheep, you'll find ten likely lads[124] who set themselves above everything, even the law: I count myself among them. If you're a better man, walk on the straight path with your head held high. But you'll have to fight envy, slander, mediocrity, the whole world. Napoleon himself ran foul of a war minister by the name of Aubry,[125] who almost had him sent to the colonies. Sound your own depths! See if you can get up each day with more will-power than you had the night before. Given the circumstances, I'm going to make you an offer that no one could refuse. Listen carefully. I have a plan, you see. My plan is to go and live the life of a patriarch on some vast estate, a hundred thousand acres or so, in the United States, in the South. I want to be a planter, own slaves, earn a few easy million selling my cattle, my tobacco, my trees, while living like a king, doing as I please, leading a life we can barely imagine here, cowering in our plaster burrows. I'm a great poet. My poetry isn't the kind you write down: it's made of deeds and feelings. At the moment I possess fifty thousand francs, which would barely get me forty Negroes. I need two hundred thousand francs, because I want two hundred Negroes to satisfy my appetite for the patriarchal life. Negroes, you see, are grown-up children and you can do whatever you like with them, without some nosy Crown Prosecutor turning up and holding you to account.[126] With this black capital, I'll have made three or four million in the space of ten years. If I make my fortune, no one will stop me and ask: "Who are you?" I'll be Mister Four-Million, citizen of the United States of America. I'll be fifty, still in good shape and I'll have my fun. In a word, if I find you a dowry worth a million, will you give me two hundred thousand francs? A 20 per cent commission, what do you say! Is that too dear? You'll make your little wife love you. Once you're married, you'll start showing signs of anxiety, remorse, you'll go round with a hangdog air for a fortnight. One night, after a few preliminaries, calling your wife "My Love!", you'll finally confess between one kiss and the next that you're in debt to the tune of two hundred thousand francs. The most distinguished young men act out this little farce every day. A young woman never refuses her purse to the man who has stolen her heart. You can't lose. You'll find a way to win your two hundred thousand francs back through some deal or other. With your money, and your brain, you'll build up a fortune as vast as any you might wish for. *Ergo*, in the space of six months, you'll have brought happiness to yourself, an attractive woman and your Uncle Vautrin, not to mention your family, who blow on their fingers in winter for want of wood for the fire. Don't be surprised by what I'm suggesting, or asking! Out of sixty fashionable weddings taking place in Paris, there are forty-seven which turn on this kind of deal. The Law Society has forced Monsieur . . .'

'What do I have to do?' said Rastignac eagerly, interrupting Vautrin.

'Hardly anything,' he replied, with a flicker of joy, the controlled delight of a fisherman who has just felt a fish bite on the end of his line. 'Listen! The heart of a poor, unhappy and needy young woman is a sponge, the most thirsty for love you will find, a dry sponge which swells as soon as it receives a single drop of sympathy. Courting a young lady who is lonely, impoverished and despairing, who has no idea that she'll be rich one day – why! – it's like having a quint and a quatorze[127] in your hand, or knowing what numbers will win the lottery; it's like playing the stock-market on a tip-off! You are laying the foundations for an indestructible marriage. When she comes into her millions, the young lady will throw them at your feet, as if they were so many bits of gravel. "Take them, my Beloved! Take them, Adolphe! Alfred! Take them Eugène!" she'll say, if Adolphe, Alfred or Eugène have had the good sense to make the odd sacrifice for her. By sacrifice I mean selling an old suit so you can treat her to mushrooms on toast at the Cadran-Bleu; then, in the evening, the Ambigu-Comique;[128] I mean pawning your watch to buy her a shawl. I hardly need mention the scribblings about love or the poppycock that so many women fall for, such as sprinkling drops of water onto your notepaper to look like tears when you're away from her: I can see you're a man with a firm grasp of the lingo of the heart. Paris, you see, is like a forest in the New World, crawling with twenty or so savage tribes – the Illinois, the Hurons – who live off the different kinds of game they hunt in society; you're a hunter of millions. To net them, you use shills, limed twigs, decoys. There are various ways of going about it. Some sniff out dowries; others lie in wait for liquidations; this man fishes for votes; that man sells his subscribers down the river, bound hand and foot.[129] He who comes home with his game-bag bulging is welcomed, celebrated, received in the highest society. To be fair to this hospitable land of ours: no other city in the world is better at turning a blind eye. If the proud aristocracies of every capital in Europe refuse to admit an infamous millionaire into their ranks, Paris welcomes him with open arms, rushes to his parties, eats his dinners and toasts his infamy.'

'But where can I find such a girl?' asked Eugène.

'She's yours, staring you in the face!'

'Mademoiselle Victorine?'

'Exactly!'

'But how?'

'She loves you already, your sweet Baronne de Rastignac!'

'She hasn't a sou to her name,' replied Eugène, stunned.

'A-ha! I'm just coming to that. A word or two more', said Vautrin, 'and all will become clear. Our man Taillefer is an old scoundrel rumoured to have murdered one of his friends during the Revolution.[130] I'd say he's one of your lone hunters. The man is a banker, senior partner in Frédéric Taillefer and Co. He has one son, to whom he intends to leave his entire fortune, leaving Victorine with nothing. Personally, I'm no fan of that sort of injustice. I'm a bit of a Don Quixote, I like to defend the weak against the strong. If it were God's will that he should lose his son, Taillefer would take his daughter back; he would want an heir of some kind, that weakness is ingrained in human nature, and I know he can't have any more children. Victorine is tender and warm-hearted, she'll soon win him over and be spinning him round like a top with a string of sweet-talk! She'll be too mindful of your love to forget you, and so you'll be married. As for me, I'll play the role of Providence, I'll guide God's will. I've a friend who owes me a favour, a colonel in the army of the Loire, who has just been posted to the Royal Guard. He has taken my advice and become an ultra-royalist; he's not one of those fools who stick to their guns. A final word of advice, my angel: never stick to an opinion any more than you would to your word. When you're asked for one, sell it to the highest bidder. A man who boasts that his opinions are unshakeable is a man who commits himself to following a straight line, a fool who believes in infallibility. There are no principles, only events; there are no laws, only circumstances: a superior man espouses events and circumstances the better to influence them. If fixed principles and laws really existed, countries wouldn't change

them as often as we change shirts. One man can't be expected
to show more sense than an entire nation. The man who has
been of least service to France is idolized, revered, because he
has always seen everything as red, when all he's fit for is to be
exhibited in the Conservatoire,[131] labelled La Fayette,[132] along
with the other machines; while the prince[133] who prevented the
partition of France at the Congress of Vienna, whose scorn for
mankind is such that he spits back in its face every oath it might
demand of him, is universally abhorred; he deserves laurels,
but they sling mud at him instead. Oh! I know exactly how
things work! I know the secrets of many a man! Let's just say
that I'll have steadfast opinions on the day when I meet three
brains who agree on the application of the same principle, and
I'll be waiting a good while yet! You won't find three judges in
the courts who share the same opinion on an article of law.
Now, this man of mine I mentioned: he'd put Jesus Christ back
on the cross if I asked him to. At a single word from Uncle
Vautrin, he'll pick a quarrel with that cad who doesn't even
have the heart to send his poor sister a hundred sous, and . . .'
Here Vautrin stood up, took his guard and mimed the lunge of
a fencing master. 'And – lights out!' he added.

'But that's horrific!' said Eugène. 'You are joking, Monsieur
Vautrin?'

'Now, now, calm down,' the other man continued. 'Don't be
such a child: although you can work yourself into a rage and
foam at the mouth if it amuses you! You can call me a black-
guard, a scoundrel, a rogue, a bandit, but I draw the line at
crook or spy! Go on, let rip, fire your broadside! I won't hold
it against you, it's only natural at your age! I was like that once
too! But consider this. You'll do worse one day. You'll toy with
the affections of some pretty woman and take her money.
That's what you have in mind!' said Vautrin, 'because how will
you get rich if your love isn't bankable? Virtue, my dear student, can't be split into parts: you either have it or you don't.
We're told to atone for our sins. There's another cunning system, which lets you get away with a crime through an act of
contrition! Seducing a woman so she'll give you a leg-up onto
a particular rung of the social ladder, stirring up all kinds of

ill-feeling among the children of a family, not to mention all the foul deeds committed out of self-interest or gratification either openly or behind closed doors, do you think these may be considered acts of faith, hope and charity? Why two months in prison for a dandy who relieves a child of half his fortune in one night, and why hard labour for some poor devil who steals a thousand-franc note with aggravating circumstances? That's the law for you. Not an article of it that doesn't verge on absurdity. A man in yellow gloves who lies through his teeth, committing murders where no blood is shed, but he has his pound of flesh all the same; an assassin jemmying open a door: both are shady customers! What I am suggesting, and what you will do one day, are exactly the same, minus the blood. You think you'll find a firm foothold in that kind of world! I say, be wary of men and keep your eyes peeled for the loopholes through which you can slide out of reach of the law. The secret of a vast fortune with no apparent cause is a crime which has been forgotten, because it was committed cleanly.'

'Enough, Monsieur, I'll hear no more; you would have me doubt myself. At the moment, all I know is what I feel.'

'As you wish, pretty child. I thought you were made of stronger stuff,' said Vautrin. 'I'll say no more. But one last word.' He gave the student a piercing stare: 'You have my secret,' he said to him.

'A young man who has refused your offer will soon forget it.'

'That was well said and gives me great pleasure. Another man, you see, might be less scrupulous. Remember what I want to do for you. I'll give you a fortnight. Take it or leave it.'

'The man has an iron will!' Rastignac said to himself, watching Vautrin stroll away with his stick under his arm. 'He has told me crudely what Madame de Beauséant expressed so delicately. He slashed at my heart with his steel claws. Why do I want to call on Madame de Nucingen? He guessed my motives as soon as they surfaced in my mind. In two words, this brigand has told me more about virtue than men and books ever have. If virtue is non-negotiable, does that mean I have stolen from my sisters?' he asked himself, throwing the bag onto the table. He sat down, and stayed there, deep in dazed thought.

'To be faithful to virtue is a sublime martyrdom! Hah! Every-one believes in virtue; but who is virtuous? Nations make freedom their idol; but where on earth is there a free nation? My youth is still as blue as a cloudless sky: if I want to be wealthy or great, must I stoop to lying, scraping, crawling, pouncing, flattering, deceiving? Must I consent to be the lackey of those who have lied, scraped and crawled? I'd have to be their servant before I could become their accomplice. Why, no. I want to work with dignity, with purity; I want to work night and day, to owe my success to my labours alone. It will be the slowest kind of success, but every night my head will rest on my pillow free of all blemished thoughts. What could be finer than to look upon one's life and find it as pure as a lily? Life and I, we're like a young man and his fiancée. Vautrin has shown me what happens after ten years of marriage. The devil take it! My mind is floundering. I must clear my head of thoughts, the heart is the truest guide.'

Eugène was brought back from his musings by the voice of big Sylvie announcing his tailor, whom he went to meet with his two moneybags in his hand, a turn of events that he did not find displeasing. After trying on his evening suit, he put his new morning wear on and found himself completely transformed. 'I'm certainly a match for Monsieur de Trailles,' he said to himself. 'At last I look like a gentleman!'

'Monsieur,' said old man Goriot, coming into Eugène's room, 'you asked me if I knew which houses Madame de Nucingen visits.'

'Indeed I did!'

'Well, next Monday, she is going to the Maréchale de Carigliano's ball. If you go, you'll be able to tell me all about it, whether my daughters enjoyed themselves, what they wore, everything.'

'How did you find out, dear old Goriot?' said Eugène, inviting him to sit by the fire.

'Her chambermaid told me. Thanks to Thérèse and Constance, I know everything they do,' he replied brightly. The old man's expression was that of a lover still young enough to delight in a stratagem that keeps him in touch with his mistress without her suspecting a thing. 'You'll actually see them!' he said, innocently expressing a pang of jealousy.

'I don't know,' replied Eugène. 'I'll go and call on Madame de Beauséant and ask her if she can introduce me to Madame la Maréchale.'

Eugène glowed inside at the thought of calling on the vicomtesse dressed as smartly as he would be from now on. What moralists call the murkiest depths of the human heart are merely the deceptive thoughts, the involuntary urges, of self-interest. These peripeteia, the subject of so many tirades, these sudden reversals, are calculated moves in the pursuit of pleasure. On seeing himself well dressed, well gloved and well heeled, Rastignac forgot his virtuous resolve. When Youth lapses into error, it dares not look into the mirror of its conscience, whereas Ripe Old Age has already seen itself reflected there: therein lies the difference between these two ages of man. Over the past few days, the two neighbours, Eugène and old man Goriot, had become good friends. Their secret friendship sprang from the same psychological phenomena that had stirred up such conflicting feelings between Vautrin and the student. The bold philosopher who sets out to establish how our feelings influence the physical world will surely find ample proof of their effect on matter in the connections they create between us and the animal kingdom. What physiognomist is a swifter judge of character than a dog deciding whether a stranger is sympathetic or not? *Elective affinity*, an adage familiar to all, is one of those facts fixed in the language that belie the philosophical rubbish filling the minds of those who like to sift through the peelings of primitive words.[134] You feel loved. That feeling leaves its mark on all things and crosses every space. A letter is a living soul, such a faithful echo of the spoken voice that discerning minds count it among the richest treasures of love. Old man Goriot, whose impulsive sensibility raised him to the sublime level of canine intuition, had sniffed out the compassion, the admiring generosity, the youthful sympathy which he had aroused in the student's heart. However, this nascent bond had not yet led them to confide in each other. Although Eugène had revealed his desire to see Madame de Nucingen, he wasn't counting on the old man for his first introduction to her; but he did hope some indiscretion might serve him well. To date, old man Goriot's only pronouncement on the subject of his daughters concerned what Rastignac had blurted out on the day he had paid his two calls. 'My dear sir,' he had said to him the next day, 'how could you possibly have thought that Madame de Restaud took umbrage at the mention of my name? My two daughters love me dearly. No father could be happier. The only flies in the ointment are my two sons-in-law who have behaved shabbily towards me. As I didn't want those dear creatures to bear the brunt of my quarrel with their husbands, I chose to see them in secret. The mystery of it makes me happy in a thousand ways, which other fathers, who can see their daughters whenever they like, are incapable of understanding. I don't have the choice, you see. So when it's fine, I find out from their maids whether my daughters are going out and I head over to the Champs-Elysées. I wait for them to go by, I see their carriages coming and my heart beats faster, I admire the way they're dressed, and as they pass, they toss me a little smile that turns everything to gold, as if struck by a dazzling ray of sun. And I stay where I am, to catch them on their way back. Here they come again! The fresh air has done them good, brought colour to their cheeks. I hear the man next to me say: "There goes a beautiful woman!" and my heart rejoices. After all, aren't they my own flesh and blood? I love the very horses that draw them and I wish I was the little dog sitting in their lap. I live off their pleasure. Every man has his own way of loving; mine harms no one, so why would the world take any notice of me? I am happy, after my fashion. Is it against the law for me to go and see my daughters in the evening, just as they're leaving for a ball? How bereft I feel if I arrive too late and am told: "Madame has already left." One evening I waited until three in the morning to see Nasie, after two days without a single glimpse. I nearly died of delight! So please, if you must mention my name, be sure to say how good my girls are to me. They're always trying to shower me with all kinds of presents; I stop them, I say, "Keep your money! What good is it to me? I have everything I need." Indeed, dear Monsieur, what am I but a poor skeleton whose soul is wherever my daughters are? When you have seen Madame de Nucingen, tell me which of the two you find most beautiful,' said the old man after a moment's silence, seeing that Eugène was preparing to go out for a stroll round the Tuileries until it was time to call on Madame de Beauséant.

This walk proved fatal to the student. He was noticed by a number of women. He was so handsome, so young, so elegantly and tastefully dressed! Seeing himself the object of such attention, even admiration, he thought no more of the sisters and aunt he had fleeced, nor of his virtuous repugnance. He had seen flying overhead that demon so easily mistaken for an angel, the iridescent-winged Satan, who scatters rubies, fires his golden arrows at palace façades, turns women crimson, adorns thrones – at bottom so simple – with fool's gold; he had listened to this pyrotechnic god of vanity whose tawdry brilliance seems to us a symbol of power. Vautrin's words, cynical though they were, had embedded themselves in his heart just as the unprepossessing face of an old pedlar-woman remains printed on a virgin's memory, once she has been foretold: 'Reams of love and gold!' After strolling around indolently for a while, Eugène went to call on Madame de Beauséant at around five o'clock and there he received one of those terrible blows against which young hearts are defenceless. Up until then he had found the vicomtesse full of the polished courtesy, the honeyed grace imparted by an aristocratic education, which are only truly accomplished when they come from the heart.

When he entered, Madame de Beauséant made a curt gesture and said brusquely: 'Monsieur de Rastignac, it is impossible for me to see you, at least not now! I have pressing business to attend to . . .'

To a keen observer, and Rastignac had swiftly become one, this sentence, her gesture, her look, the intonation of her voice, clearly told of the character and customs of her caste. He perceived the iron hand beneath the velvet glove; the temperament, the egotism, beneath the manners; the wood beneath the varnish. In all, he heard the 'I, THE KING' which rolls out from the plumes of the throne to the tip of the crest of the lowest-ranking nobleman. Eugène had too readily taken the woman's words at face value, wanting to believe in her nobility. Like all needy souls, he had signed in good faith the delightful pact binding benefactor to beneficiary, whose first article stipulates absolute equality between the generous-hearted. Charity, which makes two beings one, is a divine passion, as misunderstood and as rare as true love. Both express the profusions of a noble soul. Rastignac was determined to make it to the Duchesse de Carigliano's ball, so he took this blow on the chin.

'Madame,' he said, his voice choked with emotion, 'if it were not a matter of some importance, I would not have come to disturb you; grant me the favour of seeing you later, I'll wait.'

'Very well! Come and dine with me,' she said, a little embarrassed at the harshness of her words; for this woman really was as good as she was noble.

Although touched by her sudden change of heart, as he went out Eugène said to himself: 'Bow and scrape, do whatever it takes. What must the others be like, if, from one moment to the next, the best of women reneges on her promise of friendship and casts you off like an old shoe? So it's every man for himself? At the same time, it's true that her house isn't a shop, and it's wrong of me to need her help. I must turn myself into a cannonball, as Vautrin said.' The student's bitter musings were soon dispelled as he thought ahead to the pleasure of dining with the vicomtesse. And so, by a kind of inevitability, the slightest events in his life were conspiring to drive him in a direction, which – if the terrible sphinx of the Maison Vauquer was to be believed – would lead him, as on a battlefield, to kill or be killed, to deceive or be deceived; to leave his heart, his conscience at the gate, to wear a mask, to dupe other men mercilessly, and, as at Lacedaemonia,[135] to win his laurels by stealthily seizing his chance. Upon his return, he found the vicomtesse full of the grace and kindness she had always previously shown him. Together they entered the dining room – whose table glittered with the luxury that, as everyone knows, reached its zenith during the Restoration[136] – where the vicomte awaited his wife. Like many world-weary men, virtually the only pleasure left to Monsieur de Beauséant was that of dining well; indeed, his particular brand of *gourmandise* was on a par with that of Louis XVIII and the Duc d'Escars.[137] His table was therefore doubly sumptuous, in terms of both what was served and what it was served in. Eugène could hardly believe his eyes, for this was the first time he had dined in a house where social grandeur was hereditary. The suppers held after balls under the Empire, where military men would fortify themselves to prepare for the internal and external struggles they faced, had just gone out of fashion. Eugène had only ever been to balls. The aplomb that would later serve him so well, which he was even now beginning to acquire, stopped him short of gawping like an idiot. But the sight of the ornate silverware and the thousand elegant details of a sumptuous table, the experience, for the very first time, of discreet and soundless service, made it hard for a man with an imagination as ardent as his not to prefer this infinitely stylish life over the life of privation he had vowed to embrace that morning. His thoughts transported him to the boarding house for a moment, making him shudder with such deep revulsion that he swore to leave in January, as much to take more salubrious lodgings as to flee Vautrin, whose heavy hand he still felt on his shoulder. If a man of good sense were to cast his mind over the thousand kinds of corruption, both spoken and unspoken, that are found in Paris, he would ask himself why on earth the State builds schools there, assembles young people there, how pretty women are ever respected there and how it is that the gold flaunted by moneychangers doesn't magically take flight from their scale-pans. But considering how few crimes, or indeed misdemeanours, are committed by young men, we must surely show the greatest respect for these patient Tantalus types[138] who battle with themselves and who almost always come out victorious! If his struggle with Paris were skilfully depicted, the Poor Student would be one of the most dramatic subjects of modern times. The looks Madame de Beauséant cast at Eugène inviting him to talk came to nothing; he did not wish to speak in front of the vicomte.

'You're taking me to the Italiens this evening?' the vicomtesse asked her husband.

'Why, nothing would give me greater pleasure,' he replied

with a mocking gallantry which entirely fooled the student, 'but I have arranged to meet someone at the Variétés.'

'His mistress,' she said to herself.

'You're not seeing Ajuda this evening?' asked the vicomte.

'No,' she replied, testily.

'Well! If you absolutely must have an arm, take Monsieur de Rastignac's.'

The vicomtesse looked at Eugène, smiling. 'It would be very compromising for you,' she said.

'As Monsieur de Chateaubriand once said, *The Frenchman loves danger, for there he finds glory*,' replied Rastignac with a bow.

Moments later he was in a coupé with Madame de Beauséant, being swiftly borne towards that most fashionable of theatres, and thought he must be in a fairy tale when he entered a box in the centre and realized that, together with the vicomtesse, who was magnificently dressed, every lorgnette in the house was trained upon him. Each new delight was proving more intoxicating than the last.

'You wish to tell me something,' said Madame de Beauséant. 'Ah! look, there's Madame de Nucingen, three boxes along. Her sister and Monsieur de Trailles are on the other side.' As she was speaking, the vicomtesse glanced at the box where Mademoiselle de Rochefide ought to be, and when she saw that Monsieur d'Ajuda was not there, her face took on an extraordinary glow.

'She's lovely,' said Eugène, taking a look at Madame de Nucingen.

'She has pale eyelashes.'

'Yes, but what a pretty, slim waist!'

'She has big hands.'

'Such beautiful eyes!'

'Her face is rather long.'

'But its length has refinement.'

'Which is more than you could say about the rest of her. Look at the way she keeps raising and lowering her lorgnette! Every movement she makes betrays the Goriot in her,' said the vicomtesse, to Eugène's great astonishment.

Indeed, Madame de Beauséant was scanning the house

through her opera glasses, and, although she appeared to be paying no attention to Madame de Nucingen, hadn't missed a single gesture she'd made. The theatre was packed full of exquisitely beautiful women. Delphine de Nucingen was more than a little flattered to be the sole object of the attentions of Madame de Beauséant's young, handsome, elegant cousin: he had eyes only for her.

'If you don't stop staring at her like that, you will cause a scandal, Monsieur de Rastignac. You will never get anywhere by throwing yourself at a woman.'

'Dear cousin,' said Eugène, 'you have already shown me such kindness; if you can see your way to finishing the work you have begun, all I ask of you is a service which would mean little to you and a great deal to me. I have lost my heart.'

'So soon?'

'Yes.'

'To that woman?'

'Would my suit be heard elsewhere?' he said, looking meaningfully into his cousin's eyes. 'Madame la Duchesse de Carigliano is connected with Madame la Duchesse de Berry,' he continued after a pause; 'you are bound to see her – would you be kind enough to present me to her and take me to the ball she is giving on Monday? I'll meet Madame de Nucingen there and I'll enter the fray.'

'Gladly,' she said. 'If you've taken a liking to her already, your love affair is off to a good start. De Marsay is in Princesse Galathionne's box. Madame de Nucingen is writhing with pique. There's no better time to approach a woman, particularly a banker's wife. The ladies of the Chaussée d'Antin all yearn for vengeance.'

'What would you do, in her place?'

'I, dear cousin, would suffer in silence.'

At this point the Marquis d'Ajuda stepped into Madame de Beauséant's box.

'I've messed up my affairs to come and meet you here,' he said, 'and I'm telling you so my sacrifice isn't in vain.'

The radiance which streamed from the vicomtesse's face taught Eugène how to recognize the outpourings of genuine

love and not to confuse them with the simpering airs of Parisian coquetry. Tongue-tied with admiration, he looked at his
cousin and, with a sigh, gave up his seat to Monsieur d'Ajuda.
'How noble, how sublime a creature a woman is who loves like
this!' he said to himself. 'And here's a man would betray her for
some doll! How could anyone betray her?' His heart filled with
a childish rage. He wanted to throw himself at Madame de
Beauséant's feet, he wished for the demonic power to carry her
away in his heart, as an eagle sweeps up a white suckling kid
from the plain to its eyrie. He was ashamed to be in this great
gallery of beauty without his own painting, without a mistress
of his own. 'To have a mistress and to be as good as royal,'
he said to himself: 'these are the emblems of power!' And he
looked at Madame de Nucingen as a man who has been chal-
lenged eyes his adversary. The vicomtesse turned towards him,
discreetly expressing her heartfelt gratitude with a flicker of her
eyelids. The first act ended.

'Do you know Madame de Nucingen well enough to introduce Monsieur de Rastignac to her?' she asked the Marquis
d'Ajuda.

'I'm sure she will be delighted to meet Monsieur,' said the
marquis.

The handsome Portuguese nobleman stood up, took the student's arm and, in the blink of an eye, Rastignac found himself
at Madame de Nucingen's side.

'Madame la Baronne,' said the marquis, 'allow me to present to you the Chevalier Eugène de Rastignac, cousin of the
Vicomtesse de Beauséant. You have made such a deep impression on him that I wanted to make his happiness complete by
bringing him before his idol.'

He spoke these words in a playful tone of voice that made
palatable their rather blunt intention, albeit one which never
displeases a woman if well expressed. Madame de Nucingen
smiled and offered Eugène the seat which had just been vacated
by her husband.

'I dare not ask you to remain here with me, Monsieur,' she
said to him. 'When a man has the good fortune to be close to
Madame de Beauséant, he stays where he is.'

'I rather think, Madame,' murmured Eugène softly, 'that I will best please my cousin by staying here with you. Before Monsieur le Marquis joined us, we were speaking of you and of your distinguished appearance,' he said, raising his voice again.

Monsieur d'Ajuda withdrew.

'Monsieur,' said the baronne, 'are you really going to stay? Then we'll get to know each other. Madame de Restaud has already given me a burning desire to meet you.'

'She can't have meant it, because she had me thrown out of her house.'

'Really?'

'Madame, I'll gladly tell you why; but I must ask for your indulgence if I'm to reveal my secret. I lodge next door to your father. Not knowing that Madame de Restaud was his daughter, I was unwise enough to mention him, in all innocence, and this upset your dear sister and her husband. Madame la Duchesse de Langeais and my cousin found this display of filial disloyalty most unseemly. When I described the scene to them, they laughed until they cried. Then Madame de Beauséant spoke of you in extremely flattering terms, comparing you to your sister and saying how good you were to Monsieur Goriot, my neighbour. Indeed, how could you fail to love him? He worships you with such passion that I'm already jealous. We talked about you for two hours this morning. This evening, at dinner with my cousin, my head was so full of your father's words that I said to her you couldn't possibly be as beautiful as you were loving. No doubt wishing to encourage such warm admiration, Madame de Beauséant brought me with her tonight, mentioning with her customary delicacy that I would see you here.'

'Dear me, Monsieur,' said the banker's wife; 'so I owe you a debt of gratitude already? At this rate, we'll soon be old friends.'

'Although friendship with you must be beyond the realm of common feeling,' said Rastignac, 'I would never wish to be your friend.'

Women always find delightful the foolish stock phrases trotted out by beginners; they only seem lame when read in cold blood. A young man's gestures, looks, his intonation, give them inestimable value. Madame de Nucingen found Rastignac charming. Then, the way women do, when unable to respond to a question put as bluntly as the one the student had just left hanging in the air, she replied on another point.

'Yes, my sister has let herself down by her behaviour towards our poor father, who has been divinely generous to us both. Monsieur de Nucingen had to order me point blank not to receive my father in the morning, before I gave in. But it's been making me feel miserable for a while now. I cry whenever I think about it. His hostility, yet another example of the inhumanity of marriage, has been one of the most grievous causes of our domestic strife. Although in the eyes of the world I may be the happiest woman in Paris, in reality, I'm the unhappiest. You must think I'm mad to talk to you like this. But you know my father, which means I'm unable to see you as a stranger.'

'You can never have met anyone', Eugène said to her, 'driven by a stronger desire to live for you alone. What do all women seek? Happiness,' he continued, in a voice that went straight to the heart. 'Well then, if, for a woman, happiness means being loved, adored, having a companion in whom to confide her desires, her thoughts, her grief, her joy; laying bare her soul, with its sweet imperfections and its fine qualities, without fear of betrayal: believe me, this devoted, ever ardent heart can only be found in a young man, full of illusions, who would surrender his life at a single sign from you, who still knows nothing of the world and wants to know nothing, since you are the world for him. As for me, well, you will smile at my naivety. I've just arrived from the provinces, wholly green, having only ever known good honest souls, and never thinking to find love here. It so happens that I've met my cousin, who has revealed almost too much of her heart; she has opened my eyes to the thousand treasures of passionate love; like Cherubino,[139] I'll be in love with all women until I can devote myself to one alone. When I came in and saw you, I was drawn towards you as if magnetically. You had already been so much in my thoughts! But I never dreamed that you'd be as beautiful as you are in reality. Madame de Beauséant told me to stop staring at you. She doesn't know how irresistibly my eyes are drawn to your pretty red lips, your white skin, your soft eyes. I, too, am mad to speak such wild thoughts aloud, but let me say them anyway.'

Nothing pleases a woman more than to have such an out-pouring of sweet words murmured in her ear. The most fervent church-goer will listen to them, even if she won't allow herself to reply. Having started in this vein, Rastignac went on to recite his rosary in a low, but warm, voice; and Madame de Nucingen encouraged Eugène with her smiles, all the while keeping an eye on de Marsay, who didn't once leave Princesse Galathionne's box. Rastignac stayed sitting next to Madame de Nucingen until her husband came to take her home.

'Madame,' Eugène said to her, 'I shall have the pleasure of calling on you before the Duchesse de Carigliano's ball.'

'*Ssince Matame hass inwited you,*' said the baron, a thickset man of Alsace, whose round face had a dangerously sharp expression, '*you're pound to be vell resseeft.*'[140]

'I'm off to a good start: she didn't shy away when I asked her if she could love me. The horse has taken the bit; now we must leap astride and seize the reins,' Eugène said to himself, as he went to bid farewell to Madame de Beauséant, who had risen and was about to leave with d'Ajuda. The poor student didn't know that the baronne's thoughts had been quite elsewhere, as she was expecting one of those devastatingly conclusive letters from de Marsay. Delighted with his illusory success, Eugène accompanied the vicomtesse out to the porchway to wait for her carriage.

'Your cousin has changed beyond recognition,' said the Portuguese count to the vicomtesse, laughing, when Eugène had left them. 'He's going to break the bank. He's as slippery as an eel and I'm sure he'll go far. Only you could have picked out a woman for him at precisely the time she's most in need of consolation.'

'Although it remains to be seen', said Madame de Beauséant, 'whether she's still in love with the man who's about to jilt her.'

The student walked back from the Théâtre-Italien to the Rue Neuve-Sainte-Geneviève, making the sweetest plans. He

hadn't failed to notice how attentively Madame de Restaud
had scrutinized him, both in the vicomtesse's box and in that of
Madame de Nucingen, and he presumed that the comtesse's
door would no longer be closed to him. This meant that he was
already on the verge of acquiring four major connections – for
he was counting on winning over the maréchale – at the heart
of Parisian high society. Without dwelling too much on ways
and means, he had already worked out that in society's complex game of interests he needed a cog to ride on to get to the
top of the machine; once there, he felt he had it in his powers
to put a spoke or two in its wheel. 'If Madame de Nucingen
shows an interest in me, I'll teach her how to handle her husband. That husband of hers turns everything he touches into
gold; with his help, I could make my fortune in no time.' He
didn't put this to himself so bluntly: he wasn't yet politically
minded enough to estimate, evaluate and calculate a situation;
his ideas drifted across the horizon in the shape of light clouds,
and, although they lacked the vehemence of those of Vautrin, if
they'd been tested in the crucible of conscience they'd have
yielded nothing pure. It is by a series of transactions of this
nature that men arrive at the loose morality professed by our
current age. Today, more than ever before, they have become a
rarity, those singular men of rectitude, those strong wills that
never yield to evil, for whom even the slightest deviation from
the straight and narrow seems criminal; magnificent icons of
probity who have given us two masterpieces: Molière's Alceste
and, recently, Jeanie Deans and her father, in Walter Scott's
novel.[141] Perhaps a work portraying the opposite, a depiction
of the tortuous route taken by the conscience of an ambitious
man of the world, as he flirts with evil in an attempt to achieve
his goal while keeping up appearances, would be no less fine
or dramatic. By the time he reached the boarding house, Rastignac had fallen for Madame de Nucingen, who had seemed
so slim, as slender as a swallow. The dizzying softness of her
eyes, the silkiness of her skin, so delicately textured he could
almost see the blood that flowed beneath it, the enchanting
sound of her voice, her blonde hair: he remembered everything;
and perhaps the walk, by stirring his blood, had also played a

role in his infatuation. The student banged on old man Goriot's door.

'Neighbour,' he said, 'I've just seen Madame Delphine.'

'Where?'

'At the Italiens.'

'Was she enjoying herself? Come in, come in.' And the old man got up to open the door in his nightshirt, then immediately hopped back into bed. 'So – tell me all about her,' he demanded.

Eugène, finding himself in old Goriot's room for the first time, was unable to stop himself starting with astonishment when he saw the squalor in which the father lived, having just been admiring the daughter's finery. The window had no curtains; the paper on the walls was peeling off and curling up due to damp in several places, exposing bare plaster yellowed by smoke. The old man lay on a shabby bed covered by only a threadbare blanket and a patchwork counterpane made of scraps of material salvaged from Madame Vauquer's old dresses. The tiled floor was damp and coated with dust. Opposite the window was one of those old pot-bellied rosewood chests of drawers, with brass handles twisted into the form of climbing stems decorated with leaves or flowers; an old washstand topped with a wooden slab bearing a water jug and basin and the implements a man needs to trim his beard himself. In one corner were his boots; at the head of the bed was a bedside table with neither door nor marble top; to the side of the hearth, which showed not the slightest trace of a fire, was the square walnut-wood table upon whose crossbar Goriot had twisted his silver-gilt dish. A scuffed writing desk, which the old man used to stand his hat on, a grimy armchair stuffed with straw and two chairs completed this miserable collection of furniture. Suspended from the bed canopy, itself hanging from the ceiling by a thread, was a worn strip of red and white checked fabric. The garret of the poorest of errand boys was surely not as meanly furnished as the lodgings Madame Vauquer had allocated old man Goriot. The sight of this room made you shiver, it broke your heart, it resembled the most squalid cell in a prison. Fortunately, Goriot didn't notice the expression that flashed across Eugène's face as he set his candle down on the bedside table. Goriot turned over to lie on his side, keeping the covers pulled right up under his chin.

'Now, who do you prefer: Madame de Restaud or Madame de Nucingen?'

'I prefer Madame Delphine,' replied the student, 'because she loves you more.'

When he heard these warmly spoken words, the old man reached out an arm from under the covers and shook Eugène's hand.

'Thank you, thank you,' replied the old man, moved. 'What did she say about me?'

The student repeated what the baronne had said, with some embellishment, and the old man listened as if he were receiving God's word.

'Sweet child! Yes, she loves me. But don't believe what she said about Anastasie. The two sisters are rivals, you see; it's just further proof of their affection. Madame de Restaud loves me just as dearly. I know. A father is with his children as God is with us all: he reaches right to the bottom of our hearts and judges our intentions. They are both as loving as each other. Oh! If I'd only had kind sons-in-law, I'd have been so happy. Although perhaps earthly happiness can never be complete. If I'd lived in the same house as them, just hearing their voices, knowing they were there, seeing them come and go as they did when I had them at home with me: that would have made my heart leap with joy. Were they beautifully dressed?'

'They were, yes,' said Eugène. 'But Monsieur Goriot, with daughters as well provided for as yours, why are you living in such a hovel?'

'Dear me,' he said, with seeming unconcern, 'what difference would a little more comfort make to me? I'm hardly fit to explain these things to you; I can barely string two words together. It's all in here,' he added, striking his heart. 'My two daughters are my whole life. If they're enjoying themselves, if they're happy, finely dressed, if they have carpets to walk on, what does it matter where I lay my head and what clothes I wear? I'm never cold if they are warm and never bored if they're amused. I only suffer when they do. When you're a father, when, as you listen to your children babble, you say to yourself, "This came from me!" when you sense how those little creatures connect with every drop of your blood, and they're the finest flower that ever sprang from it, indeed they are! then you feel their skin is one with yours, you're moved by every step they take. Their voices answer mine wherever I go. One sad look from them makes my blood run cold. One day you'll understand the way their joy makes us far happier than our own. I can't explain it: something moves you inside and fills you with bliss. In short, I'm living three lives! Let me tell you something strange. When I became a father, I understood God. He is whole and present everywhere because all creation came from him. So it is with me and my daughters, Monsieur. Only I love my daughters more than God loves the world, because the world isn't as beautiful as God and my daughters are more beautiful than I. They are so near and dear to my heart that I sensed you'd see them tonight. Lord! A man who would make my little Delphine as happy as a woman is when she's truly loved: why, I'd polish his boots, I'd be his errand boy! I heard from her chambermaid what a bad lot that nasty little Monsieur de Marsay is. I've often felt the urge to break his neck. Not to love a jewel of a woman, with the voice of a nightingale and perfectly made! What on earth made her go and marry that great lump of an Alsatian? What they both need are loving, handsome young men. Well, well, they followed their fancy.'

Old man Goriot was sublime. Eugène had never before seen him lit up with the flames of fatherly love. The power of feelings to draw out what a man has in his soul is remarkable. However coarse a beast he is, as soon as he expresses strong and genuine affection, he gives off a vital fluid which changes his features, animates his gestures and colours his voice. Often, driven by passion, even the dullest creature manages to achieve the highest eloquence in his ideas, even in his language, and will seem to move in a bright sphere. At this precise moment, the old man's voice, his gestures, had all the contagious emotion of a great actor. But then, are not our noble feelings the poetries of the will?

'In that case,' said Eugène, 'perhaps it won't displease you to learn that she's about to break with de Marsay. That coxcomb has transferred his affections from her to Princesse Galathionne. As for me, I fell in love with Madame Delphine this evening.'

'Did you now!' said old man Goriot.

'Yes. She appeared to enjoy my company. We spoke of love for an hour and I'm to call on her the day after tomorrow, Saturday.'

'Oh! How much I would love you, dear Monsieur, if she took a liking to you. You're a good man, you wouldn't make her life a misery. If you betrayed her, I'd slit your throat, for a start. A woman doesn't love twice, see? Dear me! I'm talking nonsense, Monsieur Eugène. It's too cold in here for you. Dear me! So what did she tell you, what message did she give you for me?'

'Nothing,' Eugène thought to himself. Aloud, he replied, 'She asked me to send you a kiss from your loving daughter.'

'Farewell, neighbour, sleep well, sweet dreams; mine are blessed by those words. May God grant your every wish! You have been a guardian angel to me this evening; you have brought me the very air my daughter breathed.'

'Poor man,' said Eugène to himself as he went to bed; 'it's enough to melt a heart of marble. His daughter no more had a thought for him than she did for the Grand Turk.'

This conversation led old man Goriot to view his neighbour as an unhoped-for confidant, a friend. The only connection that could lead the old fellow to feel affection for another man had been established between them. One and one always makes two, when it comes to love. Old Goriot imagined he could be nearer to his daughter Delphine, he thought he would be able to visit her more often, if Eugène were to become close to the baronne. We might add that he had confided in Eugène a source of his grief. Madame de Nucingen, whose happiness he wished for a thousand times a day, had never known the sweet delights of love. Eugène was certainly, as he put it, one of the kindest young men he'd ever seen, and he had a hunch that he would give her all the pleasure of which she had been deprived. And so the friendship that the old fellow had begun to feel towards his neighbour – without which the end of this story would probably never have been known – continued to grow.

The next morning at *déjeuner*, the intent look which old Goriot gave Eugène as he sat down next to him, the few words he spoke to him and the change in his face, which usually resembled a plaster mask, were a source of surprise to the boarders. This was Vautrin's first encounter with the student since their discussion and he stared at him as if trying to see into his soul. Remembering Vautrin's scheme, Eugène, who, before falling asleep that night, had surveyed the vast field of action opening up before him, was inevitably thinking about Mademoiselle Taillefer's dowry and couldn't help looking at Victorine in the way even the most virtuous young man will look at a rich heiress. Their eyes met by chance. The poor girl didn't fail to notice how handsome Eugène looked in his new outfit. The glance they exchanged was meaningful enough to convince Rastignac that he had become the object of those confused desires that seize all young women and which they pin on the first attractive man who comes along. A voice cried out to him: 'Eight hundred thousand francs!' But he briskly threw himself back into his memories of the previous evening, thinking that his illusory passion for Madame de Nucingen would be an antidote to his involuntarily wicked thoughts.

'Last night at the Italiens they performed Rossini's *Barber of Seville*. I've never heard such delightful music,' he said. 'How wonderful to have a box at the Italiens!'

Old man Goriot snapped up these passing remarks as a dog hangs on his master's every move.

'You're like pigs in clover, you men,' said Madame Vauquer; 'you do just as you please.'

'How did you come back?' asked Vautrin.

'On foot,' replied Eugène.

'Personally,' the tempter went on, 'I wouldn't settle for half-pleasures; I'd want to go there in my carriage, in my box, and be brought home in comfort. "All or nothing!" That's my motto.'

'And a good one it is too,' replied Madame Vauquer.

'Perhaps you'll be calling on Madame de Nucingen,' murmured Eugène to old Goriot. 'I'm sure she'll receive you with open arms; she'll want to ask you a thousand little things about me. I've heard that she'd do anything in the world to be received at the house of my cousin, Madame la Vicomtesse de Beauséant. Be sure to tell her that fulfilling her wish is foremost in my mind, such is my love for her.'

Rastignac left for the Ecole de Droit[142] soon afterwards, wanting to spend as little time as possible in that hateful house. He wandered around aimlessly for most of the day, his mind full of the feverish thoughts familiar to young men tormented by overly great expectations. Vautrin's arguments had just started him thinking about life in society, when he bumped into his friend Bianchon in the Jardin du Luxembourg.[143]

'Where did you get such a long face?' asked the medical student, taking his arm as they strolled in front of the palace.

'I'm plagued with terrible temptations.'

'What kind? You can cure temptations, you know.'

'How?'

'By giving in to them.'

'You may laugh, knowing nothing of my situation. Have you read Rousseau?'

'Yes.'

'Do you remember the passage where he asks the reader what he would do if he could get rich by killing a mandarin in China solely by force of will,[144] without budging from Paris?'

'Yes.'

'Well?'

'Hah! I'm on my thirty-third mandarin.'

'I'm not joking. Look, if it were proved to you that the thing is possible and all you have to do is nod your head, would you do it?'

'Is he very old, the mandarin? Hmm. Young or old, paralytic or the picture of health, why . . . Darn it! No, I wouldn't.'

'You're a good chap, Bianchon. But if you loved a woman so much it was turning your heart inside-out, and if she needed money, a lot of money, for her gowns, for her carriage, for everything that took her fancy – what then?'

'What, you make me lose my mind, then you want me to use it?'

'Listen, Bianchon, I'm going mad, cure me. I have two sisters, beautiful, innocent angels, and I want them to be happy. Where can I find two hundred thousand francs for their dowries in the space of five years? You see, sometimes in life you have to play for high stakes instead of frittering away your luck on winning pennies.'

'Why, you're asking the question that hangs over everyone when they start out in life, only you want to cut the Gordian knot.[145] My dear friend, none but Alexander can behave like that, anyone else ends up in gaol. As for me, I'll be content to carve out a modest living for myself in the provinces, simply by stepping into my father's shoes. A man can satisfy his inclinations just as fully within the smallest circle as he can within a vast circumference. Napoleon didn't eat two dinners a night and had no more mistresses than a medical student boarding with the Capuchin friars. Our happiness, dear friend, will always fit between the soles of our feet and the crown of our head; and whether it costs us a million a year or a hundred louis, we all, inside, have the same intrinsic perception of it. My verdict is that the Chinaman should live.'

'Thank you! You've made me feel much better, Bianchon. We'll always be friends.'

'By the way,' continued the medical student, 'as I was coming out of Cuvier's lecture[146] at the Jardin des Plantes, I noticed Michonneau and Poiret on a bench in conversation with a man I saw during the riots last year near the Chamber of Deputies, who, if you ask me, is a man of the police disguised as an honest bourgeois of private means. Keep your eye on those two: I'll tell you why. Well, goodbye, I must go and answer the four o'clock roll-call.'

When Eugène arrived back at the boarding house, he found Goriot waiting for him.

'Here,' said the old man, 'you have a letter from Delphine. Such pretty handwriting!'

Eugène opened the letter and read it.

*'Monsieur, my father tells me you like Italian music. I'd be
delighted if you'd do me the pleasure of accepting a seat in my
box. As La Fodor and Pellegrini are to sing on Saturday, I'm sure
you won't turn me down. Monsieur de Nucingen joins me in
inviting you to come and dine with us informally. If you accept,
you'll be doing him a favour by relieving him of the conjugal
chore of accompanying me. Don't send an answer – come, and
accept my compliments.*

D. de N.'

'Let me see it,' said the old man to Eugène once he'd finished
reading the letter. 'You will go, won't you?' he added, smelling
the paper. 'What a sweet scent! You can tell her fingers have
touched this!'

'A woman doesn't throw herself at a man like that,' the
student said to himself. 'She wants to use me to get de Marsay
back. Only pique would make her do such a thing.'

'So,' said old man Goriot, 'what's on your mind?'

Eugène knew nothing of the delirium of vanity affecting certain women at that time and was unaware that a banker's wife
was capable of any sacrifice that would open a door for her to
the Faubourg Saint-Germain. It was a time when fashionable
opinion had begun to rate the women belonging to the Faubourg Saint-Germain set – known as the Ladies of the Petit
Château[147] – above all others. Madame de Beauséant, her friend
the Duchesse de Langeais, and the Duchesse de Maufrigneuse
ranked highest of all. Only Rastignac was oblivious to the
burning ambition among the women of the Chaussée d'Antin
to be admitted to this upper circle, where the constellations of
their sex shone brightest. But his wariness served him well: it
made him cool-headed and gave him the ambiguous power of
imposing terms rather than accepting them.

'Yes, I'll go,' he replied.

And so curiosity led him to Madame de Nucingen's door,
whereas if she'd spurned him perhaps he'd have been drawn
there by passion. Still, he waited for the next day and the time
of his departure with some impatience. A young man's first

affair may afford him as many delights as his first love. Being confident of success spawns a thousand pleasures that men never admit to and which gives certain women all their charm. Desire may be born as much of the ease of a conquest as of its difficulty. Indeed, all human passions are sparked off or fuelled by one or other of these two causes, which divide the empire of love between them. Perhaps this rift is a consequence of the greater question of temperament which, whatever anyone says, governs society. While the melancholic require the stimulation of coquetry, perhaps the choleric or sanguine lose interest when they encounter prolonged resistance. To put it another way, the elegy is as phlegmatic as the dithyramb is choleric.[148] As he dressed, Eugène savoured all the little delights a young man never dares speak of for fear of being mocked, but which tickle his self-esteem. He arranged his hair, imagining a pretty woman's gaze lingering on his black curls. He struck as many childish poses in the mirror as a young woman dressing for a ball. He eyed his slim waist with satisfaction as he smoothed the creases out of his coat.

'Well, there are certainly worse-looking men!' he said to himself. Then he went downstairs just as the regular boarders were sitting down to dinner and took in good spirit the chorus of foolish banter his elegant grooming provoked. A trait peculiar to boarding houses is the astonishment caused by smart dress. No one can wear anything new without everyone else having their say.

'Kt, kt, kt, kt,' said Bianchon, clicking his tongue against his palate, as if to spur on a horse.

'Every inch the gentleman!' said Madame Vauquer.

'Monsieur is off a-courting?' remarked Mademoiselle Michonneau.

'Cock-a-doodle-do!' crowed the painter.

'My compliments to your lady wife,' said the museum clerk.

'Monsieur has a wife?' asked Poiret.

'A wife with compartments, seaworthy, perfect finish guaranteed, priced from 25 to 40 francs, check-patterned in the latest style, washable, beautifully cut, half-yarn, half-cotton, half-wool, cures toothache and other illnesses approved by the

Royal Academy of Medicine! Also excellent for children! Better still for headaches, overeating, and other diseases of the oesophagus, eyes and ears,' cried Vautrin with the comic, unstoppable patter of a fairground quack. 'How much did this marvel cost me, I hear you ask, Gentlemen? Two sous? No. Nothing at all. A left-over from an order supplied to the Grand Mogul and which every sovereign in Europe, including the Grrrrrrrrand old Duke of Baden, has asked to see! Roll up, straight ahead there! Pay at the desk. And – music! Brooom, la la, trill! La, la, boom, boom! Oi! You on the clarinet, you're flat,' he continued in a hoarse voice. 'Watch it or I'll skin your knuckles.'

'Lord! That man is so very agreeable, indeed he is,' said Madame Vauquer to Madame Couture; 'I'd never be bored with him around.'

Amidst all the laughing and joking set off by this speech and its comic delivery, Eugène caught a furtive glance from Mademoiselle Taillefer as she leaned towards Madame Couture and said a few words in her ear.

'Your cab is here,' said Sylvie.

'So where's he dining?' asked Bianchon.

'With Madame la Baronne de Nucingen.'

'Monsieur Goriot's daughter,' replied the student.

At this they all stared at the old vermicelli dealer, who was looking at Eugène with a kind of envy.

Rastignac arrived at the Rue Saint-Lazare and entered one of those frivolous houses, with slim columns and scanty porticoes – which pass for handsome in Paris – a typical banker's house, full of expensive, affected elegance, with stucco, and marble mosaic landings.[149] He found Madame de Nucingen in a small drawing room painted in the Italian style, whose decor resembled that of a café. The baronne was downcast. The attempts she made to hide her sadness aroused Eugène's interest all the more keenly because they had nothing feigned about them. He had thought to make a woman happy by his presence and instead found her in despair. This disappointment wounded his pride.

'I have very little right to your trust, Madame,' he said, after chiding her for her troubled countenance; 'but I'm counting on your good faith to tell me honestly if I am disturbing you.'

'Stay,' she said. 'I'd be alone if you went. Nucingen is dining in town and I don't want to be alone, I need to be distracted.'

'Why, what's wrong?'

'You're the last person I'd tell,' she cried.

'I want to know, as that means this secret concerns me in some way.'

'Perhaps! No,' she continued, 'there are some domestic disputes that should stay buried at the bottom of the heart. Didn't I tell you so the other day? – I'm not happy, no, not at all. The heaviest chains are made of gold.'

When a woman tells a young man that she's unhappy, if that young man is sharp witted, well dressed, with fifteen hundred francs lying idle in his pocket, he is bound to think what Eugène thought and become conceited.

'What more could you want?' he replied. 'You are beautiful, young, loved and rich.'

'Let's not talk about me,' she said, with a miserable shake of her head. 'We'll dine here, the two of us, and then we'll go and hear some delightful music. How do I look?' she said, standing up to show him her white cashmere gown decorated in the most elegant and opulent Persian style.

'I wish you were mine and mine alone,' said Eugène. 'You look enchanting.'

'You'd be the owner of a poor estate,' she said, with a bitter smile. 'To you, there's nothing here to suggest misfortune, and yet, despite appearances, I'm in despair. My anxiety keeps me awake at night, I shall become ugly.'

'Oh, that's impossible!' said the student. 'But I'm curious to hear about these sorrows that not even devoted love would banish.'

'Ah! If I revealed what they were, you'd leave me,' she said. 'You still only love me with the gallantry a man affects out of habit; but if you really loved me, you'd be plunged into terrible despair. You see that I must keep it to myself. Please,' she continued, 'let's talk about something else. Come and see my apartments.'

'No, let's stay here,' replied Eugène, sitting down next to Madame de Nucingen on a love-seat by the fire and boldly taking hold of her hand.

She let him take it and even pressed his with one of those forceful movements that betray strong emotion.

'Listen,' said Rastignac; 'if you have troubles, you must tell me what they are. Let me prove that I love you for yourself. Either speak out and say what's wrong so I can put it right, even if it means killing six men, or I'll leave and never come back.'

'Very well,' she cried, striking her brow at a despairing thought; 'I'll put you to the test right away.' 'Yes,' she murmured to herself, 'this is the only way left.' She rang the bell.

'Is Monsieur's carriage ready?' she asked her manservant.

'Yes, Madame.'

'I'll take it. Give him mine, with my horses. Don't serve dinner until seven.'

'Let's go,' she said to Eugène, who thought he must be dreaming when he found himself sitting next to her in Monsieur de Nucingen's coupé.

'To the Palais-Royal,' she said to the coachman, 'near the Théâtre-Français.'

She seemed distracted on the way and refused to answer the thousands of questions Eugène fired at her, not knowing what to make of her stubborn, impenetrable silence.

'I might lose her at any moment,' he said to himself.

When the carriage pulled up, the baronne gave the student a look which stopped his wild words in mid-flow, for he had let himself get carried away.

'You really do love me?' she said.

'Yes,' he replied, hiding the uneasiness that was creeping over him.

'You won't think ill of me, whatever I ask you to do?'

'No.'

'Are you ready to obey me?'

'Blindly.'

'Have you ever been to a gaming-house?' she asked, with a tremor in her voice.

'Never.'

'Ah! I can breathe again. You'll have good luck. Take my purse,' she said. 'Go on, take it! You'll find a hundred francs in there; everything this happy woman owns. Go to a gaming-house; I know there are several near the Palais-Royal, although I'm not sure exactly where. Stake the hundred francs at a game called roulette and either lose the lot or bring back six thousand francs. I'll tell you why I'm unhappy when you come back.'

'I'll be damned if I have the faintest idea what I'm about to do, but I'll obey you,' he said, with a rush of exhilaration as he thought, 'She's compromising herself with me; she'll be unable to refuse me anything.'

Eugène took the pretty purse and ran to Number NINE,[150] after asking an old-clothes seller to point out the nearest gaming-house. He climbed the stairs, let his hat be taken, then went in and asked where the roulette was. The host led him to a long table. Undaunted by the astonished stares of the regulars, Eugène shamelessly asked where to put his stake.

'If you put a single louis on one of these thirty-six numbers and it comes up, you'll win thirty-six louis,' a respectable, white-haired old man said to him.

Eugène threw the hundred francs onto the number of his age, twenty-one. Before he had time to collect himself, there was a cry of amazement. He had won without realizing it.

'Take off your money,' said the old man; 'you won't win twice with that system.'

Taking the rake the old man was holding out to him, Eugène swept the three thousand six hundred francs towards him and, still not knowing how the game worked, staked them on the red. The gallery watched him enviously, seeing him play again. The wheel turned, he won once more and the croupier pushed another three thousand six hundred francs his way.

'You now have seven thousand two hundred francs,' murmured the old man in his ear. 'If I were you I'd leave; the red has come up eight times. If you're feeling charitable, you'll acknowledge this sound advice by relieving the poverty of one of Napoleon's old prefects, who is down to his last penny.'

In a daze, Rastignac let the white-haired man take ten louis, then went back down the stairs with his seven thousand francs, still knowing nothing at all about the game but staggered by his good luck.

'There! So where will you take me next!' he said, showing Madame de Nucingen the seven thousand francs as soon as the door closed behind him.

Delphine threw her arms around him wildly and kissed him warmly, although not passionately. 'You've saved me!' Tears of joy streamed down her cheeks. 'I'll tell you everything, my dear friend. You will be my dear friend, won't you? You see me as rich, wealthy, wanting for nothing or seeming to want for nothing! Well, you should know that Monsieur de Nucingen won't let me have a single sou to spend as I please: he pays for the house, my carriages, my theatre boxes, but gives me a pittance for my clothes and is secretly reducing me to poverty to serve his interests. I'm too proud to beg. Why, I'd be the lowest of creatures if I purchased his money at the price he wants to sell it at! So how have I, with my dowry of seven hundred thousand francs, allowed myself to be robbed? Through pride, through anger. We're so young, so naive, at the start of married life! The words I needed to use to ask my husband for money stuck in my throat; I never dared, I used up my savings and the money poor father gave me and then ran into debt. My marriage has been such a horrible disappointment, I can't tell you: suffice it to say that I'd throw myself out of the window if Nucingen and I didn't live in our own separate apartments. When I had to confess my debts to him, the jewels and little luxuries of a young lady (poor Father encouraged us never to deny ourselves a thing), I was racked with anxiety; but finally plucked up the courage to speak out. Didn't I have my own fortune, after all? Nucingen was furious, he said that I would ruin him, terrible things! I wanted the earth to swallow me up. As he had taken my dowry, he settled my debts, but insisted that I should in future have a fixed allowance for my personal expenses, a condition I accepted to restore peace. Since then, I have tried to be worthy of the self-regard of someone you know,' she said. 'Although he has deceived me, it would be churlish of me not to recognize the nobility of his character. But really, the way he left me was shameful! *One* should never desert a woman to whom, on a day of distress, *one* has thrown a heap of gold! *One* should love her for ever! You, with your noble twenty-one-year-old soul, so young and pure, will ask me how a woman can accept gold from a man? Why! Isn't it natural to share everything with the being to whom we owe our happiness? When you have given each other everything, why would you worry about a fraction of that whole? Money only takes on meaning at the point when feelings no longer have any. Aren't we bound to each other for life? What woman foresees a separation while believing herself to be dearly loved? You swear you will love us for ever; how could our interests be anything but shared? You have no idea how I suffered today when Nucingen absolutely refused to give me six thousand francs, a sum he gives every month to his mistress, a trollop from the Opéra! I wanted to kill myself. The wildest ideas went through my head. At times I have envied the lot of a servant, of my maid. It would have been madness to go in search of my father! Anastasie and I have bled him dry. My poor father would have sold himself if he could have fetched six thousand francs; I would have driven him to despair for nothing. You have saved me from shame and death; I was beside myself with suffering. Ah! Monsieur, I owed you this explanation: I have been insanely reckless with you. When you left me and I lost sight of you, I wanted to run away, on foot . . . Where? I don't know. This is how half the women in Paris live: wealthy on the outside, cruel cares inside their hearts. I know some poor creatures who are far worse off than I am. There are women who resort to having fake bills drawn up by their suppliers. There are those forced to steal from their husbands: some men believe that a cashmere worth a hundred louis sells for five hundred francs, others that a five-hundred-franc cashmere is worth a hundred louis. You'll find some poor women who let their children go hungry to scrape enough together for a gown. I, however, have never stooped to such vile deception. That would be my worst fear. Although some women sell themselves to their husbands to gain the upper hand, I, at least, am free! I could let Nucingen shower me with gold, but I prefer to weep with my head on the heart of a man I can respect. Ah! This evening Monsieur de Marsay will have no right to look on me as a woman he has bought.' She buried her head in her hands to hide her tears from Eugène, who uncovered her face to look at her: she was sublime in that state. 'How terrible to confuse money and feelings. You'll never be able to love me,' she said.

Eugène was deeply moved by this juxtaposition of the fine feelings that make women so noble and the misdemeanours that the current state of society drives them to commit;[151] he spoke gentle, consoling words, admiring this beautiful woman, whose cry of pain was so naively indiscreet.

'Promise you won't use this as a weapon against me,' she said.

'Ah, Madame! I could never do that,' he said.

She took his hand and pressed it to her heart in a gesture full of gratitude and warmth. 'Thanks to you, I feel happy and free again. I was living in the grip of an iron hand. I want to live simply from now on and spend nothing. You'll like me as I am, won't you, dear friend? Take this,' she said, keeping back six banknotes for herself. 'In all fairness, I owe you a thousand écus,[152] for your contribution was equal to mine.'

Eugène defended himself like a virgin. But when the baronne said, 'If you won't be my partner, I'll consider you my enemy', he took the money. 'I'll keep it in reserve as a stake for a time of need,' he said.

'That's exactly what I dreaded to hear you say,' she exclaimed, going pale. 'Should I ever mean anything to you,' she said, 'swear you'll never gamble again. Dear God! Me – corrupt you! I'd die of grief.'

They had arrived. The contrast between such woe and such wealth made the student's head spin, as he heard Vautrin's grim words ringing in his ears.

'Sit here,' said the baronne, gesturing towards a love-seat by the fire in her room; 'I'm going to write a difficult letter and I need your advice.'

'Don't write anything,' said Eugène; 'put the banknotes in an envelope, address it and have it delivered by your maid.'

'Why, you treasure of a man,' she said. 'Ah, Monsieur! That's what it is to have breeding! De Beauséant through and through,' she said with a smile.

'She's delightful,' Eugène said to himself, becoming increasingly smitten. He glanced around the room, whose sensual elegance had a touch of the rich courtesan about it.

'Do you like it?' she said, ringing for her maid.

'Thérèse, take this to Monsieur de Marsay yourself and hand it to him in person. If he's out, bring the letter back to me.'

Thérèse gave Eugène a mischievous look and went out. Dinner was announced. Rastignac gave Madame de Nucingen his arm and she led him into a delightful dining room, where he found the same glittering tableware that had left him openmouthed at his cousin's house.

'On opera days', she said, 'you must dine here and escort me to the Italiens.'

'I'd make a habit of such a pleasant way of life if it were to last; but I'm a poor student with his fortune to make.'

'It will be made,' she said, laughing. 'Look how well everything is turning out: I never expected to be this happy.'

It is in a woman's nature to prove the impossible by the possible and to quash facts with feelings. When Madame de Nucingen and Rastignac entered their box at the Bouffons, she had an air of contentment which made her so beautiful that everyone saw fit to murmur the kind of petty aspersions against which women are defenceless and which give credit to all kinds of fictitious improprieties. Those who know Paris believe nothing that is said there and say nothing of what goes on there. Eugène took the baronne's hand and the two spoke to each other with light or intense squeezes, sharing the sensations the music aroused in them. It was an exhilarating evening for both of them. They left together and Madame de Nucingen insisted on taking Eugène as far as the Pont-Neuf, all the way refusing him even one of the kisses which she had lavished upon him at the Palais-Royal. Eugène reproached her for this fickleness.

'Then,' she replied, 'it showed gratitude for your heaven-sent devotion; now it would be a promise.'

'And you'd rather not promise me anything, ungrateful woman.'

He made a cross face. With one of those impatient gestures so delightful to a lover, she gave him her hand to kiss, which he took with a bad grace she found enchanting.

'Until Monday, at the ball,' she said.

As he continued home on foot, through a beautiful moonlit night, Eugène's mind filled with serious thoughts. He was both happy and dissatisfied: happy with an adventure which would win him one of the prettiest and most elegant women in Paris, the object of his desires; dissatisfied at seeing his plans to make his fortune thwarted. He was now faced with the reality of the confused designs he had harboured the day before yesterday. Failure always bolsters the strength of our ambitions. The more Eugène enjoyed Parisian life, the less he wanted to remain poor and humble. He fingered the thousand-franc note in his pocket, inventing a thousand fallacious reasons to keep it for himself. He finally arrived at the Rue Neuve-Sainte-Geneviève and, on reaching the top of the stairs, saw a light. Old man Goriot had left his door open and his candle lit, so the student wouldn't forget to 'tell him all about his daughter', as he put it. Eugène kept nothing from him.

'Why!' cried old Goriot in a fit of desperate jealousy, 'they think I'm ruined, but I still have an annual income of thirteen hundred livres! Lord! Poor little thing, why didn't she come here? I'd have sold my stock, we'd have taken it out of the capital and I'd have set up a life annuity with the rest. My dear neighbour, why didn't you come and tell me she was in trouble? How did you have the heart to risk her poor little hundred francs at the game? It's enough to break your heart. That's a son-in-law for you! Ah! If I had them both here, I'd wring their necks. Dear Lord! Crying, you say, she was crying?'

'With her head on my waistcoat,' said Eugène.

'Oh! Give it to me,' said old Goriot. 'What! My daughter shed tears on this, my sweet Delphine, who never used to cry when she was small! Oh! I'll buy you another, don't wear it again, let me keep it. She should enjoy the use of her assets; those were the terms of her marriage contract. That's it! I'll go and see Derville, my solicitor, first thing tomorrow. I'll insist that her fortune is invested in her own name. I know the law. I may be an old wolf but I'll show them I still have teeth.'

'Take this, Father. She wanted to give me a thousand francs of the winnings. Keep them safe for her, in the waistcoat.'

Goriot looked at Eugène, stretched out a hand to take hold of his and let a tear fall onto it.

'You'll succeed in life,' said the old man. 'God is just, see? I know all about honesty, and let me tell you, there are very few men like you. So, will you be my dear child too? Off you go to bed. You'll sleep easily; you're not a father yet. She was crying, he tells me now, and there I was calmly eating my dinner like an idiot, while she was suffering; I, who would sell the Father, the Son and the Holy Ghost to spare either of them a single tear.'

'Well,' Eugène said to himself as he got ready for bed, 'I think I'll be an honest man my whole life. There's pleasure in following the promptings of your conscience.'

Perhaps only those who believe in God do good in secret; Eugène believed in God.

The next day, at the time of the ball, Rastignac went to the house of Madame de Beauséant, who was to take him with her and introduce him to the Duchesse de Carigliano. He received the most gracious welcome from the maréchale and soon caught sight of Madame de Nucingen among the guests. Delphine had dressed splendidly with the aim of pleasing all, the better to please Eugène, and was now impatiently waiting for him to look her way, deluding herself that she was hiding her impatience. A man capable of deciphering a woman's feelings revels in a moment like this. What man has not frequently delighted in keeping his opinion to himself, hiding his pleasure, seeking some revealing response to the doubt he has sown, savouring the fears he'll banish later with a smile? That evening, the student suddenly saw the full potential of his position and understood that being recognized as Madame de Beauséant's cousin gave him a certain status in society. The conquest of Madame de Nucingen, which everyone already gave him credit for, made him the focus of so much attention, that the other young men cast envious looks in his direction; on noticing one or two of these, he had his first delicious taste of conceit. As he passed through each drawing room, moving from one group to the next, he heard his good fortune being complimented. The women predicted that he would go far. Delphine, fearing to lose him, promised to grant him tonight the kiss she had so stubbornly refused the night before last. Rastignac received several invitations at the ball. His cousin introduced him to a number of women, all with fashionable pretensions, whose houses were considered to be of note; he saw himself launched into the highest and finest Parisian society. Indeed, the evening had all the charm of a brilliant debut and he would remember it until his dying day, just as a young lady remembers the ball where she first triumphed.

The next day at *déjeuner*, when Eugène was telling old Goriot and the other lodgers about his success, a devilish smile appeared on Vautrin's face. 'So you think', exclaimed that ruthless logician, 'that a young man of fashion can reside in the Rue Neuve-Sainte-Geneviève, at the Maison Vauquer? An infinitely respectable establishment by all accounts, I'll give it that, but hardly what you might call modish. It's commodious, has a fine well-to-do air, is proud to be the temporary abode of a Rastignac; but, in the end, it's in the Rue Neuve-Sainte-Geneviève and doesn't know what luxury is, because it's purely *parochialorama*.[153] My young friend,' continued Vautrin, with a mockingly paternal air, 'if you want to cut a dash in Paris, you need three horses, a tilbury for the morning and a coupé for the evening; that's nine thousand francs for your carriages alone. You'd be unworthy of your destiny if you didn't spend three thousand francs at your tailor's, six hundred francs at the perfumer's, a hundred écus at the bootmakers and a hundred écus at the hatmakers. As for your laundress, she'll cost you a thousand francs. A fashionable young man must be meticulous in the matter of his linen:[154] isn't that what he'll be judged on, after all? Love and Religion require immaculate cloths on their altars. That brings us to fourteen thousand. Not to mention what you'll fritter away at gambling, on bets, on gifts; it's impossible to get by with less than two thousand francs of ready money. I've led that kind of life, I know what it costs. Add to these essentials three hundred louis for your feed, a thousand francs for your kennel. So, child, we need to have a sweet twenty-five thousand a year lined up, or we sink into the mud, make a fool of ourselves and are relieved of our future, our successes, our mistresses! I forgot the valet and the groom! Will Christophe deliver your *billets doux*? Will you write them on the paper you use now? It would be akin to suicide. Trust an old man of experience!' he continued, with a sudden *rinforzando* boom of his bass voice. 'Either lock yourself away virtuously in a garret and wed yourself to your work, or take another path.' And Vautrin winked pointedly in Mademoiselle Taillefer's direction, with a look meant to revive and resume the seductive arguments he had planted in the student's heart to corrupt him.

Several days went by during which Rastignac led the most dissipated life. He dined almost every day with Madame de Nucingen, whom he escorted when she went out. He returned at three or four o'clock in the morning, rose at midday to wash and dress, then went and strolled in the Bois with Delphine when the weather was fine, squandering his time without being aware of its worth and absorbing all the precepts and entice-ments of luxury as eagerly as the calyx of the female date palm opens to receive the fertilizing pollen of its hymeneals. He played for high stakes, lost or won vast sums of money and with time became accustomed to the extravagant lifestyle of the young Parisian gentlemen. He took fifteen hundred francs out of his first winnings to repay his mother and his sisters, sending them handsome gifts along with the money.

Despite having announced his desire to leave the Maison Vauquer, he was still there as January drew to a close and had no idea how to extricate himself. Virtually all young men are governed by a law that may seem inexplicable, but which owes its existence to their youth itself and their frenzied pursuit of pleasure. Whether rich or poor, they never have enough money for life's necessities, but always find enough for their follies. Generous with anything they can get on credit, they're stingy with everything that requires payment up front, and seem to be avenging themselves on what they don't have by squandering everything that they could have. In a nutshell, a student takes far greater care of his hat than his suit. The tailor, whose profits are large, is ultimately more amenable to giving credit, while the modesty of the sums owed to the hatter make him one of the most inflexible figures a young man must parley with. Although the handsome young man in the balcony at the theatre puts on a dazzling display of waistcoat for the benefit of a pretty woman's opera glasses, you can be fairly sure he isn't wearing any socks; the hosier is yet another weevil in his purse. Rastignac had reached this stage. His purse – always empty for Madame Vauquer, always full for the requirements of his vanity – suffered temperamental set-backs and successes which were at variance with the most straightforward payments. If he wanted to leave this vile, stinking boarding house, this thorn in the side of his ambition, wouldn't he have to pay his landlady one month's rent and buy the furniture he needed to set himself up as a dandy? This was always impossible.

Although Rastignac knew well enough how to raise money for gambling – by purchasing watches and gold chains from his jeweller, paid for dearly from his winnings, which he then took to the Mont-de-Piété, that gloomy and discreet friend of youth – he lacked both imagination and daring when it came to paying for his food and lodgings or purchasing the tools he needed to make capital out of a life of fashion. Debts incurred for needs he had already satisfied, or for some vulgar necessity, no longer inspired him. Like many who lead the life of a chancer, he waited until the last minute to pay off debts considered sacrosanct by the middle-class citizen – like Mirabeau,[155] who never paid for his bread until it assumed the draconian form of a bill of exchange.

Around this time, Rastignac ran out of money and sank deep into debt. He began to understand that it would be impossible for him to continue this existence without having a permanent income. But even as he groaned to feel the sharp point of his precarious state, he felt unable to renounce the exorbitant pleasures of the life he was leading, and wanted it to continue at all cost. The lucky breaks he had been counting on to make his fortune were turning out to be pipe-dreams, while the real obstacles loomed ever larger. Now that he knew what went on between Monsieur and Madame de Nucingen behind closed doors, he realized he could only turn love into an instrument of fortune by drinking from the cup of shame and turning his back on the noble ideals that absolve youthful errors. This outwardly splendid life, riddled on the inside by the *taenias*[156] of remorse and whose fleeting pleasures were paid for dearly by ever-present anxieties, was the one he had chosen, and he rolled in it, making himself a bed in the soft mud of the ditch like La Bruyère's Absent-minded man;[157] but so far, like that gentleman, he had only soiled his clothes.

'So have we killed the mandarin?' Bianchon asked him one day as he stood up to leave the table.

'Not yet,' he replied, 'but he's at his last gasp.'

The medical student took this to be a joke, but it wasn't. Eugène, dining at the boarding house for the first time in a while, had remained deep in thought during the meal. Instead of leaving at dessert, he stayed sitting in the dining room next to Mademoiselle Taillefer, sending meaningful glances her way from time to time. A few guests were still at the table, eating walnuts, others were strolling around continuing discussions begun earlier. As on most evenings, each boarder left when he felt like it, depending on the level of interest he had in the conversation, or the sluggishness of his digestion. In winter, it was rare for the dining room to clear before eight o'clock, at which hour the four women stayed on alone and avenged themselves on the silence their sex forced them to keep among this gathering of men.

Intrigued by Eugène's air of preoccupation, Vautrin, who had at first seemed in a hurry to leave, stayed behind in the dining room, continually changing position to avoid being seen by Eugène, who would think he had left. Then, instead of following the last stragglers out of the room, he stationed himself stealthily in the drawing room. He had looked into the student's soul and seen the clear signs of a crisis. Indeed, Rastignac found himself in a bewildering situation familiar to many young men. Whether or not she loved him or was toying with his affections, Madame de Nucingen had made Rastignac suffer all

the pangs of genuine passion, by practising upon him every
skill known to female diplomacy in Paris. Although she had
compromised herself in public so as to bind Madame de
Beauséant's cousin to her, in private she was reluctant to grant
him the rights he appeared to enjoy. Over the past month she
had kindled Eugène's desire so effectively that its flames had
begun to lick at his heart. Although the student had believed
himself to have the upper hand in the early stages of the affair,
Madame de Nucingen had since proved the stronger of the
two, with the aid of those manoeuvres which stirred up in
Eugène all the feelings, good or bad, of the two or three kinds
of men found within a young man of Paris. Was it calculated on
her part? No; women are always genuine, even when at their
most duplicitous, for they are yielding to some natural feeling.
After allowing this young man to gain such a hold on her and
having shown him too much affection in such a short space of
time, perhaps Delphine was being true to her sense of dignity,
which made her either withdraw the privileges she had granted
or take pleasure in suspending them. It comes naturally to a
Parisienne, even as she is transported by passion, to pause as
she falls, to test the heart of the man to whom she will surrender her future!

Madame de Nucingen's hopes had already been deceived
once, and her loyalty tossed aside by a self-seeking young man.
She had good reason to be wary. Perhaps she had detected in
Eugène's manner a lack of respect caused by the peculiarity of
their situation; his rapid success had made him complacent.
No doubt she wished to appear imposing to a man of his age
and to look down on him, having for so long been made to
look up to the man who had abandoned her. She didn't want
Eugène to think she was an easy conquest, precisely because he
knew that she had belonged to de Marsay. Finally, after having
submitted to the degrading pleasure of that out-and-out monster, a young libertine, she was taking such delight in strolling
through the flowery dells of love that it must have been blissful
to admire its every aspect, to linger there listening to the leaves
sighing and to let herself be caressed by chaste and leisurely
breezes. True love was paying the price of false love. Sadly,

such misunderstandings will persist until men realize just how many flowers are cut down in a young woman's heart by the first cruel swipes of betrayal. Whatever her reasons, Delphine was playing with Rastignac and enjoying playing with him, no doubt because she knew that she was loved and would put an end to her lover's suffering whenever it was her right royal pleasure as a woman to do so.

As far as his own self-respect was concerned, Eugène didn't want to see his first skirmish end in defeat and continued in hot pursuit, like a hunter who must at all cost kill a partridge on his first Saint Hubert's day[158] outing. His fears, his wounded pride, his despair, genuine or pretended, bound him all the more closely to this woman. The whole of Paris gave him credit for the conquest of Madame de Nucingen, yet he was still no further on than the first day he saw her. As he was not yet aware that a woman's coquetry may offer a man more delights than her love may give him pleasure, he fell into foolish rages.

Although the season in which a woman contests love was bringing Rastignac an early crop of fruit, he was starting to find them as costly as they were green, tart and delicious to the taste. Sometimes, when he pictured himself without a sou, without a future, he thought, despite the voice of his conscience, about his chances of becoming wealthy by marrying Mademoiselle Taillefer, which Vautrin had led him to believe was a possibility. And so, having reached the point where the voice of his poverty was making itself heard, almost without thinking he strayed within reach of the claws of the terrible sphinx whose stare so often transfixed him. When Poiret and Mademoiselle Michonneau went upstairs to their rooms, Rastignac, thinking he was alone apart from Madame Vauquer and Madame Couture, who was knitting some woollen sleeves for herself as she dozed off next to the stove, gave Mademoiselle Taillefer a look of such tenderness it made her lower her eyes.

'Is something perhaps troubling you, Monsieur Eugène?' Victorine asked him after a moment's silence.

'All men are troubled by something!' replied Rastignac. 'If only we young men could be sure of being truly loved, with the kind of devotion that would reward us for the sacrifices we are always ready to make, then perhaps we would never have any troubles.'

In reply, Mademoiselle Taillefer gave Rastignac a look that left him in no doubt as to her feelings.

'You, Mademoiselle, may believe yourself sure of your heart today, but could you guarantee it would never change?'

A smile appeared on the poor girl's lips like a ray of light bursting from her soul and made her face glow so radiantly that Eugène was shocked at having provoked such a violent explosion of feeling.

'What! If you were to become rich and happy tomorrow, if a vast fortune fell at your feet from out of the blue, would you still love the poor young man who found favour with you when times were hard?'

She nodded prettily.

'A most unfortunate young man?'

Another nod.

'What claptrap are you talking over there?' called out Madame Vauquer.

'Never you mind,' replied Eugène; 'we understand each other well enough.'

'So it seems that Monsieur le Chevalier Eugène de Rastignac and Mademoiselle Victorine Taillefer have come to an understanding?' boomed Vautrin, suddenly appearing at the dining-room door.

'Oh! You scared me,' said Madame Couture and Madame Vauquer at the same time.

'I could do worse,' replied Eugène, with a laugh, although Vautrin's voice had just given him the worst shock of his life.

'None of your tasteless jokes please, Gentlemen!' said Madame Couture. 'Let us go upstairs to our rooms now, child.'

Madame Vauquer followed hot on the heels of her two lodgers, with a view to saving her candle and firewood by spending the evening with them. Eugène found himself alone, face to face with Vautrin.

'I knew you'd come round in the end,' said Vautrin, as unshakeably cool as ever. 'Now listen! I have just as many scruples as the next man. Don't make a snap decision, you're not yourself today. You've run up a few debts. I don't want it to be passion, or despair, but reason which brings you round to my way of thinking. Perhaps a couple of thousand écus wouldn't go amiss? Take this, here.'

That demon took a wallet from his pocket and pulled three banknotes out of it, which he fluttered before the student's eyes. Eugène found himself facing the cruellest dilemma. He had debts of honour to the tune of one hundred louis lost to the Marquis d'Ajuda and the Comte de Trailles. He didn't have the money and so didn't have the face to go and spend the evening at Madame de Restaud's house, where he was expected. It was to be one of those delightfully informal evenings where you nibble little cakes and sip tea, while effortlessly losing six thousand francs at whist.

'Monsieur,' Eugène replied, barely repressing a convulsive shudder; 'after everything you've told me, surely you must understand that it's impossible for me to come under any obligation to you.'

'Well, you'd have disappointed me had you answered any other way,' the tempter continued. 'You're a handsome young man, scrupulous, proud as a lion and as tender as a virgin. You'd be easy prey for the devil. You're a young man of calibre – I like that. A little more scheming reflection and you'll see society for what it is: a stage on which a man of superior talent acts out a couple of virtuous little scenes and thereby fulfils all his fantasies to thunderous applause from the idiots in the stalls. You'll be ours in a few days' time. Ah! If you chose to be my pupil, I'd give you everything you wanted. Every wish that came into your head would be granted immediately, whatever you might desire: honour, fortune, women. We would turn all civilization into ambrosian nectar for you. You would be our spoilt child, our youngest and dearest; we would happily efface ourselves for you. Every obstacle that stood in your way would be obliterated. Just because you're still clinging to a few scruples, you take me for a scoundrel? Well now, Monsieur de Turenne,[159] a man with as much integrity as you believe you still have, made little deals with brigands and never thought it would jeopardize his reputation. You don't want to be in my debt, eh? We won't let that stand in our way, will we?' continued Vautrin, with a smile. 'Take these bits of paper', he said, producing a stamp, 'and write on them for me, right here: *Accepted the sum of three thousand five hundred francs payable in one year's time*. And add the date! The interest is high enough to rid you of any scruples; you can call me a Jew and consider your debt of gratitude paid in full. I'll let you loathe me today because I know for certain that you'll love me later. You may find me full of those vertiginous depths, those vast pools of feeling that the foolish call vices, but you will never find me cowardly or ungrateful. In short, my boy, I'm neither a pawn nor a bishop, but a castle.'

'But what kind of a man are you?' cried Eugène. 'Were you put on earth to torment me?'

'Certainly not. I'm a decent chap who's prepared to get his hands dirty so you can steer clear of the mud for the rest of your days. You're asking yourself: why such devotion? Well, I'll tell you one day, whisper it softly in your ear. You were shocked at first when I showed you the workings of the machine and the way society rings the changes; but your initial fear will pass, as it does for any conscript on the battlefield, and you'll soon come round to the idea that men are soldiers resolved to die in the service of those who crown themselves kings.[160] How times have changed, indeed they have! Time was you could say to a cut-throat: "Here's a hundred écus; go and kill Mister So-and-so for me," then calmly carry on with your supper, consigning a man to oblivion at the drop of a hat. Today I'm offering you a fine fortune in return for a nod of the head which will leave your reputation intact, and you're hesitating. We live in a spineless century.'

Eugène signed the bill and handed it to Vautrin in exchange for the banknotes.

'That's more like it. Now, let's talk sensibly,' Vautrin continued. 'I intend to leave for America in a few months' time, to plant my tobacco. I'll send you some cigars as a sign of our friendship. If I become rich, I'll help you. If I don't have any children (as is most likely, I've no interest in making cuttings of myself to be replanted), then I'll leave you my fortune. Is that the behaviour of a friend? Why, it's love I feel for you. Besides, I have a passion for sacrificing myself for others; I've done it before. You see, my boy, I live life on a higher plane than other men. For me, all actions are means and I always keep the end in sight. What's a man to me? That!' he said, flicking his teeth with his thumbnail. 'A man is all or nothing. He's less than nothing if he's called Poiret: you can squash him like a bug; he's flat and he's foul. A man such as yourself, however, is a god, not just some machine clad in flesh, but a theatre in which the finest feelings are played out – and I live for feelings alone. What is a feeling but the whole world in one thought? Look at old man Goriot: his two daughters are his entire universe, they are the thread which guides him through the labyrinth of creation. Well, for a man like myself who has delved deep into life, there is only one true feeling and that is the friendship that exists between two men. Pierre and Jaffier, there's my passion. I know *Venice Preserv'd*[161] off by heart. How many men have you seen who, when a comrade says "Let's go and bury a corpse!", have the guts to get on with the job without saying a word or moralizing? Well, I've done that. I wouldn't talk this way to everyone, but you're a superior kind of man; I could say anything to you and you'd know what I meant. You won't be floundering around for much longer in this bog, surrounded by all these squat little toads who call it home. Well, I've said all I wanted to say. You're to be married. Let each of us press our points! Mine is made of steel and never droops, ha ha!'

Vautrin went out before the student could object, to let him off the hook. He seemed to know the secret of last-ditch resistance, the battles men stage for their own benefit and which they use to justify their wrongful deeds.

'Let him do as he likes; I certainly won't be marrying Mademoiselle Taillefer!' Eugène said to himself.

Rastignac's mind became feverish at the thought of making a pact with this man he abhorred but who was growing in stature in his eyes, due to the very cynicism of his ideas and his audacious stranglehold on society. He dressed, called for a cab and drove to Madame de Restaud's house. Over the past few days, she had shown more and more interest in this young man, whose every step brought him closer to the heart of fashionable society and who would one day surely be a force to be reckoned with. He settled up with Messieurs les Marquis de Trailles and d'Ajuda, played whist for part of the night and won back what he had lost. Being superstitious, like most men who have yet to make their way and who are more or less fatalistic, he chose to see his good fortune as a divine reward for keeping to the straight and narrow. The next morning, he hurried to find Vautrin to ask if he still had his bill of exchange. On hearing that he did, he returned the three thousand francs to him, unable to disguise his pleasure.

'Things are coming along nicely,' said Vautrin.

'But I'm not your accomplice,' said Eugène.

'I know, I know,' replied Vautrin, interrupting him. 'You're still behaving like a child. You can't see past the fancy knockers on the doors.'

CAT-O'-NINE-LIVES

Two days later, Poiret and Mademoiselle Michonneau found themselves sitting on a bench in the sun, on a secluded path in the Jardin des Plantes, talking to the gentleman whom, with some justification, the medical student had found suspicious.

'Mademoiselle,' Monsieur Gondureau was saying; 'I see no reason for you to have any qualms. His Excellency Monseigneur the Minister of Police of the realm of France . . .'

'Ah! His Excellency Monseigneur the Minister of Police of the realm of France . . .' repeated Poiret.

'Yes, His Excellency is handling this affair himself,' said Gondureau.

It might seem improbable that Poiret, retired clerk, doubtless a man of sound middle-class values, although of limited initiative, should continue to listen to a self-styled man of private means living in the Rue de Buffon, once he had blown his cover by pronouncing the word 'police' and revealing the face of an operative from the Rue de Jérusalem[162] under his mask of respectability. Yet nothing was more natural. Once we have shared a few comments made by certain observers, which have remained unpublished until now, we may gain a better understanding of the particular species to which Poiret belonged in the larger class of fools. His is the race of pen-pushers, who live crowded together on a budget ranging from the first degree of latitude – where wages of twelve hundred francs are found, a kind of administrative Greenland – to the third degree, where warmer wages of three to six thousand francs start to appear; a temperate region, one in which the bonus, although difficult to cultivate, may acclimatize and flourish. One of the characteristic

features of this lesser breed, and one which best represents its
unhealthy narrowness, is a sort of involuntary, mechanical,
instinctive respect for that Grand Lama of any ministry, known
to the clerk only as an illegible signature and the title HIS
EXCELLENCY MONSEIGNEUR THE MINISTER, five
words worth the *Il Bondo Cani* of the *Caliph of Baghdad*,[163]
and which, in the eyes of this grovelling people, are imbued with
a sacred, irrevocable power. Like the Pope for a Christian, Monseigneur is administratively infallible in the eyes of the clerk; his
every deed, his every word, not to mention every word spoken
in his name, drips with splendour; his name embroiders everything and legalizes whatever deed he orders done; his title
'Excellency', which testifies to the purity of his intentions and
the sanctity of his desires, serves as a passport for the least
admissible ideas. Whatever deed these poor people would never
perform in their own interest, they rush to carry out as soon as
the words 'His Excellency' are pronounced. The bureaucratic
system has its own kind of passive obedience, just as the army
does: a system which numbs a conscience, annihilates a human
being and ends up fixing him like a screw or a cog in the machine
of government. So it was that Monsieur Gondureau, who
seemed to know a thing or two about the human race, soon
identified Poiret as one of these bureaucratic fools and trotted
out the *deus ex machina*, the magic words 'His Excellency'. He
did so at the point when, having unmasked his guns, he needed
to dazzle Poiret, who struck him as being the male version of
Michonneau, as Michonneau was the female version of Poiret.

'His Excellency Monseigneur the Minister, in person, you
say . . . ! Well! That changes everything,' said Poiret.

'You can hear what this gentleman is saying and you appear
to have faith in his judgement,' continued the bogus man of
private means, addressing Mademoiselle Michonneau. 'Well,
His Excellency is now absolutely certain that the man who goes
by the name of Vautrin, and lodges at the Maison Vauquer, is
an escaped convict from the penal colony in Toulon,[164] where
he was known as *Cat-o'-Nine-Lives*.'

'Ah! Cat-o'-Nine-Lives! He must be a lucky man if he has
earned that title.'

'Yes indeed,' continued the operative. 'The nickname comes from his knack of escaping with his life every time he pulls off some incredible exploit. He's a dangerous man, you understand! He has certain qualities which make him extraordinary. Even his conviction earned him infinite respect from his associates . . .'

'So he's a man of honour?' asked Poiret.

'In his own way. He took the rap for another man's crime, a forgery committed by an extremely handsome young man he was fond of, a young Italian with a penchant for gambling, who has since enlisted in military service, where, as it happens, he hasn't put a foot wrong.'

'But if H.E. the Minister of Police is so sure that Monsieur Vautrin is this Cat-o'-Nine-Lives of yours, why does he need me?' said Mademoiselle Michonneau.

'Well! Yes, indeed,' said Poiret, 'if the minister, as you have done us the honour of telling us, is at all sure . . .'

'I wouldn't say he was sure; he has a hunch. You'll soon understand the challenge we face. Jacques Collin, nicknamed Cat-o'-Nine-Lives, enjoys the trust of the convicts of the three penal colonies, who have chosen him to be their agent and banker. He earns a lot by taking on this kind of business, which necessarily requires a man of mark.'

'A-ha! Did you follow the pun, Mademoiselle?' said Poiret. 'Monsieur calls him a man of *mark*, because he is a marked man.'

'The fake Vautrin', continued the operative, 'receives capital from the convicts, invests it, keeps it safe for them and makes it available to those who escape, or to their families, to whom they bequeath it in their wills, or to their mistresses, to whom they give bills drawn upon him.'

'Their mistresses! You mean their wives,' remarked Poiret.

'No, Monsieur. Convicts generally only have illegal wives, that we call "concubines".'

'You mean they all live in a state of concubinage?'

'As you might expect.'

'Well,' said Poiret, 'if I were Monseigneur, I wouldn't put up with such things. Since you have the honour of seeing His Excellency, and as you appear to be of a philanthropic bent, it's your duty to bring to his attention the immoral conduct of these people who set an extremely bad example to the rest of society.'

'But Monsieur, the government is hardly holding them up to be models of all the virtues.'

'True, true. However, Monsieur, if you'll allow me to . . .'

'Now, now, let the gentleman finish what he was saying, dearest,' said Mademoiselle Michonneau.

'I'm sure you understand, Mademoiselle,' continued Gondureau. 'It might be very much in the government's interest to seize this illicit fund, said to have swelled to a considerable amount. Cat-o'-Nine-Lives has amassed vast sums of money by not only holding capital belonging to various of his associates, but also that which comes from the Ten Thousand Club . . .'

'Ten thousand thieves!' cried Poiret, alarmed.

'No, the Ten Thousand Club is a band of top thieves, men who work on the grand scale and never take on a job unless they stand to gain at least ten thousand francs. The members of this club are our highest class of customer – those whose cases go straight to the Assize Court.[165] They know the law and never risk being sentenced to death when they're caught. Collin is their man of confidence, their representative. Thanks to his huge resources, the man has been able to create his own intelligence corps, a vast network of contacts shrouded in impenetrable secrecy. We've had him surrounded with spies for a year now, but still haven't managed to see his hand. His coffers and his talents are therefore constantly in use, making vice pay, funding crime and maintaining an army of scoundrels who wage perpetual war against society. If we could only get our hands on Cat-o'-Nine-Lives and confiscate his bank, we would strike at the root of evil. Which is why the highest-ranking State officials have a stake in this affair, one likely to bring honour to those who contibute to its success. You, Monsieur, might enter the civil service again, becoming secretary to a Police Superintendent, a position which shouldn't prevent you from drawing your pension.'

'But', said Mademoiselle Michonneau, 'why doesn't Cat-o'-Nine-Lives just make off with the cash?'

'Well, if he stole from the penal colony,' said the operative, 'wherever he went, he'd be followed by a man whose job it was to kill him. And then, you can't run off with a stash of money as easily as you can with a young lady from a good family. In any case, Collin isn't the type to play that kind of trick; he would feel it brought him into disrepute.'

'Monsieur,' said Poiret, 'you're right: it would indeed bring him into disrepute.'

'None of that tells us why you can't just turn up and clap him in irons,' remarked Mademoiselle Michonneau.

'Well, Mademoiselle, I'll tell you . . . But', he said in her ear, 'stop your man interrupting me or we'll be here all day. He's lucky anyone will listen to him, the old duffer. Cat-o'-Nine-Lives, on arriving here, slipped into the skin of an honest man, made himself an upright citizen of Paris, took lodgings in an obscure boarding house; he's a man of cunning all right – we'll never catch him without camouflage. So you see, Monsieur Vautrin is a highly regarded man, involved in affairs of high regard.'

'Of course,' Poiret said to himself.

'Should a bona fide Monsieur Vautrin be arrested by accident, the Minister would rather not have all the businessmen in Paris on his back, never mind public opinion. Things are a little shaky for the Chief of Police, he has enemies. If a mistake were made, his rivals would make the most of all the liberal yapping and grousing to have him kicked out. We need to proceed here as we did in the Coignard Affair,[166] with that fellow who passed himself off as the Comte de Sainte-Hélène; if he'd turned out to be the real Comte de Sainte-Hélène, we'd have been in a fine mess. So we need to check that this is our man!'

'Yes, and so you need a pretty woman for that,' said Mademoiselle Michonneau swiftly.

'Cat-o'-Nine-Lives wouldn't let a woman anywhere near him,' said the operative. 'I'll tell you a secret: he doesn't like women.'

'Well in that case, I can't see how I'd be able to carry out this check of yours, assuming of course that I agreed to do so, for two thousand francs.'

'Nothing could be easier,' said the stranger; 'I'm going to give you a bottle containing one dose of a preparation which makes the blood rush to the brain, simulating an apoplectic fit, but without the slightest risk. The drug can be mixed with wine or with coffee. Have your man carried to bed immediately and undress him to make sure he's not dying. As soon as you're on your own, slap him on the shoulder – wham! – and the brand will reappear.'

'Why, nothing could be simpler,' said Poiret.

'So, will you do it?' Gondureau said to the spinster.

'But, dear Monsieur,' said Mademoiselle Michonneau, 'if there is no brand, will I still get my two thousand francs?'

'No.'

'So what would I be paid?'

'Five hundred francs.'

'So little to do a thing like that. My conscience will prick me equally whatever the outcome and I must appease my conscience, Monsieur.'

'I can confirm', said Poiret, 'that Mademoiselle is endowed with a sizeable conscience, as well as being a very kind person, and an accomplished one.'

'I'll tell you what,' continued Mademoiselle Michonneau: 'give me three thousand francs if he's Cat-o'-Nine-Lives and nothing if he's a respectable citizen.'

'Done,' said Gondureau, 'as long as you finish the job tomorrow.'

'Not that soon, dear Monsieur; I need to see my confessor.'

'You're a wily bird!' said the operative as he stood up. 'Until tomorrow then. And if you need to speak to me urgently, come to the Petite Rue Sainte-Anne, at the far end of the Cour de la Sainte-Chapelle. There's only one door beneath the arch. Ask for Monsieur Gondureau.'

The rather unusual name 'Cat-o'-Nine-Lives' caught Bianchon's ear on his way back from Cuvier's lecture, and he overheard the 'Done!' uttered by the famous Chief of the Sûreté.[167]

'Why don't you get it over and done with; you'd have three hundred francs a year for the rest of your life,' said Poiret to Mademoiselle Michonneau.

'Why not?' she asked. 'Why, the matter needs some thought. If Monsieur Vautrin is this Cat-o'-Nine-Lives, there might be more advantage in coming to an agreement with him. However, asking him for money would tip him off and he'd be liable to scarper without paying his dues. And that would be a fine mess.'

'Even if he was tipped off,' continued Poiret, 'didn't the gentleman say that he was being watched? But you yourself would lose everything.'

'What's more,' thought Mademoiselle Michonneau, 'I don't like that man one bit! He never has a civil word to say to me.'

'But', continued Poiret, 'you'd be acting for the best. As he said, the gentleman – and he seems extremely respectable to me, as well as having friends in high places – if you rid society of a criminal, whatever his virtues, all you're doing is obeying the law. Once a thief, always a thief. What if he took it into his head to murder us all? Why, dash it! We'd be guilty of those murders, not to mention being the first victims.'

But Mademoiselle Michonneau was so deep in thought she didn't hear the sentences falling from Poiret's mouth one by one, like drops of water oozing from a fountain with a faulty tap. Once the old man started stringing sentences together, and as Mademoiselle Michonneau didn't interrupt him, he couldn't stop, like some wound-up piece of clockwork. He launched into one subject, but then, straying into his parentheses, found himself having to deal with other, utterly opposed subjects, without ever finishing his clauses. By the time they arrived at the Maison Vauquer, he had twisted and turned through a series of transitory passages and quotations which had brought him to the story of his testimonial in the affair of Monsieur Ragoulleau and Madame Morin,[168] when he had appeared in court as witness for the defence. As they went in, his companion was quick to spot Eugène de Rastignac deep in an intimate conversation with Mademoiselle Taillefer, which the two of them found so enthralling that they paid absolutely no attention to the two elderly lodgers as they crossed the dining room.

'That was bound to happen,' said Mademoiselle Michonneau to Poiret. 'After them making eyes at each other fit to burst all week.'

'Yes,' he answered. 'So she was found guilty.'

'Who?'

'Madame Morin.'

'I'm talking about Mademoiselle Victorine,' said Michonneau, walking into Poiret's room without realizing; 'and you answer me with Madame Morin. What has she got to do with anything?'

'So what does Mademoiselle Victorine seem to be guilty of?' asked Poiret.

'She is guilty of loving Monsieur Eugène de Rastignac and is falling head over heels, without knowing where it will all end, the poor innocent!'

That morning, Eugène had been driven to despair by Madame de Nucingen. Deep down, he had completely surrendered to Vautrin, while remaining reluctant to probe either the motives behind the friendship this extraordinary man showed him, or the future of such a partnership. It would take a miracle now to pull him out of the abyss into which he had been sinking for an hour, as he exchanged the sweetest promises with Mademoiselle Taillefer. For Victorine, it was as if she was hearing the voice of an angel, the heavens were opening for her, the Maison Vauquer was decked out in the fantastic colours set-designers use for theatrical palaces: she loved, she was loved, or at least she believed she was! And what woman wouldn't have believed what she did, had she seen Rastignac, had she listened to him for one hour, out of sight of all the Argus eyes[169] in the boarding house? As he tussled with his conscience, knowing that he was doing wrong and wanting to do wrong, telling himself that he would redeem this venial sin by making a woman happy, his despair made him more attractive and he glowed with all the fires of hell that burned in his breast. Fortunately for him, the miracle happened: Vautrin came in full of merriment and saw into the souls of the two young people he had wed through the machinations of his diabolical genius, but whose happiness he suddenly clouded by singing in his mocking, booming voice:

'*My Fanchette she is so charming*
For she is a simple lass . . .'

Victorine fled, taking as much joy with her as she had previously born grief in her life. Poor girl! A squeeze of her hand, Rastignac's hair brushing her cheek, a word spoken so close to her ear that she had felt the heat of the student's lips, her waist clasped by a trembling arm, a stolen kiss on her neck – these were the pledges of her passion, that the threat of nearby big Sylvie, likely to enter that glorious dining room at any time, made all the more ardent, intense, seductive than the most elaborate expressions of love found in the most famous love stories. These *first favours*, in the quaint words of our forebears, seem like crimes to a devout young lady who goes to Confession every fortnight! In one hour, she had poured out more of her soul's treasures than she would in later years, when she surrendered herself completely, rich and happy.

'It's in the bag,' said Vautrin to Eugène. 'Our two dandies have locked horns. Everything has gone according to plan. A difference of opinion. That pigeon of ours has called out my hawk. Tomorrow, city walls, Clignancourt. At half past eight, while she sits here quietly dipping bread and butter fingers in her coffee, Mademoiselle Taillefer will inherit her father's love and fortune. Isn't that the funniest thing? Young Taillefer is an excellent swordsman, he's as sure of himself as a man with a four-ace hand; but we'll bleed him with a stroke I invented myself, a trick of tilting up the sword and pinking your man's forehead. I'll show you that thrust of mine; it's damned useful.'

Rastignac listened like a man in a trance, incapable of replying. At this point old man Goriot, Bianchon and some of the other boarders came in.

'That's the man I thought you were,' Vautrin said to him. 'You know what you're doing. Good work, little eaglet! You'll be a ruler of men yet; you're strong, unswerving, stout of heart: you have my respect.'

Vautrin reached out to take his hand. Rastignac abruptly

withdrew his own, turned white and sank onto a chair, with the vision of a pool of blood before him.

'I see! So we're still clinging to the virtue-stained rags of our swaddling clothes,' said Vautrin in a low voice. 'Papa d'Oliban has three million; I know what he's worth. The dowry will wash you as white as a bridal gown, even in your own eyes.'

Rastignac made up his mind. He resolved to go and warn Taillefer father and son some time that evening. As Vautrin left, old man Goriot whispered in Eugène's ear: 'You look sad, dear child! I have something to cheer you up. Come with me!' And the old vermicelli dealer lit his wax taper at one of the lamps. Eugène followed him, burning with curiosity.

'Go into your room,' said the old fellow, who had asked Sylvie for the student's key. 'This morning you thought she didn't love you, eh!' he continued. 'She sent you on your way and you left her feeling angry and desperate. You ninny! She was waiting for me. Do you understand now? We had to go and put the final touches to a gem of an apartment which will be ready for you to live in in three days from now. Don't let on I told. She wants to surprise you; but I can't keep it from you any longer. You'll be in the Rue d'Artois, a stone's throw from the Rue Saint-Lazare. You'll live like a prince there. We've had it fitted out with furniture worthy of a bride. We've done plenty this past month, without saying a word to you. My solicitor has set to work: my daughter will have her thirty-six thousand francs per year, the interest on her dowry, and I'm going to see that her eight hundred thousand francs are invested in good, solid property.'

Eugène remained silent and paced up and down, arms folded, in his shabby, untidy room. Choosing a moment when the student had his back to him, Old Goriot placed on the mantelpiece a red morocco-leather box on which the Rastignac coat-of-arms was embossed in gold.

'My dear child,' said the poor old fellow; 'I'm in this affair up to my neck. But, you see, I also have a selfish reason to be interested in your change of quarters. You won't refuse me, now, if I ask you for something?'

'What is it you want?'

'Above your apartment, on the fifth floor, is a connecting bedroom. That's where I'll stay, if I may? I'm getting old; I live too far from my daughters. I wouldn't trouble you. I'd just be there. You'd tell me about them every night. You wouldn't mind doing that, would you? When you come back, I'll be in bed, I'll hear you, I'll say to myself: "He has just seen my little Delphine. He took her to the ball, he has made her happy." If I were ill, it would gladden my heart to hear you coming in, bustling around, going out. There will be so much of my daughter in you! I'd only be a short step away from the Champs-Elysées; I'd be able to see them drive past every day, where now I sometimes turn up too late. And then perhaps she'll come and see you! I'll hear her, I'll see her wrapped up warm in her morning gown, treading softly as a little cat. This last month, she has become the girl she was before, carefree and blithe. Her soul is on the mend, she owes her happiness to you. Oh! I would give you the earth. When we were on our way back, she said: "Papa, I'm so very happy!" When they stand on ceremony and call me *Father*, it makes my blood run cold; but when they say *Papa*, it's as if I'm seeing my little girls again, all my memories come flooding back. I feel more like their father. I convince myself they still don't belong to anyone!' (The poor old fellow wiped his eyes, weeping.) 'I hadn't heard her call me that for a long time; it seems an age since she last gave me her arm. Dear me, yes, it's ten years since I walked beside one of my daughters. How I love to feel her dress brush against me, to walk at her pace, to share her warmth! This morning, I escorted Delphine everywhere. I went into shops with her. And I brought her back home. Oh! Let me stay close to you both. You'll need someone to help you out from time to time: I'll be there. Oh, if only that great lump of an Alsatian would die; if his gout had the sense to rise into his stomach, my poor daughter would be happy. You would be my son-in-law, you would become her husband in the eyes of all. Bah! Her ignorance of the pleasures of this world is making her so unhappy that I forgive her everything. The good Lord must be on the side of loving fathers.'

After a pause he said, 'She's in love with you all right!' nodding his head. 'On the way there, she kept saying: "He's a good

man, Father, isn't he! He has a kind heart! Does he talk about
me?" Why, she hardly stopped for breath once between the
Rue d'Artois and the Passage des Panoramas! She poured out
her heart into mine. For one whole wonderful morning, I wasn't
old any more, I was as light as a feather. I told her you had
given me the thousand-franc note. Oh! The sweet girl, she was
moved to tears. Now then, what have you got there on your
mantelpiece?' said old man Goriot finally, dying of impatience,
seeing Rastignac standing stock still.

Eugène, stunned, looked at his neighbour with a dazed
expression. The duel, announced by Vautrin for the next day,
presented such a brutal contrast to the fulfilment of his dearest
hopes that he felt as if he was in a nightmare. He turned to face
the mantelpiece, noticed the little square box, opened it and
inside found a piece of paper tucked around a Bréguet watch.
On the piece of paper was written:

'*I want you to think of me every hour of the day*, because . . .
   DELPHINE.'

This last word no doubt referred to some scene which had
taken place between them. Eugène was moved to tears. His
coat-of-arms was enamelled onto the gold inside the watch
case. This piece of jewellery, coveted for so long, the chain, the
key, the craftsmanship, the design, was everything he could have
wished for. Old Goriot was radiant. He had no doubt promised
to report back to his daughter every last detail of the surprise
her gift would give Eugène, for he was a party to their first flush
of feeling and felt no less happy than they did. He already loved
Rastignac, for his daughter's sake, and for his own.

'You must go and see her this evening; she'll be waiting for
you. That great lump of an Alsatian is dining late with his dancer. Ha ha! What a fool he looked when my solicitor gave him
the hard facts. So he claims to worship my daughter? If he lays
a finger on her, I'll kill him. The very idea that my Delphine
belongs to . . .' (he sighed) '. . . is enough to drive me to crime;
but you couldn't call it homicide – the man is a calf's head on a
pig's body. You will take me with you, won't you?'

'Yes, dear old Goriot, you know how fond I am of you . . .'

'I can see that; you're not ashamed of me, at least! Let me embrace you.' And he hugged the student tightly. 'Promise me that you really will make her happy! You'll go to her this evening, won't you?'

'Oh, yes! Although I have to go out and attend to some pressing business.'

'Might I be able to help?'

'Why, yes! While I go and see Madame de Nucingen, perhaps you could call on the elder Monsieur Taillefer and ask him to spare me a moment this evening to discuss a matter of the utmost importance.'

'So it's true then, young man,' said old man Goriot, his expression changing, 'that you're courting his daughter, as those fools downstairs have been saying? Hell-fire! Have you any idea how hard a Goriot fist can hit? And if you were to deceive us both, it would come to blows. Oh! It's unthinkable.'

'I swear to you, there's only one woman in the world that I love,' said the student; 'I only realized it quite recently.'

'Ah, now you've made me happy!' exclaimed old man Goriot.

'But', the student went on, 'Taillefer's son is to fight a duel tomorrow, and I've heard it said that he'll be killed.'

'What is it to you?' said Goriot.

'Why, he has to be told to stop his son from going . . .' cried Eugène.

At this point, he was interrupted by Vautrin, whose voice was heard at the door of his room, singing:

'*Oh Richard, oh my King!*
The whole world has deserted you.[170]
Broom! broom! broom! broom! broom!
I've been a-roving all over the world
And I've been seen . . .
Tra la, la, la, la . . .'

'Gentlemen!' shouted Christophe, 'the soup is ready and we're waiting for you; everyone else is sitting down.'

'Ah, there you are!' said Vautrin; 'come up here and bring down a bottle of my Bordeaux.'

'It's a handsome watch, isn't it?' said old man Goriot. 'She's got good taste, eh?'

Vautrin, old Goriot and Rastignac went downstairs at the same time and, as they were all late, found themselves sitting next to each other at the dinner table. Eugène pointedly gave Vautrin the cold shoulder throughout dinner, even though that man, whom Madame Vauquer found so very agreeable, had never been so entertaining. He sparkled with wit and put all his fellow guests in good spirits. His confidence and composure filled Eugène with dismay.

'Well, you certainly got out of bed on the right side today,' Madame Vauquer said to him. 'You're as happy as a lark.'

'I'm always happy when I've done a good deal.'

'Deal?' asked Eugène.

'Why, yes. I've delivered an instalment of goods, which ought to earn me a fine commission. Mademoiselle Michonneau,' he said, becoming aware of the spinster's scrutiny; 'is there something about my face you don't like for you to turn your beady eye on me like that? Say the word! I'll change it to please you.

'Poiret, we won't fall out over this one, eh?' he said, out-staring the elderly clerk.

'Strewth! You could model as a clown and strongman,' said the young painter to Vautrin.

'Why not! As long as Mademoiselle Michonneau will pose as the Père-Lachaise Venus,' replied Vautrin.

'And Poiret?' said Bianchon.

'Oh! Poiret will pose as Poiret. He'll be the god of gardens!' quipped Vautrin. 'Deriving from pear . . .'

'Rot!' retorted Bianchon. 'Leaving you to come between the pear and the cheese.'

'Now, that's enough nonsense,' said Madame Vauquer; 'you'd be better off opening that bottle of Bordeaux wine of yours which I can see poking its nose out! That would perk us all up, besides being good for the *flabbergastation*.'

'Gentlemen,' said Vautrin, 'Her Honour is calling us to order. Madame Couture and Mademoiselle Victorine won't mind our banter; but have some respect for the innocence of old man Goriot. How about a nice *bottle-orama* of Bordeaux, going by the name of Laffitte and therefore twice as famous, although of course politics doesn't come into it.[171] Come along, cork-brain!' he said looking at Christophe, who didn't move. 'Over here, Christophe! What, can't you even hear your own name? Bring the fluids, cork-brain!'

'Here you are, sir,' said Christophe, presenting the bottle.

After filling Eugène's glass and that of old man Goriot, he slowly poured himself a few drops which he tasted as his two neighbours were drinking, and then suddenly made a face.

'Damn! damn! It's corked. Take it for yourself, Christophe, and go and fetch us some more; on the right, you know where I mean? There are sixteen of us; bring down eight bottles.'

'Seeing as you're shelling out,' said the painter, 'I'll pay for a hundred chestnuts.'

'Ho ho!'

'Boo!'

'Prrrr!'

Exclamations shot from all sides like rockets from a Catherine wheel.

'Go on, Ma Vauquer, two of your champagne,' Vautrin shouted across to her.

'Hah, that's right! Why not ask for the house? Two of your champagne! At twelve francs apiece! I don't earn enough, indeed I don't! But if Monsieur Eugène wants to pay for them, I'll throw in some cassis.'

'That cassis of hers clears you out like manna,'[172] said the medical student under his breath.

'Do be quiet, Bianchon,' exclaimed Rastignac. 'Whenever you mention manna it makes my stomach ... Yes, bring out the champagne, I'll pay for it,' added the student.

'Sylvie,' said Madame Vauquer, 'hand around the biscuits and little cakes.'

'Your little cakes have grown too big,' said Vautrin; 'they have beards. But let's have your biscuits.'

Before long, the Bordeaux was being passed around; the boarders came to life, their spirits rose twice as high. Raucous laughter was heard, suddenly cut across by a series of mimicked

animal calls. When the museum clerk took it into his head to
reproduce a Paris street-cry resembling nothing so much as the
screeching of a lovesick cat, eight voices simultaneously bawled
out the following phrases: 'Knives to grind!' – 'Chi-icky chick-
weed for your songbirds!' – 'Cream horns, ladies, cream
horns!' – 'China to mend?' – 'Oysters, oysters!' – 'Beat your
wives, beat your clothes!' – 'Old braid, hats or coats!' – 'Ripe
cherry ripe!' Bianchon brought the house down with his nasal
cry of 'Umbrella seller!' In no time at all, there was a head-
splitting row, with everyone talking at once, a live opera
conducted by Vautrin, with one eye on Eugène and old Goriot,
who already seemed the worse for wear. Leaning back in their
chairs, they watched the unusually raucous proceedings with a
serious air, drinking little; both were thinking about what they
had to do that evening and yet neither felt able to stand up.
Vautrin, following each change in their appearance with sidelong glances, chose the moment when their eyelids were
fluttering and starting to close, to lean over and murmur in
Rastignac's ear: 'A clever boy we might be, but we ain't cunning enough to outwit our uncle Vautrin, and he's too fond of
you to let you go and do something foolish. Once I've set my
mind on a thing, only the Almighty is strong enough to stop
me. Hah! So we wanted to go and warn old Taillefer, did we,
snitch like a schoolboy? The oven's hot, the flour's kneaded,
the bread's on the shovel; tomorrow we'll bite into it and
make the crumbs fly over our heads; and we want to stop it
going into the oven . . . ? No, no, we'll bake it, every bit! If
we happen to have a few little pangs of remorse, digestion
will soon take care of them. While we're having forty winks,
Colonel Comte Franchessini, with the tip of his sword, will
drop Michel Taillefer's estate into your lap. As her brother's
inheritor, Victorine will receive the tidy sum of fifteen thousand
francs per year. I've already made my enquiries and I know
that her mother's estate is worth more than three hundred
thousand . . .'

Eugène heard but could not reply to these words: his tongue
was stuck to his palate and he felt overwhelmed by drowsiness;
he could only just make out the table and the other boarders'

faces through a bright fog. The rumpus gradually abated and, one by one, the boarders left the room. Then, when only Madame Vauquer, Madame Couture, Mademoiselle Victorine, Vautrin and old Goriot were left, Rastignac, as if in a dream, became aware of Madame Vauquer busily emptying out the dregs of the old bottles to make full new ones.

'Dear me! So wild, so young!' said the widow.

This was the last phrase that Eugène managed to take in.

'Only Monsieur Vautrin could have pulled off a stunt like that,' said Sylvie. 'Just look at Christophe snoring like a pig.'

'Farewell, Ma,' said Vautrin. 'I'm off to the boulevard to admire Monsieur Marty in *Wild Mountain*, a fine play based on *The Loner*. I'll take you, if you like, along with these ladies.'

'Thank you, but no,' said Madame Couture.

'What, neighbour!' cried Madame Vauquer; 'you're turning down the chance to see a play based on *The Loner*, by Atala de Chateaubriand,[173] which we enjoyed reading more than anything, which was so pretty that we cried our eyes out over Elodie under the *ly-ums* last summer, indeed, a moral work which might be instructive for your young lady?'

'We aren't allowed to go to the theatre,' replied Victorine.

'Well, those two are certainly out for the count,' said Vautrin, comically waggling old Goriot's and Eugène's heads. Then, moving the student's head and setting it down on the chair so he could sleep comfortably, he kissed him warmly on the forehead, singing:

'Sleep, sleep, sweet loves!
I'll watch over you for ever.'[174]

'I hope he's not ill,' said Victorine.

'In that case, you should stay and look after him,' replied Vautrin. 'That', he breathed in her ear, 'is your duty as a good little woman. The young man adores you and you'll be his sweet wife, that's my prediction. In the end,' he continued aloud, '*they were loved throughout the land, had lots of children and lived happily ever after*. That's the way all love stories end. Come along Ma,' he said, turning to Madame Vauquer and putting an arm round her; 'put on your hat, that pretty dress with the flowers and the comtesse's scarf. Meanwhile

Himself will go and find a carriage for you.' And he left, singing:

'*Sun, sun, glorious sun,*
You who ripen all the pumpkins . . .'

'Dear me! Madame Couture, I swear that man would make me happy if I had to live on the roof. As for him,' she said, turning towards the vermicelli dealer, 'that old niggard never thought to take me *nowhere*. Well, he's going to come down to earth with a bump, he is! A man of his age losing his faculties, it's indecent, that's what it is! Next you'll be telling me you never lose what you never had. Sylvie, take him up to his room.'

Sylvie held the old man under his arms, made him walk and threw him fully dressed across his bed like a parcel.

'Poor young man,' said Madame Couture, parting Eugène's hair to stop it falling into his eyes; 'he's like a young girl, he doesn't know the meaning of excess.'

'Ah! Let me tell you, in the thirty-one years I've run this boarding house,' said Madame Vauquer, 'plenty of young men have been through my hands, so to speak; but I've never seen one as kind, as genteel as Monsieur Eugène. How handsome he looks, asleep! Put his head on your shoulder, Madame Couture. A-ha! He's fallen onto Mademoiselle Victorine's: there's a god for children. A bit further over and he'd have banged his head on the chair top. They make a fine couple, the two of them.'

'Dear neighbour, do please be quiet,' cried Madame Couture; 'you musn't say such things . . .'

'Pah!' retorted Madame Vauquer; 'he can't hear. Now Sylvie, come and help me dress. I'm going to wear my long-waisted corset.'

'Very good! Your long-waisted corset, on a full stomach, Madame,' said Sylvie. 'No, you'll have to find someone else to lace you in, I won't be your murderer. A piece of foolishness like that could cost you your life.'

'I don't care. I must do Monsieur Vautrin credit.'

'Do you love your heirs that dearly?'

'Come along, Sylvie, stop arguing,' said the widow as she went out.

'At her age too,' the cook said to Victorine, gesturing after her mistress.

Madame Couture and her ward, upon whose shoulder Eugène was fast asleep, were left alone in the dining room. Christophe's snoring echoed through the silent building, making Eugène's breathing seem all the more peaceful: he slept with the grace of a child. Glad to be able to permit herself one of those acts of kindness through which a woman gives vent to her feelings, one which allowed her to sense, without guilt, the young man's heart beating next to her own, Victorine took on a protective, maternal air, which made her look proud. A surge of sensual delight suddenly broke across the thousand emotions swelling her heart, stirred by the pure, youthful heat passing between them.

'Poor, dear girl!' said Madame Couture, pressing her hand.

The old lady looked with wonder and affection at that candid and long-suffering face, upon which a halo of happiness had now descended. Victorine resembled one of those naive medieval paintings, whose artist ignores all that is incidental and saves the magic of his brush – those calm, proud strokes – for the face, painted a shade of yellow, but in which the golden rays of heaven seem to be reflected.

'But he can't have drunk more than two glasses, Mama,' said Victorine, running her fingers through Eugène's thick hair.

'Well, if he was truly debauched, Daughter, he'd have held his wine like all the others. His drunkenness does him credit.'

The sound of a carriage was heard in the street.

'Mama,' said the young lady, 'Monsieur Vautrin is coming. Please move Monsieur Eugène over to your side. I don't want that man to see me like this: he says things that taint the soul and his looks make a woman feel as uncomfortable as if he were undressing her.'

'Not at all,' said Madame Couture, 'you're mistaken! Monsieur Vautrin is a decent man, not unlike the late Monsieur Couture: brusque but good, gruff but kind.'

Vautrin came in softly on cue and looked at the pretty scene made by the young man and woman, caught in the caressing glow of the lamp.

'Well, well,' he said, crossing his arms, 'here's a scene that
would have inspired some fine pages from the good Bernardin
de Saint-Pierre, who wrote *Paul et Virginie*.[175] Youth is a beautiful thing, Madame Couture. Sleep, poor child,' he said, looking
at Eugène; 'good things sometimes happen while we sleep.
Madame,' he continued, addressing the widow, 'what draws
me to this young man, what moves me, is knowing that his soul
is matched in beauty only by his face. Look, isn't he the picture
of a cherub leaning on an angel's shoulder? Now there's a man
who deserves to be loved! If I were a woman, I'd want to die . . .
(no, that would be foolish) . . . live for him. Looking at them
like this, Madame,' he murmured in the widow's ear, leaning in
close, 'I can't help thinking that God has made them for each
other. Providence moves in mysterious ways, plumbs the depths
of hearts and minds,' he said aloud. 'Seeing you together, children, united by the same purity, by every human feeling, it
seems impossible that you should ever be parted in future. God
is just. Now,' he said to the girl, 'I think I've seen your lines
of prosperity before. Will you let me look at your hand,
Mademoiselle Victorine? I know a bit about palm reading, I've
often told people's fortunes. Come along, don't be afraid. Oh!
what do I see here? I swear, as I'm an honest man, that you'll
soon be one of the richest heiresses in Paris. You'll shower the
man you love with happiness. Your father will call for you to
be near him. You'll marry a titled and handsome young man
who adores you.'

At this point, Vautrin's prophecies were interrupted by the
heavy tread of the coquettish widow coming down the stairs.

'Here comes Ma Vauquer, glittering like a star, rolled as tight
as a cigar. Aren't we suffocating, just a little?' he said, placing
his hand at the top of her stays; 'that's a well-trussed breast,
Ma. If we start crying, there'll be an explosion, but I'll pick up
the pieces as carefully as any archaeologist.'

'Now there's a man knows the language of French gallantry!'
hissed the widow in Madame Couture's ear.

'Farewell, children,' continued Vautrin, turning towards
Eugène and Victorine. 'You have my blessing,' he said, laying
his hands on their heads. 'Believe me, Mademoiselle, an honest

man's vows do count; they're bound to bring good luck, as God hears them.'

'Farewell, dear friend,' said Madame Vauquer to her lodger. 'Do you think', she added in a low voice, 'that Monsieur Vautrin has intentions towards my person?'

'Ahem, er . . . !'

'Ah! dearest Mother,' said Victorine, sighing and looking at her hands, when the two women were alone; 'if only good Monsieur Vautrin was speaking the truth!'

'Well, it wouldn't take much', replied the old lady, 'just for that monster of a brother of yours to fall off his horse.'

'Mother!'

'Goodness, perhaps it's a sin to wish your enemy ill,' continued the widow. 'Well, I'll do penance for it. In all honesty, I'll happily put flowers on his grave. The miserable coward! He's not brave enough to stand up for his mother and he's cheating you out of your share of her inheritance so he can keep it all for himself. My cousin had a huge fortune. It's just bad luck for you that her share wasn't noted in the marriage contract.'

'I couldn't bear my own happiness if it cost someone else their life,' said Victorine. 'And if, to be happy, my brother had to disappear, I'd still rather be here.'

'Lord above, as good Monsieur Vautrin says, and he's a religious man, as you've seen,' continued Madame Couture. 'I was pleased to learn he's not an unbeliever like the others. The way they talk, they seem to have more respect for the devil than for God. Well, who knows which paths Providence will lead us down?'

With Sylvie's help, the two women ended up carrying Eugène to his room, where they laid him down on his bed and the cook loosened his clothes to make him comfortable. As they left, when her guardian had her back turned, Victorine placed a kiss on Eugène's forehead with as much pleasure as this petty theft could bring her. She looked around his room, scooped up the thousand joys of the day in a single thought, so to speak, and made it into a picture that she studied at length before falling asleep the happiest creature in Paris.

The festivities, which Vautrin had used as a cover to lace Eugène and old man Goriot's wine, were his downfall. Bianchon, somewhat tipsy, forgot to ask Mademoiselle Michonneau about Cat-o'-Nine-Lives. Had he spoken that name aloud, he would certainly have alerted Vautrin, or, to give him his real name, Jacques Collin, the celebrated convict. Then, being nicknamed the Père-Lachaise Venus made Mademoiselle Michonneau decide to shop the convict, just at the point when, in anticipation of his generosity, she was weighing up whether she might be better off warning him and letting him escape during the night. She had just gone out, Poiret at her side, to meet the famous Chief of the Sûreté, in the Petite Rue Sainte-Anne, still believing herself to be dealing with a senior official by the name of Gondureau. The head of the detective division gave her a charming reception. Once they had settled the final details, Mademoiselle Michonneau asked for the potion she would use to carry out her mission and check for the brand. Judging by the satisfaction with which the great man of the Petite Rue Sainte-Anne reached into the drawer of his desk and took out the phial, Mademoiselle Michonneau guessed that there was more at stake in this raid than the straightforward arrest of a convict. After racking her brains, she began to suspect that the police had been tipped off by certain disclosures made by traitors in the penal colony and hoped to arrive in time to seize substantial sums of money. When she put her hypothesis to the old fox, he started to smile and tried to deflect the spinster's suspicions.

'You're mistaken,' he replied. 'Collin is the most dangerous *sorbonne* the thieves have ever had on their side. There's the long and short of it. Those rascals are well aware of that; he's their banner, their backer, their Bonaparte, even; they love him, one and all. That fellow will never leave his *tronche* behind on the Place de Grève.'

As Mademoiselle Michonneau hadn't understood, Gondureau explained the two slang words he had used. *Sorbonne* and *tronche* are two colourful expressions in the cant of thieves, who, above and ahead of anyone else, have felt the necessity of considering the human head from two angles. The *sorbonne* is the head of the living man, his counsel, his thought processes. The *tronche* is a derogatory word intended to express how worthless the head becomes when it is cut off.

'Collin is playing with us,' he continued. 'When we come across a man like this, as unbending as a bar of tempered English steel, we have the option of killing him if he takes it into his head to put up the slightest resistance during his arrest. We're banking on there being a little assault and battery so we can kill Collin tomorrow morning. That way we'll avoid the trial, the cost of feeding and keeping him in custody and society will be shot of him. Serving writs, subpoena-ing witnesses, remunerating them, the cost of the execution, every legal step taken to rid us of such a rascal costs far more than the thousand écus that you'll be given. It saves time. With one swift bayonet thrust in the belly of Cat-o'-Nine-Lives, we prevent a hundred crimes and avoid the spectacle of fifty bad eggs being bribed to hang around the magistrate's court, as if butter wouldn't melt in their mouths. There's good policing for you. As any true philanthropist will tell you, it's the only way to prevent crime.'

'Why, *that's* how to serve your country,' said Poiret.

'Well, well,' retorted the chief, 'you're talking sense tonight! Yes, of course, we're serving our country. Which is why the world does us such injustice. We render many a great service to society that goes unrecognized. In the end, a superior man must rise above prejudice and a Christian must bear the misfortunes that follow in the wake of good deeds which fail to conform to received ideas. Paris is Paris, you see. In those three words you have the story of my life. Your humble servant, Mademoiselle, and farewell. Tomorrow I'll be at the Jardin du Roi with my men. Send Christophe to Monsieur Gondureau's house in the Rue de Buffon, where you saw me last. Your servant, Monsieur. Should anyone ever steal anything from you, you can rely on me to recover it, I'm at your service.'

'Well,' said Poiret to Mademoiselle Michonneau, 'you meet some fools who get in a flap as soon as they hear the word police. That gentleman has a delightful manner and what he wants you to do is as easy as pie.'

The next day was to rank as one of the most extraordinary days in the history of the Maison Vauquer. Up until then, the most striking event in its peaceful existence had been the meteoric appearance of the fake Comtesse de l'Ambermesnil. But everything else would pale into insignificance next to the peripeteia of that momentous day, which was to become Madame Vauquer's pet topic of conversation *ad infinitum*. For a start, Goriot and Eugène de Rastignac slept in until eleven. Madame Vauquer, having returned from the Gaîté[176] at midnight, stayed in bed until half past ten. Christophe, having drunk to the last drop the wine Vautrin had given him, overslept, which meant that the *déjeuner* service was late. Neither Poiret nor Mademoiselle Michonneau complained about the meal being pushed back. As for Victorine and Madame Couture, they slept in. Vautrin went out before eight and came back just as the table was laid up. So no one grumbled when, at around a quarter past eleven, Sylvie and Christophe knocked on everyone's door to announce that *déjeuner* was served. While Sylvie and the servant were out of the room, Mademoiselle Michonneau, coming down ahead of the others, poured the liquor into Vautrin's silver beaker, which held the cream for his coffee and was being warmed up in the bain-marie along with the others. The spinster had counted on this peculiarity of the house to strike her blow. It took a while before the seven lodgers were finally assembled. Eugène, stretching himself, came down last of all, at which point a messenger handed him a letter from Madame de Nucingen. The letter read as follows:

'*Dear friend, I feel neither false pride nor anger towards you. I waited up for you until two in the morning. Anyone who has known the torture of waiting for a loved one will never inflict it on another. I can certainly tell that this is the first time you've been in love. Had I not been wary of revealing the deepest secrets of my heart, I'd have set out to discover what had become of you, for better or for worse. But, if I'd left the house that late, whether on foot or in my carriage, surely it would have been my ruin? How frustrated I felt, how unfortunate, to be a woman.*

Reassure me, explain why you didn't come, after everything that Father told you. I may be vexed, but I will forgive you. Are you ill? I wish you didn't live so far away. A single word, for pity's sake. I'll hear from you soon, shan't I? A single word will do if you're busy. Write: "I'm on my way now" or "I'm poorly". But if you were ill, my father would have come and told me! So whatever has happened? . . .'

'Yes, whatever has happened?' Eugène exclaimed, rushing into the dining room and crumpling the letter without finishing it. 'What time is it?'

'Half eleven,' said Vautrin, dropping sugar into his coffee.

The escaped convict shot Eugène one of those coldly mesmerizing looks that some powerfully magnetic men have the knack of giving, and which, it is said, can pacify raving lunatics in asylums. Eugène trembled in every limb. The sound of a carriage was heard in the street and a servant in Monsieur Taillefer's livery, whom Madame Couture recognized straightaway, rushed in, looking aghast.

'Mademoiselle,' he cried, 'your father wants to see you. A terrible thing has happened. Monsieur Frédéric has fought a duel, he's taken a blow to the forehead, the doctors despair of saving him; you'll barely have time to bid him farewell, he's unconscious.'

'Poor young man!' exclaimed Vautrin. 'What does anyone find to quarrel about on an allowance of thirty thousand livres? Really, young people have no idea how to behave.'

'Monsieur!' Eugène shouted at him.

'Well, what is it, child?' said Vautrin, calmly drinking the last of his coffee, a process which Mademoiselle Michonneau was scrutizing far too closely to be moved by the extraordinary event which had left everyone else stunned. 'Aren't duels fought every day in Paris?'

'I'll come with you, Victorine,' said Madame Couture.

And the two women flew out of the room without hats or shawls. Before leaving, Victorine, her eyes brimming, looked at Eugène as if to say: 'I didn't think our happiness would cost me tears!'

'Well I never! You're quite a prophet, Monsieur Vautrin,' said Madame Vauquer.

'I'm everything,' he said.

'How very odd!' continued Madame Vauquer, pronouncing a string of meaningless comments on the event. Death takes us without asking. The young often go before the old. We women are lucky not to have to fight duels, but we suffer hardships that men don't. We have children and the trials of motherhood are never ending! What a stroke of good luck for Victorine! Her father will have no choice but to recognize her now.'

'So!' said Vautrin, looking at Eugène, 'yesterday she was penniless, this morning she's worth millions.'

'Well, Monsieur Eugène,' cried Madame Vauquer, 'you've got your hand in the right jar there.'

Hearing this remark, old man Goriot looked at the student and saw the crumpled letter in his hand.

'You haven't finished it! What does that mean? That you're just like the others?' he reproached him.

'Madame, I will never marry Mademoiselle Victorine,' Eugène said pointedly to Madame Vauquer, with a look of horror and disgust that surprised them all.

Old Goriot took the student's hand and shook it, then tried to kiss it.

'Is that so!' retorted Vautrin. 'The Italians have a clever saying: *col tempo!*'[177]

'I'm to wait for your answer,' Madame de Nucingen's messenger said to Rastignac.

'Say that I'm on my way.'

The man left. Eugène was in such a state of violent agitation that he forgot the need for caution. 'What shall I do?' he said to himself aloud, without thinking. 'There's absolutely no evidence!'

Vautrin started to smile. At the same time the potion absorbed by his stomach began to take effect. Nonetheless, the convict was so tough that he stood up, looked at Rastignac and said in a hollow voice: 'Young man, good things happen while we sleep.'

Then he fell to the ground with a thud.

'Divine justice does exist,' said Eugène.

'Gracious, what's the matter with poor dear Monsieur Vautrin?'

'An apoplectic fit,' cried Mademoiselle Michonneau.

'Sylvie, hurry girl, go and fetch the doctor,' cried the widow. 'Ah! Monsieur Rastignac, quickly, go and get Monsieur Bianchon; Sylvie may not be able to find our doctor, Monsieur Grimprel.'

Rastignac, relieved to have an excuse to leave that chamber of horrors, took his leave at a run.

'Christophe, quickly, trot to the chemist and ask for something for an apoplectic fit.'

Christophe went out.

'Well, what are you waiting for, old man Goriot, help us take him up to his room.'

Vautrin was lifted, manoeuvred up the stairs and laid on his bed.

'I'm no good to you here, I must go and see my daughter,' said old Goriot.

'Selfish old man!' cried Madame Vauquer; 'go on then, and I hope you die like a dog.'

'Go and see if you can find some ether,' said Mademoiselle Michonneau to Madame Vauquer, who, helped by Poiret, had already loosened Vautrin's clothes.

Madame Vauquer went downstairs to her room, leaving Mademoiselle Michonneau mistress of the field.

'Come on, take off his shirt and turn him over, quickly! Make yourself useful for once and spare me the sight of his nudities,' she said to Poiret. 'Don't just stand there with your mouth open.'

With Vautrin face down, Mademoiselle Michonneau gave the sick man a sharp smack on the shoulder, and the two fateful letters stood out in white against the red patch of skin.

'Well, that's your three thousand francs earned with ease,' exclaimed Poiret, holding Vautrin up while Mademoiselle Michonneau put his shirt back on. 'Phew, he's a deadweight,' he continued, laying him down again.

'Be quiet. What if there's a cash-box?' said the spinster

eagerly, subjecting every last stick of furniture in the room to such intense scrutiny that her eyes seemed to pierce the walls. 'Perhaps we could open this writing desk, if we think of an excuse?' she continued.

'Perhaps that would be wrong,' replied Poiret.

'No. Stolen money, having belonged to everyone, no longer belongs to anyone. But there's not enough time,' she replied. 'I can hear Ma Vauquer.'

'Here's the ether,' said Madame Vauquer. 'My, oh my, what a day; it never rains but it pours. Gracious! That man can't be ill, he's as white as a chicken.'

'A chicken?' repeated Poiret.

'His heart's beating steadily,' said the widow, placing her hand on his heart.

'Steadily?' said Poiret, surprised.

'There's nothing wrong with him.'

'You think so?' asked Poiret.

'Why, yes! He looks like he's sleeping. Sylvie has gone to find a doctor. Look at that, Mademoiselle Michonneau, he's sniffing the ether. Humph! It's just a *pass-'im* (a spasm). His pulse is fine. He's as strong as a Turk. Just look at that thick mat of hair on his stomach, Mademoiselle; he'll live for a hundred years, that man! His wig has stayed on well, considering. Look, it's stuck on, he's got false hair; look how red it is underneath. They say that redheads are all good or all bad! He must be good.'

'For hanging,' said Poiret.

'Round the neck of a pretty woman, you mean,' snapped Mademoiselle Michonneau. 'Off you go now, Monsieur Poiret. We ladies must look after you men when you're ill. For all the use you are, you might as well go for a walk,' she added. 'Madame Vauquer and I will take care of poor dear Monsieur Vautrin.'

Poiret went off meekly and without a murmur, like a dog whose master has just given it a kick.

Rastignac had gone out to walk around, to get some fresh air: he could hardly breathe. Last night he'd wanted to stop this crime, committed at a set time. What had happened to him? What should he do? He trembled to think that he was an accessory to the act. Vautrin's sang-froid still terrified him.

'And if Vautrin were to die without talking?' Rastignac said to himself.

He hurried along the avenues of the Jardin du Luxembourg as if he had a pack of dogs at his heels and could hear them barking.

'Hey!' Bianchon shouted over to him; 'have you seen the *Pilote*?'

The *Pilote* was a radical paper edited by Monsieur Tissot, which came out in a provincial edition a few hours after the morning papers, thus bringing the day's news to the regions twenty-four hours ahead of the other papers.

'There's a cracking story in it,' said the Cochin hospital[178] house doctor. 'Taillefer's son fought a duel with Comte Franchessini, of the Old Guard, who stuck two inches of steel in his head. So our little Victorine is now one of the richest and most eligible women in Paris. How about that? If only we'd known. What a gamble death is, a regular round of Rouge-et-Noir![179] Is it true that Victorine had a soft spot for you?'

'Enough, Bianchon. I'll never marry her. I love a sweet woman, she loves me, I . . .'

'You sound as if you're having a job convincing yourself to be faithful. Show me the woman worth sacrificing old Taillefer's wealth for.'

'So every demon in hell is after me now?' Rastignac cried to himself.

'Why, whatever's the matter with you? Are you mad? Give me your hand,' said Bianchon; 'let me feel your pulse. You're feverish.'

'You're needed at Ma Vauquer's,' Eugène said to him; 'that old rascal Vautrin has just dropped down dead, at least, that's how it looked.'

'A-ha!' said Bianchon, leaving Rastignac on his own; 'you've confirmed suspicions that I'd like to look into myself.'

The law student's walk was long and sobering. He surveyed his conscience from every angle. True, he vacillated, doubted himself, hesitated, but in the end his integrity came out of this grim and terrible discussion intact, like an iron rod which has withstood every assault upon it. He remembered the secrets that old man Goriot had told him the previous evening, he recalled the apartment chosen for him, near Delphine, in the Rue d'Artois; he took up her letter, read it again, kissed it. 'A love like that will be my sheet anchor,'[180] he said to himself. 'That poor old man's heart has caused him terrible suffering. He never speaks of his sorrows, but anyone can see what they are! Well, I'll look after him like a father, I'll give him a thousand reasons to be happy. If she loves me, she'll often come to see me and spend the day near him. The Comtesse de Restaud, for all her grand airs, is despicable; her father might as well be her porter. Dearest Delphine! She's kinder to the old fellow, she deserves to be loved. Ah! This evening I'll be lucky, at last!' He took out the watch and admired it. 'Everything has turned out well for me! When two people love each other for all time, they have every right to help each other; I'm allowed to accept this. Besides, I'm bound to succeed and will be able to pay it back a hundred times over. Our liaison has nothing criminal about it, nothing that even the most virtuous woman might raise an eyebrow at. How many respectable people favour this kind of arrangement! We aren't deceiving anyone, and lies are what degrade a person most. Surely to lie is to deny all responsibility? She and her husband have been living apart for some time now. What's more, I, Rastignac, will tell that Alsatian to relinquish his claims to a woman he's incapable of making happy.'

Rastignac tussled with himself for a long time. Although youthful virtue emerged victorious, at nightfall, as the clock struck half past four, an overwhelming urge to satisfy his curiosity drew him back to the Maison Vauquer, which he had just sworn to leave for ever. He wanted to know whether Vautrin was dead.

Having come up with the idea of giving Vautrin an emetic, Bianchon had sent the substance he regurgitated to his hospital, for chemical analysis. His suspicions were strengthened by Mademoiselle Michonneau's insistence that they should be thrown away. Besides, Vautrin's recovery was so swift that

Bianchon couldn't help but suspect some plot against the jovial life and soul of the boarding house. When Rastignac came in, Vautrin was standing next to the stove in the dining room. All the boarders save old Goriot were there, brought down earlier than usual by the news of Taillefer the younger's duel, and were discussing the incident, curious to know the details of the affair and its impact on Victorine's destiny. When Eugène came in, his eyes met those of Vautrin, as imperturbable as ever. The look Vautrin gave him shot so deeply into his heart, and struck such forceful, dissonant chords there, it made him shudder.

'Well, child,' the escaped convict said, 'it looks like the old death's-head[181] will be wrong about me for a while yet. According to these ladies, I've made a magnificent recovery from an apoplexy that would have killed an ox.'

'Ooh! A bull, easily,' cried widow Vauquer.

'Perhaps you're sorry to see me still alive?' said Vautrin in Rastignac's ear, thinking to read his mind. 'The man has the strength of the devil!'

'Oh, that reminds me!' said Bianchon: 'the day before yesterday I overheard Mademoiselle Michonneau talking about a man known as *Cat-o'-Nine-Lives*; that name would suit you down to the ground.'

These words struck Vautrin like a thunderbolt: he turned white and staggered, his magnetic stare lit on Mademoiselle Michonneau like a sunburst, a blast of will-power that made her knees buckle. The spinster sank into a chair. Poiret quickly stepped between her and Vautrin, seeing the danger she was in, as the convict's face now wore a savage expression, stripped of the mask of geniality which had concealed his true nature. The other boarders looked on dumbfounded, following this dramatic turn of events without understanding a thing. Just then, a company of men was heard marching down the road, followed by the ringing sound of soldiers striking their rifles against the paving stones. As Collin instinctively scanned the windows and walls for some way out, four men appeared at the drawing-room door. The first was the Chief of the Sûreté, the other three were detective inspectors.

'In the name of the law and of the King,' said one of the

inspectors, his voice drowned out by a murmur of astonishment.

Then silence fell in the dining room as the boarders separated to let through three of the men, each with a hand on a loaded pistol in his side pocket. The detectives were followed by two gendarmes who stood guard at the drawing-room door, while another two appeared at the door leading out to the staircase. Soldiers' footsteps and guns rang out on the paving stones that ran along the front of the building. All hope of escape was therefore denied Cat-o'-Nine-Lives, towards whom all eyes were irresistibly drawn. The chief walked straight over and struck him on the head with such force that he knocked off his wig, restoring Collin's looks to their full horror. Beneath his cropped brick-red hair, his head and face, set on those powerful shoulders, took on a terrible aspect of strength and cunning and glowed with intelligence, as if lit up by the fires of hell. Everyone now understood Vautrin completely: his past, his present, his future; his implacable doctrines, his creed of self-determination, the sense of sovereign entitlement that gave him the cynicism of his thought, of his actions, and the strength of a constitution that was equal to anything. Blood rushed to his face and his eyes glinted like a wild cat's. He retaliated with a surge of such ferocious energy, he roared so loudly, that the boarders cried out in fear. In response to this lion-like behaviour, and taking advantage of the general commotion, the inspectors cocked their pistols. Seeing the gleaming hammer of each gun, Collin understood the danger he was in and suddenly showed himself capable of extraordinary human strength and self-possession – a dreadful and majestic sight! His features mirrored a phenomenon which can only be compared to the geyser whose sulphurous steam has the power to move mountains, but is dissolved in the wink of an eye by a single drop of cold water. The drop of water which cooled his rage was a thought that came to him as quick as lightning. He began to smile and looked at his wig.

'You're not having one of your polite days today,' he said to the Chief of the Sûreté. And he held out his hands to the gendarmes, beckoning them with a jerk of his head. 'Sirs, put your

cramp rings on me, wrists or thumbs. I call upon those present
to witness that I am not resisting arrest.' A murmur of admiration, prompted by the speed with which lava and fire erupted
and subsided in this human volcano, ran around the room.

'Well, that's taken the wind out of your sails, copper,' the
convict went on, staring the famous head of the detective division in the eye.

'That's enough; take off your clothes,' ordered the man from
the Petite Rue Sainte-Anne in a contemptuous tone of voice.

'Why?' said Collin, 'there are ladies present. I'm denying
nothing and I'm turning myself in.'

He paused and surveyed the gathering like a speaker letting
his audience know he has a few surprises up his sleeve.

'Write this down, Papa Lachapelle,' he said to a little old
man with white hair, who had removed the statement of offence
from a file and sat down at the end of the table. 'I confirm that
I am Jacques Collin, known as *Cat-o'-Nine-Lives*, sentenced to
twenty years in irons; and I've just proved that I earned my
name honestly. If I'd so much as raised a hand,' he said to the
boarders, 'those three beaksmen over there would have spilled
my claret all over Ma Vauquer's humble hearth. The meddling
rascals are forever laying traps!'

Madame Vauquer felt rather queasy when she heard this.

'Gracious! It's enough to make you ill; and to think I was
with him at the Gaîté yesterday,' she said to Sylvie.

'Be philosophical, Ma,' Collin continued. 'Is it so bad to
have been in my box yesterday at the Gaîté?' he cried. 'Are
you better than we are? We bear less infamy on our shoulders
than any of you do in your hearts, the withered limbs of a
gangrenous society: even the best of you were no match for
me.' His eyes came to rest on Rastignac, giving him a gracious
smile which contrasted strikingly with the harsh expression on
his face. 'Our little deal still holds, my angel, subject to accept-
ance, that is! You know the one I mean?' He sang:

My Fanchette she is so charming
For she is a simple lass.

'Don't worry,' he went on, 'I'll know how to square it. No
one tries to sharp me, they're too scared!'

The penal colony with its customs and cant, with its brusque transitions between the droll and the dreadful, its larger-than-life grandeur, its familiarity, its vulgarity, was suddenly epitomized in this calling to account, and by this man, who was no longer a man, but representative of a whole degenerate nation, an unsocialized and rational race, brutal and expedient. In the space of a moment, Collin became an ode to the inferno, a portrait of all human feelings save one, that of remorse. He had the look of a fallen archangel who will always lust after war. Rastignac lowered his eyes, acknowledging some distant kinship with this criminal to make atonement for his wrongful thoughts.

'Who betrayed me?' said Collin, scanning the assembled company with his terrible stare. And letting it settle on Mademoiselle Michonneau: 'It was you,' he said to her, 'grasping old harridan; you gave me that fake fit, poking your nose into my affairs! If I said the word, I could have your head hacked off within the week. But I forgive you, I'm a Christian. Besides, it's not you who sold me out. Who then? A-ha! So you're having a look-see upstairs, are you?' he cried, hearing the detectives opening his cupboards and seizing his possessions. 'The birds all flew the nest yesterday. And you won't get a peep out of me. My trading accounts are in here,' he said, rapping his forehead. 'Now I know who narked on me. It could only be that cove Silk-Thread.[182] I'm right, aren't I, Nabber, old man?' he said to the Chief of Police. 'That ties in only too well with the time our banknotes spent upstairs. Those little grasshoppers[183] of yours won't find a thing. As for Silk-Thread, he'll be pushing up daisies within a fortnight, even if you call out all your traps to guard him. How much did you give her, this Michonnette of ours?' he said to the policemen; 'a couple of thousand écus? I was worth more than that, you mouldy Ninon, you tattered Pompadour, you Père-Lachaise Venus.[184] If you'd tipped me off, you'd have had six thousand francs. Hah! You didn't think of that, you old fleshmonger, otherwise you'd have dealt with *me*. Yes, I'd have given you that to avoid a tedious journey which will lose me money,' he said, as they put the handcuffs on him. 'These rogues will delight in keeping me kicking my

heels, just to spur me. If they sent me straight to the penal colony, I'd soon be back to my old tricks, despite the gawpers on
the Quai des Orfèvres.[185] As soon as I get there, my lads will
put heart and soul into planning a bolt for their general, the
good Cat-o'-Nine-Lives! Can any one of you boast more than
ten thousand brothers ready to do anything for you, as I can?'
he asked proudly. 'There's good in here,' he said, striking his
heart; 'I've never betrayed anyone! You there, you old biter,
look at them,' he said to the spinster. 'They may stare at me
with terror, but you make them sick with disgust. Collect your
reward.' He paused, looking round at the boarders. 'Are you
all stupid! Haven't you ever seen a convict before? A convict of
the calibre of Collin, who stands before you, is a man who is
less of a coward than the others and who protests against the
deep disappointments of the social contract, in the words of
Jean-Jacques,[186] whose pupil I'm proud to be. You see, I stand
alone against the government with all its tribunals, gendarmes,
budgets, and I outwit the lot of them every time.'

'Devil!' said the painter; 'he'd make a fine study for a
drawing.'

'Tell me, henchman of His Eminence the Executioner,
governor of the *Widow*' (the name full of chilling poetry that
convicts give the guillotine), he added, turning to the Chief of
the Sûreté; 'be a good boy, tell me if it was Silk-Thread who
shopped me! I wouldn't like him to pay for another, it wouldn't
be fair.'

At this point, the officers who had by now opened and
inventoried everything in his rooms came back and spoke in
low voices to the leader of the raid. The statement of offence
was complete.

'Gentlemen,' said Collin, addressing the boarders, 'they're
going to take me away. You've been good company during my
stay here; I'm grateful to you for that. And so farewell. Allow
me to send you some figs from Provence.' He walked forward
a few steps, then turned to look back at Rastignac.

'Goodbye, Eugène,' he said in a sad and gentle voice that
contrasted radically with the brusque delivery of his speeches.
'Should you run into trouble, I've left you a devoted friend.'

Despite his handcuffs, he managed to take his guard, then, in the manner of a fencing master, called: 'One, two!' and lunged. 'In your hour of need, apply here. Man and money, they're all at your disposal.'

That extraordinary character pronounced these last words with such buffoonery that only he and Rastignac understood them. When every last gendarme, soldier and inspector had finally left the house, Sylvie, who was rubbing her mistress's temples with vinegar, looked at the stunned boarders.

'Well,' she said, 'he was a decent chap, all the same.'

This pronouncement broke the spell cast on them by the bewildering volume and variety of emotions the episode had provoked. Straight away, the boarders caught each other's eye and looked over at Mademoiselle Michonneau, lurking next to the stove, withered, desiccated and cold as a mummy, her eyes lowered, as if she feared that not even her eye-shade would hide what they expressed. That face, which they had found so unpleasant for so long, was suddenly explained. A low murmur rose up from the four corners of the room, in perfect unison, a sign that the feeling of disgust was unanimous. Mademoiselle Michonneau heard it but didn't move. Bianchon was the first to lean towards his neighbour.

'I'm leaving if we're to have the old girl eating with us,' he said, just loud enough for the others to hear.

Everyone except Poiret immediately approved his motion; backed by the general consensus, the medical student then approached the elderly lodger.

'You're close to Mademoiselle Michonneau,' he said to him; 'talk to her, would you, and make her understand she has to leave right away.'

'Right away?' repeated Poiret, astonished.

He went up to the old woman and spoke a few words in her ear.

'But I've settled my rent, I've paid my share like everyone else,' she said, giving the boarders a viperish glare.

'If that's all you're worried about, we'll club together to make up the amount,' said Rastignac.

'Monsieur is on Collin's side,' she replied, giving the student a poisonous and challenging look; 'it's not hard to work out why.'

At these words, Eugène sprang up as if he meant to hurl himself at the spinster and strangle her. That look, whose perfidious implications he understood, had just shone a terrifying light into his soul.

'Leave her be,' cried the boarders.

Rastignac folded his arms and bit his tongue.

'Let's have done with Mademoiselle Judas,' said the painter to Madame Vauquer. 'Madame, if you don't send Michonneau packing, we'll walk out of this dump as one and tell everyone that it's full of spies and convicts. Alternatively, if you do as we ask, we'll keep quiet about this incident, which, after all, could happen in the highest society, until the day when prisoners are branded on the forehead and banned from disguising themselves as middle-class Parisians and playing their little pranks on us.'

This speech miraculously cured Madame Vauquer of her indisposition: she stood up, crossed her arms and opened clear and apparently bone-dry eyes.

'But, my dear Monsieur, you're asking for nothing less than the ruin of my establishment. There was Monsieur Vautrin . . . Oh Lord!' she said, interrupting herself; 'I can't help calling him by his good name! That's one set of rooms empty already,' she went on, 'and you want me to have another two to rent at a time of year when everyone has found a place.'

'Gentlemen, let's get our hats and go and dine at Flicoteaux's,[187] on the Place de la Sorbonne,' said Bianchon.

Madame Vauquer decided on the most advantageous course of action in a trice and slid over to Mademoiselle Michonneau.

'Now, now, my pretty beauty, you don't want to ruin me, do you? You can see that I'm being forced by these gentlemen to consider extreme measures; why not go and spend the evening upstairs in your room.'

'For shame, that's not what we said!' cried the boarders; 'we want her to leave right away.'

'But she hasn't had her dinner, the poor demoiselle,' said Poiret pathetically.

'She can have dinner wherever she wants,' cried several voices at once.

'Out with the grass!'

'Out with the grasses!'

'Gentlemen,' cried Poiret, suddenly drawing himself up with the courage of a lovesick ram; 'have some respect for the fair sex.'

'A grass has no sex,' said the painter.

'*Sexorama* my aunt!'

'Show them the way-*outorama*!'

'Gentlemen, this is quite unacceptable. When you throw someone out, you must do so in the proper manner. We've paid, we're staying,' said Poiret, pulling his hat down and sitting on a chair next to Mademoiselle Michonneau, who was being lectured by Madame Vauquer.

'Naughty little boy,' the painter said jokingly, 'be off with you now!'

'Hurry up; if you don't go, we will!' said Bianchon.

And the boarders moved as one towards the drawing room.

'Mademoiselle, what are you trying to do to me?' cried Madame Vauquer. 'I'm ruined. You can't stay, they'll be turning violent next.'

Mademoiselle Michonneau stood up.

'Will she go!' – 'Will she stay!' – 'Will she go!' – 'Will she stay!' These two phrases were chanted in turn, and the hostility of the comments that began to rain down on her forced Mademoiselle Michonneau to leave, but not before making a few remarks to the landlady in a low voice.

'I'll be boarding with Madame Buneaud,' she said threateningly.

'Go where you like, Mademoiselle,' said Madame Vauquer, stung by this spiteful preference for an establishment that was in competition with her own and which, as a result, she detested. 'Go to Buneaud's place: you'll be served wine that would give a goat the jitters and food straight from the slop-merchant's.'

The boarders formed two rows in absolute silence. Poiret gazed at Mademoiselle Michonneau so tenderly, and looked so transparently indecisive, not knowing whether to follow her or stay, that the boarders, delighted to see the back of Mademoiselle Michonneau, caught each other's eye and started to laugh.

'Gee up, Poiret,' the painter shouted to him. 'Hup hup! Walk on!'

The museum clerk launched into a comic rendition of the opening of that well-known romance:

'*Leaving for Syria*
Handsome young Dunois . . .'[188]

'Go on, you're dying to go, *trahit sua quemque voluptas*,' said Bianchon.

' "Every Jack must follow his Jill," freely translated from Virgil,'[189] said the tutor.

Mademoiselle Michonneau was looking at Poiret and when she made as if to take his arm, he was unable to resist her appeal and let the old lady lean on him. There was a burst of applause and laughter. 'Bravo, Poiret! – Who's a pretty Poiret! – Poiret Apollo – Poiret Mars – Brave Poiret!'

At this juncture, a messenger came in and handed a letter to Madame Vauquer, who sank into her chair as she read it.

'That's it, the house may as well burn down, it's a lightning conductor. Taillefer's son died at three. That'll teach me for wishing those ladies well at the expense of that poor young man. Madame Couture and Victorine request me to send on their belongings; they're going to live with her father. Monsieur Taillefer has given his daughter permission to have widow Couture as her lady's companion. Four sets of rooms to let, five lodgers gone!' She sat down, apparently close to tears. 'Misfortune has moved into this house,' she cried.

All of a sudden they heard the sound of a carriage pulling up.

'That'll be some fresh mischief,' said Sylvie.

Goriot's face appeared soon afterwards, looking so radiant and flushed with happiness that he almost seemed a new man.

'Goriot in a carriage,' said the boarders, 'then it really is the end of the world.'

The old man headed straight for Eugène, who was sitting in a corner deep in thought, and led him away by the arm: 'Come on,' he said, bursting with joy.

'Haven't you heard?' said Eugène. 'Vautrin was a convict and has just been arrested, and Taillefer's son is dead.'

'What's that to us?' replied old Goriot. 'I'm dining with my daughter, in your rooms, do you hear me? She's waiting for you, come on!'

He tugged Rastignac by the arm and frog-marched him out with such force that he resembled a man abducting his mistress.

'Let's have dinner,' the painter called out.

Everyone immediately pulled back their chairs and sat down.

'Honestly!' said Sylvie, 'everything's gone to the dogs today; my harico of mutton has stuck to the bottom of the pan. Humph! Too bad, you'll have to eat it burnt.'

Words failed Madame Vauquer when she saw only ten instead of eighteen people sitting at her table; but everyone did their best to console her and cheer her up. Although at first the regulars talked about Vautrin and the day's events, their conversation soon snaked off in different directions, and they began to discuss duels, the penal colony, justice, laws to be remade, prisons, until finally they ended up a thousand leagues away from Jacques Collin, Victorine and her brother. Although there were only ten of them, they shouted as loud as twenty so there seemed to be more of them than usual; that was the only difference between dinner today and the day before. The habitual indifference of this selfish little world, which, the next day, would pick out other fish to fry from the daily course of events in Paris, eventually prevailed, and even Madame Vauquer allowed herself to be soothed by hope, speaking through big Sylvie.

That day, and the rest of the evening, seemed to Eugène like some fantastic vision. Despite his strength of character and generosity of mind, his thoughts were in turmoil when he found himself sitting in the carriage next to old man Goriot, whose words were so unusually joyful, and followed in the wake of such intense emotions that they boomed distantly in his ears like the words we hear in dreams.

'We finished it this morning. The three of us are going to dine together – together! What do you think of that? I haven't had dinner with Delphine, my sweet Delphine, for four years. I'm going to be near her for a whole evening. We've been at your rooms since this morning. I've been working like a navvy, with my sleeves rolled up. I helped them carry in all the furniture. Ah! you've no idea what a delight it is to dine with her, how she looks after me: "Have some of this, Papa, it's delicious." And then I can't eat a thing. Oh! It's been so long since I last enjoyed her company in peace, as we will tonight!'

'But', said Eugène, 'surely the world is upside down today?'

'Upside down?' said old man Goriot. 'Why, in all its history things have never been so right with the world. All I can see in the streets are happy people, shaking hands warmly, kissing each other, as overjoyed as if they were all about to sit at their daughters' tables and wolf down that delightful dinner she ordered before my very eyes from the chef at the Café des Anglais.[190] Hah! Why, if you're sitting next to her, even bitter aloes[191] taste as sweet as honey.'

'I can feel myself coming back to life,' said Eugène.

'What are you waiting for, driver,' shouted old Goriot, opening the front window. 'Make haste and I'll tip you a hundred sous if you take me you-know-where in ten minutes.' Hearing this promise, the coachman crossed Paris at lightning speed.

'He's a terrible slow-coach, this driver of ours,' said old Goriot.

'But where are you taking me?' Rastignac asked him.

'Home,' said old man Goriot.

The carriage stopped in the Rue d'Artois. The old man stepped out first and threw ten francs to the driver with the extravagance of a widower who, in a frenzy of delight, throws caution to the winds.

'Come on, let's go up,' he said to Rastignac, steering him across a courtyard and leading him to the door of an apartment on the third floor, at the far end of a handsome new building. Before old Goriot could ring the bell, Thérèse, Madame de Nucingen's maid, opened the door to let them in. Eugène found himself in a delightful set of bachelor rooms, made up of an entrance hall, a small drawing room, a bedroom and a closet, all looking out over a garden. In the little drawing room, whose furnishings and decoration bore comparison with the most beautiful and elegant to be found anywhere, he caught sight of Delphine in the candlelight. She stood up from a love-seat by the fire and, in a tone of voice charged with tenderness, said: 'So you had to be fetched, Monsieur, the man who refused to understand.'

Thérèse withdrew. The student took Delphine in his arms and wept for joy. This final contrast between what he was seeing and what he had seen, on a day when his heart and mind had been exhausted by so much turmoil, caused a rush of overwhelming emotion.

'I knew he loved you, I knew,' old Goriot said softly to his daughter, while Eugène, drained, sank onto the love-seat incapable of saying a word nor as yet of realizing precisely how this magic wand had been waved.

'Come and look,' said Madame de Nucingen, taking him by the hand and leading him into a bedroom whose rugs, furniture and minutest details reminded him of Delphine's, only smaller.

'There's no bed,' said Rastignac.

'That's right, Monsieur,' she said, flushing and squeezing his hand.

Eugène looked at her, and understood, young though he was, how much genuine modesty there is in the heart of a woman in love.

'You're one of those beings who must always be adored,' he whispered in her ear. 'Yes, I'm daring to say this because we understand each other so well: the more sincere and strong our love is, the more veiled and mysterious it must be. Let's not tell anybody our secret.'

'Oh! I won't be anybody, not me,' grunted old man Goriot.

'You know perfectly well that you count as one of us . . .'

'Ah! That's what I wanted to hear. You won't take any notice of me, will you? I'll come and go like a guardian spirit who is present everywhere but never seen. So, Delphinette, my Ninette, my Dedel! I was right, wasn't I, to say: "There's a lovely apartment in the Rue d'Artois, let's furnish it for him!" You didn't want to. Ah! I'm the author of your joy, just as I'm the author of your days. Fathers must always be giving to be happy. Always to be giving, that's what makes you a father.'

'What?' said Eugène.

'Yes, she had cold feet, she was scared of what people might say, as if society mattered next to her happiness! But every woman dreams of this . . .'

Old Goriot was talking to himself. Madame de Nucingen had taken Rastignac into the closet and a kiss was heard, although lightly bestowed. This room was as elegant as the rest of the apartment, which lacked for nothing.

'Have we managed to divine your wishes?' she said, as they came back into the drawing room for dinner.

'Yes,' he said, 'only too well. Alas! Such consummate luxury, such beautiful dreams-come-true, all the poetry of a life of youth and fashion – I set too much store by these things to be entirely undeserving, but I can't accept them from you and I'm still too poor to . . .'

'A-ha! You're resisting me already,' she said with an air of mock authority, pouting prettily as a woman does when she wants to make fun of some scruple or other, the better to dismiss it.

Eugène had questioned his motives only too soberly that day, and Vautrin's arrest, having shown him the depth of the abyss into which he had almost fallen, had strengthened his sense of decency and delicacy to such an extent that it was impossible for him to yield to this affectionate refusal of his noble ideas. He felt overwhelmed with sadness.

'What!' said Madame de Nucingen, 'you're considering turning me down? Do you know what your refusal would mean? That you have doubts about the future, you're reluctant to attach yourself to me. So you're afraid that you might betray my affection? If you love me, if I . . . love you, why should you be put off by such a small obligation? If you knew how much pleasure it has given me to fit out these bachelor rooms, you wouldn't hesitate, and you'd ask me to forgive you. I had money which belonged to you: I spent it wisely, that's all there is to it. You think you're being magnanimous, but you're being petty. You could ask for so much more . . .' ('Ah!' she said, catching sight of Eugène's passionate expression), 'and you're making a fuss about the silliest things. If you don't love me, then yes! yes! don't accept. My fate hangs on a word from you. Speak to me! Father, give him some good reasons,' she added, turning towards her father after a pause. 'Does he think that I'm any less concerned about our honour than he is?'

Old Goriot watched and listened to this lovers' tiff with the beatific smile of an opium-smoker.

'Child! You're on the threshold of life,' she continued, taking Eugène's hand; 'you come up against a barrier many find insurmountable, a woman's hand opens a way for you – and you shrink back! But you will succeed, you'll make a brilliant fortune, success is written all over your handsome face. Won't you be able to return to me then what I'm lending you today? In olden times, didn't ladies give their knights armour, swords, helmets, chainmail coats and horses so they could fight tournaments in their name? Well, Eugène, I'm offering you the weapons of our times, the tools needed by any man who wants to make something of himself. It must be delightful, the attic you sleep in, if Papa's room is anything to go by. So, shall we have dinner? Do you want to make me sad? Answer, will you?' she said, shaking his hand. 'Lord, Papa, help him decide, or I'll leave and never see him again.'

'I'll make you decide,' said old man Goriot, coming out of his ecstatic trance. 'My dear Monsieur Eugène, you borrow money from Jews, don't you?'

'I have to,' he said.

'Good, I've got you there,' the old fellow went on, pulling out a worn and shabby leather wallet. 'I've made myself a Jew. I paid all the bills – here they are. You don't owe her a centime for anything in here. It doesn't amount to much: five thousand francs in all. I'll lend it to you! You won't refuse me, I'm not a woman. Write me an IOU on a scrap of paper and pay me back some other time.'

Eugène and Delphine looked at each other in surprise, their eyes brimming with tears. Rastignac reached out and took the old man's hand in his.

'Well, what of it! You're my children, aren't you?' said Goriot.

'But, my poor, dear Father,' said Madame de Nucingen; 'how did you do it?'

'Ah! We're coming to that,' he replied. 'Once I'd convinced you to set him up near you, I watched you buying him his *trousseau*, so to speak, and I said to myself: "She's going to get in a pickle!" The solicitor tells me that the legal proceedings against your husband, to make him return your fortune, will take at least six months. So. I sold my perpetuity of thirteen hundred and fifty livres; with fifteen thousand francs I got myself a well-secured life annuity[193] of twelve hundred francs; and I used the rest of the capital to pay for your purchases, my children. I have a room up there which will cost me fifty écus a year; I can live like a prince on forty sous a day and I'll still have some left over. I never wear anything out and I barely need any clothes. I've been chuckling away to myself for a fortnight now, saying: "Won't they be happy!" Well, aren't you happy?'

'Oh! Papa, Papa!' said Madame de Nucingen, throwing herself at her father, who took her on his lap. She showered him with kisses, her blonde hair brushing his cheeks, and wet his radiant and delighted old face with her tears.

'Dear Father, what a good father you are to me! No, there's no other father on earth like you. Eugène already loves you so dearly, what will he feel now!'

'Why, children,' said old Goriot, who hadn't felt his daughter's heart beat next to his for ten years; 'why, Delphinette, you'll make me die of happiness. My poor heart is breaking. Now, Monsieur Eugène, we're already quits!' And the old man pressed his daughter to him so wildly, so intensely, that she said: 'Ah! You're hurting me.' – 'I've hurt you!' he said, turning white. He looked at her with an expression of superhuman pain. To paint a true portrait of this Christ of Paternity, one would need to draw comparisons with those images created by princes of the palette to show the sufferings endured by the Saviour of mankind for the sake of the world. Old man Goriot gently kissed the waist that his fingers had dug into.

'No, no, I've not hurt you,' he went on, with a questioning smile; 'it was you crying out that hurt me. It cost more than that,' he whispered in his daughter's ear, kissing it carefully, 'but I had to haul him in or he'd have kept struggling.'

Eugène, stunned by the old man's inexhaustible devotion, stared at him with that naive admiration which, at a tender age, is akin to trust.

'I'll be worthy of all this,' he cried.

'O Eugène, you've just said the most beautiful thing.' And Madame de Nucingen kissed the student's brow.

'He turned down Mademoiselle Taillefer and her millions for you,' said old man Goriot. 'Yes, she loved you, the young lady; and now, with her brother dead, she's as rich as Croesus.'[194]

'Oh! Why mention that?' cried Rastignac.

'Eugène,' Delphine said in his ear, 'that's the only regret I've felt all evening. Ah! I'll love you too, I will! and always.'

'This is the most wonderful day I've had since you were both married,' cried old man Goriot. 'The good Lord can make me suffer all he pleases, as long as it's not through you. I'll just say to myself: "In February of this year, I was happier for one moment than some men are in their whole lives." Look at me, Fifine!' he said to his daughter. 'Isn't she beautiful? Now tell me, have you met many women with her pretty colour and her sweet dimple? No, of course you haven't. Well, I made this darling woman. She'll be a thousand times more beautiful now that she has you to make her happy. I won't mind going to hell, neighbour,' he said; 'if you need my share of paradise, I'll give it to you. Let's eat, let's eat,' he went on, no longer knowing what he was saying; 'all of this is ours.'

'Poor old Father!'

'If only you knew, child,' he said, standing up and going to where she sat, taking hold of her head and kissing the crown of her hair braids, 'how little it costs you to make me happy! Come and see me sometimes; I'll be upstairs, just a step away. Promise me you will!'

'Yes, dearest Father.'

'Say it again.'

'Yes, sweetest Father.'

'Shush! I'd make you say that a hundred times if I let myself. Let's eat.'

They spent the whole evening behaving like children and old Goriot was by no means the least silly of the three. He lay down at his daughter's feet to kiss them; he kept gazing into her eyes; he rubbed his head against her dress: in all, he was as playful as the youngest and most tender lover.

'You see how it is?' said Delphine to Eugène; 'when my father is with us, he must have all of me. But it will be rather a nuisance sometimes.'

Eugène, who had already felt several pangs of jealousy, couldn't blame her for these words, which enshrined the principle of every ingratitude.

'And when will the apartment be finished?' said Eugène, looking around the room. 'We must part this evening, then?'

'Yes, but tomorrow you'll come and dine with me,' she said, delicately. 'Tomorrow is a day for the Italiens.'

'I'll be there too, in the stalls,' said old man Goriot.

It was midnight. Madame de Nucingen's carriage was waiting. On their way back to the Maison Vauquer, old Goriot and the student talked about Delphine in increasingly enthusiastic terms, which led to a curious battle of words, as each sought to express the intensity of his own passion. Eugène could not help but see that the father's love, untainted by self-interest, far outstripped his own in scope and persistence. The idol was always beautiful and pure in the father's eyes and his adoration was nourished as much by the past as the future. They found Madame Vauquer sitting alone by her stove, between Sylvie and Christophe. The old landlady had the tragic air of Marius among the ruins of Carthage.[195] She had been waiting up for her last two remaining lodgers, bewailing her lot to Sylvie. Although Lord Byron has put some fine lamentations into the mouth of Tasso,[196] they fall a long way short of the profound truth of those that now poured out of Madame Vauquer's.

'So, Sylvie, only three cups of coffee for you to make tomorrow morning. Eh! My boarding house, deserted – isn't that enough to break your heart? What's my life without my lodgers? Nothing. The house is unfurnished, stripped of its people. Life is in the furniture. What in heaven have I done to bring down so much disaster upon my head? I've laid in enough beans and potatoes for twenty people. The police, in my house! Well, in that case all we'll eat is potatoes! I'll have to sack Christophe!'

The Savoyard, who was asleep, woke up with a start and said: 'Madame?'

'Poor lad! He's like a great mastiff,' said Sylvie.

'It's the slack season; everyone has found a place to stay. They're not going to drop into my lap, are they, these lodgers? I'll go mad. And that witch of a Michonneau making off with my Poiret! What did she do to the man for him to go trotting after her like a little dog?'

'Pah! I don't know,' exclaimed Sylvie, shaking her head; 'they're up to all kinds of tricks, them old maids.'

'And then that poor Monsieur Vautrin they've gone and made a convict,' the widow went on. 'Well, Sylvie, I can't help myself, I still don't believe it. A gay dog like him, who drank his *gloria* for fifteen francs a month and always paid cash on the nail!'

'And gave good tips!' said Christophe.

'It's all a mistake,' said Sylvie.

'But, no: he confessed of his own accord,' continued Madame Vauquer. 'And to think it all happened in my house, in a street where you never see so much as a cat having a scratch! Upon my word, sure as I'm an honest woman, I must be dreaming. Because, look at it this way: we saw Louis XVI have his little accident, we saw the Emperor go, we saw him come back and go again – that was all within the realm of possibility; but what are the odds against boarding houses? We can do without a king, but we always need to eat; and when an honest woman, *née* de Conflans, puts a decent dinner on the table, as long as it's not the end of the world ... Why, that must be it: it's the end of the world.'

'And to think that Mademoiselle Michonneau, who done this to you, will get a thousand écus a year for it, so I've heard!' exclaimed Sylvie.

'Don't mention her, I can't bear it, she's a strumpet, that's what!' said Madame Vauquer. 'And to top it all, she's gone knocking on Buneaud's door! Why, there's nothing she wouldn't stoop to. I'll bet she's done some terrible things in her time, killing and thieving. They ought to pack her off to prison instead of that poor dear man . . .'

At this point Eugène and old Goriot rang the bell.

'Ah! Here come my two old faithfuls,' said the widow, sighing.

The two old faithfuls, who only dimly remembered the disasters that had struck the boarding house, unceremoniously announced to their hostess that they were moving to the Chaussée d'Antin.

'Ah! Sylvie!' said the widow, 'that's my last card played. You've struck the death-blow, Gentlemen! It has hit me right in the stomach. You've knocked all the stuffing out of me. I must have aged ten years in one day. I'll lose my mind, I swear! What am I going to do with those beans? Dear, dear! Well, if I'm going to be here all alone, you'll have to leave tomorrow, Christophe. Farewell, Gentlemen, good night.'

'What's the matter with her?' Eugène asked Sylvie.

'Bless me if all her lodgers haven't gone and left, after that business today. It's made her lose her head. Listen, she's crying. It'll do her good to have a bit of a weep. This is the first time she's ever shed a tear since I've been working for her.'

The next day, Madame Vauquer, as she herself put it, was finally *reconcealed*. Although she seemed distressed, as any woman would be who has just lost all her lodgers and whose life has fallen apart, she was clearly herself again and showed that her true grief was, at bottom, the grief of dented self-interest and disrupted routine. It goes without saying that the last lingering look a departing lover gives his mistress's house is nowhere near as tragic as the one Madame Vauquer now cast over her empty table. Eugène consoled her, saying that Bianchon, whose residency as house doctor ended in a few days' time, was bound to come and replace him; that the museum clerk had often expressed a wish to have Madame Couture's apartment and that in a few days' time she'd have a full house once again.

'May God hear your prayer, dear Monsieur! But misfortune has moved in. Death will follow within ten days, you'll see,' she

said to him, staring lugubriously around the dining room. 'Who
will he take?'

'I'm so glad we're moving out,' said Eugène to old man
Goriot, under his breath.

'Madame,' said Sylvie, running in, looking worried; 'I
haven't seen Mistigris for three days.'

'Ah! Well, if my cat is dead, if he's left us, I . . .'

The poor widow broke off, wringing her hands, and sank
back in her chair, overwhelmed by this portent of doom.

THE TWO DAUGHTERS

At around twelve, by which time postmen make it up to the Panthéon and its surrounding area, Eugène received a letter in an elegant envelope, embossed with the de Beauséant coat-of-arms. It contained an invitation, addressed to Monsieur and Madame de Nucingen, to the great ball announced a month previously, which would be held at the vicomtesse's house. Also enclosed was a short note for Eugène:

> '*I thought, Monsieur, that you would gladly undertake to communicate my sentiments to Madame de Nucingen; I am sending you the invitation you requested and would be delighted to make the acquaintance of Madame de Restaud's sister. Be sure to bring me that charming lady and try not to let her have all your affection, for you owe me a good deal in return for that which I feel towards you.*
> *Vicomtesse de BEAUSEANT.'*

'I see,' Eugène said to himself, as he read the note a second time; 'Madame de Beauséant is quite clearly telling me that she wants nothing to do with the Baron de Nucingen.' He promptly set off for Delphine's house, happy to be procuring her a pleasure for which he would no doubt be rewarded.

Madame de Nucingen was taking her bath. Rastignac waited in the boudoir, burning with the understandable impatience of a hot-blooded young man who is in a hurry to possess a mistress he has desired for two years. Emotions such as these are experienced only once in a young man's life. The first woman a man falls for who really is a woman, that is to say, one who appears before him in all the splendid trappings that fit her for Parisian society, that woman will never be rivalled. In Paris, love bears no resemblance at all to love elsewhere. Neither men nor women are fooled by the ornate caparison of commonplaces with which, for the sake of appearances, they cover up their so-called disinterested affections. In these surroundings, a woman must do more than please the heart and the senses: she knows perfectly well that she has a far greater duty to the thousand vanities life is made of. Here, more than anywhere else, love is essentially vainglorious, shameless, wasteful, flashy and false. If all the women at the court of Louis XIV envied Mademoiselle de La Vallière the great passion which made that noble prince forget that his cuffs cost a thousand écus apiece,[197] when he tore them off to assist the Duc de Vermandois' entry on the world-stage, what might we expect from the rest of humanity? Be young, rich, titled, be even better than that if you can: the more incense you burn before the idol, the more she'll favour you – if you have an idol, that is. Love is a religion, one whose worship inevitably costs more than any other; it flies past swiftly, like a child who marks his passage by leaving devastation in his wake. The luxury of feeling is the poetry of the garret; without such wealth, what would become of love? If there are any exceptions to the draconian laws of the Parisian code of conduct, they are found in solitude, in spirits who have fought against the current of social doctrine, who live near some clear spring, elusive but unceasing; who, loyal to their green shade, content to listen to the language of infinity, which they find written in themselves and in everything, patiently await their wings, pitying those who are earthbound.

But Rastignac, like most young men who have had a taste of greatness before their time, wanted to enter the lists of society fully armed; he was full of the spirit of combat, but while he may have felt strong enough to prevail, was still ignorant of either the means or the aim of his ambition. If you have no pure and sacred love to fill your life, this thirst for power can be a fine thing; simply cast off all self-interest and devote yourself to making your country great. But the student had not yet reached the vantage-point from which a man can look back on his life with a critical eye. Indeed, at this moment in time, he still hadn't entirely freed himself of the charm of the fresh and pleasing ideas that wrap themselves like foliage around the childhood of a boy raised in the country. He had continually hesitated to cross the Parisian Rubicon.[198] Even as he burned with all kinds of curiosity, he couldn't quite let go of the attractive picture of a true gentleman leading a contented life in his castle. However, his last remaining scruples had vanished the previous evening when he found himself in his new rooms. Now that he enjoyed the material benefits of wealth, as he had for so long enjoyed the moral superiority of birth, he had shed his provincial skin and smoothly made a move that pointed to a promising future. So, as he waited for Delphine, lolling in a chair in the pretty boudoir he was coming to think of as his own, he felt so far removed from the Rastignac who had arrived in Paris a year ago, and who now appeared before him by some optical illusion of the mind, that he wondered if, at that precise moment, he bore any resemblance to himself at all.

'Madame is in her room,' Thérèse came in and announced, making him jump.

He found Delphine resting on the love-seat by the fire, fresh and calm. Seeing her reclining there among billowing waves of muslin, it was impossible not to compare her to one of those beautiful Indian plants whose fruit is set inside the flower.

'Ah, at last,' she said, with emotion.

'Guess what I've brought you,' said Eugène, sitting down beside her and taking her arm to kiss her hand.

Madame de Nucingen made a gesture of delight as she read the invitation. She looked at Eugène, her eyes moist with tears, and threw her arms around his neck to pull him closer to her, in raptures of gratified vanity.

'So it's to you, Monsieur' ('to you, my darling,' she whispered in his ear; 'but Thérèse is in my dressing-room, we must be careful!'), 'to you, Monsieur, that I owe such bliss? Yes, I'll venture to call this bliss. Since it has come through you, it must be more than just a triumph for my self-esteem. Nobody would introduce me to that set. Perhaps you're thinking what a petty, frivolous, shallow *Parisienne* I am, at this moment; but you should know, dear friend, that I'm prepared to make any sacrifice for you, and that if my desire to gain access to the Faubourg Saint-Germain is stronger than ever, it's because I will find you there.'

'Don't you think', said Eugène, 'that Madame de Beauséant is saying she doesn't expect to see Baron de Nucingen at the ball?'

'Why, yes,' said the baronne, returning the letter to Eugène. 'There's no one can match those women for impertinence. But no matter, I'll go. My sister will be there; I've heard she's having an exquisite outfit made. Eugène,' she continued, lowering her voice, 'she's going because she has to clear some appalling suspicions. Haven't you heard the rumours that are flying around about her? This morning Nucingen came in and told me that everyone was talking about it quite openly last night at the Club. What a thread it hangs on, dear God! the honour of women and families! I felt attacked, wounded on my poor sister's behalf. They're saying that Monsieur de Trailles has signed bills of exchange worth around a hundred thousand francs, most of which are now overdue, and so a process has been sued out against him. They're saying that my sister, driven to extremity, sold her diamonds to a Jew, those beautiful diamonds you might have seen her wearing, which belonged to her mother-in-law, Madame de Restaud. No one has talked about anything else for the past two days. I can understand then why Anastasie might be having a splendid lamé dress made and wants all eyes to be drawn to her at Madame de Beauséant's ball, when she appears in all her splendour and with her diamonds. But I won't be looked down on by her. She has always tried to crush me; she has never done me a single good service, I who have done so many for her and have always given her money when she had none. But let's forget society: I want to be happy today.'

Rastignac was still at Madame de Nucingen's house at one in the morning. As she tenderly bade him a lovers' farewell, that *adieu* so full of the joys to come, she said to him with a melancholy air: 'I'm so afraid, so superstitious; call my premonitions what you will, but I'm terrified that I'll pay for my happiness with some terrible catastrophe.'

'Child,' said Eugène.

'Ah! So I'm the child tonight,' she said, laughing.

Eugène returned to the Maison Vauquer knowing he would be leaving it the next day, and so, on his way back, sank into the blissful day-dreams of a young man who can still taste happiness on his lips.

'Well?' old Goriot called out to Rastignac, as he walked past his door.

'Well,' replied Eugène, 'I'll tell you everything tomorrow.'

'Everything, you promise?' cried the old fellow. 'Go to bed. A life of happiness awaits us tomorrow.'

The next day, all that was preventing Goriot and Rastignac from leaving the boarding house was the tardy arrival of the remover, when, around midday, the sound of a carriage stopping right outside the door of the Maison Vauquer was heard in the Rue Neuve-Sainte-Geneviève. Madame de Nucingen stepped out and asked if her father was still at the boarding house. When Sylvie replied in the affirmative, she nimbly glided up the stairs. Eugène was in his room without his neighbour's knowledge. During *déjeuner*, he had asked old man Goriot to take charge of his belongings, saying they would meet at four in the Rue d'Artois. However, while the old fellow was out looking for porters, Eugène, having swiftly answered the roll-call at the Ecole de Droit, had come back without anyone realizing, to settle up with Madame Vauquer, not wanting to leave this to Goriot, who would, in an excess of enthusiasm, most likely have paid for him. But their landlady was out. Eugène went back up to his room to see if he had forgotten anything, and congratulated himself for having thought to do so, when, in the drawer of his desk, he found the blank bill made out to Vautrin, which he had thrown in there without thinking on the day he had paid it back. As he had no fire in the grate, he was about to tear it into tiny pieces when he recognized Delphine's voice. Not wanting to make a sound, he stopped to listen to her, thinking that there should be no secrets between them. Then, as soon as she began to speak, he found the conversation between father and daughter of too much interest for him not to listen.

'Ah! Dear Father,' she said; 'I hope to God that your idea of asking him to account for my fortune has come in time to prevent my ruin! May I speak freely?'

'Yes, the house is empty,' said old Goriot, in a choked voice.

'What's the matter, Father?' asked Madame de Nucingen.

'You've just dealt me a terrible blow,' said the old man. 'God forgive you, child! You can't know how much I love you; if you did, you wouldn't have said such a thing with so little warning, especially if the situation isn't desperate. Tell me: what has happened that is so urgent you had to come and find me here, when we were to meet later today at the Rue d'Artois?'

'Why Father! Is anyone in control of their first reaction in a catastrophe? I'm out of my mind! Your solicitor has helped us find out a little earlier about the disaster which is bound to strike later. Your long business experience will need to serve us well, and I ran to find you here, as a drowning man clings to a branch. When he found that Nucingen kept throwing endless obstacles in his way, Maître Derville threatened to sue him, saying that he would shortly obtain authorization from the magistrate. Nucingen came to see me this morning and asked me if I wanted to bring about both his ruin and my own. I replied that I didn't know what he was talking about, that I had a fortune, that I ought to be in possession of my fortune and that everything to do with this affair was being handled by my solicitor, that I knew nothing at all about anything and was therefore unable to discuss the slightest detail. Wasn't that what you told me to say?'

'Good,' replied old man Goriot.

'Well,' continued Delphine, 'he let me know the state of his affairs. He has invested all his capital and mine in ventures which are only just starting out and for which he has had to put aside vast sums of money. If I were to force him to pay me back my dowry, he'd be obliged to declare himself bankrupt; whereas if I decide to wait another year, he has promised on his honour

to repay me with a fortune double or triple my own, by invest-
ing my capital in property schemes, leaving me in possession of
all the assets upon completion. Dear Father, he meant what he
said; he has frightened me. He asked me to forgive him for
what he'd done, he gave me back my freedom, he said I could
do whatever I want, as long as I let him manage the business
concerns in my name. To prove his good faith, he promised to
consult Maître Derville as often as I like, to judge whether the
deeds making the property over to me are properly drawn up.
In other words, he has placed himself in my hands, bound hand
and foot. He wants to run the household for another two years
and has begged me not to spend any more on myself than my
allowance permits. He assured me that it's all he can do to keep
up appearances, that he's sent away his dancer and that he's
going to have to exercise the strictest economy, if his speculations are to come to maturity without his credit being affected.
I made it hard for him, I cast doubt on everything, pushed him
to the limit so I'd find out more: he showed me his books, he
even cried. I've never seen a man in such a state. He lost his
head, said he'd kill himself, he was beside himself. I felt sorry
for him.'

'And you believe his nonsense,' cried old Goriot. 'He's
putting it on! I've dealt with Germans in business before: most
are men of good faith and integrity, but when they start being
tricksy and cunning beneath that sincere and good-natured air,
they're better at it than anyone else. Your husband is fooling
you. He can feel the hounds closing in, he's playing dead; he
has more control in your name than in his own and wants to
keep it that way. He'll make the most of the situation to cover
himself against the risks of his profession. He's as devious as he
is dishonest; he's a bad lot. No, no, I won't end up in Père Lachaise[199] and leave my daughters destitute. I still know a thing or
two about business. He has, so he says, invested in a number of
ventures. Well, in that case, the interests he holds correspond
to securities, surveys, contracts! Let him show them and come
to a settlement with you. We'll choose the best speculations,
run the risks ourselves and have the shares marked in our name
as *Delphine Goriot, wife of Baron de Nucingen, with separate*

assets.[200] Does the man take me for a fool? Does he really think that I could stand the thought of leaving you without money, without bread, for even two days? I couldn't bear it for a single day, for a night, two hours! If I thought there was any truth in the idea, it would be the end of me. What! Are you telling me that I've worked for forty years, broken my back lugging sacks around, poured with sweat, done without all my life for you, my angels, who made any burden, any toil seem light, only to see my entire fortune, my whole life, go up in smoke today! I could die of rage. By all that's most sacred in heaven and on earth, we'll get to the bottom of this; we'll check his books, his coffers, his business ventures! I won't sleep, I won't rest, I won't eat, until I've found proof that your fortune is intact. Thank God your estate is separate and Maître Derville will represent you – luckily he's an honest man. As God's my witness, you'll keep hold of your sweet little nest-egg million, your fifty thousand livres a year, until the end of your days, or I'll kick up such a rumpus in Paris! Hah! And if the tribunals brushed us off, I'd take it to the Chamber of Deputies. Knowing that you had no worries or concerns about money soothed all my ills and eased my grief. Money is life. If you have cash, you can do anything. What's he playing at, that great lump of an Alsatian? Delphine, don't give so much as a quarter of a liard to that monster, who has shackled you and brought you down. If he needs you, we'll knock him into shape and make him walk the straight and narrow. Lord, my head is on fire, there's a burning inside my skull. My Delphine, without a penny! Oh! my Fifine, you of all people! Sapristi! Where are my gloves? Come on! Let's go, I want to see it all immediately: books, business, accounts and correspondence. I won't have any peace until I have proof that your fortune is no longer at risk and have seen it with my own eyes.'

'My dear Father! We must be cautious. If you show even the slightest desire for vengeance in this matter and reveal that your intentions are hostile, I'll be lost. He knows you, he thought it only natural for me to be concerned about my fortune, when prompted by you; but I swear to you, my money is in his hands and that's exactly where he wants it to be. I wouldn't put it past him to make off with the capital and leave us stranded, the scoundrel! He knows full well that I won't bring my own name into disrepute by taking him to court. His position is both strong and weak. I've looked at it from every angle. If we push him to the limit, I'll be ruined.'

'Why then, he's nothing short of a rogue?'

'Yes, Father,' she said, throwing herself onto a chair and weeping. 'I didn't want to tell you, to spare you the sorrow of having married me to such a man! His conscience and his private behaviour, his body and soul, they all lead to the same conclusion! It's dreadful: I detest and despise him. Yes, I can no longer respect that crook Nucingen, after all that he's told me. Any man who's mixed up in the kind of underhand schemes he's told me about must be entirely lacking in scruples, and if I'm afraid, it's because I've seen what's in his soul. That man, my own husband, explicitly offered me my freedom – you know what that means? – if I was willing to be a tool in his hands should his plans go awry, in other words, as long as I let him use my name as cover.'

'But we have laws! But we have a Place de Grève[201] for sons-in-law who behave like that,' cried old man Goriot; 'why, I'd guillotine him myself if there was no executioner to be had.'

'No, Father, there are no laws against him. Listen to what he's really saying when you strip his words of all their niceties: "Either you lose everything, you end up penniless, you're ruined – because I couldn't possibly find another accomplice – or you allow my projects to come to fruition." Is that clear enough? He still needs me. Having a wife who has integrity reassures him; he knows that I'll leave him to his fortune and be content with my own. I must consent to this dishonest, wicked association or be ruined. He's buying my conscience and paying for it by allowing me to be Eugène's wife, in my own way. "I'll let you commit misdemeanours; let me commit crimes and ruin the poor!" Is that plain enough language for you? Do you know what he calls a deal? He buys up vacant lots in his own name, then has men of straw build houses on them. These men strike deals for the buildings with contractors, paying the latter in long-dated bills of exchange. Then, for a small fee, the men of straw acknowledge receipt of payment by my husband – making him the owner of the houses – and then liquidate their debt towards the duped contractors by going bankrupt. The name of the firm of Nucingen is used to dazzle the poor contractors. I understood that much. I also understood that, in the event that he should ever need to prove he had paid out vast sums of money, Nucingen has transferred huge amounts of securities to Amsterdam, London, Naples, Vienna.[202] How would we ever get hold of them?'

Eugène heard a heavy thud as old Goriot fell to his knees on the tiled floor.

'Lord, what have I done to you? My daughter at the mercy of this wretch; he'll stop at nothing to get what he wants. Forgive me, Daughter!' cried the old man.

'Yes, if I'm ruined, perhaps it is partly your fault,' said Delphine. 'We have so little sense when we marry! Do we know anything about the world, business, men or morals? Our fathers should think for us. Dear Father, I don't blame you at all, forgive me for what I said. This is all my fault. No, don't cry, Papa,' she said, kissing her father on the forehead.

'Don't you cry either, my little Delphine. Bring yourself over here and I'll kiss the tears from your eyes. There! I'm going to screw my head back on and untangle this web of affairs your husband has been weaving.'

'No, let me do things my way; I'll know how to bring him round. So he loves me – well then, I'll use the hold I have on him to make him invest some capital in properties for me, as soon as possible. Perhaps I'll make him buy Nucingen, in Alsace, in my name: he loves that place. But come tomorrow to examine his books, his affairs. Maître Derville doesn't know anything about commerce. No, don't come tomorrow. I don't want to get in a fret. Madame de Beauséant's ball is the day after tomorrow: I must do everything I can to be beautiful and rested when I go, so I'll be a credit to my darling Eugène! Let's go and look at his room.'

At this point another carriage stopped in the Rue Neuve-Sainte-Geneviève and Madame de Restaud's voice was heard in the stairwell, asking Sylvie: 'Is my father here?' This fortunate circumstance saved Eugène, who was already thinking about leaping into bed and pretending to be asleep.

'Ah! Father, have you heard about Anastasie?' asked Delphine, recognizing her sister's voice. 'Apparently there are some strange goings-on in her domestic life too.'

'What!' said old man Goriot; 'this will be the death of me. My poor head can't take a double dose of misfortune.'

'Good morning, Father,' said the comtesse, as she came in. 'Ah! You're here, Delphine.'

Madame de Restaud seemed disconcerted by her sister's presence.

'Good morning, Nasie,' said the baronne. 'You're surprised to find me here? *I* see Father every day.'

'Since when?'

'If you ever came to see him, you'd know.'

'Don't goad me, Delphine,' said the comtesse in a pitiful voice. 'I'm quite wretched. I'm lost, dear Father! Oh yes, well and truly lost this time!'

'What's the matter, Nasie?' cried old Goriot. 'Tell us everything, child. She's gone white. Delphine, quickly, help her. Be good to her and I'll love you even more than I do already, if that's possible!'

'Poor Nasie,' said Madame de Nucingen, helping her sister to a seat; 'speak. You have in us the only two people who'll always love you enough to forgive you everything. You see, family ties are the strongest.' She held smelling salts under her nose and the comtesse came round.

'This will be the death of me,' said old Goriot. 'Now,' he continued, poking his tan-turf fire, 'come closer both of you. I'm cold. What's the matter Nasie? Tell me quickly, you're killing me . . .'

'Well,' said the poor woman, 'my husband knows everything. Think back, Father, some time ago: do you remember that bill of exchange of Maxime's? Well, it wasn't the first. I'd already paid many more. At the beginning of January, Monsieur de Trailles seemed terribly low. He didn't say anything to me, but it's so easy to see into the heart of someone you love; it takes just the slightest thing – and then, you have premonitions. Well, I'd never known him more loving, more tender, I couldn't have been happier. Poor Maxime! In his head, he was saying goodbye; he told me that he wanted to blow his brains out. So I pleaded with him and begged him relentlessly; once I even spent two hours on my knees. He told me he owed a hundred thousand francs! Oh Papa! A hundred thousand francs! I was out of my mind. You didn't have them; I'd swallowed up everything you had.'

'No,' said old man Goriot, 'I wouldn't have been able to raise that kind of money, short of stealing it. But I would have done it, Nasie! I will.'

When they heard how mournfully he gasped out these words, with a groan like the rattle of a dying man, laying bare the agony of a father who finds himself powerless, the two sisters paused. Who, however selfish, could have remained indifferent to this cry of despair, which, like a stone thrown into a chasm, revealed its depth?

'I raised it by selling something which didn't belong to me, Father,' said the comtesse, bursting into tears.

Delphine, moved, wept with her head pressed against her sister's neck.

'So it's all true,' she said to her.

Anastasie bowed her head; Madame de Nucingen threw her arms around her and kissed her tenderly, pressing her against her heart: 'In here, you will always be loved without being judged,' she said to her.

'My sweet angels,' said Goriot weakly, 'why do you only ever embrace each other in times of misfortune?'

'To save Maxime's life, which is to say, everything my happiness depends on,' the comtesse went on, encouraged by these signs of warm and heartfelt tenderness, 'I went to that pawnbroker you know, Monsieur Gobseck, a man made in hell, for nothing can soften his heart, and took him the family diamonds which Monsieur de Restaud holds so dear: his, mine, the lot, I sold them. Sold them! Do you hear me? He was saved. But, as for me, I'm dead. Restaud knows everything.'

'Who told him? How? I could kill them!' cried old Goriot.

'Yesterday, he called me into his room. I went in . . . "Anastasie," he said to me in a certain tone . . . (oh! his voice was enough, I guessed immediately) . . . "Where are your diamonds?" "In my room." "No," he said, looking at me, "they're over there on my dresser." And he showed me the jewel case, which he'd covered with his handkerchief. "Do you know where they came from?" he asked me. I fell to my knees . . . I wept, I asked him what death he would have me die.'

'You said that!' shouted old Goriot. 'In the sacred name of God, any man who lays a finger on either of you, for as long as I live, may rest assured that I'll roast him alive! Yes, I'll rip him to pieces like . . .'

Old man Goriot ran out of breath, his words rasping in his throat.

'In the end, dear Sister, he asked me to do something harder than dying. May heaven spare any other woman from having to hear what I did!'

'I'll murder that man,' muttered old Goriot. 'But he only has one life and he owes me two. Tell us, what was it?' he continued, looking at Anastasie.

'Well,' continued the comtesse after a pause; 'he looked at me: "Anastasie," he said, "I'll draw a veil over this affair, we'll stay together, we have children. I won't call out Monsieur de Trailles, I might miss, and if I rid myself of him any other way I'd have human justice to answer to. To kill him in your arms would bring dishonour on the children. But if you don't want to see either your children, their father or myself destroyed by this, you must meet two conditions. Tell me: are either of the children mine?" I said yes. "Which one?" he asked. "Ernest, the eldest." "Good," he said. "Now, swear to me that you will obey me in one respect." I swore that I would. "You will sign your assets over to me when I ask you to do so."'

'Don't sign,' cried old Goriot. 'Never sign such a thing. Hah! Pah! You, Monsieur de Restaud, have no idea how to make a woman happy: she'll find happiness where she can, and you think you can punish her for your own pathetic impotence? Enough; what about me, I'm still here! He'll find me blocking his way, Nasie, you can rest assured. Ah, so he values his heir, does he? Well, well. I'll kidnap his son, who after all, dammit, is my grandson. Don't I have a right to see him, the brat? I'll take him to my village, I'll make sure he's well looked after, you can be sure of that. I'll bring that monster to his knees, I'll say to him: "This is between the two of us! If you want your son, give my daughter back her fortune and let her do exactly what she wants."'

'Father!'

'That's right, your father, that's who I am! Ah! I'm a true father. I won't let that rascally toff mistreat my daughters. Damn it! I must have the blood of a tiger in my veins, I could eat them both alive. Oh children! Is this your life? It will be the death of me. How will you fare when I'm no longer here? Fathers should live as long as their children. Lord, this world of yours is so badly made! And yet you have a son yourself, or so we're told. You should prevent us from suffering for our children. My dearest angels, how can it be! You only come here when you're in trouble. You only ever tell me about your tears. Yes, yes, you love me, I can see that. Very well, bring your sorrows here! My heart is vast, there's room for them all. Yes, go ahead and tear it to shreds: each shard will become a whole new father's heart. I want to bear your burdens, to suffer for you. Ah! You were so happy when you were little . . .'

'Those were our only good times,' said Delphine. 'Do you remember how we'd tumble down off the sacks in the big granary?'

'Father! There's more,' said Anastasie in Goriot's ear, making him jump. 'I didn't get a hundred thousand francs for the diamonds. Maxime has been served with a writ. We only have twelve thousand francs left to pay. He has promised to be good, to stop gambling. His love is all I have left in the world and I've paid for it so dearly I would die if I should lose that too. I've sacrificed fortune, honour, peace of mind and children for him. Oh! At least let Maxime keep his freedom and his honour, so he can remain in society where he'll be able to make a name for himself. He doesn't just owe me my happiness now: we have children who could be fortuneless. If he ends up in Sainte-Pélagie,[203] all is lost!'

'I don't have the money, Nasie. Nothing left, nothing, nothing at all! The end of the world has come. Oh! The world is falling to pieces, there's no doubt about it. Run, save yourselves! Ah! I still have my silver buckles, and six pieces of cutlery, the first I ever owned in my life. After that, all I have left is a life annuity of twelve hundred francs . . .'

'What have you done with your perpetuity?'

'I sold it and kept back this little bit of income for my needs. I had to find twelve thousand francs to furnish some rooms for Fifine.'

'At home, Delphine?' Madame de Restaud said to her sister.

'Oh! What does that matter!' old Goriot went on; 'the twelve thousand francs have gone.'

'I can guess,' said the comtesse. 'For Monsieur de Rastignac. Ah! Poor Delphine, don't do it. Look what has become of me.'

'My dear, Monsieur de Rastignac is not the kind of young man who would ruin his mistress.'

'Thank you, Delphine. Given the dire straits I'm in, I might have expected better from you; but then, you've never loved me.'

'Of course she loves you, Nasie,' cried old Goriot; 'she told me so just before you arrived. We were talking about you and she said that you were beautiful, whereas she was just pretty!'

'Pretty, her!' retorted the comtesse; 'she's as cold as charity.'

'That's as may be,' said Delphine, flushing, 'and what of your conduct towards me? You disowned me, you made sure every door would be closed to me, wherever I wanted to go; in short, you've never passed over the slightest opportunity to hurt me. And as for me, have I been coming here, as you have, to bleed our poor father – a thousand francs here, a thousand francs there – of his entire fortune and reduce him to the state he's in now? This is your handiwork, Sister. *I* have seen father as often as I could, I never showed him the door and I didn't come and suck up to him whenever I needed something. I didn't even know that he'd spent those twelve thousand francs on me. *I* live within my means, as you know. What's more, I've never angled for the gifts Papa has given me.'

'You were luckier than me: Monsieur de Marsay was rich, as you have reason to know. You've always been as filthy as lucre. Farewell. I have neither sister, nor . . .'

'Hold your tongue, Nasie!' shouted old Goriot.

'What kind of a sister repeats gossip that everyone knows to be unfounded? You're a monster,' Delphine said to her.

'Children, children, hold your tongues, or I'll kill myself here and now.'

'Come, Nasie, I forgive you,' continued Madame de Nucingen; 'you're upset. But I won't stoop to your level. To say that to me at a time when I was prepared to do anything to help you, even share my husband's bed, something I wouldn't do for myself nor . . . That's on a par with every other wrong you've done me these past nine years.'

'Children, children, give each other a kiss and be done!' said their father. 'You're angels, both of you.'

'No, let go of me,' cried the comtesse, brushing her father's hand off her arm as he tried to hug her. 'She cares about me even less than my husband does. To hear her talk, you'd think she was a model of all the virtues!'

'I'd rather people thought I owed money to Monsieur de Marsay, than have to confess that Monsieur de Trailles has cost me over two hundred thousand francs,' replied Madame de Nucingen.

'Delphine!' cried the comtesse, moving towards her.

'I'm telling you the truth, whereas you are slandering me,' retaliated the baronne, coldly.

'Delphine! You . . .'

Old Goriot sprang forward to restrain the comtesse and put his hand over her mouth to stop her finishing her sentence.

'Good Lord, Father! Whatever have you been handling this morning?' Anastasie asked him.

'You're right, that was a mistake,' said her poor father, wiping his hands on his trousers. 'But I didn't know you were coming. I'm moving out.'

He was happy to have earned himself a reproach which would deflect his daughter's anger onto him.

'Ah!' he went on, sitting down, 'you've split my heart in

two. I'm dying, children! The inside of my skull feels as if it's on fire. Be good now, be kind to each other! You'll be the death of me. Delphine, Nasie, come: you're both right, you're both wrong. Now, Dedel,' he went on, turning to the baronne, his eyes full of tears, 'she needs twelve thousand francs, let's see if we can find them. Don't look at each other like that.' He went down on his knees before Delphine. 'Do it to make me happy, ask her to forgive you,' he said in her ear; 'she's the worst off here, isn't she?'

'Dearest Nasie,' said Delphine, horrified by her father's wild, stricken look, pain written all over his face; 'I've wronged you, kiss me . . .'

'Ah! balm for my bleeding heart,' cried old man Goriot. 'But where will we find twelve thousand francs? What if I enlisted in the reserves?'

'Ah! Father!' said the two daughters, putting their arms around him; 'no, no.'

'God will reward you for that thought; we could never do so in our lifetimes! Isn't that so, Nasie?' said Delphine.

'Poor Father, it would in any case be a drop in the ocean,' the comtesse pointed out.

'Can nothing be done then, with this blood of mine?' the old man cried out in desperation. 'I'll swear allegiance to the man who saves you, Nasie! I'll kill a man for him. I'll be like Vautrin, I'll do time! I . . .' He stopped as if struck by lightning. 'Nothing left!' he said, tearing his hair out. 'If only I knew a place to rob, but even then it's hard to know what to steal. And you need time and people to take on the Bank.[204] Well, all that's left is death. I may as well die. Yes, I'm a wreck. I'm no longer a father! She asks, she needs! And I have nothing, wretch that I am. "Ah! You've money tied up in your life annuity, you mean old rascal, and you have daughters! Why, don't you love them? Die, die, like a dog, for that's what you are!" Yes, I'm worse than a dog – a dog wouldn't be capable of this! Argh! My head! It's boiling!'

'Why, Papa,' cried the two young women, putting their arms around him to stop him banging his head against the wall; 'pull yourself together.'

He started sobbing. Eugène, in horror, snatched up the bill endorsed to Vautrin,[205] stamped as valid for a larger amount; he corrected the figure and made it out to Goriot, turning it into a genuine bill of exchange for twelve thousand francs, then went in.

'Your money, Madame, in full,' he said, handing her the paper. 'I was asleep; your conversation woke me and so I found out what I owed Monsieur Goriot. Here's the security, which you can convert into cash; I'll pay it off faithfully.'

The comtesse, rigid, held the paper in her hand.

'Delphine,' she said, pale and shaking with fury, rage and wrath, 'I would have forgiven you everything, as God is my witness, but now this! What? Monsieur was here and you knew it? You were petty enough to take your revenge by letting me reveal my every secret, every detail of my life, my children, my shame, my honour! Hah! You mean nothing to me now, I hate you, I'll do you as much harm as I can, I . . .' She choked, her throat dry with rage.

'Why, he's my son, our child, your brother, your saviour,' cried old Goriot. 'Kiss him, Nasie! Look, I'll kiss him,' he continued, throwing his arms around Eugène in a kind of frenzy. 'Oh! child! I'll be more than a father to you: I'll be a whole family. If only I were God, I'd throw the universe at your feet. Go on, Nasie, kiss him! He's no mere mortal, but an angel, truly an angel.'

'Ignore her, Father, she's acting like a madwoman at the moment,' said Delphine.

'Madwoman! Madwoman! What does that make you, then?' retorted Madame de Restaud.

'Children, I'll die if you go on like this,' cried the old man, falling onto his bed as if struck by a bullet. 'They're killing me!' he murmured.

The comtesse looked at Eugène, who stood there, stunned at the violence of the scene: 'Monsieur,' she said, with a challenging gesture, tone of voice and expression, paying no attention to her father, whose waistcoat Delphine had quickly unbuttoned.

'Madame, I'll pay up and say nothing,' he replied, before she could phrase her question.

'You've killed our father, Nasie!' said Delphine, showing the old man, unconscious, to her sister, who ran out of the room.

'I'll willingly forgive her,' said the old fellow, opening his eyes; 'she's in a dreadful mess and it would muddle a stronger head than hers. Console Nasie, be gentle with her, promise your poor dying father that?' he asked Delphine, squeezing her hand.

'Why, what's the matter with you?' she asked, frightened.

'Nothing, nothing,' replied her father, 'it will pass. There's something pressing against my forehead, a migraine. Poor Nasie, what a future!'

At this point, the comtesse came back and threw herself at her father's knees: 'Forgive me!' she cried.

'Stop it', said old man Goriot, 'or you'll hurt me even more.'

'Monsieur,' said the comtesse to Rastignac, her eyes misted with tears, 'my suffering made me unjust. Will you be a brother to me?' she went on, holding out her hand to him.

'Nasie,' Delphine said, hugging her, 'little Nasie, let's forget all this.'

'No,' she said, '*I* will always remember!'

'Angels,' cried old Goriot, 'you are lifting the fog that covered my eyes, your voices are bringing me back to life. Kiss each other again. Well, Nasie, will this bill of exchange save you?'

'I hope so. Now, Papa, would you be so good as to sign it?'

'Dear, dear, how stupid of me to forget that! But I didn't feel so good, Nasie; don't hold it against me. Send someone to let me know that you're out of trouble. No, I'll go myself. No, no, I won't go; I'll never be able to look your husband in the eye without killing him on the spot. As for carving up your assets, I'll be there. Go quickly, child, and make that Maxime of yours behave himself.'

Eugène was dumbfounded.

'Poor Anastasie has always had a violent streak,' said Madame de Nucingen, 'but her heart's in the right place.'

'She only came back for the signature,' Eugène muttered in Delphine's ear.

'Do you think so?'

'I wish I didn't. Don't trust her,' he replied, looking heaven-wards as if confiding in God the thoughts he dared not speak aloud.

'Yes, she has always been a bit of an actress, and my poor father allows himself to be taken in by her grimacing.'

'How are you, dear old Goriot?' Rastignac asked the old man.

'I feel sleepy,' he replied.

Eugène helped Goriot to lie down. Then, once the old man had fallen asleep holding her hand, his daughter withdrew.

'We'll meet at the Italiens this evening,' she said to Eugène, 'and you'll tell me how he is. Tomorrow, Monsieur, you'll be moving. Let me see your lodgings. Oh! how dreadful!' she said, going in. 'Why, your room is even worse than my father's. Eugène, you behaved well. I'd love you even more if it was possible; but, child, if you want to make your fortune, you can't just throw twelve thousand francs out of the window like that. The Comte de Trailles is a gambler. My sister refuses to see it. He'd have gone in search of his twelve thousand francs wherever it is he always goes to win or lose mountains of gold.'

A groan brought them back to Goriot's room; he looked as if he was sleeping, but when the two lovers came nearer, they heard him say: 'They aren't happy!' Whether he was asleep or awake, the intonation of this phrase touched his daughter's heart so deeply that she approached the pallet on which her father was sleeping and kissed his forehead. He opened his eyes, saying: 'It's Delphine!'

'So, how are you feeling?' she asked.

'Fine,' he said. 'There's no need for you to worry, I'll get over it. Off you go, children; off you go, enjoy yourselves.'

Eugène escorted Delphine home, but, concerned by the state in which he had left Goriot, he chose not to dine with her and instead returned to the Maison Vauquer. He found old Goriot up and about, well enough to sit down to dinner. Bianchon had positioned himself so that he could study the old vermicelli dealer's face carefully. As he watched him pick up his bread and sniff it to work out what flour it was made from, the student, noting the total absence of what you might call conscious design in this gesture, shook his head ominously.

'Come and sit next to me, dear doctor,' said Eugène.

Bianchon came over all the more willingly as it brought him closer to the elderly lodger.

'What's the matter with him?' asked Rastignac.

'Unless I'm mistaken, it's all over for him! Some extraordinary event must have taken place inside him; I'd say he seems to be at risk of suffering an imminent serous apoplexy.[206] Although the lower part of his face is relatively peaceful, look how his upper facial features are being pulled up towards his forehead, involuntarily! And then, his eyes have that particular condition which indicates an effusion of serum in the brain. They look as if they're full of fine dust, wouldn't you say? I'll know more tomorrow.'

'Is there no cure?'

'None whatsoever. We might be able to delay his death, if we find a way to provoke a reaction in the extremities, in the legs; but if he still has these symptoms tomorrow evening, the poor old fellow is lost. Do you know what has caused his illness? He must have suffered some violent shock which has sapped his mind.'

'Yes,' said Rastignac, remembering how the two daughters had fought tooth and nail over their father's heart.

'At least Delphine loves her father,' Eugène said to himself.

That evening, at the Italiens, Rastignac chose his words carefully, so as not to cause Madame de Nucingen undue alarm.

'Don't worry,' she replied, as soon as Eugène began to speak; 'my father is as strong as a horse. We just shook him a little this morning. Our fortunes are in jeopardy, can you not see the scale of the catastrophe? If my life is still worth living, it's because your affection has made me impervious to what I once would have considered to be mortal fear. Today, the only fear, the only catastrophe that could strike me, would be to lose the love which has made me feel the joy of being alive. I'm indifferent to everything except that feeling, I care for nothing else in the world. You're everything to me. My wealth only brings me happiness inasmuch as it allows me to bring you greater pleasure. To my shame, I'm more of a lover than a daughter. Why? I don't know. My entire life is in you. My father gave me a heart, but you made it beat. Let the whole world judge me, what do I care! As long as you, who aren't permitted to hate me for the crimes which the strength of my feeling compels me to commit, find me not guilty. Do you think I'm an unnatural daughter? Oh, no, it's impossible not to love a father as good as ours. Could I have prevented him from seeing the inevitable consequences of our lamentable marriages? Why didn't he stop them? Shouldn't he have done our thinking for us? Today, I know, he's suffering as much as we are; but what can we do about it? Comfort him! We have no comfort to offer him. Our resignation has cost him more pain than the harm our reproaches and complaints would cause him. Some situations in life are bitter through and through.'

Eugène was struck dumb, stirred to tenderness by this candid outpouring of true feeling. Parisian women may often be artificial, drunk on vanity, self-centred, coquettish, cold, but you can be sure that when they truly love, they sacrifice more feelings in the flames of their passions than other women; they rise above their pettinesses and become sublime. Eugène was struck, too, by the depth and soundness of judgement a woman shows towards her most natural feelings, when a propitious state of mind separates her from them and gives her some distance. Madame de Nucingen was unsettled by Eugène's prolonged silence.

'Tell me what you're thinking,' she asked him.

'I'm still listening to what you've just said. Up until now, I thought I loved you more than you loved me.'

She smiled and steeled herself against the pleasure she felt, so as to keep their conversation within the bounds of propriety. She'd never heard an impassioned declaration of youthful, sincere love like this before. A few more words and she'd have been unable to contain herself.

'Eugène,' she said, changing the subject, 'have you heard what's happening? The whole of Paris will be at Madame de

Beauséant's tomorrow. The Rochefides and the Marquis d'Ajuda have agreed to keep it to themselves, but the King is going to sign the marriage contract tomorrow and your poor cousin still knows nothing about it. She'll have no choice but to play the hostess and the marquis won't be at the ball. No one can talk about anything but this affair.'

'And society finds such infamy amusing and wallows in it! Don't you see that this will be the death of Madame de Beauséant?'

'No,' said Delphine, smiling, 'you don't know the kind of woman she is. But all Paris will be at her house, and so will I! I owe that pleasure to you.'

'But', said Rastignac, 'couldn't it just be one of those absurd rumours that are always doing the rounds in Paris?'

'We'll find out the truth of the matter tomorrow.'

Eugène did not go back to the Maison Vauquer. He was unable to resist the lure of his new rooms. Whereas the night before he had had to leave Delphine at one in the morning, this time it was Delphine who, at around two, left him to go home. The next day he slept late and waited in for Madame de Nucingen, who came to take *déjeuner* with him at around midday. As eager to enjoy these sweet pleasures as a young man will be, he had almost forgotten old Goriot. The day was one long celebration for him, as he acquainted himself with each and every one of his elegant new belongings. Madame de Nucingen's presence made everything all the more precious. However, at around four, the two lovers spared a thought for old man Goriot, remembering the happiness he was hoping for on coming to live in this house. Eugène remarked that they'd need to bring the old fellow there as soon as possible, should he be ill, and, leaving Delphine, he went straight to the Maison Vauquer. Neither old Goriot nor Bianchon had come down to dinner.

'Well now,' the painter said to him; 'old man Goriot has been wounded in action. Bianchon is tending to him upstairs. The old fellow saw one of his daughters, the Comtesse de Restau*rama*. Then he decided to go out and took a turn for the worse. Society is about to be deprived of one of its finest ornaments.'

Rastignac rushed towards the stairs.

'Hey! Monsieur Eugène!'

'Monsieur Eugène! Madame is calling you,' shouted Sylvie.

'Monsieur,' said the widow; 'you and Monsieur Goriot, you were meant to leave on the fifteenth of February. We're three days past the fifteenth, it's the eighteenth; you'll need to pay me another month's rent, for you and for him, but, if you can vouch for old man Goriot, your word will be enough.'

'Why? Don't you trust him?'

'Trust! If the old chap lost his marbles and died, his daughters wouldn't give me a single liard and his worldly possessions wouldn't even fetch ten francs. This morning he sold the last of his silver, I don't know why. He was all got up like a young man. God forgive me, I'll swear he was wearing rouge, he looked younger to me.'

'I'll vouch for everything,' said Eugène, with a shiver of dread, sensing a catastrophe.

He went up to Goriot's room. The old man was recumbent on his bed and Bianchon was sitting with him.

'Hello, Father,' said Eugène.

The old man gave him a gentle smile, turned his glazed eyes towards him and responded, 'How is she?'

'Well. And you?'

'Not bad.'

'Don't tire him out,' said Bianchon, leading Eugène into a corner of the room.

'So?' Rastignac said to him.

'Only a miracle could save him; he's displaying all the symptoms of serous congestion. We're applying mustard poultices;[207] he can feel them, which is a good sign they're having some effect.'

'Can we move him?'

'Impossible. He must stay here and avoid any physical exertion or emotional upheaval . . .'

'Bianchon, dear friend,' said Eugène, 'we'll look after him together.'

'I've already called out the senior doctor from the hospital.'

'And?'

'He'll be able to tell us more tomorrow evening. He's promised to come as soon as he's finished his rounds for the day. Unfortunately, the blessed old chap went and did something rash this morning and is refusing to tell me anything about it. He's as stubborn as a mule. Whenever I open my mouth, he pretends not to hear and goes to sleep so he won't have to reply; or if he has his eyes open, he starts groaning. He left first thing and went somewhere in Paris on foot, we don't know where. He took everything he owned of any value and seems to have been on some fool's errand that was quite beyond his strength! One of his daughters came to see him.'

'The comtesse?' asked Eugène. 'A tall brunette, with bright, deep-set eyes, dainty feet and a slim waist?'

'Yes.'

'Give me a moment alone with him,' said Rastignac. 'I'll get him to talk; he'll tell me everything.'

'I'll go and have my dinner in the meantime. But try not to over-excite him; there's still a glimmer of hope.'

'Don't worry, I won't.'

'They're going to have such a good time tomorrow,' said old Goriot to Eugène, as soon as they were on their own. 'They're going to a grand ball.'

'So what did you do this morning, Papa, that has made you so poorly this evening that you have to stay in bed?'

'Nothing.'

'Has Anastasie been to see you?'

'Yes,' answered old man Goriot.

'Come, don't hide anything from me. What did she ask you for this time?'

'Ah!' he went on, summoning up the strength to speak; 'she was terribly upset, the poor child! Nasie hasn't had a sou since that business with the diamonds. She has ordered – especially for the ball – a lamé gown which is bound to suit her down to the ground. Her dressmaker, a nasty piece of work, wouldn't let her have it on credit and so her maid put down a thousand-franc deposit on the dress. Poor Nasie, to be reduced to that! It broke my heart. But when the maid saw that Nasie had lost Restaud's trust, she was afraid she would lose her money and made a deal with the dressmaker not to hand over the gown unless the thousand francs were repaid. The ball is tomorrow, the dress is ready. Nasie is in despair. She wanted to borrow my silver to pawn. Her husband wishes her to go to the ball and show all Paris the diamonds she's rumoured to have sold. Can she now say to that monster: "I owe a thousand francs, will you pay them for me?" No. I understood that perfectly. Her sister Delphine will be there, superbly dressed; Anastasie mustn't be beneath her younger sister. And she can't stop crying, my poor daughter! I was so ashamed not to have had the twelve thousand francs yesterday that I'd have given what's left of my wretched life to make good that wrong. Do you see? I'd been strong enough to take anything, but not having the money was the last straw, it broke my heart. Oh! Why! I didn't even stop to count to two, to one. I pulled myself together and smartened myself up. I sold my silver and buckles for six hundred francs, then I made over a year's annuity payments to uncle Gobseck, for a one-off payment of four hundred francs. Pah! I'll eat bread! That was good enough when I was young, that will do me now. At least my Nasie will have a wonderful evening. She'll be there in all her finery. I've put the thousand-franc note under my pillow. It makes me feel warm to know that here beneath my head I have something that will make poor Nasie happy. She'll be able to sack that no-good Victoire of hers. What's the world coming to when servants no longer trust their masters! I'll be better tomorrow, Nasie is coming at ten. I wouldn't want them to think I was ill, or they wouldn't go to the ball: they'd stay and look after me. Tomorrow Nasie will kiss me as she would her child, her caresses will cure me. After all, I'd have spent a thousand francs at the apothecary's, wouldn't I? I'd rather give them to my Heal-All, my Nasie. At least I'll bring her some solace, in the wretched state she's in. That will make up for the wrong I did her when I got myself an annuity. She's at the bottom of the pit and I'm not strong enough any more to pull her out. Oh! I'll go back into business. I'll go to Odessa to buy grain. Wheat costs three times as much here as it does there. They may have banned grain imports as natural produce, but the clever lot who made the laws didn't think to ban by-products made of wheat. Heh heh! . . . I came up with that one this morning! There are some good moves to be made in the starch trade.'

'He's mad,' Eugène said to himself as he looked at the old man. 'Come, rest now, no more talking . . .'

Eugène went down to dinner when Bianchon came back up. Then, throughout the night, they took it in turns to care for the sick man, keeping themselves busy, the one reading his medical books, the other writing to his mother and sisters. The next day, the patient's symptoms, according to Bianchon, tended towards a favourable prognosis, but required constant treatments that could only be administered by the two students and which it is impossible to describe without offending against the euphemistic phraseology of the day. The leeches fixed on the old man's wasted body were accompanied by poultices, foot baths and medical procedures that required all the strength and devotion of the two young men. Madame de Restaud didn't come; she sent a messenger to pick up her money.

'I thought she'd come in person. But perhaps it's just as well; it would only have upset her,' said the father, seeming to view this in a positive light.

Thérèse came at seven in the evening, bringing a letter from Delphine.

'Tell me, what are you doing, my love? Having recently become your beloved, am I to be so soon neglected? When we poured out the secrets of our hearts to one another, you revealed to me a soul of such beauty that you must surely be one of those who are faith-ful for ever, having seen how many nuances a feeling can have. As you said when you heard Moses' prayer:[208] "For some it's all on one note, for others it's the infinity of music!" Don't forget that I'm expecting you to come and escort me to Madame de Beauséant's ball this evening. Monsieur d'Ajuda's contract was finally signed at court this morning and the poor vicomtesse only found out at two. The whole of Paris will flock to her house, like the crowds that swarm into the Place de Grève to watch an execution. How abominable, to go and see whether the woman will manage to hide her grief, whether she'll manage to die gracefully! I would *certainly not go, my love, if I'd already been admitted to her house; but this will probably be the last time she holds a reception and otherwise I'll have made all this effort for nothing. My situation is quite different from that of other people. Besides, I'm going for you, too. I'll be waiting for you. If you are not at my side in two hours' time, I'm not sure I'll be able to forgive you such a betrayal.'*

Rastignac picked up his pen and replied as follows:

'I'm waiting for the doctor to hear how long your father has to live. He's dying. I'll bring you the verdict myself – I'm afraid it might be a death sentence. Then you'll be able to see whether you can go to the ball. With all my most tender affection.'

The doctor came at half past eight and, although his opinion wasn't favourable, didn't think that death was imminent. He predicted alternating recoveries and relapses on which the old man's life and faculties would be contingent.

'It would be better for him if he died quickly,' were the doctor's final words.

Eugène left old Goriot in Bianchon's care and set off to bring Madame de Nucingen the sad news, which, to his mind, still imbued with a sense of family duty, must surely defer all pleasure.

'Tell her to enjoy herself no matter what,' old Goriot called after him, sitting up despite his drowsiness, just as Rastignac was leaving.

The young man arrived at Delphine's house with a heavy heart, to find her with her shoes on and her hair done, ready and dressed apart from her ballgown. But, like the final brushstrokes a painter applies to a picture, the finishing touches were taking longer than the actual composition of the canvas.

'What, aren't you dressed yet?' she said.

'But Madame, your father . . .'

'My father again,' she cried, cutting in. 'Why, it's not for you to tell me what I owe my father. I've known my father a long time. Not a word, Eugène. I won't listen to you until you're dressed. Thérèse has laid everything out for you in your rooms; my carriage is ready, take it; come straight back. We'll talk about my father on the way to the ball. We must leave in good time; if we get stuck in the queue of carriages, we'll be lucky if we make our entrance before eleven.'

'Madame!'

'Hurry! Not a word,' she said, running into her boudoir to fetch a necklace.

'Well, what are you waiting for, Monsieur Eugène, you'll vex Madame,' said Thérèse, giving the young man a push that sent him on his way, appalled by this parricide committed in the name of fashion.

He went off to dress, his head full of the saddest and most dispiriting thoughts. Society now looked much like an ocean of mud into which a man sank up to his neck if he so much as dipped a toe in. 'Only the pettiest crimes are committed here!' he said to himself. 'Vautrin was greater than that!' He had now seen the three main factions of society: Obedience, Struggle and Rebellion; the Family, the World and Vautrin. And he didn't know which to join. Obedience was tedious, Rebellion impossible and Struggle uncertain. His thoughts took him back to the bosom of his family. He remembered the pure feelings of that quiet life, he thought of the days he had spent surrounded by people who loved him. By conforming to the natural laws of domestic life, those dear creatures found a happiness that was whole, constant and free of care. Despite his fine thoughts, he wasn't quite brave enough to go to Delphine and profess his faith in the purity of souls, while ordaining her to the office of Virtue in the name of Love.

The education upon which he had embarked was bearing fruit. His love was already selfish. His intuition allowed him to recognize the nature of Delphine's heart. He sensed that she would walk over her father's dead body to get to the ball, and he had neither the strength to play the role of reasoner, nor the courage to displease her, nor sufficient honour to leave her. 'She'd never forgive me for proving her wrong in this particular case,' he said to himself. Then he reinterpreted the doctor's words: he convinced himself that old Goriot wasn't as seriously ill as he thought; in all, he stacked up one seductive argument after the other to vindicate Delphine. She was unaware of her father's state of health. The old man would send her off to the ball himself if she went to see him. The laws of society, so implacably formulated, frequently condemn in cases where an apparent crime may be excused by any number of extenuating circumstances within a family, arising from differences in personality or divergent interests and situations. Eugène wanted to deceive himself, he was ready to sacrifice his conscience for his mistress.

In two days, everything in his life had changed. The woman had wreaked havoc, she had eclipsed his family, she had seized everything for herself. Rastignac and Delphine had met in the right conditions for them to afford each other the greatest pleasure. Their well-prepared passion had finally reached maturity through that which tends to deaden passions: gratification. Possessing this woman had made Eugène realize that he had merely desired her up to that point; he only loved her the day after she had made him happy: perhaps love is simply the acknowledgement of pleasure. Whether despicable or sublime, he adored this woman for the dowry of sensual pleasures he had given her, and for all those he had received in return; similarly, Delphine loved Rastignac much as Tantalus[209] would have loved the angel that came to satisfy his hunger or to quench the thirst of his parched throat.

'So, how is my father?' Madame de Nucingen asked him, when he returned dressed for the ball.

'Seriously ill,' he replied. 'If you want to prove that you love me, let us hurry and go to him.'

'Very well,' she said, 'but after the ball. Dear Eugène, be kind: don't lecture me, it's time to go.'

They left. Eugène remained silent for part of the way.

'What's the matter?' she said.

'I can hear your father's death-rattle,' he replied, angrily. And, with the heated eloquence of youth, he recounted the destructive course of action to which Madame de Restaud's vanity had driven her, the fatal crisis triggered by her father's final act of devotion and what Anastasie's lamé gown had cost. Delphine wept.

'I'm going to look ugly,' she thought. Her tears dried. 'I'll go and look after my father, I won't leave his bedside,' she said.

'Ah! That's how I wanted you to be,' cried Rastignac.

The lanterns of five hundred carriages illuminated the approach to the Hôtel de Beauséant. Two gendarmes guarded the brightly lit door, mounted on spirited horses. The *beau monde* had turned out in such great numbers, and everyone was so eager to see this fashionable woman at the moment of her downfall, that the reception rooms on the ground floor of the mansion were already full by the time Madame de Nucingen and Rastignac were announced. Not since the time the whole court rushed to see the *Grande Mademoiselle*,[210] when Louis XIV snatched her lover away from her, had there been an affair of the heart as spectacularly catastrophic as that of Madame de Beauséant. In this case, the last daughter of the near-royal House of Burgundy showed herself to be superior to the wrongs done to her, and, to the last, held sway over the society whose vanities she had only tolerated as long as they served the triumph of her passion. The most beautiful women in Paris made her reception rooms sparkle with their dresses and their smiles. The most distinguished courtiers, ambassadors, ministers, all kinds of illustrious figures, decorated with crosses, medals and many-coloured sashes, thronged around the vicomtesse. The melodies played by the orchestra echoed off the gilt mouldings of this palace, which, as far as its queen was concerned, was deserted.

Madame de Beauséant stood at the entrance to her outer drawing room to receive her so-called friends. Dressed in white, without a single ornament in her simply braided hair, she seemed calm and showed neither pain, nor pride, nor feigned gaiety. No one could read what was in her soul. She might have been a Niobe made of marble.[211] The smiles she gave her closest friends may have been a little derisive at times; but she seemed to everyone to be so very much herself, and did such a good job of appearing just as she was when at her happiest, that even the hardest-hearted were full of admiration for her, just as young Roman women would applaud the gladiator who managed a smile as he took his last breath. Fashionable society appeared to have turned out in all its finery to bid farewell to one of its sovereigns.

'I was afraid you wouldn't come,' she said to Rastignac.

'Madame,' he replied, in a voice choked with emotion, hearing a reproach in her words; 'I have come and will be the last to leave.'

'Good,' she said, taking his hand. 'You're possibly the only person here that I can trust. Dear friend, be sure to fall in love with a woman you'll always be able to love. Never leave a woman in the lurch.'

She took Rastignac's arm and led him to a sofa in the drawing room where the gaming tables were.

'Go and call on the marquis,' she said. 'Jacques, my valet, will take you there and give you a letter for him. I'm asking him to return my correspondence. I'd like to believe that he'll give you all of it. If you come back with my letters, go up to my room. Someone will come and tell me.'

She rose to greet the Duchesse de Langeais, her best friend, who had also just arrived. Rastignac left and asked for the Marquis d'Ajuda at the Hôtel de Rochefide, where he was due to spend the evening, and where he found him. The marquis took him to his house, handed the student a box and said: 'They're all in there.' He seemed inclined to talk to Eugène, perhaps to ask him about the events of the ball and the vicomtesse, perhaps to confess that he was already in despair at his marriage, as he would be, later; but his eyes had a proud glint in them and he was, regrettably, brave enough to keep his finest feelings to himself. He clasped Eugène's hand with sadness and affection and sent him on his way.

Eugène went back to the Hôtel de Beauséant and was let into the vicomtesse's room, where he watched the final preparations for her departure. He sat down by the fire, stared at the cedarwood casket and sank into the deepest melancholy. In his eyes, Madame de Beauséant had taken on the dimension of a goddess in the *Iliad*.

'Ah! Dear friend,' said the vicomtesse as she came in, pressing Rastignac's shoulder with her hand.

He turned to see his cousin in tears, her eyes raised, one
hand trembling, the other lifted. She abruptly took hold of the
box, put it on the fire and watched it burn.

'Everyone is dancing! They arrived on time, but death will
come late. Sshh! dear friend,' she said, putting her finger to
Rastignac's lips to stop him speaking. 'This is the last I'll see of
Paris and fashionable society. At five o'clock in the morning,
I'm going to leave and bury myself in deepest Normandy. I've
had since three o'clock this afternoon to make my preparations, sign documents, see to my affairs; I've been unable to
send anyone to . . .' She stopped. 'I never doubted that he'd be
with . . .' She stopped again, overcome with grief. At times like
these, all is suffering and certain words cannot be spoken aloud.
'Anyhow,' she went on, 'I was counting on you for this final
service tonight. I'd like to give you a token of my friendship. I'll
think of you often, you who have seemed to me so good and
noble, so young and candid, in a world where these qualities
are so hard to find. I hope you will think of me from time to
time. I'd like you to have this,' she said, looking round; 'it's the
box I kept my gloves in. Each time I took a pair from it on my
way out to a ball or to the opera, I felt beautiful, because I was
happy, and only ever left some pleasant thought inside when I
touched it: there's a lot of me in there, a whole other Madame
de Beauséant who no longer exists. Please accept it; I'll have it
brought to your rooms in the Rue d'Artois. Madame de Nucingen is on fine form this evening, love her well. Although we'll
never see each other again, dear friend, you who have been so
good to me, be sure that I'll pray for you. Let's go down; I don't
want them to think I'm crying. All eternity lies before me, I'll
be alone there and no one will ask me to account for my tears.
Let me take one last look at this room.' She paused. Then, after
covering her eyes with a hand for a moment, she dabbed them,
bathed them in cold water and took the student's arm.
'Onwards!' she said.

Rastignac had never felt such strong emotion as he did
now, sensing so much nobly contained suffering in the pressure of her hand on his arm. On returning to the ball, Eugène
accompanied Madame de Beauséant on a turn around the

room, a last, thoughtful gesture on the part of that generous woman.

He soon spotted the two sisters, Madame de Restaud and Madame de Nucingen. The comtesse looked magnificent with all her diamonds on display, although they must have been burning into her; this was the last time she would ever wear them. Despite the strength of her pride and her love, she was finding it hard to hold her head up high with her husband's eyes upon her. It was a sight which did nothing to lessen the sadness of Rastignac's thoughts. Behind the two sisters' jewels, he could see the pallet on which old man Goriot lay dying. The comtesse, mistaking his melancholy air, took her arm out of his.

'Off you go! Don't let me stand in the way of your pleasure,' she said.

Eugène was soon claimed by Delphine, delighted with her success and keen to lay at his feet the tributes she had received from these people whom she hoped would accept her.

'What do you think of Nasie?' she asked him.

'She has cashed in[212] everything up to and including her father's death.'

At around four in the morning, the crowds in the reception rooms began to thin. The music petered out soon after. Rastignac and the Duchesse de Langeais found themselves alone in the main drawing room. The vicomtesse, thinking to find the student alone there, came in after bidding farewell to Monsieur de Beauséant, who eventually went to bed, still saying to her: 'You're wrong, my dear, to go and shut yourself away at your age! Stay here with us.'

When she saw the duchesse, Madame de Beauséant was unable to suppress a cry.

'I've found you out, Clara,' said Madame de Langeais. 'You're leaving, never to return; but I won't let you go before you've heard what I have to say and we've understood each other.' She took her friend by the arm, led her into the next room and there, looking at her with tears in her eyes, put her arms around her and kissed her on both cheeks. 'I don't want to bid you a cold farewell, my dear; the remorse would be too heavy to bear. You may count on me as you would yourself.

You showed true greatness this evening, I felt worthy of you and want to prove it. I have done you wrong at times, I haven't always behaved well towards you. Forgive me, my dear: I disavow everything that might have wounded you, I wish I could take back my words. Our souls are united by a common grief and I don't know which of us will suffer more. Monsieur de Montriveau wasn't here this evening and you know what that means. No one who has seen you tonight at the ball, Clara, will ever forget you. I myself shall make one last attempt.[213] If I fail, I'll enter a convent! Where will you go?'

'To Normandy, to Courcelles, to love and to pray, until the day when God releases me from the world.'

'Come in, Monsieur de Rastignac,' said the vicomtesse, her voice choked with emotion, remembering that the young man was waiting. The student went down on one knee, took his cousin's hand and kissed it. 'Farewell Antoinette!' Madame de Beauséant went on; 'be happy. As for you, you are happy, you're young, you have something to believe in,' she said to the student. 'I'll depart this world with sacred, sincere feelings around me, as the dying sometimes do, if they have that good fortune.'

Rastignac left at around five o'clock in the morning, after seeing Madame de Beauséant into the berlin she was to travel in and after she'd bid him a last tear-washed *adieu*, proving that not even the highest-ranking members of society are exempt from the laws of the heart and do not live free of all sorrows, as those who pay court to the common people would have them believe. Eugène returned to the Maison Vauquer on foot, in cold, wet weather. His education was coming to an end.

'There's no hope for poor old Goriot,' Bianchon said to Rastignac when he stepped into his neighbour's room.

'My friend,' Eugène said to him, watching the old man sleeping, 'keep on following the humble destiny to which you have limited your desires. I myself am in hell and must stay there. Whatever terrible things you hear about society, believe them all! Not even a Juvenal could do justice to the horrors that lurk beneath its gold and jewels.'

VI
DEATH OF THE FATHER

The next day, Rastignac was woken at two in the afternoon by Bianchon, who needed to go out, and asked him to look after old man Goriot, whose condition had sharply deteriorated that morning.

'The old man doesn't have two days, maybe not even six hours, left to live,' said the medical student, 'and yet we can't stop fighting the illness. He needs expensive treatments. We can nurse him here, but I haven't a sou. I've turned his pockets inside out, looked in his cupboards – nothing. I questioned him in one of his more lucid moments and he told me he didn't have a liard to his name. How much have you got?'

'I only have twenty francs, but I'll go and gamble them and win more.'

'What if you lose?'

'I'll ask his sons-in-law and his daughters for the money.'

'And what if they don't give you any?' replied Bianchon. 'At the moment, finding money isn't the most urgent priority; the old man needs his legs wrapping in a hot mustard poultice from his feet to the middle of his thighs. If he cries out, it means there's life in him yet. You know what to do. Christophe will help you. In the meantime, I'll go to the apothecary's and stand surety for the medication we need. It's a shame the poor old man couldn't be moved to our hospice; he'd have been more comfortable there. Now, come with me so I can settle you in and don't leave him until I'm back.'

The two young men went into the room where the old man lay dying. Eugène was appalled at the change in his face, now pale, contorted and deeply debilitated.

'Papa?' he said, leaning over the straw bed.

Goriot lifted his distant eyes towards Eugène and looked at him attentively without recognizing him. The sight was too much for the student to bear and his eyes welled up with tears.

'Bianchon, surely the windows should have curtains.'

'No. Atmospheric conditions no longer affect him. If only he did feel hot or cold, that would be encouraging. However, we do need a fire to make infusions and to prepare various treatments. I'll have some faggots sent up to you; that will do until we manage to get some wood. Yesterday and last night I burned all the tan-turf that you and the old man had. It was so damp in here, there was water running down the walls. I've only just managed to dry the room. Christophe has swept it out; it really is a midden. I had to burn juniper to mask the smell.'

'Dear God!' said Rastignac, 'and to think he has daughters!'

'Here, if he asks for something to drink, give him this,' said the house doctor, showing Rastignac a big white pot. 'If he sounds like he's in pain, and his stomach is hot and hard, call Christophe to help you to administer . . . you know what. If he starts to seem over-excited, if he talks a lot, if he has a touch of dementia, leave him be. That wouldn't be a bad sign. But send Christophe to Cochin hospital. Either our doctor, my colleague or myself will come and apply moxas.[214] This morning, when you were asleep, we had a long consultation with one of Doctor Gall's trainees, a senior doctor from the Hôtel-Dieu, and our doctor. These gentlemen thought they recognized a couple of unusual symptoms and we're going to follow the progress of the illness, which should cast light on some important scientific issues. One of these gentlemen maintains that the pressure of the serum, should it affect one organ more than another, might lead to the development of strange phenomena. So if he does speak, listen to him carefully in order to establish what category of ideas his speech belongs to: whether the impressions of memory, of perception, of judgement; whether he's concerned with material things, or feelings; whether he's calculating, whether he's going back over the past: in all, stay alert and give us a precise report. It's possible that the congestion may occur suddenly, that he'll die in the imbecile state he's in at the moment. These kinds of illnesses are always so unpredictable! Should the bomb explode here,' said Bianchon, pointing at the back of the sick man's head, 'we've seen some strange effects: the brain recovers a few of its faculties and death comes more slowly. The serosities divert away from the brain and follow paths whose directions may only be revealed by an autopsy. At the Incurables, there's an old man who has lost his wits; in his case, the fluid has travelled down his spinal column; he's in terrible pain, but he's still alive.'

'Did they enjoy themselves?' said old man Goriot, recognizing Eugène.

'Oh! All he can think about is his daughters,' said Bianchon. 'Last night he must have said to me: "They're dancing! She has her gown!" more than a hundred times. He cried out their names. The way he called for them brought tears to my eyes, I swear to you! "Delphine! My little Delphine!" "Nasie!" Believe me,' said the medical student, 'it was all I could do not to break down and weep.'

'Delphine,' said the old man, 'she's here, isn't she? I knew it was her.' And his eyes rolled wildly as he tried to recover enough energy to look at the walls and the door.

'I'll go down and tell Sylvie to prepare the mustard plasters,' cried Bianchon; 'this is a good time.'

Rastignac stayed alone with the old man, sitting at the foot of the bed, his eyes riveted to the dreadful, painful sight of that face.

'Madame de Beauséant is leaving, this man is dying,' he said. 'A noble soul can't abide this world for long. How, indeed, could a lofty sensibility ever be reconciled with this petty, shallow and mean-spirited society of ours?'

Visions of the ball he had just attended surfaced in his memory, contrasting with the pitiful sight of the death-bed scene before him. Bianchon suddenly reappeared.

'Listen, Eugène. I've just seen our senior doctor and ran all the way back. If he shows signs of lucidity, if he talks, lie him on a long poultice so he's wrapped in mustard from the nape of his neck to the small of his back, and send for us.'

'Dear, kind, Bianchon,' said Eugène.

'Oh! It's all in the interests of science,' replied the medical student, with the enthusiasm of a neophyte.

'I see,' said Eugène; 'so I'm the only one looking after the old man out of affection.'

'You wouldn't say that if you'd seen me this morning,' replied Bianchon, unruffled by the remark. 'Practising doctors only see the disease; *I* still see the patient, dear fellow.'

He went out and Eugène was left alone with the old man, fearing a crisis, which soon began to manifest itself.

'Ah! It's you, dear child,' said old Goriot, recognizing Eugène.

'Are you feeling any better?' asked the student, taking hold of his hand.

'Yes, my head felt like it was gripped in a vice, but it's easing a little now. Have you seen my daughters? They'll be here soon, they'll come rushing over as soon as they know I'm ill; they looked after me so well when we lived in the Rue de la Jussienne! Dear me! I wish my room were clean and fit to receive them. That young man has burnt all my tan-turf.'

'I can hear Christophe,' said Eugène; 'he's bringing you up some wood sent by that same young man.'

'That's all very well! But how will I pay for the wood? I don't have a sou, child. I've given everything away, everything. I'm reduced to charity. But the lamé gown was beautiful, wasn't it? (Ah! My head!) Thank you, Christophe. God will reward you, boy; I myself have nothing left.'

'I'll see you and Sylvie right,' Eugène whispered in the boy's ear.

'My daughters did say they were coming, didn't they, Christophe? I'll give you a hundred sous to go to them again. Tell them I'm not feeling well, that I want to kiss them, see them one last time before I die. Tell them that, but don't go frightening them.'

Rastignac motioned to Christophe to leave.

'They'll come,' the old man went on. 'I know them. Sweet, kind-hearted Delphine: if I die, how sad I'll make her! Nasie too. I don't want to die, not if it makes them cry. Dying, dear Eugène, means never seeing them ever again. I'll feel so empty

there, wherever it is we end up afterwards. For a father, hell is
being without his children, and that's a lesson I've been learning since the day they got married. Our house in the Rue de la
Jussienne was my paradise. Although who knows, if I do go to
heaven, perhaps I'll be able to come back to earth in spirit and
be with them. I've heard talk about that sort of thing. But is
there any truth in it? I can see them now, just as they were at
home in the Rue de la Jussienne. They'd come down in the
morning and say, "Bonjour, Papa." I'd sit them on my lap, I'd
tease and tickle them a thousand times. They'd give me the
sweetest cuddles. We took our *déjeuner* together every morning, and dinner; that's how it was – I was a father, my children
were my delight. When they lived in the Rue de la Jussienne,
they never questioned anything, they knew nothing of the
world, they loved me dearly. Dear God! why didn't they stay
small for ever? (Oh! My head, that stabbing pain.) Aah! aah!
Forgive me, Daughters! I'm in such agony and this must be real
pain, for you've hardened me against mere heart-ache. Dear
God! if I could only hold their hands in mine, I'd stop feeling
the pain. Do you think they're coming? Christophe is such a
dolt! I should have gone myself. He will find them, won't he?
Why, you were at the ball yesterday. Tell me, how were they?
They didn't know I was ill, did they? They wouldn't have been
out dancing, poor little mites! Oh! I can't afford to be ill any
more. They still need me too much. Their fortunes are hanging
in the balance. And to think they're at the mercy of those husbands of theirs! Heal me, cure me! (Oh! My head, the pain!
Aah! aah! aah!) I must get better, because they need money, you
see, and I know where it can be made. I'm going to go and
make starch-powder in Odessa. I'm ahead of the game, I'll
make millions. (Oh! The pain, I can't bear it.)'

Goriot fell silent for a moment, seeming to put his every
last effort into summoning up enough strength to endure the
pain.

'If they were here, I wouldn't be complaining,' he said, 'so
why complain?'

He fell into a fitful sleep which lasted for some time.

Christophe came back. Rastignac, believing old Goriot to be

asleep, let the boy report back on his errand without lowering his voice.

'Monsieur,' he said, 'I went to see Madame la Comtesse first, but was unable to speak to her; she was with her husband, discussing some great matter. When I insisted, Monsieur de Restaud himself came out and said, in these very words: "So Monsieur Goriot is dying: well, that's the best thing he can do. I need Madame de Restaud here to finish some important business; she'll leave when it's complete." He looked angry, he did, the gentleman. I was just going out, when Madame came into the ante-room through a door I hadn't noticed, and said: "Christophe, tell my father I'm tied up with my husband, I can't leave now; it's a matter of life and death for my children; but I'll come as soon as it's over." As for Madame la Baronne, now that's another story! It was out of the question to see her, never mind speak to her. "Ah!' said her maid, 'Madame came home from the ball at a quarter past five, she's asleep; if I wake her before midday, she'll scold me. I'll tell her that her father's condition is worse when she rings for me. Bad news can always keep for later." No matter how much I begged! So that was that. I asked to speak to Monsieur le Baron, but he was out.'

'Neither of his daughters will come!' cried Rastignac. 'I'll write to them both now.'

'Neither of them,' replied the old man, sitting bolt upright. 'They have business to attend to, they're asleep, they won't come. I knew it. You have to be dying to find out what your children are really like. Ah, my friend, don't marry, don't have children! You give them life, they give you death. You bring them into the world, they hound you out of it. No, they won't come! I've known that for ten years. I said as much to myself from time to time but couldn't bring myself to believe it.'

A tear welled up on each red rim of his eyes without falling.

'Ah! If I were rich, if I'd kept hold of my wealth instead of giving it to them, they'd be here now, falling over each other to kiss my cheeks! I'd be living in a grand house, I'd have fine rooms, servants, a fire, all to myself; and my daughters, their husbands, their children, would all be here, in tears. All of that would be mine. Instead, nothing. Money buys everything, even daughters.[215] Oh! my money, where has it all gone? If I still had a fortune to leave them, they'd be dancing attendance on me, they'd be looking after me; I'd hear them, I'd see them. Ah! my dear child, my only child, destitute and abandoned as I am, I'd rather have it this way! At least when a poor man is loved, he knows he really is loved. No, let me be rich; at least I'd see them. Although, who knows? They both have hearts of stone. I gave them too much love, they kept none back for me. A father must always have means, he should keep a child on a tight rein, like a skittish horse. And I worshipped them. The wretched pair! This crowns their behaviour towards me for all of ten years. If you knew what a fuss they made of me when they were newly wed! (Aah! The pain, it's torture!) As I'd just gifted them both eight hundred thousand francs or thereabouts, neither they, nor their husbands, could very well behave ungraciously towards me. I was welcomed with "Darling Father, this", "Dear Father, that". A place was always laid for me at their tables. In those days I dined with their husbands, who treated me with the greatest respect. They thought I was still a man of means. Why? Simply because I'd kept quiet about my affairs. A man who gives his daughters eight hundred thousand francs is a man to be cultivated. And so they made a fuss of me, but it was only for my money. Fashionable society has its ugly side and I saw it soon enough! They'd take me to the theatre in their carriages and I'd stay at their parties for as long as I wished. In all, they said they were my daughters and acknowledged me as their father. But I still had my wits about me and I didn't miss a trick. They only ever thought of themselves and it broke my heart. I saw perfectly well that it was all for show; but there was no way to put things right. I felt no more at ease in their homes than I do at that dinner table downstairs. I was always saying the wrong thing. So whenever some man of fashion murmured in my son-in-law's ear: "Who on earth is that man over there?" – "He's their father, the one who made a fortune, he's a rich man" – "A-ha! Is that so!" they said and looked at me with all the respect that bundles of banknotes command. Maybe I did cramp their style at times, but I paid dearly for my faults! Besides, is anyone perfect? (My head feels as if it's been split open!) At present I'm racked with the agonies a man must endure when he's dying, dear Monsieur Eugène; well, that's nothing compared to the pain I felt the first time Anastasie gave me a look that told me I'd just said something stupid and mortified her; it made my heart bleed. Maybe I was poorly educated, but what I did know for certain was that I'd be a thorn in her side for the rest of my days. The next day I called on Delphine, hoping to console myself, and went and made some silly blunder that made her lose her temper with me. I thought I was losing my mind. For that whole week I didn't know what to do with myself. I didn't dare go and see them, fearing I'd be rebuffed. And that's how I found myself banished from my daughters' houses. O God! You who know how much misery, how much suffering, I've endured; you who have witnessed each twist of the knife in my heart, how these past years have aged me, changed me, drained me, greyed me: why make me suffer today? I've already atoned for the sin of loving them too much. They themselves have taken revenge on my fondness, they tortured me, they were my executioners. Ah, how foolish a father is! I loved them so much, I kept going back for more, just as a gambler returns to the game. Only my vice was my daughters; they were my mistresses, in a manner of speaking, they were everything to me! Whenever they needed the slightest thing, some piece of finery or other, their maids would come and tell me and I'd give it to them, in return for a warm welcome! But they still couldn't resist teaching me a few little lessons on how I ought to behave in polite society. Oh! they didn't wait long. I soon became an embarrassment to them. That's what comes of giving your children a proper education. At my age I couldn't very well go to school. (Lord, the pain, terrible pain! Doctor! Doctor! If you split my head open, it wouldn't hurt as much as this.) Anastasie! Delphine! My daughters, my own daughters, I must see them. Let them be brought here by force, by the police! Justice is on my side, everything's on my side, the laws of nature, the civil code. I won't stand for it. If fathers are to be trampled underfoot, the country[216] will go to the dogs. No doubt about it. Everything, society, the whole world, hinges on fatherhood; and if children no longer love their fathers, everything will fall apart. Oh! to see them, to hear them, no matter what they say, simply to hear their voices, especially Delphine's, that would ease my pain. But tell them, when they come, not to look at me so coldly. Oh! Monsieur Eugène, my dear friend, you don't know what it's like when the gold in a look suddenly turns to lead. Ever since the day their eyes stopped shining on me, I've been living in winter, in this room; I've had nothing but sorrows to gnaw on and I've gnawed them to the bone! I've existed only to be humiliated, insulted. I love them so much that I swallowed every indignity, the cost of the few shameful, shabby little pleasures they sold me. A father having to hide so he can see his daughters! I gave them my life and today they won't give me an hour of their time! I'm thirsty, I'm hungry, I'm burning, and they won't come and help me bear the pain of my passing, because I am dying, I can tell. Why, don't they know what it means to walk over their father's dead body? There's a God in heaven: he'll avenge us fathers, against our wishes. Oh! they must come! Come, my darling girls, come and kiss me once more, one last kiss, a viaticum[217] for your father, who'll pray to God for you, who'll tell him you've been good daughters, who'll plead for you! You are innocent, after all. They're innocent, my friend! Be sure to make that clear to everyone, so they're not given any trouble on my account. It's my own fault entirely: I taught them to walk all over me. I enjoyed it, didn't I? It concerns no one else, neither human justice, nor divine justice. God would be wrong to punish them because of me. I didn't know how to behave, I was stupid, I surrendered my rights. I'd have stooped to anything for them! What do you expect! The finest nature, the best of souls, would have been corrupted by such facility in a father. I'm a wretch; it's right I should be punished. I alone have caused my daughters' excesses, I spoiled them. Today they want pleasure, as they used to want sweets. When they were small, I always indulged their every fancy. At fifteen, they had their own carriages! They never encountered the slightest resistance. I alone am guilty, although guilty because of love. Their voices stripped my heart of its defences. They're on their way, I can hear them. Oh! they will come, yes. A child is required by law to come and see her father die, the law is on my side. Why, all it will cost them is the fare. I'll pay for it. Write and say I have millions to leave them! I swear it's true. I'll go and make Italian pasta in Odessa. I know how to do it. There are millions to be made from this scheme of mine. No one has thought of it yet. There's no risk of it spoiling in transit like wheat or flour. Eh, eh, and what about starch? There's millions in that too! You won't be lying, tell them millions and even if they only come out of greed, I'd rather be deceived; I'd see them, at least. I want my daughters! I made them! They're mine!' he said sitting up, turning towards Eugène a face with threat written all over it, framed by wispy white hair.

'There now,' said Eugène, 'lie down again, dear old Goriot, I'm going to write to them. I'll go and fetch them myself as soon as Bianchon is back, if they don't come.'

'If they don't come?' the old man repeated, sobbing. 'But I'll be dead, dead in a fit of rage, yes, rage! I'm seething with anger! I can see my whole life before me now. I've been a fool! They don't love me, they've never loved me! It's obvious. If they haven't come by now, they'll never come. The longer they delay, the less likely it is that they'll decide to bless me with their presence. I know them. They've never been aware of my sorrow, my pain, my needs, so why would they be aware of my death; the secret of my affection quite simply escapes them. Yes, I see now that for them my habit of holding nothing back rendered worthless everything I did. If they'd wanted to pluck out my eyes, I'd have said: "Pluck them out!"[218] I'm such a fool. They think all fathers are like theirs. Always make yourself seem valuable. Their children will avenge me.[219] But it's in their own interest to come here. Warn them that they're endangering the peace of their own passing. To commit this one crime is to commit every crime. Go on, go and tell them now that it would be parricide not to come! The list of their wrongdoings is long enough without adding that particular one. Summon them, say this: "Hey, Nasie, hey, Delphine! Come to your father who's been so good to you and who's in terrible pain now!" Nothing, nobody. So I'm to die here like a dog? This is my reward, to be abandoned. They're loathsome, they're wicked; I despise them, I curse them; I'll rise up out of my coffin at night to curse them over and over again, because, after all, friends, am I wrong? Their behaviour couldn't be any worse! Eh? What am I saying? Didn't you tell me that Delphine is here? She's the better of the two. You have truly been a son to me, Eugène! Be a father to her, love her. Her sister is as wretched as she could be. And their fortunes! Ah, dear God! I'm at my last breath, the pain is too much for me to bear now! Cut off my head, but leave me my heart.'

'Christophe, go and find Bianchon,' shouted Eugène, horrified at the new pitch the old man's sobs and groans were beginning to reach, 'and fetch me a cab.

'I'm going out to find your daughters, dear old Goriot; I'll bring them back here to you.'

'Force them to come, force them! Call out the guards, the battalion, the lot! The lot,' he said, looking at Eugène with one last glimmer of lucidity. 'Tell the government, the Crown Prosecutor, to have them brought to me, I want them here!'

'But you cursed them.'

'Whoever said such a thing?' replied the old man, stunned. 'You know very well that I love them, I adore them! If I could only see them, I'd be cured . . . Go, good neighbour, my dear child, go, you've a kind heart; I wish there was some way to thank you, but I've nothing left to give you but the blessings of a dying man. Ah! I wish I could at least see Delphine to tell her to repay my debt towards you. If the other one won't come, bring her. Tell her that if she doesn't come you won't love her any more. That will make her come, she loves you so dearly. Something to drink, I'm burning inside! Put something on my head. One of my daughters' hands, that would save me, I know it would . . . Dear God! Who will rebuild their fortunes if I go? I have to go to Odessa for them, to Odessa, to make pasta.'

'Drink this,' said Eugène, raising the dying man and supporting him with his left arm while holding a cup of tisane in the other hand.

'You must love your father and mother!' said the old man, squeezing Eugène's hand with his two shaky ones. 'Can you believe that I'll die without seeing my daughters? Always thirsty and never able to drink, that's how I've lived for the past ten years . . . My sons-in-law killed my daughters. Yes, they stopped being my daughters as soon as they were married. Fathers, tell the Chambers to pass a law against marriage! Whatever you do, don't marry off your daughters if you love them. A son-in-law is a scoundrel who spoils everything we love in a daughter, he sullies everything. An end to marriage! It robs us of our daughters, so that we die without them. Make a law to protect dying fathers. Ah, it's a dreadful thing! Vengeance! It's my sons-in-law who're stopping them coming. Kill them! Kill Restaud, kill that Alsatian, they're my murderers! Death or my daughters! Ah! it's all over, I'm dying without them! My daughters! Nasie, Fifine, hurry, what's keeping you! Your papa is on his way out . . .'

'Dear old Goriot, calm down, hush now, keep still, don't get upset, don't think too much.'

'Not seeing them is my mortal agony.'

'You are going to see them.'

'You're right!' cried the old man, rambling. 'Oh! See them! I'm going to see them, hear their voices. I'll die happy. Ah! yes, I've no wish to live any longer, I'd lost the taste for life, my sorrows only ever increased. But if I could see them, touch their dresses, ah! even if it was just their dresses, it's not much to ask; just to touch something that belongs to them! Let me touch their hair . . . hai . . .'

His head fell back on his pillow as if he'd been struck by a club. His hands moved restlessly across the blanket as if searching for his daughters' hair.

'They have my blessing,' he said, making an effort, '. . . blessing.'

His body suddenly sagged. At that point Bianchon came in.

'I met Christophe on the way,' he said; 'he's gone to fetch you a carriage.' Then he looked at the sick man, drawing up his eyelids; the two students saw how his eyes were now glazed and lifeless. 'He won't recover from this,' said Bianchon, 'not in my opinion.' He felt for his pulse and placed a hand on the old man's heart.

'The machine is still going, but in his case that's a bad thing; it would be better for him if he died!'

'Yes, I think you're right,' said Rastignac.

'What's the matter with you? You're as pale as death.'

'Friend, I've just heard the most unspeakable sobbing and groaning. There is a God! Yes, there has to be! There is a God, and he's made a better world for us, or this earth of ours makes no sense whatsoever. If it hadn't been so devastating, I'd weep, but my heart and stomach are in knots.'

'Listen, we're going to need lots of extra things; where's the money going to come from?'

Rastignac removed his watch.

'Here, pawn that as soon as you can. I'd rather not stop on the way; I don't have a minute to lose and Christophe should be here soon. I don't have a liard – the coachman will need to be paid when I get back.'

Rastignac rushed down the stairs and set off for Madame de Restaud's house in the Rue du Helder. On his way there, his imagination, struck by the terrible scene he had just witnessed, fired up his indignation. When he arrived in the antechamber and asked for Madame de Restaud, the answer came back that she was not available.

'But I've come with a message from her dying father,' he said to the valet.

'Monsieur le Comte has given us the strictest orders, Monsieur . . .'

'If Monsieur de Restaud is in, tell him what his father-in-law's condition is and let him know that I must speak to him immediately.'

Eugène waited a long time.

'Perhaps he's drawing his last breath even now,' he thought.

The valet showed the student into the outermost drawing room, where Monsieur de Restaud received him standing, without inviting him to be seated, in front of a hearth in which no fire had been lit.

'Monsieur le Comte,' said Rastignac; 'as we speak, your

father-in-law is dying in a squalid little room, without even a liard for wood; he is on the very brink of death and is asking for his daughter . . .'

'Monsieur,' the Comte de Restaud replied coldly; 'you may have noticed that there is no love lost between myself and Monsieur Goriot. He has compromised both his reputation and that of Madame de Restaud, he has been the cause of my misfortune, he has destroyed my peace of mind. I have not the slightest interest in whether he lives or dies. That is my position towards him. The world may condemn me, but I really couldn't care less. I have more important things to do at the moment than to concern myself with the opinions of fools and complete strangers. As for Madame de Restaud, she's not in any fit state to go out. What's more, I do not wish her to do so. Tell her father she'll come and see him as soon as she has done her duty by me and my son. If she loves her father, she could be free in a few minutes' time . . .'

'Monsieur le Comte, it's not for me to judge your conduct; you are your wife's lord and master. But may I appeal to your sense of fairness? Well then! Promise me you'll simply tell her that her father won't live to see another day and has already cursed her for not being at his bedside!'

'Tell her yourself,' replied Monsieur de Restaud, impressed by the heartfelt indignation he heard in Eugène's voice.

Rastignac followed the comte into the drawing room in which the comtesse usually received visitors; he found her in floods of tears, sunk deep in an armchair like a woman who wishes she could die. He felt sorry for her. Before meeting Rastignac's eye, she looked at her husband, her fearful glance indicating that all her strength had been crushed by sustained mental and physical tyranny. The comte gave a nod and she plucked up the courage to speak.

'Monsieur, I heard everything you said. Tell my father that he'd forgive me if he knew what a terrible situation I'm in. Nothing could have prepared me for such torture, it's more than I can stand, Monsieur; but I'll resist right to the end,' she said to her husband. 'I am a mother. Tell my father that my behaviour towards him is beyond reproach, despite what it looks like,' she cried out in despair to the student.

Eugène bade the pair farewell, guessing at the terrible dilemma the wife was facing, and left the room, stunned. Monsieur de Restaud's tone had made it clear that his efforts would come to nothing and he saw very well that Anastasie had lost her freedom.

He ran to Madame de Nucingen's house and found her in bed.

'I'm not well, my poor sweet,' she said to him. 'I caught a chill on my way back from the ball; I'm afraid I might have pneumonia, I'm waiting for the doctor . . .'

'Even if your lips were turning blue,' said Eugène, interrupting her, 'you should drag yourself to your father's side. He's calling for you! If you could hear even the faintest of his cries, you'd no longer feel the slightest bit ill.'

'Eugène, my father may not be quite as sick as you say he is; but I couldn't bear to find the slightest fault in your eyes, and I'll do as you wish. As for my father, I know that he'd die of grief if my illness took a fatal turn as a consequence of this outing. So I'll set off as soon as the doctor has been. Oh! why aren't you wearing your watch?' she asked, seeing him without his chain. Eugène flushed. 'Eugène! Eugène, if you've sold it, lost it already . . . oh! that would be terrible of you.'

The student leaned over Delphine's bed and said in her ear: 'You want to know why? Then let me tell you! Your father has nothing left to pay for the shroud we'll wrap him in this evening. Your watch is at the pawnbroker's: I had nothing else.'

Delphine immediately leaped out of bed, ran to her writing desk, took her purse and held it out to Rastignac. She rang the bell and cried: 'I'll go, I'll be there, Eugène. Just let me dress; why I'd be a monster not to! You go on ahead, I'll arrive before you! Thérèse,' she cried to her maid, 'tell Monsieur de Nucingen to come up. I need to speak to him immediately.'

Eugène, glad to be able to tell the dying man that one of his daughters was coming, arrived back at the Rue Neuve-Sainte-Geneviève feeling almost joyful. He delved into the purse to pay the coachman directly. That young woman, so rich, so elegant, had all of seventy francs in her purse. When he got to the top of the stairs, he found old Goriot raised up, supported by

Bianchon, while the hospital surgeon, watched by the doctor, was burning his back with moxas, that futile medical remedy of last resort.

'Can you feel them?' the doctor asked.

Old man Goriot, catching sight of the student, said: 'They are coming, aren't they?'

'Perhaps he'll pull through,' said the surgeon; 'he's talking.'

'Yes,' said Eugène, 'Delphine is right behind me.'

'That's the spirit!' said Bianchon; 'he's been talking about his daughters and calling out for them as a man being burned at the stake cries out for water, so they say . . .'

'That's enough,' said the doctor to the surgeon; 'there's nothing else we can do, we won't save him now.'

Bianchon and the surgeon laid the dying man down again on his squalid pallet.

'The bed linen must be changed,' said the doctor. 'Even though there's no hope, his human dignity must be respected. I'll come back later, Bianchon,' he said to the student. 'If he starts to groan again, rub opium on his diaphragm.'

The surgeon and the doctor left.

'Now, Eugène, courage, old son!' said Bianchon to Rastignac when they were alone; 'we need to put a nightshirt on him and change his bed. Go and tell Sylvie to bring up some sheets and to come and help us.'

Eugène went downstairs and found Madame Vauquer busy laying the table with Sylvie. As soon as Rastignac began to speak, the widow sidled over to him, with the honeyed yet embittered manner of a shrewd saleswoman who wishes neither to lose money, nor to vex her customer.

'My dear Monsieur Eugène,' she replied; 'you know as well as I do that old man Goriot is broke. Giving sheets to a man who's about to kick the bucket means kissing them goodbye, not least because one of them will be sacrificed for the shroud. As it is, you already owe me a hundred and forty-four francs, so if we add, say, forty francs worth of sheets and a few bits and bobs, the candle Sylvie's going to give you, then that all comes to at least two hundred francs, and a poor widow like me can't afford to lose that much money. Believe me! Be fair,

Monsieur Eugène; I've already lost enough in the last five days, since that jinx moved in here. I'd have given ten écus for the old fellow to be leaving, like you said he was going to. It's bad for my boarders. I'd pack him off to the almshouse at the drop of a hat. After all, put yourself in my shoes. My boarding house comes first: it's my livelihood.'

Eugène hurried back upstairs to old man Goriot's room.

'Bianchon, where's the money from the watch?'

'Over there on the table, there are three hundred and sixty odd francs left. I took out enough to pay off everything we owed. The pawn-ticket's under the money.'

'Here, Madame,' said Rastignac, with loathing, after racing down the stairs again; 'let's settle our accounts. Monsieur Goriot won't be staying here much longer, and I . . .'

'Yes, he'll be leaving feet first, poor old chap,' she said, counting out her two hundred francs with a half-cheery, half-gloomy air.

'Now let's get on,' said Rastignac.

'Sylvie, fetch the sheets and go upstairs to help the gentlemen. You won't forget Sylvie, will you,' Madame Vauquer said in Eugène's ear; 'she's been up all hours for two nights now.'

As soon as Eugène's back was turned, the old woman hurried over to the cook and said in her ear: 'Use the sheets you've just turned over in number seven. Lord knows, that's good enough for a dead man.'

Eugène, who was already halfway up the stairs, didn't hear what the old landlady had said.

'Right,' said Bianchon, 'let's put on his nightshirt. Hold him up.'

Eugène stood at the head of the bed and supported the dying man while Bianchon took off his nightshirt. The old man reached a hand towards his chest as if to hold something there and uttered plaintive, inarticulate cries, as an animal does when in terrible pain.

'Oh! I know!' said Bianchon, 'he wants a little hair chain and locket that we took off earlier so we could apply his moxas. Poor man! We'd better put it back on him. It's on the mantelpiece.'

Eugène went to fetch the plaited chain of ash-blonde hair,

presumably belonging to Madame Goriot. On one side of the locket was engraved 'Anastasie' and on the other 'Delphine': a mirror-image of his heart, which always lay against it. The curls it held were so fine that they must have been cut when the two girls were very small. As he felt the locket touch his chest, the old man let out a long, deep sigh of such contentment, it was unbearable to watch. This was one of the last echoes of his sensibility, which then seemed to retreat to that unknown core from which our sympathies are drawn out or towards which they tend. The expression on his contorted face was that of a man sick with joy. The two students, devastated by the blinding force of feelings so strong they could outlast the faculty of thought, shed hot tears on the dying man, who uttered a cry of anguished delight.

'Nasie! Fifine!' he said.

'He's still alive,' said Bianchon.

'What for?' asked Sylvie.

'To suffer,' replied Rastignac.

Gesturing to his friend to do the same, Bianchon kneeled down and slipped his arms behind old Goriot's knees, while Rastignac kneeled on the other side of the bed so he could slide his hands under the sick man's back. Sylvie stood waiting, ready to pull off the sheets as soon as the dying man was lifted up, and to replace them with the ones she'd brought up. Fooled as he was by those tears, Goriot put every scrap of strength he had left into stretching out his hands until he found the students' heads on either side of the bed and violently grasped their hair. A faint 'Ah! My angels!' was heard. Two words, two murmurs given intonation by the soul taking flight as they were uttered.

'Poor, dear man,' said Sylvie, her heart softened by this cry, the expression of a loftiness of feeling that the most cruel, the most unintentional of lies had exalted for the last time.

The father's final sigh was to be one of joy. That sigh was the summation of his entire life: he was deceived to the last. Old man Goriot was respectfully laid back down on his pallet. From this point onwards, his features would bear the painful imprint of the ensuing struggle between death and life, in a system now devoid of the cerebral awareness which determines human feelings of pleasure and pain. It would only be a matter of time before there would be a complete collapse.

'He'll stay like this for a few hours and will die without our noticing; we won't even hear a death-rattle. His brain must be completely congested.'

Just then they heard the footsteps of a young woman, out of breath from the stairs.

'She's come too late,' said Rastignac.

It wasn't Delphine, but Thérèse, her chambermaid.

'Monsieur Eugène,' she said; 'a terrible scene blew up between Monsieur and Madame, over the money my poor mistress requested for her father. She fainted, the doctor came, she had to be bled, she kept calling out: "My father's dying, I want to see Papa!" Why, she was weeping and wailing fit to break your heart.'

'Enough, Thérèse. Even if she came now, there'd be no point. Monsieur Goriot is no longer conscious.'

'The poor dear old gentleman, so he really is that ill!' said Thérèse.

'You don't need me any more – got to go and get my dinner, it's half four,' said Sylvie as she went out, almost colliding with Madame de Restaud at the top of the stairs.

The comtesse appeared, a grave and terrible apparition. She looked at the poorly lit death-bed with its one candle and was moved to tears to see her father's mask-like features, still twitching with the last tremors of life. Bianchon withdrew discreetly.

'I didn't get away in time,' the comtesse said to Rastignac.

The student gave her a nod full of sadness. Madame de Restaud took hold of her father's hand and kissed it.

'Forgive me, Father! You used to say that my voice would summon you from the grave; please then, come back to life for just a moment and bless your repentant daughter. Please hear me. This is terrible! No one on earth but you will ever bless me again. Everyone hates me; you alone love me. Even my own children will despise me. Take me with you; I'll love you, I'll look after you. He can't hear me any more, I must be mad.' She fell to her knees and stared wild-eyed at her father's poor exhausted body.

'My misery is complete,' she said, looking at Eugène. 'Monsieur de Trailles has gone, leaving huge debts behind him, and I have found out that he was deceiving me. My husband will never forgive me and now has complete control over my fortune. I've lost all my illusions. Alas! Why did I forsake the only heart' (here she gestured towards her father) 'that held me in adoration! I ignored him, I pushed him away, I did him a thousand wrongs, despicable creature that I am!'

'He knew,' said Rastignac.

Just then old Goriot opened his eyes, but it was only the effect of a convulsion. The comtesse's desperate lurch of hope was no less dreadful a sight than that of the dying man's eyes.

'Could it be that he can hear me?' cried the comtesse. 'No,' she said, sitting down next to the bed.

As Madame de Restaud seemed to want to sit with her father, Eugène went downstairs for something to eat. The boarders were already assembled at the table.

'Well, well,' said the painter, 'so it seems there's to be a bit of a *deathorama* upstairs?'

'Charles,' said Eugène, 'perhaps you could find a less morbid topic for your jokes.'

'What, can't we have a laugh round here any more?' retorted the painter. 'What difference does it make? Bianchon says the old chap isn't *compos mentis*.'

'Meaning', said the museum clerk, 'that he'll die as he has lived.'

'My father is dead,' cried the comtesse.

Hearing Madame de Restaud's terrible wail, Sylvie, Rastignac and Bianchon rushed upstairs and found her in a faint. Once they had brought her round, they helped her into her carriage, which was still waiting. Eugène handed her into Thérèse's safekeeping, giving orders to drive to Madame de Nucingen's house.

'Ah! Yes, he's dead all right,' said Bianchon, as he came downstairs.

'Come along, Gentlemen, hurry up and sit down,' said Madame Vauquer; 'the soup's going cold.'

The two students sat down side by side.

'What do we do now?' said Eugène to Bianchon.

'Well, I've closed his eyes and laid him out. Once we've had his death recorded and certified by the doctor at the town hall, he'll be sewn up in a shroud and we'll bury him. What else is there for him?'

'He'll never go sniffing his bread again, like this,' said one boarder, mimicking the face the old man used to make.

'For the love of God, Gentlemen,' said the tutor, 'just leave old man Goriot be and stop stuffing him down our throats, because you've been dishing him up with every possible sauce for the past hour. One of the privileges of the fine city of Paris is that you can be born, live and die here without anyone paying the blindest bit of notice to you. Let us therefore reap the benefits of civilization. There were sixty other deaths today: why don't you go and weep over the hecatomb of all Paris? If old man Goriot has snuffed it, good for him! If you're that fond of him, go and take care of him and leave the rest of us to eat our dinner in peace.'

'Oh! I agree,' said the widow. 'Good for him! After all, he had nothing but troubles all his life, the poor man.'

This was the only funeral oration spoken for a man who, in Eugène's eyes, was Fatherhood incarnate. The fifteen boarders started chatting away as if nothing had happened. The clashing of forks and spoons, the laughter and banter, the expressions that flickered across those greedy and unconcerned faces, their indifference, made Eugène and Bianchon shudder with disgust. As soon as they had eaten, they set off to find a priest to keep vigil and pray by the dead man's bedside through the night. They had to measure out the last respects to be paid to the old man against the paltry sum they could spare to pay for them. At around nine in the evening, the body was placed on the slats of the bedstead, between two candles, in that bare room, and a priest came to sit with it. Rastignac had asked the cleric the price of the service and the pallbearers, and, before going to bed, wrote to the Baron de Nucingen and the Comte de Restaud, requesting them to send sufficient funds through their representatives to meet the costs of the burial. He dispatched Christophe with the notes, then went to bed and fell fast asleep, utterly exhausted.

Next morning, it fell to Bianchon and Rastignac to go and register the death, which was certified around midday. Two hours later, neither of the two sons-in-law had sent any money, nobody had turned up to represent them and Rastignac had already been obliged to pay the priest. As Sylvie had requested ten francs for laying the old man out and sewing him into a shroud, Eugène and Bianchon worked out that if the dead man's relatives refused to contribute anything at all, they would be pushed to cover the costs. The medical student therefore decided to lay out the corpse himself and had a pauper's coffin brought from the hospital, which he'd been able to buy at a discount.

'Let's play a prank on those rascally relatives of his,' he said to Eugène. 'Go and buy a plot of earth in Père Lachaise, for five years, and order a third-class funeral[220] at the church and at the undertaker's. If the sons-in-law and the daughters refuse to pay you back, then have the stone engraved with: "Here lies Monsieur Goriot, father of the Comtesse de Restaud and of the Baronne de Nucingen, whose burial was paid for by two students."'

Eugène held off following his friend's advice until he had called on Monsieur and Madame de Nucingen, and Monsieur and Madame de Restaud, without success. He made it no further than the doorstep. The valets had received strict orders.

'Monsieur and Madame', they said, 'will see no one; their father has died and they are in the deepest mourning.'

Eugène now had enough experience of Parisian society to know not to insist. He felt a strange pang of emotion when he found himself cut off from Delphine.

'Sell some of your jewellery,' he wrote to her in the porter's lodge, 'so that your father may be decently consigned to his last resting-place.'

He sealed the note and persuaded the baron's porter to give it to Thérèse for her mistress; but the porter handed it over to the Baron de Nucingen, who threw it straight in the fire. Once he had made his final preparations, Eugène returned to the boarding house at around three and wept to see the coffin left stranded outside the openwork gate, draped in a black cloth that barely covered it, propped on two chairs in the empty road. A cheap holy-water sprinkler,[221] as yet untouched, lay submerged in a silver-plated brass bowl of holy water. The door hadn't even been draped in black. This was a pauper's death, with no ceremony, no followers, no friends and no relatives. Bianchon, who was needed at the hospital, had left a note for Rastignac, letting him know what he'd decided about the church. The house doctor informed him that a Mass was too expensive, that they'd have to make do with the cheaper service at Vespers and that he'd sent Christophe with a note for the undertaker. As Eugène finished reading Bianchon's hastily scribbled message, he caught sight of Madame Vauquer fingering the circular gold locket which held the two daughters' locks of hair.

'How could you dare to take that!' he said to her.

'Gracious! Did you want it to be buried with him?' replied Sylvie. 'It's made of gold.'

'Of course!' Eugène said indignantly; 'let him at least take with him the one thing that may stand in for his daughters.'

When the hearse came, Eugène had the coffin lifted up, then prised it open and reverently put back on the old man's chest the locket that held the likeness of a time when Delphine and Anastasie were young, untainted and pure, and 'never questioned anything', in the anguished words that he had cried out as he was dying. Rastignac and Christophe, with two undertakers, were the only followers of the hearse that took the poor man to Saint-Etienne-du-Mont, a church near the Rue Neuve-Sainte-Geneviève. When they arrived, the body was displayed in a small, dark, low-ceilinged chapel, around which the student looked in vain for old man Goriot's daughters or their husbands. Apart from him, the only person there was Christophe, who felt obliged to pay his last respects to a man who had sent a few good tips his way. As they waited for the two priests, the altar-boy and the verger, Rastignac squeezed Christophe's hand, unable to speak.

'Yes, Monsieur Eugène,' said Christophe, 'he was a decent and an honest man, who never raised his voice, never harmed a soul and never did any wrong.'

The two priests, the altar-boy and the verger arrived and did everything that can be done for seventy francs in an age when the Church isn't rich enough to pray free of charge. The clergymen chanted a psalm, the *Libera*, the *De profundis*.[222] The service lasted twenty minutes. There was one funeral carriage, for one of the priests and the altar-boy, who consented to take Eugène and Christophe with them.

'There's no one following,' said the priest; 'we can go fast so we won't finish late, it's half past five.' However, just as the body was placed in the hearse, two emblazoned but empty carriages, belonging to the Comte de Restaud and the Baron de Nucingen, turned up and followed the convoy to Père Lachaise.[223]

At six o'clock, old man Goriot's body was lowered into his grave, watched by his daughters' servants. As soon as the clergyman had said the short prayer for the dead man that the students' money had purchased, they disappeared, and so did he. The two grave-diggers threw a few shovelfuls of earth onto the lid of the coffin, then straightened up and turned to Rastignac to ask for their tip. Eugène delved into his pockets, but, finding them empty, was forced to borrow twenty sous from Christophe. This detail, so slight in itself, filled Rastignac with unbearable sadness. Night was falling, the damp, drizzling dusk sapped his mind, he looked at the grave and buried in it his last young man's tear, a tear that springs from the sacred emotion of a pure heart, the kind that splashes up from the ground where it falls and rises into heaven. He folded his arms and stared at the clouds. Seeing him thus preoccupied, Christophe left him.

Alone now, Rastignac walked up towards the cemetery's highest point and saw Paris below him, winding along the banks of the Seine, its lights beginning to sparkle. His eyes came to rest almost greedily on the area between the column on the Place Vendôme and the dome of the Invalides, the home of the *beau monde*, which he had been so determined to enter. He gave the droning hive a look that seemed to drain it of its honey in advance and pronounced these grand words: 'Now let us fight it out!'

And by way of firing an opening shot at Society, Rastignac went to have dinner with Madame de Nucingen.

Saché,[224] September 1834

Notes

1. *Geoffroy Saint-Hilaire*: Balzac was an admirer of the famous 'visionary naturalist' Etienne Geoffroy Saint-Hilaire (1772–1844), some of whose theories presaged Darwin. In his preface to the *Human Comedy*, Balzac declares his intention to apply scientific methods to the study of 'social species', which 'have existed and always will exist, just as there are zoological species'. As a keen observer of the natural history of humanity, he is concerned with the way species adapt, or fail to adapt, to the ever-changing milieux in which they find themselves. See note 146 on Georges Cuvier and Introduction p. xx.

I. A RESPECTABLE BOARDING HOUSE

2. *Rue Neuve-Sainte-Geneviève*: Today, Rue Tournefort, running parallel to the Rue Mouffetard, south of the Panthéon. Balzac's description does not tally exactly with the street layout at that time; he highlights features that emphasize its isolation and drabness.
3. *Faubourg Saint-Marceau*: Balzac uses 'Marceau' here, 'Marcel' elsewhere. The district – named after Saint Marcel or Marceau (Bishop of Paris AD 417–36) – was known by both names.
4. *drama . . . tear-strewn literature*: The *drame romantique*, which exploited the effects of melodrama, was in vogue at that time, and Balzac had recently written a review of Victor Hugo's *Hernani*. 'Tear-strewn' perhaps refers us to that strand of popular Romantic literature whose intense emotion and despairing melancholy tended to tip over into sentimentality.
5. *intra muros et extra*: Latin, 'within and without the city walls'. A quotation from Book I of Horace's *Epistles*.
6. *Jaggernaut*: A reference to the Indian god Jagannatha, worshipped at Puri (Orissa) in the bay of Bengal. Jagannatha,

'Lord of the World', is one of the titles of Krishna (the eighth avatar of Vishnu). Every year, during the *Rathayātrā* festival, the deity is drawn through the streets of Puri on a richly decorated chariot, so huge and heavy that it takes hundreds of pilgrims to pull it. Accidents are frequent – hence the origins of the word 'Juggernaut', denoting a force that crushes whatever lies in its path.

7. *All is true*: The alternative title of Shakespeare's *Henry VIII* and the one by which it was known to its first audiences. Balzac may have taken this from an article on the play which preceded one of his short stories, 'The Red Inn', in the *Revue de Paris*, 1831.

8. *Val-de-Grâce ... Panthéon*: The first is a military hospital founded during the Revolution on the site of a seventeenth-century abbey; the second, originally a church dedicated to Sainte-Geneviève, founded by Louis XV, became a 'pantheon' during the Revolution, that is, a secular monument devoted to the memory of the 'great men of the nation'.

9. *a stone's throw away*: At the Hôpital des Capucins, a former convent, where venereal diseases were treated.

10. *on his return to Paris in 1777*: In fact, Voltaire returned – after twenty-eight years in exile – on 10 February 1778, just a few months before his death. He wrote this rhyming couplet for his friend the Marquis de Maisons.

11. *tapering fruit trees*: Literally, 'quenouille-trained', a French pruning method where the fruit tree's branches are trained to bend downwards, forming a conical or distaff shape.

12. *haircloth*: A fabric popular with middle-class families and establishments in the nineteenth century, as it was extremely strong and long-wearing, but had a sheen which emulated the effect of expensive silk upholstery at a fraction of the cost.

13. *Telemachus*: The scenic paper in question was designed around 1818 and blockprinted by the Paris firm Joseph Dufour et Cie. It was a long strip landscape paper (a continuous scene of non-repeating panels) based on Fénelon's popular work *Les aventures de Télémaque* (1699), which recounts the education of Ulysses' son by Athena, disguised as Mentor, who oversees his transformation from selfish youth to model ruler (it also operated as a commentary on the bellicosity and excesses of Louis XIV). The same paper was to be found at the Château de Saché, where Balzac wrote *Old Man Goriot*.

    Calypso was the nymph who imprisoned first Ulysses, then his son Telemachus – when he came in search of his missing

father – on the island of Ogygia. She gave both food and promised them immortality. Balzac's choice of wallpaper is not without
significance, and humour.

14. *moiré*: Ordinary tin plate treated with acids to give it a varie-
gated appearance, otherwise known as crystallized tinplate. The
moiré métallique technique was discovered in France in 1814.

15. *Argand lamps*: The Argand oil lamp was invented in France in the
early 1780s, and represented a significant breakthrough in household lighting, as it produced as much light as nine candles.

16. *discounter*: Also 'bill-discounter'. Someone (often Gobseck, in
the *Human Comedy*) who purchases a bill of exchange (note 70)
at a discount (that is, minus the difference between its present
value and its value on the date it falls due) then sells it for its full
worth at maturity, to make a profit.

17. *Georges and Pichegru*: Vendean (royalist) leader and former
revolutionary general whose plot to assassinate Napoleon was
uncovered in 1804, when they were both betrayed for a reward.
Georges Cadoudal was guillotined, Jean-Charles Pichegru died
in prison (murder or suicide).

18. *Commissary-General*: A kind of quartermaster. One of Balzac's
uncles held this post during the Revolution.

19. *La Bourbe and La Salpêtrière*: These began as hospitals in the
older sense of the word, namely, institutions or asylums for the
poor and indigent. The former abbey in Rue de la Bourbe (literally, 'Muddy Road', named for its general insalubrity) was first a
foundling then a lying-in hospital (it provided poor women with
a place to give birth); La Salpêtrière, a converted saltpetre manu-
factory and former women's prison, took in old, incurable and
insane women. The area defined here lies between the Observa-
toire and the Quai d'Austerlitz.

20. *fichus*: Triangular pieces of colourful fabric or lace, covering the
head or neck.

21. *a dealer in second-hand finery*: An ambiguous profession. These
women who went from door to door offering clothes and jewellery for sale were also reputed to engage in shadier activities on
the side.

22. *the audacious tribe of the sons of Japet*: Balzac's rendering of
'audax Iapeti genus' comes from a famous line in one of Horace's
Odes (I.3.27), which considers all mankind as descended from
Prometheus, son of Iapetus, who made man in the likeness of the
gods. The Boulevard des Italiens was one of the most fashionable
streets in Paris.

23. *cats . . . fire*: Reference to the fable by La Fontaine, 'The Cat and the Monkey' (*Fables* IX.17). The cat (Raton) pulls the chestnuts out of the fire, while the monkey (Bertrand) eats them; that is, the monkey uses the cat as a tool to accomplish a self-serving purpose. Hence the English expression 'to be the cats-paw of someone'.

24. *chlorosis*: A type of anaemia affecting pubescent females – and notably the heroine of Balzac's roman de jeunesse *Wann-Chlore* – which was fashionable at that time. Also known as 'green sickness', for the pallid complexion it induced.

25. *a certain piercing and steely look*: Balzac was interested in the ideas of Franz-Anton Mesmer (1734–1815) on second sight and thought transmission, notably his theory of 'animal magnetism' (or 'mesmerism').

26. *gloria*: Coffee with a dash of eau-de-vie (brandy), so called because it comes at the end of a meal, just as the Gloria Patri comes at the end of the psalms during Mass.

27. *Juvenal*: Roman poet, born AD 55–60?, author of the vitriolic *Satires*, which targeted the rich and powerful in ancient Rome.

28. *verdigris*: The green rust which forms on copper and brass. The comparison with a counting-house underlines the pragmatically commercial character of Madame Vauquer's establishment.

29. *armoires . . . 'ormoires'*: An 'armoire' is a wardrobe or safe. According to Balzac, in *César Birotteau*, the corruption '*ormoire*' comes from the idea that women kept their gold (*or*) in their wardrobes along with their dresses.

30. *marks*: A mark was a European measure mainly used to weigh gold and silver, equivalent to eight ounces.

31. *Grand-Livre*: The register of all those who hold Government Stock.

32. *Macouba*: High-quality snuff from the Macouba plantations in Martinique.

33. *Choisy, Soissy, Gentilly*: Three villages on the outskirts of Paris known for their many *guinguettes*, or open-air taverns, popular with Parisians on Sunday outings.

34. *free ticket in July*: Summer emptied Paris theatres of fashionable audiences. Free tickets were distributed by authors or producers to friends or official 'claqueurs' (applauders), so that their play would appear to be a success (Balzac writes about this system in *Lost Illusions*).

35. *Galeries de Bois*: Shops made of wooden boards, which once stood on the site of the present-day Galerie d'Orléans.

36. *La Petite Jeannette*: A shop selling novelties established in 1833, on what is today 3 Boulevard des Italiens.

37. *Boeuf à la mode*: The reference is to a famous restaurant near the Palais-Royal whose sign showed a bullock dressed up in a shawl and hat, a pun on the signature dish from which the restaurant took its name.

38. *lamb . . . stag*: Both are stock-market terms for outsiders. The first is a dunce who speculates and loses his money; the second a speculator who poses as a bona fide investor but only buys shares to sell them immediately at a profit.

39. *prunella*: A strong fabric (silk or worsted), usually black, used in women's footwear.

40. *Rue de l'Estrapade*: As we know from the opening passage, horses rarely entered the Rue Neuve-Sainte-Geneviève, because of the inconvenient slope.

41. *ell*: An obsolete length measurement.

42. *drab*: A type of woollen cloth mainly worn in the winter.

43. *facial angle*: From phrenology; the angle formed by a horizontal line (nostril to ear) and a vertical line (nostril to forehead). Then thought to be an indicator of the degree of development of the mental faculties or intelligence. See also note 75 on Franz Joseph Gall.

44. *Capiferae*: That is, of the 'genus' of cap-wearers.

45. *Réaumur scale*: Thermometric scale introduced by the French physicist René-Antoine Ferchault de Réaumur around 1730, according to which water freezes at 0° and boils at 80°.

46. *Prado . . . Odéon*: The Prado, situated in Rue de la Barillerie (today, Boulevard du Palais), was a ballroom popular with students. The Odéon reopened after being entirely rebuilt in October 1819, and so Rastignac would theoretically have attended the first balls that took place there.

47. *tan-turf*: Spent oak bark from the tan-pits which was pressed into bricks to make cheap fuel.

48. *the Faubourg Saint-Germain*: Balzac provides his own definition in the *History of the Thirteen*.

> What in France goes by the name of the Faubourg Saint-Germain is neither a quarter of Paris, nor an institution, nor anything clearly definable. The Place Royale, the Faubourg Saint-Honoré and the Chaussée d'Antin also possess mansions in which the atmosphere of the Faubourg Saint-Germain prevails. Thus the Faubourg is not strictly confined to its own territory. People born far beyond its sphere of influence can feel it and be part and parcel of this

world, whereas certain others born inside it may be forever excluded from it. The manners, speech, in a word the Faubourg Saint-Germain tradition, has been in Paris, during the last forty years, what the Court formerly had been, what Hôtel Saint-Paul had been in the fourteenth century, the Louvre in the fifteenth, the Palais, the Hôtel Rambouillet, the Place Royale in the sixteenth, then Versailles in the seventeenth and eighteenth centuries. In every phase of history the Paris of the upper classes and the nobility has had its own centre, just as plebeian Paris will always have its own special quarter.

(Tr. Herbert J. Hunt, Penguin Classics, 1974)

49. *rout*: In its nineteenth-century sense, a large fashionable gathering or evening reception.

50. *quadrille*: A French square dance for four couples, divided into five sections, each of which is a separate dance.

51. *the Bois . . . the Bouffons*: The Bois de Boulogne, to the west of Paris, was where members of high society would drive out to promenade in their carriages; the Bouffons is another name for the Théâtre-Italien or Italiens, the fashionable place to be seen by night, where Parisians went to hear performances of *opera seria* sung in Italian (rather than French).

52. *the Marquis de Montriveau . . . Duchesse de Langeais*: The full story of these two lovers is told in the second section of Balzac's *History of the Thirteen*: 'The Duchesse de Langeais' (tr. Hunt, 1974). The story's original title was 'Don't touch the axe!'

53. *Chaussée d'Antin*: The name of a road situated just east of what is today the Opéra. The reference here is to an entire district, at the time home to wealthy financiers and bankers, or nineteenth-century right-bank new money (as opposed to the old aristocracy of the left-bank Faubourg Saint-Germain). Anastasie de Restaud lives in the Rue du Helder; her sister Delphine de Nucingen close by in the Rue Saint-Lazare.

54. *the Code*: The Code Civil, introduced in 1804 (later known as the *Code Napoléon*), constituted a comprehensive reformation and codification of French civil law. After the Revolution, it became possible, and necessary, to replace the many conflicting legal systems that had previously co-existed (Roman law, customary law, canon law, case law, royal decrees), as the old power structures were replaced by the new. Under the Code, all male citizens were equal. However, for women, the new laws were retrograde, subordinating them to their fathers and husbands,

who decided on the fate of children, had control of all property and were favoured in divorce proceedings. The paterfamilias even had the right to imprison his child for a month, while illegitimate children were barred from any right to inherit. Victorine Taillefer, and Goriot's daughters, suffer from the impact of these laws in *Old Man Goriot*.

55. *a Saint Joseph*: A carpenter.

56. *King Augustus of Poland*: Augustus II 'the Strong' (1670–1733, reigned from 1697) was reputed to have fathered 300 children (all illegitimate save the son who succeeded him).

57. *list slippers*: Made from the selvage, or border, of a length of cloth, woven to produce a more robust finish, so less likely to fray. They were worn around the house in situations where a quiet tread was required, for example, in nurseries and sick rooms. Here, the circumstance is clearly suspicious; the wearer is engaged in some surreptitious activity.

58. *Saint-Etienne*: The church of Saint-Etienne-du-Mont, not far from the Maison Vauquer (and still to be seen today near the Panthéon in the fifth arrondissement).

59. *Michonnette ... Poireau*: Sylvie is referring to Mademoiselle Michonneau and Monsieur Poiret in a jokily disrespectful way: '-ette' is a familiar form, and *poireau* is a leek.

60. *two liards*: A liard was a French coin of small denomination, worth a quarter of a sou. See Note on Money for an overview of the different currencies in circulation at that time in France.

61. *packet-boat*: More precisely, the 'Compagnie des Messageries impériales'. This was a private company (with state authorization) founded in 1805, which had the monopoly of public transport abroad until 1826.

62. *Rue des Grès*: Today, Rue Cujas, in the fifth arrondissement, near the Panthéon. Strategically located near the Sorbonne, where Gobseck is well placed to ensnare students living beyond their means, such as Rastignac.

63. *a Jew, an Arab, a Greek, a Bohemian*: Nineteenth-century terms for, respectively, someone who drives a hard bargain, a moneylender, a card-sharper and a gypsy (gypsies were thought to have come from Bohemia).

64. *A quietus*: A receipt issued when a debt has been paid off.

65. *O innocent ... women*: The phrase comes from a popular spoof melodrama, a four-act pantomime first performed in 1811.

66. *roux*: Used for thickening soups and stews, usually a mixture of butter and flour.

67. *déjeuner*. In nineteenth-century Paris, this referred to a morning
     meal of some kind. 'Breakfast (*premier déjeuner* . . .) was taken
     immediately after waking. It consisted of a cup of milk, coffee,
     tea, or chocolate together with a *flûte* (thin loaf) or round of
     toast' (see pp. 8–10, where it is served at seven). In this particular
     instance, the lodgers are having their 'Second breakfast' (*deux-
     ième déjeuner*). This 'was served between ten and noon. It
     consisted of hors-d'oeuvres, cold meats, and other snacks. Roast
     meats and salad were served only if the hour was somewhat
     advanced' (*A History of Private Life*, vol. 4, ed. Philippe Ariès
     and Georges Duby). *Deuxième déjeuner* could be taken as late as
     twelve in high society; the middle classes tended to take it closer
     to ten.

68. *Gobseck*: Madame de Restaud's visit to the usurer is described in
     Balzac's short story 'Gobseck', published in 1830, prior to *Old
     Man Goriot*.

69. *Mont-de-Piété*: In France, the name given to a state-run pawn-
     broker offering loans to the poor at low interest.

70. *bills of exchange*: Widely used in the nineteenth century, a bill of
     exchange functioned a little like a post-dated cheque or IOU,
     with the unique feature that it was negotiable, that is, the bill
     could be endorsed to a third party, and sold on. In simple terms,
     it was a payment order in writing addressed by one person
     (drawer) to another (drawee), the former instructing the latter to
     pay a specific sum of money on a given date to a specified person,
     or to the current bearer of the bill. The drawee signed the bill to
     accept responsibility for payment. There was no limit on how
     many times the bill could change hands before the due date. The
     more remote the due date, the lower the purchase price of the bill
     (and thus the greater the profit the third party stood to make).
     The third party, or endorsee (in this case, the bill-discounter),
     could speculate on the value of the bill to make a profit, either by
     waiting for the due date to make a gain equal to the difference
     between the value of the bill at purchase and at maturity, or by
     selling it on before the due date, ideally at a higher price (passing
     on the risk of default at the same time). The advantage of the
     transaction for the drawee was that they could defer payment to
     a later date. The advantage for the drawer was that they could
     convert the bill into cash without waiting for the due date. And
     the advantage for each successive endorsee was that they could
     speculate on the value of the bill with a view to making a profit.
     The amount at which the bill was discounted (sold for less than

its value at maturity) could also depend on the perceived risk of default by the drawee at maturity. If the drawee defaulted, the bill was 'protested', that is, legally declared dishonoured by the holder of the bill.

71. *paraded on the square*: That is, wearing the carcan or iron collar, still in use at the time (abolished in 1848).

72. *fiacre*: The French equivalent of the hackney cab, a small four-wheeled carriage.

73. *Diorama ... Panoramas*: The Panorama and Diorama prefigured modern cinema and mass entertainment, allowing anyone at all to admire alpine views, or see famous battles from the perspective of their generals. Both were spectacles based on large-scale paintings staged in purpose-built theatres. The Panorama created a spatial illusion: spectators stood on a static viewing platform and were presented with a 360-degree view of a topographical subject – an imposing landscape or famous city – painted on a huge circular canvas. The Diorama, with its revolving turntable, was more dynamic and theatrical, exploiting the dramatic possibilities of lighting to create convincing atmospheric effects (clouds, sunrise, sunset, storms) and thereby the illusion of temporal change and movement.

The British painter Robert Barker took out the first patent for a Panorama in 1787, and also coined the term by which it became known. It was initially popularized in Paris by James Thayer and the painter Pierre Prévost, whose assistant, Louis Jacques Mandé Daguerre, a former set designer (and future inventor of the Daguerrotype), went on to create the hugely successful Diorama in 1822. The Panorama enjoyed renewed popularity in Paris in the 1830s, when Charles Langlois, a former Napoleonic colonel, opened his Panorama de Navarin (criticized by Balzac for its 'mechanical charlatanism'), which gave spectators the chance to view a depiction of a sea battle from the deck of a real French battleship.

74. *usque ad talones*: Meaning 'into my heels'; a French/Latin student joke (*'avoir l'estomac dans les talons'* means 'to be starving').

75. *Doctor Gall's system ... bumps of Judas*: German physician Franz Joseph Gall (1758–1828) came to Paris in 1807 and established himself as medical practitioner and lecturer on phrenology. He saw the brain as being divided into twenty-seven (later thirty-seven) separate 'organs' and believed that the external appearance of the skull could be linked to specific mental functions and capacities (such as poetic talent, wit, forethought, obstinacy,

compassion, reproduction instinct and so on) and the extent of
their development. Geoffroy Saint-Hilaire (the dedicatee of this
novel) supported Gall's unsuccessful 1821 application to the
Académie des Sciences. Bianchon's comment on Mademoiselle
Michonneau's 'bumps of Judas' is a joke, suggesting that 'treach-
ery' is written all over her, although no such correlation is made
by Gall.

76. *A rose . . . dawn*: From 'Consolation à M. du Périer' (1598) by
     François de Malherbe (1555–1628), a well-known poem he
     wrote for a friend on the death of his daughter.

77. *cornute*: The noun describes a vessel with a long neck, bent
     downwards, used in distillation; the adjective denotes a cuckold.
     The French is *cornue*, which also sounds like *corps nu* (naked
     body). The jokes that follow all play on the idea (or innuendo)
     of Goriot's nose being long, red or a strange shape. 'Cornemuse'
     is the French term for the bagpipe

II. TWO CALLS ARE PAID

78. *Talleyrand-esque sayings*: Charles-Maurice de Talleyrand-Périgord
     (1754–1838) was a talented statesman and survivor; he held
     political or diplomatic office under five successive regimes in his
     lifetime. His inexhaustible humour and ironic wit were legend-
     ary (and enjoyed by such exacting companions as Madame de
     Staël and Lord Brougham).

79. *Charente*: One of the 83 French *départements* founded in 1793,
     comprising the former province of Angoumois, with Angoulême
     as its administrative seat, in the south-west of France. Balzac
     chose to set the estate of Rastignac in this region. He had stayed
     in Angoulême with his friend Zulma Carraud and her husband
     in 1832.

80. *bergère*: An armchair with a canework back, sides and seat, and
     loose cushions.

81. *thirty drawers*: Balzac's metaphor is inspired by Gall's system of
     phrenology. See note 75.

82. *Compagnie des Indes*: 'Company of the Indies', one of the names of
     the prosperous trading company originally founded by Louis XIV
     and Colbert in 1664, and dissolved by the National Conven-
     tion (which governed France 1792–5) on 24 August 1793. The
     company's role was to manage French trade with India, eastern
     Africa, the East Indies and other territories in the Indian Ocean.

83. *Vengeur . . . Warwick*: The *Vengeur* started life as the *Marseillois*, a French 74-gun man-of-war that saw action against the English in the American War of Independence (France signed a treaty in 1778 backing the Americans). The ship was renamed the *Vengeur de Peuple* in 1794, and was part of the republican fleet commanded by Admiral Villaret de Joyeuse during the Revolutionary Wars. She was sunk by the HMS *Brunswick* during the *Bataille du 13 Prairial an II* (the Glorious First of June). The *Warwick* was a British ship captured in 1756 off Martinique by the French frigate the *Atalante*, then recaptured in 1761 by Admiral Alexander Hood commanding HMS *Minerva*.

84. *morganatic*: In German law, the term designated a marriage between a man and a woman of unequal rank, in which the offspring would have no succession rights. There is no French legal equivalent, but the term was used to describe the 'secret marriages' contracted within the Royal Family During the Ancien Régime, for example, that between Madame de Maintenon and Louis XIV. As such, the term came to be associated with illicit liaisons.

85. *C-a-a-ro . . . non dubitare*: A duet from Cimarosa's *Il Matrimonio segreto* (after David Garrick's play *The Clandestine Marriage*), which was performed at the Théâtre-Italien in 1819–20.

86. *porter*: In French, a *suisse* or 'Swiss'. Porters of grand houses were called this because their richly coloured uniforms looked like those worn by the Swiss Guard, who protected the French Royal Family before the Revolution.

87. *coupé(s)*: A short, closed carriage with four wheels and two seats inside. The driver sat outside.

88. *stallion . . . scent of equine love on the breeze*: A reference to Virgil's *Georgics* III.5.250–51. The section deals with the dangers of desire.

89. *the Elysée*: Then the residence of the Duc de Berry (son of the future Charles X). As Montriveau is a member of the Royal Guard, Madame de Beauséant says that he was there because he was on duty, implying that he was not there to meet the duchesse.

90. *Ejusdem farinae*: Latin, literally, 'of the same flour', a denigratory term implying 'they're all as bad as each other'. Louis XVIII had a reputation for wit.

91. *five or six hundred thousand francs*: There is some discrepancy as to the exact amount. Delphine says it is 700,000, Goriot 800,000, later rounding off the sum to 'un bon petit million'.

92. *Lamartine*: Rather than a specific quotation, a reference to the poet's style. Alphonse de Lamartine (1790–1869) was a politician

and poet. His *Méditations poétiques* (1820) established him as a pivotal figure in the French Romantic movement.

93. *wield love like an axe*: The Duchesse de Langeais is the eponymous heroine of a story by Balzac, whose original title, echoed here, was 'Don't touch the axe!' See note 52.

94. *Foriot*: A fashionable ploy among French aristocracy and high society at the time was to wilfully mispronounce commoners' names, pretending to be unable to remember them.

95. *president of his section*: In 1790, forty-eight revolutionary 'sections' replaced the old system of urban parishes.

96. *intendant*: The person who manages a nobleman's household.

97. *his kind*: That is, forestallers, or the farmers and manufacturers who, from 1793, withheld necessary commodities from circulation and hoarded them. The subsequent threat of famine drove up prices drastically and provoked widespread rioting in Paris in 1795. The workers and lower classes suffered most – their destitution contrasting with the ostentatious wealth of a new class of rich profiteers (*accapareurs*), who became the public enemy.

98. *Committee of Public Safety*: The notorious *Comité de salut public* in fact dealt ruthlessly with profiteers, sending many to the guillotine.

99. *royalist leanings*: The novel is set in 1819, during the Bourbon Restoration, five years after Louis XVIII had ascended to the throne (following Napoleon's abdication and exile to Elba in 1814, then escape, defeat at Waterloo and banishment to St Helena, a year later). Louis XVIII had the support of the right-wing 'ultra-royalists'. Balzac wrote the novel in 1834–5.

100. *veteran of '93*: 1793 was the year in which the Reign of Terror began. The sans-culottes ousted the politically élitist Girondins from the Convention, and the socially radical Jacobins (including Robespierre, Danton, Marat) took over the Committee of Public Safety.

101. *when the Bourbons were reinstated*: See note 99. From a royalist point of view, Goriot's survival, through his revolutionary involvement (mentioned earlier), taints him.

102. *Ariadne's thread*: A reference to the Greek myth where Ariadne helps Theseus to slay the Minotaur by giving him the magic ball of thread left her by Daedalus. He ties the end to the entrance door of the labyrinth and the thread leads him to the Minotaur. After slaying the monster, he finds his way out again by rolling the thread back into a ball.

103. *ultima ratio mundi*: Latin, 'the world's final sanction'. An echo

of the famous motto Louis XIV had inscribed on the royal cannon: *ultima ratio regum*, 'the final argument of kings'. That is, money prevails where other measures fail. There are interesting echoes here of views expressed by the republican thinker and writer Benjamin Constant in his 1819 speech *De la liberté des anciens comparée à celle des modernes*:

> Today [by contrast with the ancients], private individuals are stronger than political authorities; wealth is a force more readily available at all times, more readily applicable to all interests, and is consequently far more real, and more readily obeyed. Power threatens; wealth rewards. We can evade power by deceiving it, but to obtain the favours of wealth, we must serve it. Ultimately, the latter will prevail.

104. *asymptotes*: In mathematics, rather than being a parallel, as Balzac seems to imply here, an asymptote is actually a line which approaches a curve without ever reaching it.

105. *Dolibans*: Monsieur d'Oliban is the main character – a foolish father – in a play by Choudard-Desforges performed in 1790. In earlier versions of the text, Balzac wrote 'Caliban'.

106. *Rue Oblin*: This road ran from the Rue Coquillière to the circular Corn Exchange building.

107. *the Holy Roman Empire*: The name by which the Empire of Germany was known from 800 to 1806, until the abdication of Emperor Francis II, following the formation of the Confederation of the Rhine, which recognized Napoleon as its protector.

III. AN INTRODUCTION TO SOCIETY

108. *cannons of elder*: Being hollow stemmed, elder twigs are ideal for making blowpipes or pea-shooters.

109. *There is talk . . . silence as to the rest*: A witty misquotation from Corneille's *Cinna* (IV. 1290).

110. *twenty thousand livres per year*: Balzac appears to suggest that a canny tailor recognizes that the clothes he provides allow a young man to make his fortune, and that his return may not ultimately be in money, but in reputation. As Robb observes in his biography (*Balzac*, p. 137), Balzac scatters flattering references to his own tailor, Buisson, throughout the *Human Comedy*, as a 'novel way of paying bills "without spending any money"'.

111. *Rue Saint-Jacques ... Rue des Saints-Pères*: That is, the Latin Quarter, centred around the Sorbonne.

112. *projected thoughts ... catch us unawares*: Balzac's ideas on thought, will and energy reflect his interest in Emanuel Swedenborg's system of spiritual philosophy and Franz Mesmer's theory of animal magnetism (and are exposed in detail in his novels *Louis Lambert* and *Séraphîta*).

113. *the cause of his death*: Joachim Murat (1767–1815) came from the Lot region in south-west France. He served Napoleon effectively in the coup d'état of 1799 and was rewarded with the hand of his younger sister Caroline. Murat distinguished himself with daring acts of bravery in the most important battles of the age: Marengo, Austerlitz, Jena, Eylau, and was made King of Naples in 1808. However, after the battle of Borodino, he wavered in his loyalty to Napoleon and abandoned the retreating army, in an unsuccessful bid to save his kingdom from the Austrian troops. In October 1815 he made a last reckless bid to recover Naples, almost unaided, but was taken prisoner and shot.

114. *the Midi*: The south of France, or the area below an imaginary line dividing France east–west at Brive-la-Gaillarde and Valence (roughly corresponding to the old north–south language divisions of *Oïl* and *Oc*).

115. *King of Sweden*: The reference is to Jean-Baptiste Bernadotte (1764–1844), one of Napoleon's most controversial marshals, who was born in Pau, in the Pyrenees. He married Désirée Clary, Bonaparte's former fiancée, and was elected Crown Prince and regent of Sweden in 1810. When France occupied Swedish Pomerania in 1812, he switched allegiances and joined the Sixth Coalition (Great Britain, Russia, Prussia, Sweden, Austria, German states) against Napoleon. He became King Charles XIV of Sweden in 1818, founding the present royal dynasty.

116. *Cellini*: The memoirs of the famous (and notorious) Florentine sculptor and goldsmith (1500–1571) were published in French in 1822. Berlioz was also an admirer: his opera *Benvenuto Cellini* was first performed in Paris in 1838.

117. *in the nets at Saint-Cloud*: Nets were cast into the Seine at Saint-Cloud to catch the corpses of the drowned as they floated downstream.

118. *I've spent some time in the Midi*: This is explained at note 164 to avoid revealing elements of plot.

119. *the Code*: See note 54.

120. *T for thief*: French convicts were branded with the initials 'T.F.' for *Travaux Forcés* ('hard labour').

121. *Villèle ... Manuel*: That is, falsifying election results by 'reading' the wrong name on the ballot. 1819 was a general election year. Joseph Villèle was an ultra-royalist leader and (Restoration) government supporter; Jacques-Antoine Manuel was a republican lawyer and member of the opposing 'Independent' or liberal faction.

122. *on the shelf*: The French refers to the custom of calling a woman a *catherinette* if she reached twenty-five and was still single on St Catherine's day (25 November). The term originated with seamstresses, who would make a special hat to wear to the *bal des catherinettes*.

123. *Longchamp*: Not a reference to the racecourse, which didn't exist at the time the novel was written, but most likely to the fashionable custom of promenading carriages through the Bois de Boulogne, from Porte Maillot to Longchamp.

124. *ten likely lads*: A reference which brings to mind the Thirteen: 'They were thirteen kings – anonymous, but really kings; more than kings: judges and executioners too, they had equipped themselves with wings in order to soar over society in its heights and depths, and disdained to occupy any place in it, because they had unlimited power over it' (from Balzac's preface to *History of the Thirteen*, tr. Hunt, 1974).

125. *Aubry*: During his time in charge of military operations on the Committee of Public Safety between April and August 1795, François Aubry relieved Bonaparte of the artillery command of the Italian army. However, he himself was deported to Cayenne (French Guiana) after the coup of 18 Fructidor (4 September 1797).

126. *I want ... holding you to account*: Slavery was first abolished in France in 1794 by the Convention, restored in 1802 by the Consulate (Bonaparte), and definitively abolished in 1848 by the Second Republic. Balzac's younger brother Henri married a Creole woman and owned around thirty black slaves on the island of Mauritius. He returned to France in 1834, financially ruined.

127. *a quint and a quatorze*: In the card game Piquet, a *quint* is a sequence of five cards of the same suit counting as fifteen and a *quatorze* is a set of four aces, kings, queens, knaves or tens, counting as fourteen.

128. *Cadran-Bleu ... Ambigu-Comique*: The Cadran-Bleu restaurant

took its name from a sign with a clock-face showing four o'clock. Situated on the Boulevard du Temple, it was frequented by a bourgeois rather than fashionable clientele. The Ambigu-Comique, on the same road, was one of the largest theatres in Paris and attracted mainly working-class audiences to the melodramas it showed.

129. *Some sniff out dowries . . . bound hand and foot*: Vautrin suggests four methods of making money: marrying a rich woman, profit-taking on the liquidation of business concerns (just as Grandet turns his dead brother's liquidation to his own account, in *Eugénie Grandet*), vote-rigging in an election, or selling a newspaper, whose subscribers are committed for a certain amount of time, and powerless to protest.

130. *Taillefer . . . the Revolution*: This story is told in Balzac's 'The Red Inn' (included in *Selected Short Stories*, tr. Sylvia Raphael, Penguin Classics, 1977).

131. *the Conservatoire*: The Paris museum known as the Conservatoire des Arts et Métiers was founded in 1794 and houses collections of machines, scientific instruments and inventions.

132. *La Fayette*: The Marquis de La Fayette (1757–1834) was a soldier and statesman, of Liberal ideals. He fought in the American Revolution (becoming a lifelong friend of George Washington), and was involved in drafting the Declaration of the Rights of Man and of the Citizen in July 1789.

133. *the prince*: A reference to Talleyrand, the French statesman whose skilled diplomacy at the Congress of Vienna (1814–15) secured better-than-expected terms for France. Balzac was an admirer. See note 78.

134. *primitive words*: In grammar or philology, original or radical words, from which others are formed, as opposed to derivative words; or alternatively, the primeval stage of a parent language.

135. *Lacedaemonia*: The ancient Greek name for Sparta, whose ruling class turned from the arts, philosophy and literature towards war and diplomacy, to build up the most powerful army in Greece. The warrior class rewarded bravery with glory, and trained its young men to be ruthless and cunning.

136. *the Restoration*: See note 99.

137. *the Duc d'Escars*: Royalist general and renowned gastronomist, who was made a duke by Louis XVIII and became his senior maître d'hôtel. He reputedly died of indigestion in 1822.

138. *Tantalus types*: See note 209.

139. *Cherubino*: The Count's desiring and desired adolescent page, in Beaumarchais' satirical comedy *Le Mariage de Figaro* (Paris,

1784), upon which the Mozart comic opera, *Le Nozze di Figaro* (Vienna, 1786), was based.

140. *Ssince . . . vell resseeft*: Balzac is said to have modelled Nucingen's Teutonic accent on that of the powerful banker James de Rothschild.

141. *Alceste . . . Jeanie Deans*: Alceste, the main character in Molière's play *The Misanthrope* (1666), makes himself unpopular through his determination to flout social convention and be honest at all costs. Jeanie Deans is the principled heroine of Walter Scott's *The Heart of Midlothian* (translated into French in 1818 as *La Prison d'Edimbourg*), who sees her sister sentenced to death rather than tell a white lie.

142. *Ecole de Droit*: The law faculty of the Sorbonne university.

143. *Jardin du Luxembourg*: A large public park in the sixth arrondissement not far from the Sorbonne.

144. *asks the reader . . . by killing a mandarin in China solely by force of will*: The passage appears to come from Chateaubriand's *Le Génie du christianisme* (1802), I.6.2, rather than Rousseau.

145. *Gordian knot*: 'An intricate knot tied by Gordius, king of Gordium in Phrygia. The oracle declared that whoever should loosen it should rule Asia, and Alexander the Great overcame the difficulty by cutting through the knot with his sword' (*OED*).

146. *Cuvier's lecture*: The renowned naturalist Georges Cuvier (1769–1832) began his career in Paris as the protégé of Geoffroy Saint-Hilaire, the dedicatee of this novel, but later in life became his rival. Their bitter clash of ideas in 1830 caused great controversy: both sought to explain the diversity of nature, but (roughly), Cuvier focused on function (and the differences between species), Saint-Hilaire on structure (and the similarities). Both positions found their way into Darwin's theory of evolution. Balzac admired and was influenced by both men. He attended Cuvier's lectures at the Natural History Museum in 1818. The Jardin des Plantes (botanical gardens) is in the fifth arrondissement, near the Gare d'Austerlitz. See also note 1.

147. *the Ladies of the Petit Château*: A clique of high-ranking noblewomen close to the king's brother (who would become Charles X in 1824, on the death of the former king, Louis XVIII).

148. *elegy . . . choleric*: The concept of the four 'complexions' or 'temperaments' – melancholic, phlegmatic (or lymphatic), sanguine and choleric – was founded on that of the four humours (black bile, phlegm, red blood and yellow bile respectively). The

elegy is a poetic form traditionally used to lament the dead (hence Balzac associates it with the watery and insipid temperament of a phlegmatic); the dithyramb is 'a Greek choric hymn, originally in honour of Dionysus or Bacchus, vehement and wild in character; a Bacchanalian song' (*OED*), and is thus fit to express the tempestuous and enthusiastic (choleric) sentiments of a Rastignac.

149. *a typical banker's house . . . marble mosaic landings*: A reference to the grand houses built in this area at the end of the eighteenth century, designed by architects such as Claude-Nicolas Ledoux (1736–1806), according to neoclassical or Palladian ideals. Many were demolished later in the nineteenth century.

150. *Number NINE*: At the time, there were five gaming-houses near the Palais-Royal: Numbers 9, 36, 113, 129 and 154. In the course of the *Human Comedy*, Balzac's characters turn up at four of them.

151. *the misdemeanours . . . drives them to commit*: The Code Civil (note 54) reduced women to the status of children in the eyes of the law. In *La Physiologie du Mariage* (1829), Balzac argues that women should have greater freedom, particularly in legal terms.

152. *a thousand écus*: Rastignac returns to the carriage with 7,000 francs in winnings, having given the old man 200 francs (ten louis) in return for his advice. Delphine needs 6,000 francs to pay back de Marsay. So all she can give him is 1,000 francs, while wishing that it was 1,000 écus (calculating here in the pre-revolutionary écu, equal to six livres, so approximately 6,000 francs). See Note on Money.

153. *parochialorama*: Balzac writes *patriarcalorama* ('patriarchalorama'), perhaps because the boarding house is home to unfashionable old men such as Goriot and Poiret.

154. *meticulous in the matter of his linen*: In his *Traité de la vie élégante* ('Treatise of Fashionable Life', 1830), Balzac considers clothes as markers of social standing, developing an idea previously introduced in the *Code des gens honnêtes* ('Code for Respectable People', 1825): 'Speak, walk, eat or dress, and I'll tell you who you are'. On the specific matter of linen, he quotes one of the mottos of Regency dandy Beau Brummell: 'no perfumes, but very fine linen, plenty of it'. Balzac himself paid great attention to his linen, and ran up huge laundry bills.

155. *Mirabeau*: Honoré Gabriel Riqueti, the Comte de Mirabeau (1749–91), was a skilful orator and one of the leading political

figures of the earliest phase of the Revolution, despite his aristocratic background. He led a life of dissipation as a young man, running up huge gambling debts and conducting scandalous love affairs.

156. *taenias*: Tapeworms, parasites that suck their host dry.

157. *Absent-minded man*: One of the satirical sketches of various human types in Jean de la Bruyère's *The Characters* (1688), although the episode mentioned here doesn't feature in it.

158. *Saint Hubert's day*: This fell on 3 November, and opened the hunting season. Saint Hubert is the patron saint of hunters and hunting.

159. *Monsieur de Turenne*: A reference to one of Louis XIV's greatest marshals, Henri de la Tour d'Auvergne, Vicomte de Turenne (1611–75).

160. *those who crown themselves kings*: Such as Napoleon Bonaparte, who on 2 December 1804, in the presence of the Pope, crowned himself Emperor of the French, signalling that he owed his position to his own efforts, and that he recognized no overlord.

161. *Venice Preserv'd*: A tragedy by Thomas Otway (1652–85), which first appeared in 1682. The two main characters, Pierre, a foreign soldier, and Jaffier, a Venetian nobleman, form an intimate bond which ends in suicide. Vautrin's take on the play reveals his values, the importance that the bonds between men, in life and in love, have for him, and provides one of many hints in the novel as to (the nature of) his homosexuality.

IV. CAT-O'-NINE-LIVES

162. *Rue de Jérusalem*: In other words, the Préfecture de Police (police headquarters), situated on the Ile de la Cité, not far from the Palais de Justice.

163. *Caliph of Baghdad*: In this comic opera by François-Adrien Boieldieu (first performed in 1800), the caliph, Isaoun, assumes the name 'Il Bondocani', which has a kind of magic power, so that he can roam the streets freely at night in disguise.

164. *the penal colony in Toulon*: This explains Vautrin's earlier oblique allusion (note 118), to having 'spent some time in the Midi'.

165. *Assize Court*: In France, the court dealing with major offences or felonies (*crimes*), such as murder and rape, and, until the abolition of capital punishment in 1981, those which incurred a death sentence.

166. *Coignard Affair*: Pierre Coignard was an escaped convict who rose to the rank of Lieutenant-Colonel by pretending to be the émigré Comte de Sainte-Hélène. He was arrested in 1819.

167. *the Sûreté*: 'The French police department of criminal investigation' (*OED*).

168. *Ragoulleau ... Morin*: A contemporary case of attempted murder. Madame Morin was sentenced to twenty years of hard labour in 1812 for having tried to kill Monsieur Ragoulleau.

169. *Argus eyes*: Argus Panoptes, the 'All-Seeing', had a hundred eyes. He was chosen by Hera to watch over the beautiful Io, whom Zeus had turned into a white cow. After he was decapitated by Hermes, Hera placed his eyes in the tail of a peacock. Hence 'Argus' has come to designate a spy or a guardian.

170. *Oh Richard ... The whole world has deserted you*: A famous aria from the first act of Grétry's popular opera *Richard Coeur de Lion* ('Richard the Lionheart', 1784), sung by the troubadour Blondel, the squire of the imprisoned king. According to the *Mémoires* of the Duchesse d'Abrantès, Napoleon sang it to himself, taking the air one night, on his way through France to Elba.

171. *Laffitte ... politics doesn't come into it*: Jacques Laffitte (1767–1844), with two 'f's and two 't's, was a famous banker and politician, and Louis-Philippe's first prime minister. The equally famous Bordeaux claret Château-Lafite (no relative) is spelled with one of each.

172. *manna*: 'A sweet pale yellow or whitish ... juice obtained from incisions in the bark of the Manna-ash, *Fraxinus ornus*, chiefly in Calabria and Sicily; used in medicine as a gentle laxative' (*OED*). It would seem that Madame Vauquer's cassis is the opposite of manna from heaven.

173. *Wild Mountain ... The Loner ... Chateaubriand*: *Le Mont Sauvage* ('Wild Mountain', 1821) was a play by Pixérécourt, adapted from the sentimental novel *Le Solitaire* ('The Loner') by the Vicomte d'Arlincourt. René de Pixérécourt (1773–1844) was a prolific writer of popular melodramas. He knew his audience – 'J'écris pour ceux qui ne savent pas lire' ('I write for those who cannot read') – and, alongside the more sensational elements in his plays, sought to provide moral guidance that would be understood by the manufacturing classes. The boulevard theatres had an important social and imaginative function for the sub-literate (the literacy rate in France didn't start to rise until 1925). Madame Vauquer mistakenly attributes the novel to François-

René de Chateaubriand (1768–1848), and confuses his first name with the title of his novel *Atala* (1801). (In French you might refer to the book as 'L'*Atala* de Chateaubriand', hence Atala de Chateaubriand.) Chateaubriand was a high Romantic writer concerned with the social and aesthetic benefits of Christianity. Madame Vauquer's confusion is comic but almost understandable: Pixérécourt's melodramas, while appealing to a different sensibility, perhaps occupied similar imaginative terrain to high Romantic drama, as writers of all kinds attempted to come to terms with France's new emerging social values.

174. *Sleep . . . for ever*: A refrain from Scribe's vaudeville, *Le Somnam bule* ('The Sleepwalker', 1819).

175. *Paul et Virginie*: A popular utopian novel by Jacques-Henri Bernardin de Saint-Pierre (1737–1814), published in 1787. Set on the island of Mauritius, it tells the tragic tale of two innocent young lovers.

176. *Gaîté*: The Théâtre de la Gaîté on the Boulevard du Temple, where Vautrin took Madame Vauquer to see *Mont Sauvage* (note 173). A carnival atmosphere reigned on the Boulevard, which, along with its theatres, was packed with cabarets, cafés and street entertainers.

177. *col tempo*: Italian, 'with time'.

178. *Cochin hospital*: In the Rue du Faubourg Saint-Jacques. Founded in 1779 as a hospice for the poor by Jean-Denis Cochin, priest of the parish of Saint-Jacques-du-Haut-Pas, and later named after him.

179. *Rouge-et-Noir*: Another name for the card game known as *trente et quarante*, in which thirty and forty are by turns the winning and losing numbers. *Rouge-et-Noir* is named after the table at which it is played, which has two red and two black diamond-shaped marks on which players place their stakes. Hence, an unpredictable, high-risk game of chance where one person's ruin is another's gain.

180. *sheet anchor*: The largest of a ship's anchors, used only in an emergency. Figuratively, 'That on which one places one's reliance when everything else has failed' (*OED*).

181. *the old death's-head*: In French, *la camuse* or *la camarde* – from *camus*, having a snub or flattened nose. The death's-head is depicted as a face stripped of flesh, a skull whose nose appears flat, as reduced to its bridge of bone.

182. *Silk-Thread*: A literal translation from the French. English thieves'

cant expressions around silk perhaps have similar associations. According to Eric Partridge's *Dictionary of the Underworld*, a 'silk' is a swindler (whose talk is 'smooth as silk'); a 'silk-hat', a high-class con-man or a gangster who affects respectability and elegance. In *Splendeurs et misères des courtisanes* ('A Harlot High and Low'), we learn that this convict's real name is Sélérier.

183. *grasshoppers*: In English thieves' cant, a 'grass', rhyming on 'coppers'.

184. *Ninon ... Pompadour ... Père-Lachaise Venus*: The first two references are to famous courtesans. Despite being a woman of independent means, Ninon (Anne) de Lenclos (*c.* 1620–1705), a renowned intellect, was perhaps given this tag because of her open sexuality and her rebuttal of patriarchal authority. Antoinette Poisson, Marquise de Pompadour (1721–64), a well-educated woman of wealthy bourgeois stock, was Louis XV's most famous and cherished mistress; a patron of the *philosophes*, her political and cultural influence was considerable. Although history has since refreshed the reputations of these women, Vautrin's intention is to imply that Mademoiselle Michonneau is a prostitute who is past her best, while 'Père-Lachaise Venus' ('Vénus de Père-Lachaise') also suggests that she is more cemetery statue (see note 199 on Père Lachaise) than Venus de Milo.

185. *Quai des Orfèvres*: The famous French equivalent of Scotland Yard (Criminal Investigations Department) is located on the left-bank side of the Ile de la Cité, near the police headquarters and the law courts.

186. *Jean-Jacques*: Jean-Jacques Rousseau (1712–78), the Swiss writer and thinker, whose immensely influential – and controversial – work *The Social Contract* (1762) rejects the assumption that any human being has the authority to wield power over another, positing instead the idea of the state as a pact between citizens. His ideas on freedom, virtue, law and equality have been widely (mis)interpreted over the centuries.

187. *Flicoteaux's*: An establishment described in detail in *Lost Illusions* (Part II, Chapter 2):

> Flicoteaux is a name inscribed in many memories. Few are the students who, having lived in the Latin quarter during the first twelve years of the Restoration, did not frequent this shrine of hunger and poverty ... What has no doubt prevented Flicoteaux the friend of youth from making a colossal fortune is a certain feature in his

programme . . . thus stated: BREAD AT YOUR DISCRETION –
an indiscretion as far as restaurant-proprietors are concerned.
(*Lost Illusions*, tr. Herbert J. Hunt, Penguin Classics, 1971)

As we know, Madame Vauquer keeps a sharp eye on how much
bread her student boarders consume.

188. *Leaving for Syria . . . Dunois*: 'Partant pour la Syrie' or 'Le beau
Dunois' was a song written in the medievalizing Romance or
Troubadour style which originated during the First Empire. The
poem tells the story of a crusader who, on the eve of his departure for Syria, prays that his bravery in battle will be rewarded by
the love of a beautiful woman. Composed by Bonaparte's step-
daughter, Hortense de Beauharnais, the song was a huge popular
success, played by hurdy-gurdies on street corners everywhere. It
also became a Bonapartist rallying cry during the Restoration.

189. *trahit sua quemque voluptas . . . Virgil*: From *Eclogues* II.65.

190. *the Café des Anglais*: Situated on the corner of the Boulevard des
Italiens and the Rue de Marivaux, this establishment, noted for the
quality of its food and wine, was frequented by the Parisian elite.

191. *bitter aloes*: 'A drug of nauseous odour, bitter taste and purga-
tive qualities' (*OED*).

192. *love-seat*: A small sofa for two, known in French as a 'causeuse',
from *causer*, 'to chat'.

193. *perpetuity . . . life annuity*: Two different kinds of bond that
yield the investor a yearly interest payment. The payments on the
former continue for ever (at a lower rate), and on the latter cease
at the death of the investor (at a higher rate). Goriot's wealth is
now almost at its lowest level. We know that prior to retirement
his income was 60,000 livres (francs) a year, with comparatively
modest yearly expenses of twelve hundred francs. He gives his
daughters dowries of 800,000 francs each (by his own account,
less by other people's), and when he moves into the Maison Vauquer, he is left with an annual income of eight to 10,000 francs,
already a significant reduction. Now, his income is reduced to
twelve hundred francs a year – equivalent to the amount he paid
Madame Vauquer in rent on his arrival – and the interest he'll
receive will only just cover 50 écus' (250 francs) rent per year,
and daily expenses of 40 sous (2 francs). To place Goriot's sacrifice in perspective, see Note on Money.

194. *Croesus*: King of Lydia during the sixth century BC, famous for
his wealth.

195. *Marius . . . Carthage*: Caius Marius, Roman general and polit-

ician (*c.* 156–86 BC). Following an initially successful career, he was outlawed from Rome by his rival Sulla, and escaped to Africa. The image of Marius in exile, sitting on the ruins of Carthage, came to symbolize the unpredictable swings in human fortunes (and Balzac uses it more than once in the *Human Comedy*, for example, in *Cousin Bette*). Marius returned from Africa to capture Rome and ordered the massacre of his opponents.

196. *Tasso*: Byron's *The Lament of Tasso*, describing the sufferings of the great Italian poet in Ferrara, was translated into French in 1830 by Amédée Pichot.

V. THE TWO DAUGHTERS

197. *cuffs . . . a thousand écus apiece*: Louise de La Vallière reputedly ripped the king's lace cuffs as she clung to him in agony during labour throes. Later replaced as his mistress by Madame de Montespan, she withdrew to a convent. Balzac had a particular (and personal) interest in fine linen and its costs (see note 154).

198. *Rubicon*: The name of the small stream which marked the southern boundary between Cisalpine Gaul and Italy, on the east coast of northern Italy. It was forbidden for a general to cross it with his army; Caesar, in doing so, effectively declared war against Pompey. Hence, proverbially, the expression 'to cross the Rubicon' means 'to take a decisive or final step' (*OED*).

199. *Père Lachaise*: This famous cemetery is situated in the present-day twentieth arrondissement in eastern Paris; when it was founded in 1804, it was on the outskirts of the city. It was a destination Balzac often aimed for as he walked the streets of Paris, during his early years as a writer, when he lived in the Rue Lesdiguières (near the Place de la Bastille). See also note 223.

200. *separate assets*: Goriot is clutching at straws. Even under the terms of this kind of contract, the law stipulated that a wife was not allowed to sell or mortgage her property without her husband's signature, whereas the husband was able to dispose of his wife's property as he wished without involving her. See note 54 on the Code Civil.

201. *Place de Grève*: Historically, it was on this square, on the right bank of the Seine, that judicial executions were carried out. The last was held in 1830 and the name was subsequently changed to Place de l'Hôtel de Ville.

202. *men of straw . . . duped contractors . . . Vienna*: In this scam, it

seems that some kind of fake sale is taking place between the men of straw and Nucingen. The former acknowledge receipt of payment, i.e. that Nucingen has purchased the buildings from them, even though he hasn't paid full price for them. The men of straw then go bankrupt and default on the bills used to pay the contractors, so the latter foot the cost of construction. As Nucingen appears to have legal ownership of the buildings, and as no direct agreement exists between him and the contractors, they have little or no recourse. To cover his tracks further he transfers some of his wealth abroad so that, if he's ever questioned, he can claim that the money was spent on purchasing the houses, and his books will appear to balance.

203. *Sainte-Pélagie*: Debtors prison, located in the present-day fifth arrondissement, opposite the boarding house on which Balzac may have modelled the Maison Vauquer.

204. *the Bank*: The Banque de France, founded under Napoleon in 1800 to stabilize the French financial system, following the hyperinflationary trauma of the post-revolutionary years caused by excessive note issue (the unpopular *assignats*).

205. *the bill endorsed to Vautrin*: In return for cash from Vautrin, Rastignac had originally signed a promissory note undertaking to pay back a certain sum by a certain date. It seems likely that at this stage the bill was endorsed 'in blank', that is, payable to 'the bearer' (Vautrin). Rastignac payed Vautrin back in full the next day, so Vautrin returned the bill to him. Rastignac (drawee) now turns it into a bill of exchange by making it out to Goriot, who becomes the drawer, and Goriot then endorses it to the comtesse, so she can sell it on and convert it into cash. For more on bills of exchange, see note 70.

206. *serous apoplexy*: The medical theory Bianchon refers to here, of apoplexy caused by an effusion of serum to the brain, was accepted at that time, but has since been discredited. The closest modern equivalent would appear to be a brain haemorrhage, which is caused by blood invading the brain. Balzac's description of Goriot's symptoms seems to indicate that he is suffering from a stroke (severe headache, confusion, tiredness).

207. *mustard poultices*: In the nineteenth century, mustard poultices were used in threatened cases of apoplexy or paralysis, to 'rouse the system' (*Savory's Compendium of Domestic Medicine*, 7th edn, 1865).

208. *Moses' prayer*: An aria from Rossini's opera *Moses in Egypt*, of which Balzac appears to have been fond (he also refers to it in

'La Duchesse de Langeais' and 'Massimilla Doni'). It was first
performed in Paris in 1822.

209. *Tantalus*: In ancient mythology, a mythical king of Phrygia who
revealed the secrets of the gods. His punishment, which was
unending, was to endure unquenchable thirst and unsatisfied
hunger. No angel came to bring him solace.

210. *the Grande Mademoiselle*: That is, Mademoiselle Montpensier
(a cousin of Louis XIV). In December 1670, the king gave his
consent to her marriage with the Duc de Lauzun (an adventurer),
only to retract it three days later and have her lover imprisoned
instead.

211. *Niobe made of marble*: In Greek myth, the daughter of Tantalus,
who was turned into stone as she wept for the loss of her
children.

212. *cashed in*: Literally, 'discounted'. The implication of this powerful image is that Anastasie views everything, including Goriot's
life, as a kind of bill of exchange – and she has cashed in
(discounted) the latter before its maturity date. Not only has
she already spent all of his capital (which he needs in order to
live) before he has been able to bequeath it to her upon his
death, she has devalued his quality of life and his estate in the
process.

213. *I . . . shall make one last attempt*: A reference to the equivalent
episode in Balzac's story 'The Duchesse de Langeais' (see note
52), where the duchesse finally realizes she is in love with Montriveau and sends him a letter saying that she will retire from
society if he doesn't come back to her. When he fails to appear,
she withdraws to a convent.

VI. DEATH OF THE FATHER

214. *moxas*: A moxa (from the Japanese *mokusa* 艾) is a preparation
of mugwort herb (*Artemisia moxa*), or an inflammable substance
such as a roll of cotton, used in the practice of moxibustion,
whereby the substance is burned and applied to the skin. An
ancient Chinese medical practice, it is used to stimulate circulation and energy, particularly in the case of debilitated or geriatric
patients; it was popular in France in the nineteenth century.

215. *Money buys everything, even daughters*: The echoes of *King
Lear* in the novel are perhaps most audible in these closing passages. Here, the tragic realization Goriot shares with Lear is that

purchased affections are only as shallow and short lived as the money that bought them. Fool (II.4):

> Fathers that wear rags
>> Do make their children blind,
> But fathers that bear bags
>> Shall see their children kind.

Money can buy the words that flatter a father's vanity, but not the honest filial love the words stand in for, where loyalty and devotion are given unbidden and freely. Where Delphine and Anastasie display the selfishness of a Regan or Goneril, perhaps Victorine Taillefer shows a Cordelia-like loyalty to her father. It is known that performances of *King Lear* and other Shakespeare plays were held in Paris in 1827–28, and caught the attention of contemporaries such as Alexandre Dumas, Alfred de Vigny, Victor Hugo and Hector Berlioz.

216. *the country*: In French, *la patrie*, which has overtones of 'fatherland', resonating with the novel's theme of paternity.

217. *viaticum*: The Eucharist, or, in other religious traditions, voyage provisions, given to the dying, to help them on their journey as they depart this world. Sometimes this takes the form of a coin, the obolus that pays Charon for passage across the river Acheron in Greek mythology, for example. But money has lost all meaning for Goriot – all he wants is a kiss. (In French, the word is also used to denote comfort or sustenance.)

218. *Pluck them out!*: Another echo of *Lear*. Gloucester, betrayed by his bastard son Edmund, is blinded when Goneril orders Cornwall to 'Pluck out his eyes' (III.7).

219. *Their children will avenge me*: Lear, cursing Goneril (I.4):

> Hear, nature, hear: dear goddess hear:
> Suspend thy purpose if thou didst intend
> To make this creature fruitful.
> Into her womb convey sterility,
> Dry up in her the organs of increase,
> And from her derogate body never spring
> A babe to honour her. If she must teem,
> Create her child of spleen, that it may live
> And be a thwart disnatured torment to her.
> Let it stamp wrinkles in her brow of youth,
> With cadent tears fret channels in her cheeks,

Turn all her mother's pains and benefits
To laughter and contempt, that she may feel
How sharper than a serpent's tooth it is
To have a thankless child.

220. *a third-class funeral*: In France, undertakers divided funerals into nine classes according to their expense. A third-class funeral was moderately expensive.

221. *holy-water sprinkler*: At a Roman Catholic funeral, the coffin is sprinkled with holy water by a priest, and by the mourners, as a symbol of purification. No one has yet performed this ritual for Goriot.

222. *Libera ... De profundis*: The Libera Nos (prayer) and the De Profundis (Psalm 129) are both part of the Mass for the dead, here tacked on to the daily Vespers service.

223. *Père Lachaise*: See note 199 on the location and origins of this cemetery. Balzac himself was buried here on his death in 1850, not far from the spot where Rastignac stands and watches Goriot's coffin being lowered into the ground. His was a third-class funeral, like Goriot's. However, Balzac's was attended by a vast crowd of friends, writers and admirers, who listened and mourned as Victor Hugo pronounced his funeral oration, calling Balzac a member of 'the powerful race of revolutionary writers' (Robb, *Balzac*, p. 412).

224. *Saché*: Balzac began writing *Old Man Goriot* in September 1834, at the Château de Saché in Touraine, where he stayed as the guest of Jean de Margonne and his wife. He completed it on 26 January 1835. It was first published in the *Revue de Paris* in four instalments, between December 1834 and February 1835. See Introduction, pp. xv–xviii.

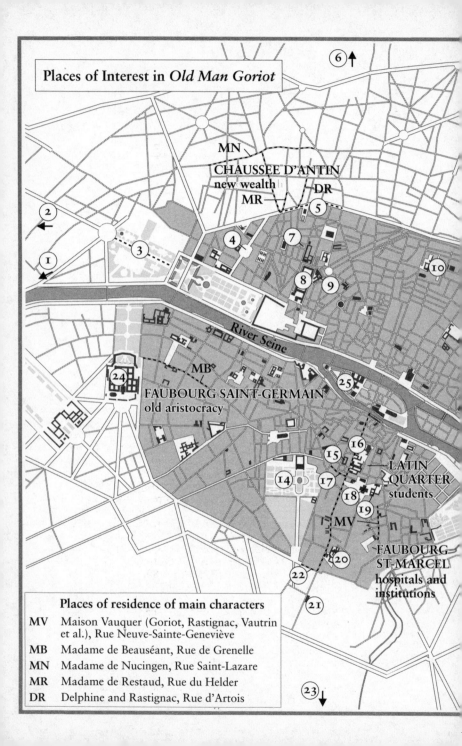

Places of Interest in *Old Man Goriot*

MN
CHAUSSEE D'ANTIN
new wealth
MR
DR

FAUBOURG SAINT-GERMAIN
old aristocracy

MB

River Seine

LATIN
QUARTER
students

MV

FAUBOURG
ST-MARCEL
hospitals and
institutions

Places of residence of main characters

MV Maison Vauquer (Goriot, Rastignac, Vautrin
    et al.), Rue Neuve-Sainte-Geneviève
MB Madame de Beauséant, Rue de Grenelle
MN Madame de Nucingen, Rue Saint-Lazare
MR Madame de Restaud, Rue du Helder
DR Delphine and Rastignac, Rue d'Artois

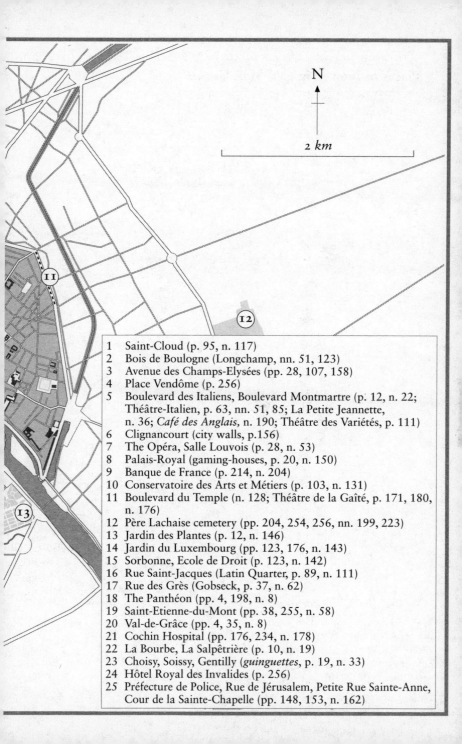

N

2 km

PENGUIN CLASSICS

MADAME BOVARY
GUSTAVE FLAUBERT

'Oh, why, dear God, did I marry him?'

Emma Bovary is beautiful and bored, trapped in her marriage to a mediocre doctor and stifled by the banality of provincial life. An ardent devourer of sentimental novels, she longs for passion and seeks escape in fantasies of high romance, in voracious spending and, eventually, in adultery. But even her affairs bring her disappointment, and when real life continues to fail to live up to her romantic expectations the consequences are devastating. Flaubert's erotically charged and psychologically acute portrayal of Emma Bovary caused a moral outcry on its publication in 1857. It was deemed so lifelike that many women claimed they were the model for his heroine; but Flaubert insisted: 'Madame Bovary, c'est moi'.

This modern translation by Flaubert's biographer, Geoffrey Wall, retains all the delicacy and precision of the French original. This edition also contains a preface by the novelist Michèle Roberts.

'A masterpiece' Julian Barnes

'A supremely beautiful novel' Michèle Roberts

Translated and edited with an introduction by Geoffrey Wall
With a Preface by Michèle Roberts

PENGUIN CLASSICS

SENTIMENTAL EDUCATION
GUSTAVE FLAUBERT

'He loved her without reservation, without hope, unconditionally'

Frederic Moreau is a law student returning home to Normandy from Paris when he first notices Madame Arnoux, a slender, dark woman several years older than himself. It is the beginning of an infatuation that will last a lifetime. He befriends her husband, an influential businessman, and their paths cross and re-cross over the years. Through financial upheaval, political turmoil and countless affairs, Madame Arnoux remains the constant, unattainable love of Moreau's life. Flaubert described his sweeping story of a young man's passions, ambitions and amours as 'the moral history of the men of my generation'. Based on his own youthful passion for an older woman, *Sentimental Education* blends love story, historical authenticity and satire to create one of the greatest French novels of the nineteenth century.

Geoffrey Wall's fresh revision of Robert Baldick's original translation is accompanied by an insightful new introduction discussing the personal and historical influences on Flaubert's writing. This edition also contains a new chronology, further reading and explanatory notes.

Translated with an introduction by Robert Baldick
Revised and edited by Geoffrey Wall

read more

PENGUIN CLASSICS

NOTRE-DAME DE PARIS
VICTOR HUGO

'He was like a giant broken in pieces and badly reassembled'

In the vaulted Gothic towers of Notre-Dame lives Quasimodo, the hunchbacked bellringer. Mocked and shunned for his appearance, he is pitied only by Esmerelda, a beautiful gypsy dancer to whom he becomes completely devoted. Esmerelda, however, has also attracted the attention of the sinister archdeacon Claude Frollo and, when she rejects his lecherous approaches, Frollo hatches a plot to destroy her that only Quasimodo can prevent. Victor Hugo's sensational, evocative novel brings life to the medieval Paris he loved, and mourns its passing in one of the greatest historical romances of the nineteenth century.

John Sturrock's clear, contemporary translation is accompanied by an introduction discussing it as a passionate novel of ideas, written in defence of Gothic architecture and of a burgeoning democracy, and demonstrating that an ugly exterior can conceal moral beauty. This revised edition also includes further reading and a chronology of Hugo's life.

Translated with an introduction by John Sturrock

PENGUIN CLASSICS

THE MISANTHROPE AND OTHER PLAYS
MOLIÈRE

Such Foolish Affected Ladies/Tartuffe/The Misanthrope/The Doctor Despite Himself/The Would-be Gentleman/Those Learned Ladies

'Let's not worry about the manners of the age and make more allowance for human nature. Let's judge it less severely and look more kindly on its faults'

The six plays collected in this volume illustrate Molière's broad range of comic devices, from satire and farce to slapstick and sophisticated wit and wordplay. In *Tartuffe* and *The Doctor Despite Himself,* Molière shows us the foolishness of those taken in by a religious hypocrite and a bogus physician, while *Such Foolish Affected Ladies* and *Those Learned Ladies* are a humorous attack on the excessive refinement and pedantry of the Parisian smart set. And in *The Misanthrope* and *The Would-Be Gentleman* Molière warns us of the dangers of obsession and intolerance. Exposing duplicity, mocking snobbery and revealing the horrors of hypocrisy, Molière's plays are masterly studies in the absurdities of human nature.

All of the humour and panache of the original French has been preserved in John Wood's translation. In his introduction, David Coward discusses the reception each play received when it was first performed and how this has changed over the centuries. This edition also includes a chronology, a bibliography and notes.

Translated by John Wood and David Coward with an introduction and notes by David Coward

PENGUIN CLASSICS

GERMINAL
ÉMILE ZOLA

'Buried like moles beneath the crushing weight of the earth, and without a breath of fresh air in their burning lungs, they simply went on tapping'

Etienne Lantier, an unemployed railway worker, is a clever but uneducated young man with a dangerous temper. Compelled to take a back-breaking job at the Le Voreux mine when he cannot get other work, he discovers that his fellow miners are ill, hungry and in debt, unable to feed and clothe their families. When conditions in the mining community deteriorate even further, Lantier finds himself leading a strike that could mean starvation or salvation for all. The thirteenth novel in Zola's great Rougon-Macquart sequence, *Germinal* expresses outrage at the exploitation of the many by the few, but also shows humanity's capacity for compassion and hope.

Roger Pearson's lively and modern new translation is accompanied by an introduction that examines the social and political background to Zola's masterpiece, in particular the changing relationship between labour and capital. This edition also contains a filmography, chronology and notes.

Translated and edited by Roger Pearson

PENGUIN CLASSICS

NANA
ÉMILE ZOLA

> 'Her slightest movements fanned the flame of desire,
> and with a twitch of her little finger she could stir men's flesh'

Born to drunken parents in the slums of Paris, Nana lives in squalor until she is
discovered at the Théâtre des Variétés. She soon rises from the streets to set the
city alight as the most famous high-class prostitute of her day. Rich men, Comtes
and Marquises fall at her feet, great ladies try to emulate her appearance, lovers
even kill themselves for her. Nana's hedonistic appetite for luxury and decadent
pleasures knows no bounds – until, eventually, it consumes her. Nana provoked
outrage on its publication in 1880, with its heroine damned as 'the most crude
and bestial sort of whore'. Yet the rich atmosphere and luminous language of this
'poem of male desire' transform Nana into an almost mythical figure: a destructive
force preying on a corrupt, decaying society.

George Holden's lively translation is accompanied by an introduction discussing
Nana as a key work in Zola's Rougon-Macquart cycle, representing a powerful
critique of France's Second Empire.

Translated with an introduction by George Holden

PENGUIN CLASSICS

THE COUNT OF MONTE CRISTO
ALEXANDRE DUMAS

'On what slender threads do life and fortune hang'

Thrown in prison for a crime he has not committed, Edmond Dantes is confined to the grim fortress of If. There he learns of a great hoard of treasure hidden on the Isle of Monte Cristo and he becomes determined not only to escape, but also to unearth the treasure and use it to plot the destruction of the three men responsible for his incarceration. Dumas's epic tale of suffering and retribution, inspired by a real-life case of wrongful imprisonment, was a huge popular success when it was first serialized in the 1840s.

Robin Buss's lively English translation is complete and unabridged, and remains faithful to the style of Dumas's original. This edition includes an introduction, explanatory notes and suggestions for further reading.

'Robin Buss broke new ground with a fresh version of *Monte Cristo* for Penguin'
The Oxford Guide to Literature in English Translation

Translated with an introduction by Robin Buss

PENGUIN CLASSICS

THE HOUSE OF THE DEAD
FYODOR DOSTOYEVSKY

'Here was the house of the living dead, a life like none other upon earth'

In January 1850 Dostoyevsky was sent to a remote Siberian prison camp for his part in a political conspiracy. The four years he spent there, startlingly re-created in *The House of the Dead*, were the most agonizing of his life. In this fictionalized account he recounts his soul-destroying incarceration through the cool, detached tones of his narrator, Aleksandr Petrovich Goryanchikov: the daily battle for survival, the wooden plank beds, the cabbage soup swimming with cockroaches, his strange 'family' of boastful, ugly, cruel convicts. Yet *The House of the Dead* is far more than a work of documentary realism: it is also a powerful novel of redemption, describing one man's spiritual and moral death and the miracle of his gradual reawakening.

This edition includes an introduction and notes by David McDuff discussing the circumstances of Dostoyevsky's imprisonment, the origins of the novel in his prison writings and the character of Aleksandr Petrovich.

Translated with an introduction and notes by David McDuff

PENGUIN CLASSICS

THE IDIOT
FYODOR DOSTOYEVSKY

> 'He's simple-minded, but he has all his wits about him,
> in the most noble sense of the word, of course'

Returning to St Petersburg from a Swiss sanatorium, the gentle and naive Prince Myshkin – known as 'the idiot' – pays a visit to his distant relative General Yepanchin and proceeds to charm the General, his wife and his three daughters. But his life is thrown into turmoil when he chances on a photograph of the beautiful Nastasya Filippovna. Utterly infatuated with her, he soon finds himself caught up in a love triangle and drawn into a web of blackmail, betrayal and, finally, murder. In Prince Myshkin, Dosteyevsky set out to portray the purity of 'a truly beautiful soul' and to explore the perils that innocence and goodness face in a corrupt world.

David McDuff's major new translation brilliantly captures the novel's idiosyncratic and dream-like language and the nervous, elliptic flow of the narrative. This edition also includes an introduction by William Mills Todd III, further reading, a chronology of Dostoyevsky's life and work, a note on the translation and explanatory notes.

Translated by David McDuff with an introduction by William Mills Todd III

THE STORY OF PENGUIN CLASSICS

Before 1946 ... 'Classics' are mainly the domain of academics and students; readable editions for everyone else are almost unheard of. This all changes when a little-known classicist, E. V. Rieu, presents Penguin founder Allen Lane with the translation of Homer's *Odyssey* that he has been working on in his spare time.

1946 Penguin Classics debuts with *The Odyssey*, which promptly sells three million copies. Suddenly, classics are no longer for the privileged few.

1950s Rieu, now series editor, turns to professional writers for the best modern, readable translations, including Dorothy L. Sayers's *Inferno* and Robert Graves's unexpurgated *Twelve Caesars*.

1960s The Classics are given the distinctive black covers that have remained a constant throughout the life of the series. Rieu retires in 1964, hailing the Penguin Classics list as 'the greatest educative force of the twentieth century.'

1970s A new generation of translators swells the Penguin Classics ranks, introducing readers of English to classics of world literature from more than twenty languages. The list grows to encompass more history, philosophy, science, religion and politics.

1980s The Penguin American Library launches with titles such as *Uncle Tom's Cabin*, and joins forces with Penguin Classics to provide the most comprehensive library of world literature available from any paperback publisher.

1990s The launch of Penguin Audiobooks brings the classics to a listening audience for the first time, and in 1999 the worldwide launch of the Penguin Classics website extends their reach to the global online community.

The 21st Century Penguin Classics are completely redesigned for the first time in nearly twenty years. This world-famous series now consists of more than 1300 titles, making the widest range of the best books ever written available to millions – and constantly redefining what makes a 'classic'.

The Odyssey continues ...

The best books ever written

PENGUIN 🐧 CLASSICS

SINCE 1946

Find out more at www.penguinclassics.com